DANI SANCHEZ

AND THE

THE SEVEN DEADLY SINS

SEQUEL NOVEL

B.C. TAYLOR

NOSLRAC PUBLISHING, LLC

Copyright Page

Dani Sanchez and the Seven Deadly Sins
Published by Noslrac Publishing, LLC
Copyright 2025 B. C. Taylor
Cover designed by B. C. Taylor
Image generated by Canva

This book is a work of fiction. Though some actual towns, cities, and locations may be mentioned, they are used in a fictitious manner and any names, characters, events and occurrences are a product of the imagination of the author. Any similarities of characters or names used within to any person, past, present, or future, are coincidental.

ISBN 978-1-959090-25-0
Library of Congress Control Number: 2025911511
First Edition paperback 2025

Noslrac Publishing
authorBCtaylor@gmail.com
brooklynctaylor.com

*To me. For choosing to love after the world
broke my heart again and again.*

TABLE OF CONTENTS

Disclaimer

It is recommended to read this sequel novel after the main series, Hayden Black and the Salem Witch Trials, as this content contains major spoilers.

A glossary of terms and powers can be found at the end of this book.

Reading Order

The Lost Witch

The Dark Mother

The Nephilim's Glory

The Earth's Curse

The Warrior Witch

The Salem Witch... Prequel Novella

Dani Sanchez and the Seven Deadly Sins... Sequel Novel

CHAPTER ONE

RETURN OF THE WITCH

It all started at the end…

At the end of the Salem War two years ago, Hayden Black offered Dani Sanchez a spot in her circle. The most powerful circle to ever exist.

Optimistically, Dani had been hoping—praying even—that Hayden Black would return to the witching town of Asylum and welcome her into her circle. But Hayden hadn't been to Asylum in over a year. Her and Jamie Bishop were off traveling the world, only visiting Asylum on rare occasion to see their friends. Most of the time, the couple was stealth. They'd appear and disappear before anyone knew and whisperings of their visit propagated for weeks. The gossip mill in Asylum was worse than any human paparazzi—and less accurate.

Dani was losing hope of Hayden returning to give her purpose. She released a solemn sigh. Her breath fogged in the frigid air as she swept away the snow with her elemental water magic as she trudged down State Street with her brother, Damien, to the cathedral for witch church.

Despite the cold, the street bustled with witches running in and out of stores for hot coffee, tea, or breakfast before the service. Two years after the war, the witches of Asylum were the happiest they had been since Alice Parker, Asylum's founder and a previous Salem Witch, settled the witching town in a magical land hidden within what is now the state of Wisconsin.

Lilith, the Mother of Demons and villainess in the Salem War, was defeated, and while millions of demons roamed loose in the world, they couldn't penetrate the wards surrounding Asylum—the magical enchantments constructed by Alice Parker's special Nephilim and Salem Witch powers to protect the town.

Alice Parker founded Asylum in 1693 as a safe haven for witches after the horror of the hangings in Salem. Alice had led the pilgrimage from Salem, Massachusetts to a land that is now within the state of Wisconsin, in a town called Salem. Over three hundred years ago, the land had not yet been settled by the Europeans, but was inhabited by the Winnebago Tribe. Instead of encroaching on their lands, Alice combined her Nephilim-Salem Witch magic with the Tribe's knowledge of Olde Earth Magic to create Asylum, which existed within a pocket of magic that allowed the town to exist within the human lands without consuming the lands.

Only Hayden's loyal demons were permitted past the wards, which disgruntled some witches, but the townies had reached an easy peace with the demons, who frolicked in the December snow, and many had attached themselves to witches, almost like familiars—a magically bonded pet.

Dani smiled at a young hellhound the size of a sedan playing with a group of five year olds in the snow. He rolled onto his back, his tongue lolling out of his mouth as the kiddos rubbed his belly.

"Do you want anything?" Damien gestured to the coffee shop nestled into the line of stores edging the street.

"Coffee. Black."

Damien rolled his eyes at his sister. "What seventeen-year-old girl drinks black coffee? There's something wrong with you."

Dani elbowed him sharply in the ribs. "It matches my soul."

Her brother rolled his eyes hard enough to see his brain, if he had one. "Sis, I know you think you're tough and all, but your soul can't even touch Hayden's. And she's a demon princess."

Rolling her own eyes, she shoved her brother. "Just get the coffee."

Normally, Dani would go inside to warm up, but one look through the floor-to-ceiling windows had Dani deciding she'd rather freeze. Crowds and Dani did not vibe together. She got claustrophobic standing in an empty elevator alone. Instead, she watched the kids playing with the hellhound, a smile on her face.

Goosebumps rose on her skin, not from the frigid Wisconsin winter, but from the eerie feeling of being hunted. Dani slipped a hand into her coat to grip her wooden wand as she scanned the street for a sign of something out of the ordinary. Finding none, she relaxed her grip on her wand and turned to head inside despite the crowd, but a glint of light off of what might have been a thin steel blade stole her attention. The light flashed once, originating from between two pillars of a Colosseum arch. Squinting, Dani strained her eyes toward the flash of light, but as quickly as it had come, it was gone again, and shadows lurked around the arena.

The bell chimed as the door swung open, breaking the tension hovering around Dani, and Damien sauntered out, carrying two travel mugs of piping hot coffee. Well, hers was coffee. His was sugar and milk with a dash of coffee.

One look at her face, and Damien's sassy smile dropped into a concerned frown. "What's wrong?"

Dani shook herself, glanced over her shoulder at the Colosseum archway, then faced her brother. "Nothing."

But Damien tracked her gaze to the shadows between the Colosseum pillars. His eyes narrowed as if he could see through the darkness. Without breaking his gaze, he handed Dani's coffee to her, then withdrew his wand and gave it a twirl, sending a cutting breeze blowing across the street and into the alcove. But nothing rustled. Only the giggles of the children and the usual chatter of gossiping witches reached their ears.

The Sanchez siblings shared an uneasy look.

It had been two and a half years since Hayden defeated Lilith and demolished her dark army of demons, but Apalla—a Prophetess gifted with True Sight to see visions of the future—had warned that another storm was brewing. And Hayden had seemed to know all about it. A thrill of excitement rushed through Dani at the memory. Hayden had indicated she would need a full circle, and Dani had the spot as the water witch, if she wanted it.

And Dani wanted it.

Shaking his head as though he could shake away the dark thoughts plaguing him, Damien grumbled, "Come on, let's get to the cathedral." But the worry remained etched on her older brother's face as he gnawed his bottom lip.

They walked the rest of the way in silence, their physical and magical senses alert. Dani couldn't quite shake the feeling of being watched. Why her? Why would someone in Asylum be stalking her?

Unless they weren't from Asylum.

The thought unnerved her, but a twisting in her gut told Dani she was onto something. As she sipped her coffee, the dark liquid scalding her throat, she couldn't shake the feeling that she should be afraid. Very afraid.

But what would something—like a demon not loyal to Hayden or Elliot Fox, the traitor witch—want with Dani Sanchez? She hadn't been welcomed into Hayden's circle yet. Why wouldn't the stalker go after Apalla?

Apalla Nomad—a Daughter of Apollo— currently served on Asylum's Athenian Council as High Priestess. Her mother, Isleen, had been the previous High Priestess before she passed in the war against Lilith—a.k.a. the First Eve. Both Apalla and Isleen were powerful air elementals—witches with the power to control the wind—with colorful magic, which only manifested for the most powerful of witches. Apalla's magic colors were gold and pink. Gold for her powers of sunlight magic gifted from Apollo, and pink for her air magic.

Dani certainly wasn't powerful enough to have colorful magic.... No wonder Hayden never returned for Dani after her graduation from St. Salem's Spellery—Asylum's magical school for witches.

If Elliot had returned, wouldn't he seek revenge on Hayden by attacking her best friend? Apalla had been a key warrior in the Salem War and a powerful air elemental who opposed Elliot. Elliot, who had been born and raised a witch, was an air witch like Apalla, but unlike Apalla, his magic warped and twisted when he chose to follow Lilith, the Mother of Demons and the grandmother of Hayden Black.

Hayden, having been born as the Salem Witch, the only witch with the power of all five elements, was chosen by the Creator to defeat Lilith and end her reign in Hell. So, yeah, Elliot hated Hayden's guts, but for some reason, Hayden allowed him to escape from Asylum after the war ended.

What if he came back?

Apalla wasn't the only mega powerful witch in Hayden's circle. A circle was composed of five witches who represented the five elements—air, fire, water, earth, and Spirit.

Jamie Bishop wasn't just the best fire witch in Asylum.... As the Nephilim son of the Messenger Archangel, Gabriel, Jamie was the most powerful fire elemental in the world. And as the soulmate of Hayden Black, the Warrior Witch, he had the blessing of the Warrior Archangel, Michael, so Jamie was scary talented on the battlefield. Dani witnessed first-hand how

Jamie mercilessly slaughtered his enemies in war, so if Elliot was lurking in the shadows, Jamie would obliterate him.

But nobody had heard anything about the Salem Witch or her soulmate in months, so the likelihood of them dropping by Asylum now...

Dani tried to shake the thought from her mind as she glanced over her shoulder. The only people following them were other witches on their way to the cathedral. People Dani had known since she moved to Asylum to attend the Spellery years ago.

After graduating the Spellery last summer, Dani moved out of the student apartments into a townie apartment with her older brother, Damien, who happened to be friends with the Salem Witch. Damien had graduated from the Spellery a few years ago, then assumed the position of Air Representative on the Athenian Council after Hayden defeated Lilith, but Dani had absolutely no idea what she wanted to do with her life.

Except serve as the water witch in Hayden's circle.

Then there was Harbor Bishop.... Water witch and the twin sister to Jamie, making her the Nephilim daughter of Gabriel. She was the most fearless circle member, more fearless than Hayden herself, because Harbor had sacrificed her life to use her Glory—the ability of a Nephilim to channel their heavenly parent's full power—to banish Lilith to Hell for a year before Lilith could swallow the world in darkness. Hayden had needed more time to train with the elements... she hadn't been the walking powerhouse of magic that she was now. And Harbor, in all her wisdom, knew that. The caveat... using her Glory severed the ties binding her soul to her mortal body, and Harbor Bishop died. Her immortal soul now resided in the eternal Garden of Eden.

How was Dani supposed to live up to those wild standards? Who could dream to fill Harbor's shoes as the next water elemental in Hayden's circle?

And would Jamie hate Dani forever if she accepted the position that rightfully belonged to Harbor?

As Dani followed Damien through the massive double doors and entered the radiating warmth of the cathedral, she glanced over her shoulder one last time, casting a wary eye to the shadows watching her.

Since Damien was the Air Representative on the Athenian Council, he and Dani usually sat at the front of the cathedral along with the other Council members, which included Kova Parker, the Ethereal Bloodline Representative and the name Alice Parker used to hide her true identity from the rest of the world. Basically, Kova was Alice Parker is disguise.

Since each witching community was governed by an Athenian Council, most didn't have access to an immortal Nephilim like Kova, so the Ethereal Bloodline Representative usually had diluted celestial blood—like Elizabeth Black, Hunter Black's mother—who served on the Supreme Council who oversaw every Athenian Council in the witching world.

And for once, the red-haired witch attended witch church, a rarity in the last few months. Despite the never-ending gossip mill in Asylum, nobody seemed to know exactly why Kova Parker was missing service.

But this was Dani's opportunity to talk to her.

"Hi, Dani," Kova greeted her warmly as the younger witch sank into the pew next to the Resigned Salem Witch. During the Salem War, Kova's secret identity had been leaked to the rest of Asylum—insufferable gossips—but Asylumnites were loyal to their own and not a whisper of Kova's true identity as Alice Parker, the immortal Nephilim child of Uriel—the Archangel of Earth—was uttered outside of these wards.

"Hi, Kova. Nice to see you at church service for once."

Kova shot her a sheepish smile, but didn't say anything.

Comfortable silence fell over the duo as Damien chatted with Harlan Bishop, oblivious to Dani worrying her lip.

"Kova?" Her questioning tone drew the older witch's attention. "It's probably nothing, but when Damien and I were walking here..." She hesitated. "Never mind, I'm probably overreacting."

Kova's hunter green eyes were sharp and alert as the woman straightened in the pew. "Don't dismiss your intuition, Dani. What happened?"

"I can't be sure, but it felt like someone was following me. Watching me. Damien sensed it, too."

Surging to her feet, Kova strode to where Apalla Nomad stood at the pedestal at the front of the cathedral with a Holy Grimoire and said something to the High Priestess, whose gaze snapped to Dani. Dani couldn't make out any of their conversation through the chatter filling the cathedral.

An explosion sounded in the distance, silencing the crowd as witches hit the floor or dove under pews. Kova and Apalla shared a look, then drew their weapons. Green light flashed, and the women disappeared as Kova spooked—the witching ability to disappear from one place and reappear in a new location.

Dani had no idea where the women disappeared to, but as screams sounded from outside the cathedral, Dani jumped to her feet. Unsheathing her falchion sword, she dodged her brother's hand as he reached for her and sprinted out of the cathedral. Others followed her lead, some of them Knights, some of them Dani's peers from her time at the Spellery, and others ordinary witches, but all witches had a wand and a weapon.

Sinister black smoke darkened the sky.

Dani and the others broke into sprints.

Black smoke meant one thing. The town was on fire, and not a normal fire or a magical fire, but a demonic fire. If it were caused by Hayden's demons—demons who were blessed with a soul by Heaven for their loyalty to the righteous side—then it would be extinguished already. This was not friendly fire.

Rounding the corner, Dani slid to a stop in the town square.

Black blood was splattered everywhere as soul-blessed demons tore through demons loyal to Hell.

Dani charged into the fray.

Cornered, a hellhound stood over a mother and her two small children, the family cowering as the blessed demon protected them like a family dog. Its deadly fangs sank into a brimstone demon's neck as the hellhound chomped its head off.

Across the square, a group of teenagers Dani recognized from the Spellery fended off a swarm of demons, but those water elementals weren't the fighting type. As the previous Water Major—the student water witch with the most magical prowess—Dani knew all the water witches. These three were more interested in healing than fighting, but they were holding their own against the inferni and brimstone demons.

Dani sprinted toward her old classmates.

A rapier blade sliced in front of her, nearly skewering her. Ducking under the blade like she was doing the limbo, Dani swiped her falchion through the air to clang against her opponent's blade. As she pivoted and rose to her full height, her gaze found her opponent's.

Black eyes. Entirely black eyes without an iris or pupil.

Dani's jaw dropped open.

Elliot Fox had returned to Asylum.

And he had come for her.

A blackish-blue hue hovered around Elliot, the scent of putrid decay wafting off him as though his soul was rotting inside his body. With his blade in hand, he stalked toward her with a vindictive smile, no doubt thrilled for the opportunity to finally cut her down like he tried to do when she defied him during the Salem War, right before Hayden Black smoked him with a bolt of lightning and ended Lilith's immortal reign in Hell.

Dani's falchion crashed against Elliot's thin rapier blade, making it warble from the force. She kicked out, slamming her heel into his shin, but the blow barely affected him. He shot a fist at her face, but Dani dodged, and his punch sailed over her head. Dani spun under his arm and sliced her blade across his ribs, earning a hiss from the demon.

Elliot's elbow rammed into the back of Dani's head. She stumbled forward, her back to Elliot. Catching herself after two steps, Dani slipped into her stance again and pivoted on one foot. Spinning, she raised her other foot and kicked it across his cheek. His neck nearly snapped from the force of her blow, but his body spun with his face.

Pushing off the ground, Dani thrust her blade at Elliot, intending to skewer him through the abdomen, but he side-stepped her at the last second. Wind blasted into her back. A wall of ice rose between them as her element protected her.

The water melted with a wave of her hand. Unlike most witches, including Damien, Dani didn't need a wand to control her elemental magic. Her water magic had been stronger than anybody else's at the Spellery, except Harbor Bishop. Elliot gave himself over to the demons in his lust for power, but the Goddess's magic gifting lived strongly inside of Dani.

She shot a dagger of ice at Elliot, striking him in the shoulder. Dani sprinted at him as he recovered from the elemental attack. Their blades crashed together again, ground apart, then clashed again. Metal clanged against metal as their swords met again and again, neither landing a blow against the other.

"Miss." Elliot's voice was a hiss on the wind.

Dani's falchion slipped past Elliot, striking air. Her eyes widened in surprise. How did she miss?

Elliot's fist slammed into her sternum, throwing her backward with the force of a wind powering his punch.

Dani crashed to the ground, the air rushing from her lungs as her falchion flew from her grasp. Precious seconds were lost as she struggled to breathe in, and by the time oxygen filled her lungs, Elliot's shadow fell over her, a maniacal grin twisting what could have been handsome features—if not for the evil tainting his energy.

The point of his rapier stabbed toward her.

Desperate to live, Dani slashed a hand through the air, frantically calling out to her water magic to seize hold of the snow surrounding her. An icicle speared out of the ground, the tip so sharp, it sank into Elliot's wrist like a knife into butter.

Crying out in pain, Elliot dropped his sword before it could skewer Dani, and he pulled his wrist free from the spear of ice. Blood as dark as night seeped from the hole in his arm as Elliot pressed his other hand to the wound. He may have been demonic, but he was still a witch and mortals could feel pain.

Dani dove for his sword before he could recover. As soon as the rapier was in her hand, Dani planted her hands in the snow and kicked her legs over her head in a backward somersault, landing on her feet.

Dark blue light tainted with ugly grey surrounded Elliot as he glared at her, shaking his wrist as though he were shaking off the pain. Dani stared in horror as the wound stitched itself together, flesh regrowing to fill in the gaping hole.

"You'll pay for that, you little witch," Elliot growled, stepping toward her as dark blue magic magnified around him.

Raising Elliot's rapier, Dani braced herself. She had no idea what Elliot was capable of, or how much his powers had grown since the Salem War.

She charged, raising the blade overhead to cut him down.

"Stop." The single word was laced with power. Power that Dani couldn't counter.

She froze against her will, the rapier raised as she gripped it fiercely with both hands, one foot holding her weight as she paused midstride with the other leg raised in front of her. Her leg cramped from the prolonged position, threatening to buckle under her, but no matter how hard she tried to move, to swing the sword, she couldn't.

Fear clawed at her chest.

Elliot was a Charm Speaker…. A rare gifting for witches, but as a demon… the Devil perverted what was good to suit his wicked ways, and Elliot was the latest depravity with the tongue of a serpent.

His twisted blue magic wrapped around Dani, holding in her place as Elliot continued to mutter something, but Dani couldn't hear through the blood pounding in her ears.

A vindictive smile twisted his pale lips as he approached and ripped his rapier from her grasp, leaving her weaponless. Not that it mattered since she was frozen against her will.

Elliot traced the tip of his blade down her cheek. The skin split open, and warm blood dribbled down the side of her face. War raged around her, but nobody saw her, nobody would come to save her as they fought for their lives. If they did try to help her, the witch turned demon could stop them with his demonic Charm Speak.

His blade fell away from her skin as Elliot's cold, pale hand wrapped around her throat.

Dani tried to throw herself away from him. She raged and fought and bit and clawed inside, but not a muscle twitched to throw her away from him, her self-preservation instinct completely overridden by his demented magic.

"Do you know what I'm going to do to you, Dani Sanchez?" Elliot spoke softly, his voice crawling over Dani's skin. She would have shuddered from the sound, but her subconscious reaction was blocked. He leaned into her. "I won't kill you." He clicked his tongue. "No. No, that would be too merciful for what I have planned for you." He leaned away from her, so his black eyes bored into hers, and he smiled a twisted, triumphant smile. "Of course, a Virtue would defy the Dark Mother. But you stood against *me*, you foolish girl. And now you will pay the price for defying Darkness, for not bowing to the power that is greater than you, you filthy peasant."

The wind blew fiercely from the east, raging into a Midwestern tornado, as black lightning danced in the darkening sky.

Wait... black lightning?

Maniacal feminine laughter resounded through the air as silver fire burst to life in a circle around Elliot, separating him from Dani. A ghost's hand seized Dani by the collar and ripped her from Elliot's grasp. Dani gasped in a breath as she was sucked into the ether, then reappeared on the outside of the ring of flames, safe from Elliot and freed from his demonic magic that kept her paralyzed at his mercy.

A violent swell rose from Lake Luna, then crashed down on Elliot, smashing him into the ground under the force of a waterfall. The Salem Witch unleashed the worst the sky and sea could manifest.

Elliot lurched to his feet, releasing a roar as he spun in a circle, searching for the Salem Witch. A low growl escaped his lips as his black eyes fell on Kova, mistakenly blaming her for the elemental attack.

But Kova was battling an abyss demon, shooting an endless stream of golden lightning into the open maws of the demon as it tried to open a portal to Hell.

That same wicked laughter rang through the air as black lightning struck the ground behind Elliot. A woman as pale as a ghost with jet black hair appeared like a wraith in the night, a haunting sight to behold. A large male with golden bronze hair stood behind her in silent threat, making her that much more terrifying with her Nephilim protector. Hayden Black reached out a finger to lightly tap Elliot on the shoulder.

He spun around in a rage.

"Boo."

Jamie Bishop decked Elliot in the face with brass knuckles. Elliot flew backward, and with a flourish of her hand, Hayden commanded the air to slam him to the ground and knock the wind out of him.

Dani stared in awe, even as her brother slid to a stop in front of her, throwing his arms up to shield her. But she didn't need shielding. Hayden Black was here, standing in black jeans and a sports bra with a black sword sheathed at her hip and the five elements swirling around her. Not to mention the Nephilim of Fire shadowing her, his hair alight with white holy flames.

She flicked her fingers, and vines sprang forth from the earth, snapping like whips to lash Elliot.

Red flames danced along the edge of Jamie's broadsword as he unsheathed it. Black magic rolled out of Hayden's open palms, creeping over the ground like a wandering fog. Her lips curled into a feral smirk.

Creepy didn't even begin to describe her.

These were the warriors who had gone to war and come out the victors. No. Hayden Black was the angel who went to Hell and returned with her halo intact.

And as Elliot clamored upright, the petrified look on his face said he knew it. His magic sputtered pathetically at his fingers. It was the equivalent of bringing a water gun to a gunfight. And Hayden Black was a military grade bazooka. Elliot turned on his heel and plunged into the crowd of demons.

Hayden snapped her fingers, and bolts of black lightning shot from the elemental storm brewing overhead to strike a hundred demons, dusting them instantly.

With a wild grin, she unsheathed her longsword and amulet athame and charged through the circle of holy flames into the army of demons, Jamie by her side, wielding his holy flames. With lethal grace, Hayden slaughtered the demons by the dozen, her blades flashing as lightning crackled overhead.

Was a yellow hellhound ripping the head off a brimstone demon? The oversized beast must have been the size of a sedan. Oh, Goddess, that wasn't a hellhound. It was Salem—Hayden's familiar had been a Yellow Labrador that sacrificed herself to save Hayden, only to be reborn as an immortal dog with her animal spirit intact.

Sunlight beamed from Apalla's palms, searing demons. The light glinted off the blood spraying in Hayden's wake as the High Priestess followed the Salem Witch.

Thea—the Heart of Earth—swept her emerald-studded staff in an arc, commanding the earth to spear into the hearts of demons.

Wings of silver Spirit burst from Hayden's back like she was an avenging angel. She was so fearsome, so powerful, she didn't need to attach magical feats to physical gestures. The elements whirled around her as she fought, fighting for her as though they had their own minds.

Hayden laughed aloud. She actually laughed as she slaughtered demons. Her own army of darkness followed in her wake, obliterating their old comrades who did not join the light.

And Dani just sat there, on the ground, with her older brother sheltering her. Hayden's laughter cut to Dani's soul, pulling her from her reverent stupor. Pushing Damien off her, Dani surged to her feet, then sprinted after Hayden and her circle. If Elliot was here for Dani, then she wanted to know why.

Water magic swirled around Dani's hands as she shot daggers of ice at the lesser demons. As the ice pierced their eye sockets, Dani made the dagger explode, sending shards of ice cutting through their insides. Demons exploded into dust as Dani smoked them. As larger, more threatening demons intercepted her, Dani used her falchion to fend off the fiends.

By the time she caught up with Hayden, the Salem Witch had cornered Elliot between her and the Asylum wards. Hayden and her circle had driven the demons from the town square to Asylum's South Gate.

Black lightning shot off the Warrior Witch, blasting demons to bits as they charged her. It was as if the lightning had a mind of its own, because Hayden's full rage was focused entirely on Elliot, so there was no way she was directing her magic.

As Dani went to stab another pit demon through its black heart, lightning struck, and the demon exploded into ash before Dani could kill it.

"You may be a witch, Elliot, but you are no longer welcome here." Hayden's voice was ice.

"And what are going to do about it, Hayden?" the traitor witch taunted. "You made a Devil's Bargain with Lucifer. You can't kill me. You can't harm me."

"I made no such promise, boy," Kova growled, appearing between him and Hayden in a flash of green light. "Your predecessor was the King of Demons, who fell easily to the might of the Creator within me. Your power is *nothing* compared to mine."

Golden lightning exploded out of her to strike Elliot in the chest and send him flying backward through the wards. As the traitor was expelled from Asylum, hundreds of demons charged toward the South Gate, fleeing after their leader.

Joining hands, Kova and Hayden combined their magic. A yellowish-colored bolt of lightning rocketed from the witches' hands, bouncing from demon to demon and dusting them to piles of ash. Elliot's demonic army was decimated in a flash of lightning. Literally.

Beyond the wards, Elliot was on his feet, staring at the Salem Witches with wide black eyes.

And then he disappeared in the blink of an eye.

Post battle silence hung in the air. Asylum felt suddenly empty with the lack of enemy demons.

"Hayden Black," Kova's authoritarian voice cut through the silence. "What on earth are you wearing?"

CHAPTER TWO

THE CHASE

"What on earth are you wearing?" Kova shrieked when she noticed Hayden standing there in black jeans and a black sports bra. "Why don't you have a shirt on?"

With an eye roll, Hayden snapped her fingers, spooking a black t-shirt into her hand. "Relax, Kova. Jamie and I were training in the lagoon, and I was sweating. He had time to put his shirt on."

"Since when does the heat bother you?" Kova grumbled.

But Hayden rolled her eyes again as she pulled her shirt over her head. As she flipped her hair out from under the collar, Dani noticed the graphic tee read, "Pretty Good at Bad Decisions," in jagged red letters.

As Dani raised her gaze to Hayden's face, she nearly stepped backward. The Salem Witch's piercing, crystal blue eyes were staring directly into Dani's chocolate brown ones, as though the demon princess could see into her soul.

All of Asylum followed Hayden's gaze to stare at Dani. Floundering, Dani looked around, squirming under the penetrating gaze of the Salem Witch, but found no relief from the stares.

Damien's head snapped between Hayden and his sister. "Uh, Hays, care to explain what's going on? What was Elliot doing here? And what does he want with Dani?"

Katrina Pierce, a water witch and healer who attended the Spellery with Damien and a generally unappealing person, hiked her hands onto her hips, and in her bratty, nasally tone, demanded, "And why haven't you killed him yet? You gloat about being this big, powerful witch, yet you can't beat a measly air witch." Katrina flipped her high blonde ponytail over her shoulder.

Ugh. How did she always manage to push her nose where it didn't belong? Dani clung to her grudge against Katrina after failing to beat the witch in the State Competition for the Grimoire Games five years ago, but Katrina was still the worst.

Hayden's cold stare cut into Katrina the way a knife slices through flesh, and Dani had to resist the shudder of fear threatening to wrack her body. It was no secret that Hayden and Katrina despised one another, but one would think Katrina would have learned by now to not mess with Hayden Black if she possessed any instinct for self-preservation.

"We don't kill mortals," Hayden said simply, her tone cold and monotone, but with an edge that brooked no argument. Hayden ignored Katrina and strode toward Dani with Jamie following as her shadow, ever the protector.

"You." Hayden pointed at Dani, then waved her hand in a gesture to follow. "Come with me." The Salem Witch marched past Dani. "Damien, you, too. Everyone—you are safe to return to your lives. Elliot and his demons will not return while I'm here."

Everyone's shoulders sagged, as if the town breathed a sigh of relief all at once. Wands and swords were sheathed, and the Knights began to deal with the aftermath of the battle, helping the injured to healers and directing the townspeople away from the South Gate.

Whimsically, Apalla swept after her best friend with the grace and elegance befitting a High Priestess, and the rest of the Athenian Council followed. A teenager with dark skin and emerald green eyes pulsing with power followed behind them, her hair swinging with every move. Tightly woven braids extended in neat rows along her scalp and down to her hips. Today, the braids were restrained with a leather band, but Dani knew the girl could fight as easily with her hair worn loose.

Thea... well, Dani didn't actually know Thea's last name because she wasn't exactly a normal witch. Thea was the Heart of Earth—the mortal incarnation of the celestial goddess that was Mother Earth. She split her essence into fragments and manifested a mortal body for herself in the mortal realm so she could train Hayden in earth magic.

Gods and goddesses without the capital "G" were deities manifested by the one and only, all-powerful Creator, who was comprised of the God and Goddess, the Masculine and Feminine Divine, and these lower deities were simply a product of the Creator's power manifested. As a goddess, Thea was ridiculously powerful, more powerful than was possibly conceivable.

Dani stared after the powerful witches, dumbfounded.

A warm hand landed on Dani's shoulder, and the young witch looked into the hunter green eyes of Kova Parker. "It's okay, Dani, Hayden won't smite you." She smiled warmly at Dani, and the tension unwound from her body as dark green light surrounded her.

The next instant, Dani appeared in what must have been the Council's private quarters in the Parthenon. Her knees buckled from the impact of her boots slamming into the floor.

Nausea overwhelmed Dani as she dropped to the floor, and she retched, throwing up the coffee she drank earlier. Acid burned her throat. Embarrassment stained Dani's cheeks as her face heated. Did everyone see her puke?

"Spooking newbie?" Hayden drawled casually from where she sat at the head of the long, rectangular table, her feet propped up on the table as she leaned back in her chair. A thick black eyebrow quirked up as she grinned slyly. "Don't worry, it gets easier. I did the same thing the first time I spooked with Kova."

Such simple words drove away Dani's humiliation. If Hayden Black, the most powerful witch of all time had gotten sick the first time she spooked, then what was there to be ashamed of?

Pushing to her feet, Dani straightened to her full height of five-foot-five and mustered all the confidence she could as the Athenian Council—including Damien since he was the Air Representative on the Council—and Hayden's circle stared at her.

"Take a seat, Dani." Hayden gestured to the seat at the head of the table across from her. "Damien, you should sit, too."

As if in a daze, Damien sank into the seat on Dani's right, wedging himself between his sister and Kova.

Dani could see the gears whirling in Damien's mind as he stared blankly at the wooden tabletop.

If he didn't know what was going on...

Dani couldn't sit still, letting her gaze bounce around the table. Zola, the Earth Representative, sat to Dani's left with his apprentice, Harlan Bishop, Jamie's cousin. It was well known that Harlan was extremely likely to take over for Zola on the Council within the next election cycle, especially since he had served as an apprentice since the Salem War.

Bridget Bishop, Jamie's mortal mother was in attendance as the Water Representative, sitting next to Dante, the Fire

Representative. Those two whispered in hushed tones with their heads together.

On the other side of Fire and Water sat Jamie at Hayden's right hand, and across from him sat Apalla, on Hayden's left. Shockingly, Kelsey Kensington, the Asylum Ambassador who traveled between this town and other witching communities throughout the nation, sat next to Apalla. Between her ambassador duties and attending the human college in the local city, Kelsey was a rare sight in Asylum these days.

On her other side was Thea, who hadn't lived in Asylum permanently in the last three years, at least not to anyone's knowledge. Goddess only knew what the circle was up to when they weren't in Asylum.

Between the child goddess and Damien sat Greyson Valentino, the General of the Asylum Knights, elected after Kane Corso died in the battle against Lilith. Greyson—Grey for short—was a kind gentleman, well-liked by the entire town. He was normally warm and welcoming, but when it came to business, he was as unmoving as a boulder, his face a mask of stone. Typical earth elemental. But they made for the best Generals. Kane and Hunter Black, the two Generals before Grey, had both been earth witches, too. Something about earth elementals' personalities suited them to serving in the witch military.

And then there was Hayden... the Salem Witch, who wielded incomparably great power. The only witch with the power of all five elements, the Salem Witch was chosen by Heaven's angels to fight the Darkness threatening the world, and they only appeared once every thousand years or so.

Except for Hayden, who was chosen a few mere centuries after Alice Parker, the Salem Witch who ended the Massachusetts Salem witch trials. Until Hayden, Alice Parker—

a.k.a. Kova—had been the most powerful Salem Witch, making her the most powerful witch in existence. The powers bestowed upon the Salem Witch came from the Creator, meaning the God and Goddess decide which powers and how much to give each Salem Witch, but Alice was special. They endowed extreme power to her on top of her Nephilim powers inherited from her mother, Uriel, the Archangel of Earth.

But the thing about Nephilim... they had the power to resurrect. While Harbor Bishop chose to remain in the Garden of Eden to live in peace with her soulmate, Alice Parker sacrificed life in the Garden to return to Earth and end the Salem witch trials. But resurrection came with a cost for Nephilim—Alice could never die. Her and her soulmate were doomed to an endless cycle of her living forever on Earth while he reincarnated lifetime after lifetime. But for the first seventeen years of his life, he didn't remember her.

And the last reincarnation of Alice's soulmate went by the name of Hunter Black... the adoptive father of Hayden Black. It was weirdly fitting that Hayden's mentor of the last seven years was also her father's soulmate.

Alice Parker's magical wards—protective enchantments— surrounded Asylum, keeping demons out and preventing humans from discovering the town and magic safely hidden. Which made Elliot's ability to enter Asylum and breach the wards for other demons all the more concerning, and based on the pinched look on Kova's face, she was contemplating the same issue. They were her wards, after all.

Dani's eyes shot to Hayden, who engaged in quiet conversation with Kova and the rest of her circle. Straining her ears, Dani attempted to eavesdrop on their conversation, but someone cast a spell to prevent her from hearing.

That wasn't nerve wracking at all.

What could they possibly be talking about that was so important for Dani to not hear? As much as she wished it, she knew it was unlikely that Hayden would actually want Dani to join her circle. But could it be...?

"Dani," Hayden's voice cut through the whispers of the room, jarring Dani from her thoughts to meet the Salem Witch's crystal blue eyes.

Hayden's tone wasn't cruel, but her voice held a certain intensity that intimidated grown men, and Dani wondered if the woman knew how terrifying she was, even when trying to be kind.

All eyes were on Dani.

Swallowing roughly, she cleared her throat, giving her mind time to catch up with what was happening. Nothing had really happened, but sitting in front of the Athenian Council and Hayden's circle, with all attention on her, the weight of the world pressed on the teenager's shoulders.

"Yes?" she asked, her voice meeker than she intended. She winced.

"Dani, you're not in trouble," Apalla assured her with a soft smile.

If Hayden was a brewing tempest, Apalla was a sunny day. You couldn't find two more opposite women, yet they fit together all the same.

Hayden gave Dani what may have been an attempt at a reassuring smile, but if Dani didn't know Hayden, she would have been traumatized.

"For the love of Goddess, would someone *please* tell us what is going on?" Damien whined. He thrust a finger at Hayden, then pointed to Apalla. "You two know more than you're letting on. Per usual." He pinned them with a glare.

Hayden merely waggled her eyebrows in light-hearted response, but the look she shared with Kova made concern claw at Dani's chest.

Silent communication passed between Hayden and her circle before she finally turned to Dani and asked, "What do you know of the Seven Deadly Sins?"

Dani blinked at her. "Uhh, you mean like wrath and lust and those?"

"Sorta." Hayden dropped her feet from the table. "I'm more referring to the seven Princes of Hell."

"Not much," Dani admitted. Should she know about them? What did this have to do with her. "All I know is that they're crazy powerful fallen angels who followed Lucifer in the Fall and aligned themselves with Darkness."

"About sums it up." Hayden nodded. "Each Prince is associated with a particular Sin. Seven princes. Seven Sins. Together, these Sins spread chaos and darkness throughout the world, and the more evil they spread, the stronger they become. But there are entities working against them. Do you know anything about the Seven Heavenly Virtues?"

"Even less than I know about the princes." Dani shifted in her seat. She hadn't expected to be tested on the lore of Heaven and Hell. Was this a test to be welcomed into Hayden's circle?

But Hayden nodded again. "Most witches do not know about the Virtues. At least not in detail, because they only reappear once every seven hundred years. But the Virtues are different than the Sins in more than one way. While the Sins tie themselves to a single vessel—preferably an immortal like the fallen angels—the Virtues exist as entities unconstrained to a physical vessel. Their essences are less concentrated but can spread over more of the world. They cover more ground but are weaker in any one place. The Sins could choose to do this as well, but they desire the power of a physical vessel."

Dani licked her lips. "During the Salem War, didn't you say Elliot descended into a Prince of Hell?"

"Yes," Hayden agreed curtly. "He now embodies the Sin of Lust, who lacked a physical vessel for the last three hundred or so years thanks to Alice Parker"—Hayden gestured at Kova, sharing a smirk with her mentor—"destroying the fallen angel, Asmodeus. The other princes remain in Hell, their fallen angel bodies banished there."

"But not for much longer," Apalla spoke softly, a dark warning in her sweet voice. Golden light flashed through her hazel eyes, a sign that she saw a vision.

Tense silence hung in the air.

"What?" Damien shrieked, leaning forward to brace his arms on the table. "What does that mean? 'Not for much longer'? Girl, you *cannot* give us a cryptic message without explanation."

Hayden sucked in a sharp breath, then blew it out slowly. "Every seven hundred years, the Sins and their physical vessels are released from Hell to wage war against the Seven Holy Virtues in a battle known as the Apokalyptic War. Seven months before the war, the Sins are released into the mortal realm to prepare for the battle. At the same time, seven chosen champions of Heaven are imbued with the full powers of their Virtue. Once every seven hundred years, the Virtues assume a physical vessel to concentrate their essence into a manifestation powerful enough to fight the evil of the Sins. But unlike the Sins, the Virtues choose mortal vessels, so when the mortal dies, the Virtue is released to become an entity."

Hayden's crystal blue gaze pierced Dani, and she fought the urge to shrink away from the intensity in Hayden's eyes.

"You are one of these Virtues, Dani."

"She's *what*?" Damien shrieked, his face paling three shades as green tinged his skin, like he was going to be physically ill.

While Damien outwardly panicked, yelling at Hayden and her circle and demanding answers, Dani sat in stunned silence.

She was a Virtue? What did that mean? Hayden said she would have the full powers of a Virtue.... What would Dani's power be? She didn't know what she was, let alone what her powers were.

"Which one?" Dani asked quietly, but her words echoed around the chamber, silencing her brother's endless blathering and drawing every eye to her. Clearing her throat, Dani mustered the courage to ask again, louder this time, "Which Virtue am I?"

Hayden's eyes sparkled with mischief and delight, and Dani couldn't decide if that was a good sign, or a sign she should be scared for what came next.

"Chastity."

"The Virtue who opposes the Sin of Lust," Kova said with a victorious smirk. "Like me."

Dani's jaw dropped open. Oh Goddess. Alice Parker had destroyed the Prince of Hell, Asmodeus, in 1692. And now, Dani had to face the same Sin, except this Sin...

"Lust is now Elliot," Hayden reminded her. "He is *mortal*," she emphasized the word, like it should reassure Dani. "The Sins have two advantages over the Virtues because the Sins are immortal fallen angels. They're stronger, more powerful, and deadlier than any Virtue. And the same fallen angels have fought this battle since the Fall. But now that Lust is Elliot, his vessel is weaker. *You* are already stronger than him, Dani," Hayden said with unwavering confidence. "Once your Virtue powers kick in, you will defeat him with ease."

"I think I need to sit down," Dani said as the room spun.

Hayden's wicked smirk turned down. "You are sitting."

The room spun faster as Dani's head grew warm.

Golden light flashed around Apalla's head, but Dani was too dizzy to register what it meant.

"Uh oh, somebody catch her, she's gonna—"

The room went black as Dani fainted.

Pleasant warmth from a burning fire beat against Dani's face. She wasn't a fire elemental, but Dani enjoyed the heat, and waking up from her nap to a cozy fire was the perfect start to a cold wintery day.

Her chocolate brown eyes fluttered open to stare into the emerald flames flickering in the hearth.

Green flames? What the—

Dani jerked upright, pushing the blanket off her body as she swung her feet off the couch and leaped to her feet. Her toes sank into the plush rug in front of the hearth, and warmth seeped into her skin. Someone had removed her combat boots and placed them to the side of the hearth.

She started toward them but stopped in her tracks as a familiar voice spoke.

"Feeling better?" Hayden drawled from where she lounged lazily in the armchair to the side of the fire, a polishing rag in one hand and Nightmare, the longsword magically bonded to her, in the other.

Rubbing her face with her hands, Dani recalled the events from earlier that day. Before church, Dani felt as though she was being watched, and then Elliot infiltrated Asylum and attacked Dani, then Hayden told her...

"Elliot attacked me because he knows I'm one of the Virtues, doesn't he?" Dani asked, staring at her feet.

Sheathing her blade in the scabbard on her hip and tossing the rag away, Hayden stood and stretched like a feline, then joined Dani in front of the fire to warm her hands. Black magic danced at her fingertips, mingling and coaxing the perpetually burning green flames.

"You're not gonna faint again, are you?" Hayden asked, the corners of her lips tilting up.

"No."

Hayden shot her an amused grin.

Silence fell upon the two teenagers. Sometimes it was hard to remember Hayden was two years older than Dani. At nineteen, the Warrior Witch seemed so... beyond.

"He wanted to kidnap me, not kill me." It wasn't a question.

"Yes."

"Why?"

"Because you're the only Virtue the Sins have identified. I suspect he wanted to kidnap you to draw out the other Virtues. You see, the Sins can identify one another. The same is true for the Virtues. With you, Elliot was probably hoping to identify the other Virtues before they inherit their full powers."

"How did Elliot know I'm Chastity? I didn't even know."

"Just as Virtues can sense other Virtues, Sins and Virtues can sense their counterpart. When you come into contact with one another, your energies identify each other. Since Elliot was aware of his identity as a Prince and a Sin, I believe he sensed the truth of your nature when you defied him during the Salem War."

Hayden turned from the fire to face Dani fully, her pale face framed by dark curtains of her midnight black hair, a strikingly beautiful contrast. Hayden Black was stunning, but Dani sensed that Hayden either didn't know, didn't care, or both.

Dani tucked a curly strand of black hair behind her ear. She had always loved her hair with its large, voluminous curly and thick, coarse texture. But suddenly, she felt self-conscious next to Hayden, who never had a hair out of place, even while fighting. Dani could only imagine how wild her hair looked after napping on the couch.

"Well, you don't look like you're going to pass out again," Hayden said with a smirk.

Dani snorted. "No, I don't think so. I was just so shocked... I never thought..."

"Never thought you'd have the fate of the world resting on your shoulders? Tell me about it." Hayden's smile was terse as black lightning crackled in her hair. Did she even realize the magic constantly surrounding her? Dani suspected Hayden manifested her magic absentmindedly. It was part of her, as natural as breathing. "I'm sorry if I overwhelmed you earlier. Sometimes I forget how momentous these occasions can be, and the danger and peril can be lost on me. Especially after the last two years."

"You mean because you're immortal?"

"When you're immortal, danger starts to lose its meaning. At least for me and Jamie. My fear is for the lives of others. Mortals are more fragile than me, and after the Salem War... Once you meet the Creator, you realize there is nothing to fear, for It is greater than all else."

Quiet, Dani stared into the green flames, wondering if she would ever be as fearless as Hayden. But Hayden didn't press her to talk, just stood silently beside the young witch, her intimidating presence a calming reassurance to Dani. Though Hayden was two years older, the immortal witch stood with an authority that transcended age.

"So, what's next?" Dani asked, letting determination steel her nerves.

Hayden smirked wickedly. "I'm so glad you asked. Pack your bags, Dani. We're going on a little trip."

The eternal magic of Alice Parker's wards shimmered like golden glitter as Dani stared at the JEEP truck on the other side of the protective enchantments.

Hayden flicked her wrist, and the JEEP's engine turned over, the lights flickering to life.

"Whoa," Dani breathed. "Did you do that with your electricity magic?"

"Nope." Hayden held up a car fob. "Remote start. This thing is amazing."

Dani's jaw dropped. The Salem Witch, the most powerful witch in the world who could summon lightning and grant souls and resurrect from the dead, relied on a human invention to start her car?

Jamie's hand clasped around Hayden's to wrestle the fob away from her, causing her to pout. Ignoring her, Jamie strode through the wards and settled into the driver's seat behind the wheel. Salem, the massive Yellow Labrador whose size must have come from the magic imbued in her reincarnated soul, jumped in the bed of the truck, making the vehicle dip under her weight.

"Salem, you're too heavy—out, girl! Plus, you can teleport." Reluctantly, Hayden admitted, "Technically, it is Jamie's JEEP. We keep it outside the wards so the random magic flying around Asylum doesn't fry the electronics, but with what we're about to do, my electricity magic will protect the wiring so the vehicle doesn't die."

"Wait." Dani looked at the older witch with alarm. "What are we about to do?"

"We're leaving Asylum." Apalla floated up next to Dani and gestured to the circle.

"What? Why?"

Hayden ignored her, her eyes narrowed at the horizon as though she was waiting for something.

"To join the other Virtues," Thea answered simply, appearing next to Dani from thin air.

Dani's heart jumped out of her chest. How did the sixteen-year-old move so silently?

"Why can't they come to Asylum? It's the safest place for witches."

"Because the Apokalypsis War occurs in a specific location, which is not Asylum."

"Then where—"

"Let's move." Hayden cut her off.

Black shadows engulfed her, and Dani nearly vomited up her stomach again—albeit, the sensation was significantly less nauseating than the first time—before reappearing in the passenger seat of the JEEP. Before she could so much as blink, Jamie buckled her in.

Dani wasn't allowed to say goodbye to her brother. The last time she saw Damien was right before she passed out in front of the Athenian Council. That was embarrassing.

Several "thumps" sounded behind them as Hayden and Apalla dropped into the back end. Thea and Kova spooked into the rear seat in a flash of green light. More pounding sounded overhead as Hayden slammed a fist against the roof of the car, and Jamie revved the engine.

A mass of black and white and silver magic burst to life a quarter mile in front of the JEEP, blocking out the light of the setting sun. That's when Dani noticed the darkness swarming in the sky.

Holy. Demons.

"Remind me why we can't spook directly to wherever it is we are going?"

"Wards prevent spooking or portaling in and out of the compound," Kova answered. "If we modified our wards to allow magical transport, it would create a gap in the magic the demons could leverage to infiltrate the safe house. Strict restrictions keep the Sins out." She shrugged. "With mine and Hayden's powers, the compound may be safer than Asylum."

Dani gulped. "Right." What in the endless Universe did Goddess get her into?

The JEEP lurched forward as Jamie slammed his foot on the gas pedal. The wheels spun in the dirt for a second before finding purchase. Dani's head nearly slammed into the top of the JEEP as they jostled over the treacherous terrain outside Asylum's wards.

Demons dropped from the sky above, plunging toward the truck while terrestrial demons charged toward them.

White holy flames flew in front of the truck to incinerate the demons before they reached the witches. Sunlight beamed from Apalla's hands. Demons hated daytime sunlight, but Apalla's concentrated beams were lethal. The legion of demons retreated or died under Hayden's and Apalla's magical attacks. They were going to make it. The demon army was retreating.

And then the traitor witch emerged from the shadows beside the portal. Elliot's malicious grin flashed a half second before he slammed his hand against the portal, his dark blue magic spreading. Before anyone could react, the JEEP soared through the magical portal. Dani blinked as she emerged on the other side, in a completely new location.

"Hayden!" Jamie roared from behind the wheel, yanking it to spin the JEEP ninety degrees. Jamie swerved before he crashed into the side of a brick building. Dani braced herself against the window to keep her head from smacking the glass. Tires screeched as they spun before coming to stop in a parallel parking spot on the side of the street. Dani glanced at the lines in the road, impressed at Jamie's professional driving maneuver.

The Salem Witch cursed loudly from where she remained standing in the bed of the truck. "Meddling demons! Elliot redirected my portal."

"How is that possible?" Dani asked, but the other witches merely scowled.

Hayden swore again outside, then appeared inside the cabin with Apalla, sitting wedged between Thea and Kova.

"Thea switch, please." The Heart of Earth disappeared in a flash of green to spook to the outside of the truck.

"Apalla—"

"Already done, but I have to hold the spell."

"Elliot's magic tainted my portal. It wasn't enough to mess us up too bad, but we have to drive through the city to get to the compound."

A screech punctured the air.

"We have company," Kova pointed out the rear window at the giant wyvern demon in the sky.

"On it." Hayden disappeared from the back seat. Dani expected her to appear in the bed of the truck again, but she didn't.

Instead, the wyvern's slowly decaying body slammed into the truck seconds after Thea bailed. White holy flames burst to life and devoured the body.

"Thanks for the warning," Thea grumbled before hopping back in the truck bed.

"There's gonna be a lot more," Hayden warned. "Jamie, let's move. We've got more than five miles between us and the compound, and more are coming."

Jamie's foot hit the gas, and he spurred the JEEP into the thick traffic of whatever city they ended up in. If Dani had to guess, they were somewhere on the east coast based on the weather and the quaint, small-town charm of the brick buildings and elegant chapels with steeples and old-time architecture.

But Dani's attention was wrenched from her surroundings as a hellhound appeared running beside the truck. Before she could react, a tongue of white fire shot down its throat, incinerating it from the inside.

She didn't dare look out the rearview windshield as she heard the sickening squelch of a sword sinking into flesh. Did she want to know how many demons Hayden was fighting? And what kind? Because some demons from Lilith's army had been absolutely repulsive. Like vomit-rific.

Jamie turned a corner at a terrifying speed, then slammed on the breaks. Whipping around, he shared a look with Kova, then faced forward and hit the gas again, but less aggressively as he approached the stalled traffic with caution.

The first vehicle they approached moved backward as they squeezed past. Dani marveled at the use of magic, but three dark figures in the sky pulled her gaze.

"Uh, guys?" Dani pointed to the three wyvern demons in a nose dive toward the JEEP as Jamie slowly weaved it through the traffic while Kova used her Salem Witch powers to move the cars as gently as possible so they didn't crash. Honking and cursing greeted them as the wove through the traffic of enraged humans. Lots of middle fingers were flipped for being that jerk.

Hayden disappeared from the bed again, no doubt to deal with the wyverns, leaving Thea to blast green magic from the emerald in her staff at the demons attacking from the rear.

Something slammed onto the top of the cabin. Four hairy legs clamped onto the side of the JEEP as a hairy black head turned upside down to glare through the window at Dani. Another did the same thing on the other side, and Thea battled a third in the back.

Dani *hated* spider demons. They were her least favorite of the creepy crawlies because of their legs. Eight legs just weren't natural.

Speaking of legs—the spider demon rammed its leg into Dani's window, fracturing the glass in a spiderweb pattern.

The spider demon retracted its leg preparing to strike. Jamie threw a hand out, ready to scald it with holy flames, but Dani was faster. Calling upon her water magic, she formed it into a frozen spear.

The demon's leg crashed through the window. Glass rained on Dani's lap, cutting through the thick denim of her jeans.

Dani threw the javelin of ice, spearing it through the demon's head as it pushed the bulbous appendage through the window to bite her. Free of the spider demon, Dani used her water magic to heal the cuts on her legs, which stung as the magic cleansed the wounds.

"Nice." Jamie shot her an impressed look before fixating his eyes on the road again, swerving around human pedestrians and cars as Hayden and Thea blasted magic at the flying demons. How were humans so oblivious?

"Illusion magic," Kova answered from the back seat, pointing a thumb at Apalla, who sat with her eyes closed, her hands pressed together as though in prayer as she muttered under her breath. "Keeps the humans from seeing anything supernatural so we don't have to wipe their memories." She flinched, as though remembering something extremely unpleasant.

"Are you kidding me?" Jamie swore, then shot white holy flames out of his driver's side window at the massive killer bee demon diving at them with its stinger ready to plow through the windshield.

The flames roasted the bee in a torrent, but the demon didn't disintegrate fast enough, and its black, gooey body slammed into the windshield. Goo splattered across the glass, obscuring Jamie's vision.

Air magic pushed the demon off the windshield, but the goo remained, and Dani summoned a blast of water to wash away the demon residue.

Jamie hit the lever for the wipers and put them on high speed until the demon bits finally rinsed off.

"Incoming." Kova pointed over Dani's shoulder at the gray brick building they sped toward at breakneck speeds.

"Crap," Jamie cursed, yanking on the wheel as Kova summoned a ramp of earth. Jamie hit the ramp as the JEEP turned and the vehicle flew into the air sideways.

Two wheels scraped against the top of the brick wall, almost finding purchase, but they had too much momentum. The JEEP careened over the edge, flipped once, then slammed into the ground. The vehicle bounced off the rubber wheels, but Kova's air magic had added so much force that the JEEP spun midair and slammed into the inside of the brick wall.

Airbags deployed, smacking Dani full in the face. Her nose crunched under the impact, and hot liquid gushed down her chin. Turns out, airbags were *not* soft. Despite being filled with air, the bags packed a punch. If anybody suggested air witches couldn't fight as well as other witches because their element was incorporeal, Dani would make them drive a truck into a wall. The airbag deflated.

"At least we made it to the compound," Apalla groaned from the back seat.

"Ugh, we've got to work on our driving and magic combination," Jamie groaned.

"Don't blame me," Kova grumbled as she unbuckled herself in the back seat. "I've hated these monstrosities since Carl Benz invented the first automobile. Back in my day, we had wagons and horses. I never would have ridden in this death trap if it wasn't for you youths."

"Back in your day, indoor plumbing didn't exist," Apalla quipped.

Ignoring their banter, Dani touched a hand to her tender skin and winced. Summoning water magic, she pressed her hand to her nose and healed the bone and skin. The healing was less than pleasant as the bones moved into position and fused correctly. By the end, Dani had washed away the blood staining her mouth and chin, too.

Her passenger side door wrenched open, and Jamie appeared in the door frame. He cut the seat belt off her and scooped her into his arms to carry her away from the wreckage to where Kova and Thea stood unharmed outside the vehicle.

"Welcome to the Salem, Oregon Witches' Compound," Jamie nodded a head to the courtyard's four stone walls.

"Your JEEP," Dani mourned as Jamie set her on her feet.

"When you're dating Hayden, you insure *everything*. There's a reason her name isn't on the title. I'd never get coverage." Jamie winked at her. "I can replace it. *Divination Insurance* probably already knows." He winced and scratched the back of his neck. "In my defense, they knew what they were taking on when they accepted me as a client."

Hayden reappeared like a murderous sentry, her face darkened by the shadows surrounding her.

Jamie lifted a single eyebrow at her in a silent question.

"It's so annoying that I can't use my full powers against him," she said in a huff.

"Not what I was asking."

"I know, but I wanted to complain." She sneered and added with a grumble, "And yes, I handled it," then blew a hair out of her face. "It will take a while for him to escape the bottom of the ocean."

"Oh, Goddess. You abandoned someone at the bottom of the ocean? He will *die*," shrieked a blonde woman not much older than Dani.

Hayden rolled her eyes hard enough for them to roll out of her head. Kova snorted, but didn't say anything.

"That one is as pleasant as Thea described," Apalla muttered under her breath.

"Hayden!" A burly man with a buzz cut and a full beard swept Hayden into a hug, then spun her in a circle and dropped her to the floor. He made to do the same with Jamie, but the Son of Fire stopped him by forcing a handshake instead. "Welcome back to Salem."

"Salem?" Dani asked, glancing between the other witches. "This doesn't look like Massachusetts."

"Because it's not the east coast," a fit woman in her later forties answered as she approached. "We are in Salem, Oregon."

Dani's jaw dropped. "Oregon? As in the state?"

"No, as in the country." The snobby blonde rolled her eyes. "Of course, Oregon the state."

Dani instantly disliked her.

"Enough." Hayden's voice cut through the chatter of the people who had surrounded them, which was a handful of Knights, their weapons drawn, and six other witches dressed as civilians. The six plus Dani... together they were the Seven Holy Virtues. "Unless you all want to die—"

A demonic roar tore through the night, drowning out Hayden's words as a shadow in the shape of a dragon fell over the assembled witches. Dani had fought plenty of wyvern demons, but had never seen one so massive. Its shadow stretched the entire length of the courtyard they stood in.

The Salem Witch disappeared so fast that Dani didn't see her sink into the shadows. Appearing overhead, Hayden wrapped her arms around the wyvern's throat. Black and silver lightning zapped out of her, electrocuting the demon as her lightning bounced from scale to scale.

The demon's long, serpentine neck thrashed and bucked, trying to throw her free as the electricity sank through its scales. Its muscles contracted and twisted painfully as Hayden's magic coursed through its body.

Going limp, the wyvern fell, but shadows swallowed it at Hayden's command.

"Three, two, one..."

Hayden reappeared beside Jamie, panting slightly, as the last word passed his lips.

"As I was saying. Unless you want to die, I suggest you listen up."

CHAPTER THREE

THE CALLING

"Who are you?" a man who appeared to be in his early thirties asked in awe, his eyes widening behind his glasses.

"Demon to some, angel to others," Hayden answered nonchalantly, her gaze trained on the sky above as though waiting for the stars to give her a sign.

"She's Hayden Black," Dani answered. How did these witches not know who she was? "The Reigning Salem Witch."

"Don't let her innocent face fool you." Jamie Bishop shot a smirk over at the frightening warrior woman. "She's really a demented demon."

"Princess of Hell," Hayden corrected, not flinching at the accusation. "And Daughter of Heaven. So good news, I'm pretty much who I say I am. Bad news... yeah, I'm pretty much who I say I am. Depends on how you look at it." She pointed to the sky as a glowing full moon withdrew from hiding behind a cloud, its silvery light illuminating the courtyard. "In other news, you're about to channel your Virtue powers."

"Our *what*?"

"Yeah..." Hayden drew out the word. "Sorry about that. Thought we'd arrive sooner, and I'd have time to explain. But demons." She shrugged. "What can you do?"

The man who spoke earlier gawked at her, his jaw hanging loose.

"Dani, stand here." Hayden pointed to a spot on the ground, and Dani obliged, running to assume her position while Hayden spooked, grabbed one of the Virtues and positioned them, then grabbed the next one and moved them into position until all seven Virtues—or soon to be Virtues— stood in a circle.

"What now?" The girl with platinum blonde hair stood next to Dani.

But Hayden ignored her from where she stood in the center of the circle, staring up at the light of the silver full moon. "Three. Two. One..." She spooked in the blink of an eye.

Dani lifted her gaze to stare at the moon as Hayden had, but instead of the moon's normal silver, the orb glowed with a red tinge. And Dani was mesmerized.

Her body went rigid, her eyes widened, and she didn't blink as she engaged in a staring contest with the moon, the representation of the Goddess. Dani's muscles spasmed, contracting and releasing, not uncomfortably, but she stood rooted to the spot. Electricity zapped down her spine—no, not the spine, but the two muscles to either side, the muscles that would control an angel's wings, if Dani had any.

Her spine arched to just shy of painful. A mix of silver and red light beamed down from the moon and struck Dani in the chest. She tried to brace herself, expecting to fall backward from the blow, but the light didn't hit her with any force. Instead, it sank into her body. She hardly felt it if not for the electricity zapping her skin. Bolts of blue lightning danced over her skin.

Lightning! That was Hayden's Spirit power made manifest.

Dani was being imbued with Spirit magic.

Pale blue light haloed around her, expanding to stretch ten feet to either side of her, stopping where it met the purple and teal auras of the female witches to either side of her.

And then the paralyzing magic released her, and Dani stumbled forward a step. Whipping her head around, she stared at the other Virtues who were alight with different colored light.

The burly man with a barrel chest was surrounded by red light. He must have been the opposite of Wrath. He was Patience. At least, that's what Dani's gut told her, like an instinctual knowledge existed inside her.

A man in his upper twenties, built like a body builder and dressed in a cutoff and jeans, glowed with orange magic. He was Temperance, the opposer of Gluttony.

A small Hispanic girl, standing no taller than five-foot-two and dressed in a simple yet flattering flannel dress, glowed yellow with the Virtue of Charity, who opposed Greed.

The young man with glasses who had gawked at Hayden earlier pulsed with neon green magic. The Virtue of Kindness and opposite of Envy.

The snobby platinum-haired girl exuded the teal magic of Diligence, the underminer of the Sin of Sloth.

And the final Virtue, Humility, glowed with purple magic around the woman in her late forties. Humility, the downfall of Pride.

Dani's blue light faded, receding into her body, as did the other Virtues, until no more magical light shined and the moon returned to its silver glow.

Hayden appeared in front of Dani, scanning her with a critical eye. "You okay?"

Dani nodded. "I don't feel any different."

Apalla Nomad appeared behind Hayden's shoulder, studying Dani. "Her power hasn't manifested yet."

The blonde girl slapped her hands on her hips. "What was that? And who are you?" she demanded.

Wow, that was a lot of sass.

Apalla and Hayden outright ignored the girl, except for Hayden shooting a threatening look to silence the mouthy witch.

"And the others?" Hayden pivoted on her heel to monitor the other five Virtues.

"I did." The older witch next to Dani said the words calmly.

Hayden spun to stare at her. A broad grin split her face. "Excellent, Ronnie! Whatcha get?" She rubbed her hands together like a greedy little kid.

The woman looked at the air around Hayden rather than directly at the Warrior Witch. Was she nervous about meeting Hayden's eye? Maybe. But her gaze flitted around, bouncing like a ping pong ball to various, random places in the air.

"I can see auras."

"Second Sight!" Apalla's hazel eyes flashed with golden light. "Oo, yes, I'm gonna have fun training you."

"Dani." Hayden grabbed her arm and guided her to the older witch. "This is Verona Hawthorne."

"Hawthorne? As in—"

"Yes." Verona sighed and shook her head. "As in Nathaniel Hawthorne who changed his last name because of *that* Hathorne."

Judge Hathorne who had sentenced nineteen people to die for the sin of witchcraft in Salem, Massachusetts. Dani couldn't stop herself from glancing to Kova.

"Oh, sorry." Heat flooded Dani's cheeks. "I didn't mean it like that."

"I know. I can read your aura."

"Oh. Is that how you knew what I was going to ask?"

Verona let out a mix of a laugh and a snort. "No. I knew because I've been asked that question by every single witch I've met, except that one." She gestured to Hayden, then held out her left hand to Dani in a show of respect between witches. "Verona Hawthorne, Virtue of Humility. But I go by Ronnie."

"Ronnie it is." Dani accepted the woman's handshake by slipping her left hand past Ronnie's to grip her wrist in the traditional witch handshake. "I'm Daniella Sanchez, Dani for short. The Virtue of Chastity and water witch."

"I'm a water witch as well." Ronnie inclined her head and beckoned Dani to follow her to Diligence.

"Hi, I'm Ronnie. Humility." She offered her hand to the blonde girl like she had done for Dani, but the other girl stuck her nose in the air. "Noted. I'm Milena Wardwell. I go by Mila. Air witch and apparently the Virtue of Diligence. How I know, I don't have a clue, but apparently, we got a cosmic download along with yet to be determined powers." She sniffed and looked at Dani. "And you are?"

"Dani Sanchez. Chastity."

"Lovely. Who is the wraith?" Mila pointed a perfectly manicured finger at Hayden, and Dani had to bite down a laugh. "And why are *you* so buddy-buddy with her?"

"You haven't met her?" Dani assumed Hayden had brought in all the Virtues.

"Why would I have met her?"

"Because she's Hayden Black, the Salem Witch," Dani said, but it came out sounding like a question. She looked at Ronnie. "You knew her."

Ronnie shrugged. "Hayden hunted me down about a year ago, explained the Virtues and the Apokalypsis War, and I agreed to move here."

"Well, she didn't do that for me. Me and my sisters"—she pointed to two girls who looked like exact replicas of Mila, only a few years younger—"moved here a month ago with a group of Knights to get away from the demon attacks in L.A."

"So, you didn't know you were a Virtue?"

"Nope." She popped the 'p'. "I know about the Apokalypsis War, but I didn't know I'd be dying in it." She rolled her eyes. "If you excuse me, I'm done with tonight." Without waiting for a response, she sauntered over to join her sisters.

Dani shared a look with Ronnie. That girl had issues.

The body builder who glowed orange earlier approached Dani and Ronnie and held out his left hand. "I see you've met Milena." He grimaced. "She's a hard one to get to know."

"You don't say." Dani accepted his handshake and introduced herself. Ronnie did the same.

"Emmett English. Earth elemental." He paused, then laughed and rubbed the back of his head. "And Virtue of Temperance, now, I suppose. Still a bit of a shock. When Hayden recruited me, I thought the Warrior Witch was recruiting new Knights. I had no idea I'd be one of the Virtues." He shook his head. "Crazy. Anyway, the others are manifesting their powers, too." Emmett pointed to where the other Virtues—Patience, Charity, and Kindness—still glowed with their colorful, holy magic. Hayden, Apalla, and Kova each accompanied a Virtue, coaching them through channeling their powers for the first time. "But I haven't figured mine out, yet."

"Me neither." Dani answered, and Ronnie explained her Second Sight powers to Emmett as the trio approached Hayden and the short Hispanic girl.

Silver flames shot from Hayden's open palm like a flare, and the three halted their approach. Maybe they didn't want to get close to whatever was happening there.

Hayden turned and waved them closer, a crap-eating grin on her face. "Dudes, this is Raphaela Jacobs."

The girl remained silent as she waved shyly.

"Charity Virtue." Hayden shot her a disapproving look as though she had wanted the girl to introduce herself. "And guess what her power is?" She vibrated with excitement. Literally. "Amplifier!"

"Amplifier of what?" Emmett asked, eyeing Hayden like she was a grenade after her fiery display.

"Of magic."

Ronnie let out a slight gasp. "Ah. I can see it. You can increase the magical abilities, be it Virtue or elemental magic.

It is a unique and wonderful ability to have. You shall wield it well."

Raphaela blushed at the praise, but remained silent, crossing her arms over her abdomen.

"And Walker here is an Astral Walker." Apalla clapped a hand on the shoulder of the guy with glasses. He had glowed green. The Virtue of Kindness. "He can astral project and create and walk through doors to other dimensions."

"Took a while to anchor him to his body," Kova added. "But he's in control now."

Walker looked a little shaky, but he composed himself to introduce himself. "I'm Walker Burroughs."

The other Virtues acknowledged him, though apparently he and Ronnie had already met.

At long last, the burly-chested Virtue of Patience joined them. "You must be Chastity." Patience grabbed Dani's left hand and shook so furiously, she was afraid he would dislocate her shoulder. "I'm Axel Redd. Virtue of Patience and earth witch. Pleasure to meet you. You're the only Virtue I haven't met yet, so we've been anticipating this for a while."

"You knew you were a Virtue?"

"Of course I knew." He scoffed. "The Salem Witch appears randomly out of nowhere and I'm supposed to believe it was coincidence that the most powerful witch in history knows my name and story and wants me to join her in Salem, Oregon? I know enough about witching history to know the Apokalypsis War was approaching, so it wasn't hard to follow the thread. What I didn't know is that the powers I received tonight would be hypnosis. Imagine hypnotizing those little buggers into a daze and dusting them! But what is your name, child?"

"Dani Sanchez. Water witch."

"And where are you from?"

"Asylum."

"Ah! No wonder you were the last to arrive. Those wards are mighty fine." He let out a whistle. "I haven't visited in nearly a decade. Family trip with my brothers when we were in our thirties. It was a few years before that one showed up." He jabbed his chin at where Hayden had been whispering conspiratorially with Jamie and the rest of her circle, but she was gone.

"Looking for me?" the Salem Witch drawled from behind them with a disgruntled Mila at her side. "How about we share a meal in the dining hall?"

Hayden snapped her fingers and shadows converged around the group. Nausea tugged at Dani's stomach, but it was less than the last time she spooked, and it was over even faster.

Her boots slammed into the wood floor of the dining hall, alongside the other Virtues and Hayden's circle. Apparently, spooking was allowed within the compound, but not between the inside and outside worlds.

Dani was surprised to find Kelsey Kensington seated in the second chair to the left of the head seat. When did she arrive? The other Virtues cast her wary looks, but nobody asked, and nobody offered an explanation for the former witch of terror's presence. But Hayden had a reason. She always had a reason, no matter how insane. At least, that's what Damien always said.

Wordlessly, Hayden and her circle sat, Jamie glued to Hayden's right side. Apalla sank into the chair between Hayden and Kelsey then gestured for the Virtues to sit.

Dani followed their instruction, spotting the sigil inscribed in the wood in the center of the table. She slammed a hand down on the sigil and her magic flared as she ordered a cheeseburger and fries.

Jamie scowled as the hot food magically arrived.

All of Asylum knew he was a health nut, so of course he judged Dani's diner food as he indulged in a... salad. The man couldn't have been more opposite his soulmate who tore off half her burger in a single bite and swallowed without chewing.

"Eat," she said through a mouthful of fries. "You need your energy."

Those were the last words for half an hour as everybody ordered their food from the sigil and indulged in their midnight meal. One of the things Dani loved about magic was how it made the mundane so much more alive.

Sigil magic was a symbol imbued on a material. The intent was captured in the sigil itself, but the magic was fueled by the witch. There was power in the symbol, and with a touch of magic, Dani could conjure whatever food she wanted. Of course, kitchen witches cooked all the food. The sigil merely summoned it.

Basically, she had a free meal plan at the Spellery every day for her tween and teen years. Thank Goddess they had sigils here, too, otherwise Dani would starve to death.

"Thank Goddess they have sigil magic here. I would starve to death if I had to cook." Hayden echoed Dani's thoughts

"No, no, definitely not." Jamie waggled a finger at her. "No cooking."

She held up her hands in surrender, then clapped them together. "So, Virtues. I'm sure you have questions." Hayden shoved the other half of her burger into her mouth.

"Why did you tell some of us that we're Virtues and not others?" Mila demanded.

Hayden shrugged. "Some of you weren't ready. The anticipation would have caused too much anxiety. As the oldest of you, Ronnie and Axel have the most life experience, and I knew they could handle the pressure. For the rest of you, it was best to give you time to settle into living here before upending your lives cataclysmically."

Mila opened her mouth to argue, but Ronnie cut her off with a question. "How long do we have?"

"Seven months," Kova answered. "Seven Virtues against Seven Sins with seven months to prepare before you do battle under the Blood Moon Eclipse on the seventh day of the seventh month. Angels like to stick to their holy numbers."

"Seven months of training to defeat the Sins." Walker wiped his sweaty palms on his jeans. "Right. No pressure."

"About that." Hayden shared a look with Kova. "The final battle takes place under the Blood Moon Eclipse, but the Sins can engage you before that."

"Well, duh. Seems kind of obvious." Mila sneered.

"I don't think it's that simple." Axel frowned.

"Because it's not," Kova agreed. "There are cosmic laws keeping you and the Sins in check. The Rules of Engagement state the Sins and Virtues can engage in battle thrice after they receive their powers and before the final battle. However, there are no restrictions on where or how. The only restriction is that you cannot engage in a battle to the death within three days of another battle."

"Then let's take the fight to them before they can bring it to us." Emmett pounded a fist against the top of the table.

"Whoa, horsey." Hayden raised flat palms. "Slow down. You're not ready. Not even close."

"And how would you know?" Mila shot back. "Not like you've been here to assess our skills." She leaned back in her chair with a smug look on her plastic face. "You'd be surprised by what some of us are capable of."

"I'm sure I won't be," Hayden said flatly. "But it's not your powers and combat finesse I'm worried about."

"Some of us are experienced warriors, but many of us are not hardened by battle," Axel agreed. "But that will change. With training, I'm sure—"

"None of you have faced a Sin before," Kova interrupted. "It's not that they're physically superior—and they are. Sins are fallen angels. They have strength, agility, speed, and thousands of years of experience beyond that of any mortal."

"Says the mortal." Mila rolled her eyes.

"She has a point," Emmett agreed. "You're one to talk, seeing as you've never faced a Sin."

Ronnie pursed her lips, studying Kova through narrowed eyes.... Because she could see auras. Could she see what Kova was hiding? What Asylum kept secret for Kova?

"Have any of you faced a Sin?" Walker asked not unkindly.

"Yes, but Elliot is the only mortal Sin," Jamie admitted. "Which is a recent development."

Mila huffed out an undignified laugh. "You ethereal bloodlines are all the same, so high and mighty and self-righteous, living on your pedestal. Just because you're a descendant of Alice Parker doesn't mean you get to tell the rest of us what to do," Mila snapped. "You think you're better than the rest of us witches." She slammed her palms on the table. "News flash. You're not. You don't get to tell us how to fight this war. We're the Virtues. We're special. Not you. Deal with it."

Hayden's circle shared a strained glance with Kova, seemingly communicating without speaking.... And they probably were. Kelsey had developed telepathy from her mind control—she probably opened a channel of communication between them.

And Dani had a good guess as to what the topic of conversation was.

Kova's true identity.

At long last, Kova inhaled a ragged breath through her nose and waved a hand at Hayden with an exasperated eye roll.

"Here's the thing guys..." Hayden glanced uncertainly at Kova, like she wasn't sure about the next part. "There are ethereal bloodline witches who do think they're better—like the House of Black," she added with a grumble. "Kova isn't harping on you guys because she thinks she's better. You should heed Kova's advice because she's lived a lot longer than any of you."

Axel scoffed. "It's cute that you children forget my age. No offense, Kova. I know you're, what, twelve years my junior, but you're only thirty-three."

"It's cute that you think three Nephilim who have died and resurrected are *children*."

Mila rose to her feet, pushing her chair forcefully. Boy, did that girl have issues with authority. "Immense power does not make you an adult. Nineteen years of life does not make you an adult."

"And what does three centuries make me?" Kova asked with a deadly calm.

Crickets chirped in the eerie silence.

Kova sighed, shaking her head. "I am Alice Parker, the Resigned Salem Witch and Resurrected Nephilim daughter of Uriel."

Mila gawked. All of them, except Ronnie and Dani, gawked. The Virtue of Humility merely let out a content, "Ah," and settled in her chair, as though she were content with merely solving the mystery.

"You say we are children compared to your fifty years, but by the time I was seventeen, I mastered the elements, died and resurrected, ended the Massachusetts Salem Witch Trials and the witch burnings in the Old World, then returned to the New World to lead the expedition from the Plymouth Colony to the lands that are now called Salem, Wisconsin, where I founded Asylum, naming it so witches everywhere would recognize it as a safe colony, free from the fear of persecution. And pray tell, what did you accomplish by seventeen?"

Crickets chirped again.

But Goddess, Mila wanted to fight. It was like she woke up on the wrong side of the bed and chose violence today.

"So, what? You're the daughter of Uriel. A Nephilim. Whoo-hoo." Mila glared at her. "Don't expect us to worship the ground you walk on. And don't think you can walk all over us. We're not your puppets. I've met your kind before." She sneered. "Nothing about your lineage makes you special from what I can see."

"Kova wasn't chosen as the Salem Witch because she was the daughter of Uriel, just like I wasn't chosen because I'm the daughter of Michael," Hayden said calmly. Our Nephilim blood means nothing in the Creator's choice. She was chosen because the Creator knew her soul, both the Dark and the Light, and the same is true of me." Black hellfire ignited in the Salem Witch's locks, like a crown of fire encircling her head. "After all, Goddess refused to take my demon blood, and she chose me as Heaven's champion." Hayden grinned maniacally and the temperature dropped ten degrees at her declaration, a deadly reminder that Hayden Black was no ordinary witch, even compared to the Virtues, who were extraordinary in their own right.

She extinguished the flames in her hair and motioned for Mila to take her seat again. Begrudgingly, the Virtue of Diligence decided *not* to double down.

"Listen, guys. Magic is neither good nor evil, and neither is the witch. It is the intention with which the witch casts the magic, but the same isn't true of the Sins and the Virtues. The powers gifted to you are inherently pure. Patience gives clarity of mind so one can exhibit sound judgement and composure, and in doing so, can separate right from wrong, good from evil. Temperance finds a middle ground between extremes. It brings balance. It protects against extremes, especially Evil, which seeks to tip the scales. Kindness... well, that one is kinda self-explanatory. Charity seeks to improve life for all, to fight for the common good, and to bring light and love into the world. Diligence is more complicated in that it requires faithfulness and dedication to do good despite life's challenges. Chastity is the Virtue of self-control such that evil cannot dominate our lives, and it allows love to grow in places where Evil seeks shelter. Humility allows us to recognize our own shortcomings so we are not so self-centered, and we can see the value others bring to life."

"But I haven't manifested my powers yet," Dani said.

"But you will, and when you do, it will cancel out the evil of Elliot's Sin, too."

"If our powers cancel out the Sins, then why isn't the War a draw? How have the Virtues won the past wars?" Walker asked.

"Because it's not just the magnitude of your power. It's how you wield it, how you wield your elemental magic, and how you fight. It's contingent on your intelligence, instincts, and intuition." Hayden's expression darkened. "Here's the thing about the Sins... they will use the things you love against you. They play dirty, but Virtues play clean. And it puts you at a disadvantage.

"But here's the good thing. Virtue powers don't consume energy the way elemental power does. When you wield the elements, it uses the energy of your magic. Virtues are infinite. The more you use it, the more energy there is. The Sins are different. They consume and devour, stealing the life forces of beings to fuel their demonic powers, burning through the energy to manifest."

"Who are the Sins?" Ronnie asked. "Besides being fallen angels and Princes of Hell. What are their names? Their powers?"

Between her age and her Virtue ability, Ronnie deduced the right questions to ask. She had a sharp mind. Quiet, but maybe that allowed her to see more clearly.

"The Sins are Princes of Hell, fallen angels. They were the Seven who followed Lucifer and led the others to Fall from Grace. The Seven Deadly Sins are the most powerful, possessing the greatest gifts of Evil."

"Then how are we supposed to kill them?" Emmett asked. "They're *immortal*."

"Yeah." Mila slapped her hands on her hips. We're mortals. We can die. They can't."

"You can't kill a Sin, but you can kill a fallen angel." Hayden shrugged. "Well, I can."

Mila rolled her eyes. "That's just fantastic for you," she drawled sarcastically. "What about us? Plus, what you said doesn't even make sense."

"Sins and the fallen angels aren't one and the same. The fallen angels are merely vessels for the Sins. Sins are entities that can exist outside of a physical vessel, and entities can never die. But the host can. When the original Seven fell, the entities bound with the immortal fallen angels because of the sheer power offered by such a vessel. A vessel that *can* perish, albeit, it's hard to kill the fallen angels. In return, the Sins imbued their powers on the Seven."

"Which are what?" Axel crossed his meaty arms over his chest.

"Wrath for Abaddon," Hayden answered. "Gluttony for Beelzebub."

"Asmodeus was bonded to Lust, until I killed him," Kova explained. "Now, Lust has bonded to Elliot Fox, a witch turned traitor during the Salem War. He sided with Lilith and, with Lucifer's help, descended to a Prince of Hell through demonic actions, including drinking demon blood until his heart beat black."

"Ugh," Mila grimaced. "That's disgusting."

"Belial is Pride," Jamie continued, and Dani realized they were explaining the Sins whom their respective parents had driven out of Heaven during the Fall.

Dani had learned all about it during Zola's *Angels* course at the Spellery. Michael, the Warrior Archangel and Hayden's biological father, defeated Abaddon. Jamie's father, Gabriel, the Messenger Archangel, defeated Belial. And Uriel, the Archangel of Earth and Kova's mother, defeated Asmodeus, which was super fitting since Kova was the one to eventually kill him.

"Mammon is Greed," Apalla said. He was defeated by Raphael, the Archangel of Air. "And Leviathan is the ugly green monster, Envy." Jophiel, the Archangel of Heavenly Beauty, defeated the monster. How fitting.

"And Belphegor is Sloth," Thea finished. Chamuel, the Archangel of Heavenly Relationships, renounced him from Heaven.

"Each Sin has a unique power, magic gifted to them by Darkness. But they all possess the physical abilities of fallen angels. Immortal and nearly invincible, they're the most terrifying opponent you'll cross blades with." The dead seriousness of Hayden's tone made claws of cold ice wrap around Dani's heart. "Abaddon's gift is superior strength, even greater than the supernatural strength of an angel. Beelzebub is a siphon, meaning he can steal power from anything or anyone and use it for his own. Mammon is an alchemist. He can transmute matter, mostly metal, but he is limited by distance. It becomes problematic when you try to fight him with weapons.

"Leviathan... he's a monster. A monster who can open portals to Hell. Oh, and as the King of Monsters, he can control other demons. Belphegor possesses temporary time magic, but he is limited to a small range—six feet—and it holds for six seconds. Again, avoid close proximity. Their physical strength alone can wreck you.

"Elliot was born with mind control powers as a witch. Darkness corrupted that power to demonic Charm Speak. He can mind control telepathically, depending on the witch and the circumstances, but typically, he must speak the commands aloud. Belial uses his illusion powers to make fears come to life."

Walker rubbed his temples with his fingers. "My head hurts."

"That was... a lot," Emmett agreed, scrubbing his hands over his face.

Mila's face was sheet-white, and for once she didn't say anything.

"Then let's call it a night." Hayden rose from her seat, the chair legs scraping over the floor. "It's been a long day, and it's almost to the witching hour. Go to your rooms. Get some sleep. Tomorrow, we train."

She disappeared with her soulmate in a flash of red light.

Dinner had long since finished, and Ronnie had shown Dani to her new bedroom two hours ago. It was past four in the morning, but Dani couldn't sleep. She had tried but gave up after an hour of tossing and turning. Now, she busied herself by doodling with a pencil on a spare piece of paper she had found in the desk drawer in her room.

It was a simple room. The whole compound was simple. It was a military base, after all. Gray brick characterized the entire building, only brightened by the medieval tapestries and faded murals painted on random walls, like someone had tried to enliven the place years ago but eventually lost against the dullness of life.

The compound was large—large enough to house the countless Knights flocking here based on Hayden's call to prepare for the pending war. But it seemed small compared to the Spellery, which was an actual castle. But having more Knights around made Dani feel safer, even knowing both Kova and Hayden had painted layer upon layer of protective wards on the compound. The courtyard they had crashed into earlier was the training grounds where Dani would be spending every day for the next seven months of her life.

The compound was a military fortress. Located in the heart of Salem, Oregon, in Wilson Park, the compound was stationed a block from the Capitol Building, and hidden in plain sight thanks to glamour magic.

And what a sight it would have been. Ugly, gray, and dull, it contradicted the aesthetic charm of the human buildings in downtown Salem. But Dani supposed it wasn't meant to be pretty. Especially since it looked like an abandoned insane asylum... and Dani wasn't certain that it wasn't...

The room was bleak. A rickety frame raised the bare twin mattress off the floor. A sheet and a thin blanket decorated the bed. Her desk was worn, but sturdy wood, and the curtains on her windows did little to block out the lights streaming in from the street outside the compound. A simple three-drawer dresser was pushed against the wall next to the desk, but it would have been empty if not for Raphaela, who stopped by earlier to lend Dani bed clothes and clean socks and brand new underwear. The girl hadn't said much, but she did speak to Dani, which was a major improvement over when they had channeled their Virtues in the courtyard earlier.

"Dani." Hayden's voice startled the Virtue of Chastity from the doorway.

Bracing a hand over her beating heart, Dani faced the girl dressed in head-to-toe black with a shoulder leaning against the doorframe. Even leaning, Hayden was taller than Dani, who wasn't short at five-foot-five, but wasn't tall.

"Sorry." She grimaced. "I forget how silent I can be."

"Does Jamie?" Dani teased.

The Warrior Witch snorted and pushed away from the door to enter the room. Closing the door behind her, she said, "Oh, it infuriates him to no end that I sneak up on him. Don't tell him, but I have to use air magic so he doesn't hear me. He still hasn't figured it out." Hayden shot her a wink.

"Maybe he should try putting a magical bell on you."

Hayden tossed her head back and roared with laughter. "Tell him that, and I guarantee the next time you see me, he will have attached a bell to my charm bracelet." She gestured to the charm bracelet filled with miniaturized weapons she could enlarge to life-size with a transfiguration spell. "Anyhoo, I wanted to talk to you."

"About what?"

Hayden flopped down on Dani's bed, making herself right at home. Holding up a hand, she snapped her fingers, and a bowl of popcorn appeared. She shoveled a handful into her mouth and offered the bowl to Dani, who accepted and gracefully folded herself into a seated position next to Hayden. Dani could have sworn Hayden didn't chew before swallowing her entire mouthful of popcorn.

"How you holding up?" she asked, throwing a single piece of popcorn into her mouth.

Dani shrugged. "The same as everyone else. I mean, it was a shock to us all."

"Yes," Hayden mused. "But you're the youngest Virtue by a few years and the others have been living here for months. You arrived today, were attacked by demons and one of the Sins, then channeled your Virtue and met the rest of your comrades in the matter of"—she held up her silver wand as though she were checking the time—"like seven hours, tops."

Dani breathed out a heavy sigh and leaned against the wall. "When you put it like that..."

"It's been a *lot*." Hayden offered her more popcorn.

"Like Salem Witch a lot?"

Hayden considered for a moment. "Not like a Trial, because those absolutely sucked."

"You mean getting thrown off a fourteen-story building and shattering every bone in your body didn't feel great?"

"At thirteen? Nope." She shrugged. "But today was heavy, kind of like the day I found out I was the Salem Witch." She set down the popcorn bowl and faced Dani. "Look, what I'm getting at is that the others have had time to acclimate. Yes, they're surprised they're Virtues, but they're at least settled in here. This is all being thrown at you, and you've been handling it like a champ, but there always comes a breaking point."

Dani raised an eyebrow. "You think a little demon battle and manifesting new magical powers will break me?"

"No." Hayden answered, dead serious. "But it will happen. Believe me. I've broken down more times than I can count."

Dani's eyebrows flew up. Hayden Black? Breaking down? She couldn't imagine it. Hayden, who was always so in control, who had unfathomable power at her fingertips, broke down mentally or emotionally?

Hayden continued, "Now, I don't pick favorites, but you're definitely my favorite." She winked one crystal blue eye. "I know I'm 'scary and intimidating and generally unapproachable'"—she rolled her eyes as she made air quotes with her fingers—"but I do care about you, Dani. So, if you need anything, my door is always open. Figuratively, not literally. Knock first."

Hayden rose from the bed, then glanced around the room with a frown. She snapped her fingers and black light flashed around the room. Was that black light or shadows? Either way, Dani couldn't see, then blinked as the magic disappeared. Her eyes focused, and she gasped.

"Hayden, you..." She spun in a circle. Her dorm room from the Spellery student apartments in Asylum was here. Hayden had spooked in everything, even her water globe collection. Tears welled in her eyes as she spotted her brother's sweatshirt flung over her desk chair. "Thank you," she said through the thickness in her throat. "You're right. Today was a lot. But this makes it easier to call Salem home."

CHAPTER FOUR

BITTER WORK

"You know, normal people don't have a personal collection of weapons."

"Let alone enough to fill an entire dungeon."

"Who said I was normal?" Hayden winked mischievously at Dani. "Anyhoo, for those of you who lack a bonded weapon"—she swept her arms out to her side—"choose wisely."

Not every witch bonded with a weapon. Most at the Spellery did, but many witches fought with a regular sword. Dani was lucky to have bonded with her falchion immediately. Dani stared down at her falchion, at the plain, ordinary metal of her blade.

"Ordinary is a frame of mind," Hayden said softly, taking the blade from Dani to examine it. Upon finishing her inspection, she returned it to Dani's sheath. "A falchion." She smiled kindly. "Like your brother's bonded sword."

Dani nodded in response.

"It shall serve you well."

"So, are these weapons, like, special?" Mila asked as she eyed a pair of twin shortswords. "To help us defeat the Sins?"

"No." Hayden removed the shortswords from their mount on the wall and handed them to Mila, encouraging her to give them a swing. "The weapons themselves are not special except in that they bond to you. They possess no powers to renounce the Sins."

"Renounce the Sins..." Raphaela said softly, as though she were speaking to herself. "What does that mean?"

"It means to defeat them," Hayden answered, a softer edge to her normally abrupt tone. "There are two ways to renounce the Sins. Either banish them to Hell or kill their hosts and the entity will be banished."

"Not exactly," Kova corrected her. "If you kill a Sin before the Apokalypsis War, only Spirit magic"—she pointed to herself and Hayden—"can banish it to Hell. But during the Blood Moon Eclipse, different laws constrain the Sins, and they will be banished to their realm."

"In the past, the Virtues merely banished the Sins to Hell."

"Not that that always worked," Kova grumbled.

"Then how do the Sins exist in the world today?"

"It takes decades, centuries sometimes, for a Sin to escape Hell in the form of their physical host. Once they do, they remain weak for decades. But when the Apokalypsis War comes around every seven hundred years, the Sins are released from Hell."

"When we got our powers last night..." Understanding hit Dani like a ton of bricks.

Hayden nodded. "The Sins were released from Hell."

"What about Elliot?" she asked. "You said he was a Prince of Hell, but he's been roaming the earth for years."

"He wasn't always a Prince of Hell. He was born mortal, but over time, he became so corrupted that the Sin of Lust escaped Hell and chose him as its new physical host."

"Mortal because Alice Parker killed Asmodeus, the Prince hosting the Sin of Lust, in the last Salem War?"

"Correct," Kova answered, not correcting Walker that she was Alice Parker. "Fallen angels can be killed. I proved that. And now you will do the same." Her green irises sparkled with golden light or was it Dani's imagination? "You will kill the six remaining Princes of Hell and renounce the Seven Deadly Sins."

"Normally, hundreds, if not thousands, of years pass before the need for a Salem Witch arises." Kova shrugged. "You just so happen to be lucky that Hayden and I both resurrected within the last few centuries."

"Oh goodie." Mila rolled her eyes. "Ethereal snobs swelled with pride at your power?"

"Not at all." Hayden didn't flinch at Mila's attitude from where she perched on the edge of the practice ring in the center of the Salem compound courtyard.

The courtyard was similar to the Colosseum in Asylum, only much smaller than the massive architectural masterpiece, but it accommodated a legion of Knights training in magical combat simultaneously as Hayden and her circle instructed the Virtues in sword and sorcery.

"But the Apokalypsis War does take place on July seventh, which coincides with my twentieth birthday and the third anniversary of the Salem War, down to the day I defeated Lilith." She shrugged, her foot dangling below her to brush along Salem's hackles. "Could be a coincidence." Her demeanor conveyed it was anything but.

"Was Lil... Lil..." Walker couldn't spit out her name. Her ruthlessness still preceded her, striking fear into the hearts of witches. "Was the First Eve worse than the Sins?"

"Lilith was the progenitor demon. The Mother of All Demons. But the Sins came before her. Lucifer and the Sins fell before Lilith and Adam were created. Worse than the Sins?" She shrugged. "She wasn't a great grandmother. But the degree of their evil is so far gone that it's not worth comparing."

"Hayden," Kova prompted.

"Oh, right. Totally not the point. The point was that unlike the previous Virtues, you aren't going to banish the Princes."

"You're going to kill them." Kova's face was dead serious.

"If previous Virtues couldn't kill the Sins, what makes you think we can?" Walker fidgeted nervously.

"Because the previous Virtues didn't have stacked a team of Heaven-blessed witches," Dani answered. She had seen first-hand what Hayden and her friends could do.

"What she said." Hayden pointed at Dani.

"We know Hayden and I are capable of killing the Sins because I did it in single combat against Asmodeus."

"Elliot is mortal. We won't be killing him—"

"What?" Mila startled.

"Aye. I'm inclined to agree with Diligence on this one." Axel inclined his head. "The boy made his choice. He's with the Sins."

"He's not with the Sins. He *is* a Sin," Emmett emphasized. "If we're aiming to kill them, wouldn't he be the weakest link?"

"Yes, he's the weakest link," Jamie answered, then rolled his eyes as he said the next part. "But *someone* made a Devil's Bargain and promised *not* to kill him."

Hayden sneered. "Not like I wanted to agree to that. But it doesn't matter. We don't kill mortals."

"But—"

Hayden held up a hand, silencing Walker's rebuke. "If it is in self-defense, fine. But we do not seek to kill. Where you see Sin, the Goddess sees one of Her children gone terribly astray. He is lost, yes, but lost does not mean irredeemable." Hayden's crystal blue eyes cut into Dani. "Ultimately, it is up to you, as the Virtue of Chastity, to decide what happens to him."

"I don't understand. Why wouldn't the Creator take away Elliot's mind control?" Walker asked.

"Because the Creator's gifts and the call of the God and Goddess are irrevocable," Kelsey answered. "It is up to us to make good decisions with the free will we are granted to advance the Kingdom of Light." She shrugged. "The mercy of the Creator is greater than you can imagine. Goddess can take the worst of us, even those of us who have abused our power, and transform us into powerful weapons against the reign of Darkness."

"You speak from experience." Axel didn't ask it as a question.

"I do." She nodded. "Elliot and I share the same power—mind control. We're two sides of the same coin, him and I, only he chose wrong. I did not."

"Kelsey speaks wisely," Hayden agreed. "Listen to her. Meanwhile, let's train. Virtues, pair off with someone from my circle, then we'll rotate." She pointed her black sword at Ronnie. "Since there are six of us, one of the Virtues can rest. Ronnie, you rest first. Dani, you're with me." She rose to her feet then jumped over the rubbed bands encircling the combat ring at the center of the courtyard, and Dani followed.

Positioning herself opposite Hayden, Dani drew her blade and slid into her stance.

Hayden moved without warning.

Dani gasped, her eyes barely able to track the Warrior Witch as she moved in a blur. Dani raised her sword in time to block Hayden's black Nightmare. The obsidian longsword slammed into Dani's falchion so hard, it sent warbling vibrations down the steel and into Dani's arm.

Dani threw her free fist, coated with frosty ice, at Hayden, but the Warrior Witch ducked with easy grace. Dani blocked her next blow, then stabbed at her opponent. Hayden slid her blade down the length of Dani's, but the younger witch pushed off Hayden and spun away from her.

Water surged around her in a mini hurricane to protect her back, then disappeared as Dani wrapped around Hayden's back and kicked out. Her combat boot was about to collide with Hayden's head, but Hayden ducked at the last minute, spun, and wrapped a hand around Dani's ankle.

Dani should have been on her butt, but Hayden locked eyes with her, nodded, released her foot, and backed away while Dani slipped into her stance again.

They charged one another. Falchion met longsword again, but this time, Dani struck out with a spear of ice. Hayden glided around the spear, but another ice dagger sailed at her head while Dani swung her sword simultaneously at Hayden's hip.

Hayden dropped to the ground, dodging under both attacks. Then Dani was sailing through the air. A second passed as she remained suspended in the air, then she dropped. Her back slammed into the ground, knocking the air from her lungs, but she held onto her sword.

She raised the falchion in a desperate attempt to protect herself while her muscles fought to inhale a breath of air. Pain radiated down her arm, and the sword slipped from her grasp as sweet air filled her lungs.

Dani gasped and rocketed upright to find herself on the pointy end of Hayden's sword.

She lost.

Stupid fast. What was that? Two minutes?

"How bad was that?" Dani grimaced as Hayden lifted her to her feet.

"Honestly?" Hayden scrunched her face. "Not bad for a mortal. But the Sins would kill you in less than five minutes."

"I could have used less brutality in that honesty."

"I didn't promise your brother that I'd coddle your feelings. I promised him that I'd keep you alive, so that's what I'm trying to do. If that means I have to be brutal and unyielding, then so be it. I'd rather you hate me, because at least that means you're alive. I'll coddle you after the war, how about that?"

Dani snorted as she rubbed out the kink in her neck. "Hey, can ask you a question?" Dani stopped Hayden before she sauntered to the next Virtue.

The Warrior Witch turned back around, all of her attention resting on Dani. "Of course."

"How do you deal with the darkness?" Dani asked. "I mean, as Princess of Hell, you must have more demons than anyone. Uh, no offense."

"None taken." She hiked her blade up, letting the flat rest against her shoulder. "There was a time… when I was younger… I almost caved to my darkness. My demons tried to drown me." Hayden's lips pulled into a tight smile. "Good thing I can breathe underwater. But that isn't why you're asking."

Dani licked her lips nervously, the salt from her sweat stinging her tongue. "It's just that you said I would have to make the decision of what to do with Elliot."

"You're wondering if you can live with yourself if you kill him?"

Dani nodded. "And wondering how I can defeat him if I don't."

"I can't answer that question for you, Dani. All I can say is that I committed that sin when I killed Cain as revenge against him for killing my father." Sorrow pinched her face at the memory. "It is a scar that haunts me, but my Water Trial was all about self-forgiveness, so it's something I'm working through. Just know that taking a life… it leaves a scar. One that doesn't heal easily…. To answer your question on how I deal with the darkness that plagues me…. One breath at a time. One day at a time. It got easier with Spirit." She smiled as silver light glowed around her. "But every day, I start fresh by giving my life to the Creator who made me."

Hayden closed the distance between her and Dani. "Do the world a favor, Dani. Don't hide your magic." Hayden swept Dani's braid of thick black hair behind her shoulder. "The Creator chose you for a reason. Have the courage to be exactly who you were created to be without apology. You're the kind of girl who doesn't settle for anything less than your best. Keep not settling, and I promise you, the Creator is working within and around you."

"What if I choose wrong?" Dani blurted out. "What if I mess it up, and everyone hates me? What if they don't forgive me?"

Hayden cocked her head. "When you decide to kill or not to kill Elliot, will you choose the option you think is moral?"

"Yes."

"Then never apologize for doing the right thing, Dani, no matter who tells you otherwise." Hayden's hand landed on Dani's shoulder. "Even me."

Hiking her black longsword, Nightmare, onto her shoulder, Hayden left Dani to skip to where Jamie and Kova dueled Axel and Emmett.

"Hey," Dani said as she approached Humility. "Your powers allow you to see auras, right?"

Humility shrugged. "Yes. It's part of the whole clear perspective of Humility, I guess. Why?"

Dani chewed her bottom lip. "I was wondering..."

Humility raised an eyebrow.

"What does Hayden's aura look like?" Dani blurted out.

Humility looked at her quizzically. "Why such an interest?"

Dani glanced over at Hayden, who was trying to lick hot sauce off her shirt that said "Good Heart. Bad Temper." while double fisting chicken tenders as Jamie shamed her with a deadpan look.

"You mean you aren't curious how one minute she can be the petrifying Princess of Hell and the next minute she's... that?" Dani gestured at Hayden as she finally cleaned the hot sauce off her shirt, leaving a red stain over the white words.

Humility chortled. "I see your point." Ronnie's face scrunched as she narrowed her gaze at the Princess of Hell. "Her soul is like the night sky—the darkest of blacks, but with specks of light and a white light around the edges. Normally, a black tinge around an aura indicates sickness, disease, or demons, but with her..." Humility hesitated. "It's almost poetic. I'm not sure how exactly to describe it."

"I wouldn't let Hayden catch you talking about her aura."

Dani jumped out of her skin at the sound of Apalla's voice behind her.

"We were... um, we were just talking about—"

"Don't bother lying, Dani." Apalla waved a flippant hand at her as her eyes flashed gold. "I witnessed your conversation in a vision. Comes with the Prophetess gig."

Ronnie eyed Apalla warily, not used to Apalla the way Dani was since Humility wasn't an Asylumnite. "How extensive are your powers, exactly?" she asked, her voice rough.

But Apalla hardly seemed to notice the edge in Ronnie's tone, regarding the older woman with a hint of amusement. "Not so different from your own," she remarked with a sad smirk. "Like you, I see everything. That is my curse." Apalla perched on the pillar of the battle ring beside Dani, watching Humility with piqued curiosity. "I suspect you can relate."

"I don't know what you're talking about."

"Don't you?" Apalla raised a single eyebrow and crossed her arms over her chest. It was such a Hayden gesture, it seemed wrong on sweet Apalla. "Your gift is to peer into the souls of the humans and witches around you. You can see their heart's every desire—both wicked and virtuous. Makes it difficult to trust anyone, doesn't it?"

Humility swallowed roughly, lowering her gaze to her hands in her lap.

"It is a powerful gift," Apalla spoke softly. "But it is not an enviable one. Ignorance is bliss, so for those of us who have knowledge forced upon us, ignorance is a futile wish."

"Then there is no hope at all."

"I didn't say that," Apalla said firmly, but not unkindly. Her hazel eyes shot pointedly over to Hayden. "It takes a long time, but eventually, you will meet a soul who is not pure but does not try to hide its darkness and never stops in her pursuit of a better world." Apalla's gaze cut to Dani's chocolate brown eyes. "You can see the truth of that person's soul, so that is how you know when you've found the kind of soul you want in your life."

Raphaela, the quiet, shy Virtue of Charity, trailed behind Kelsey, who approached with a golden wand clutched in her hand. "Palla, Damien wand called."

The Prophetess tipped her head back and groaned. "Do I even want to know?"

"Probably not."

"Who do they need?"

"Three of us."

"My brother called you?" Dani asked eagerly. She hadn't heard from her brother except for a few brief wand messages exchanged back and forth. "Is he okay?"

"He's fine," Kelsey said with a kind smile. "But it seems Elliot and the other Sins have deployed an army of demons in Salem township."

"The human town?" Ronnie asked, straightening her spine. "Isn't that where Hayden grew up?"

Of course gossip about the Salem Witch spread beyond Asylum's borders. It was amazing Kova kept her secret identity secret.

"It is," Apalla answered. "And she will be furious if anything happens to it."

"Greyson deployed our Knights. They beat the army easily, but as soon as our witches returned to Asylum, another wave attacked Salem. They're trying to wear down our forces so Asylum is vulnerable."

Apalla's eyes flashed with golden light as she channeled her powers of divination, or True Sight as Apollo, the god of visions, had called it the day he claimed her. "I don't think so." Her frown deepened. "I think he's trying to draw us out. Split our forces between here and Asylum."

"Well, it's working." Kelsey scowled. "Damien said he needs at least two of us. Preferably three."

Apalla sighed, sending her golden waves shaking. "Then Kova may as well come with. We need someone to portal us home."

"How do we help?" Dani asked, a fierce edge to her tone as she gripped her sword hilt. If the Sins were attacking her home, she would do anything to protect it. To protect her brother.

"Stay here," Hayden commanded, her tone brooking no argument as she approached the group with the others in tow.

"But—"

"The Sins want to distract us, divide us so we're too distracted to train you properly."

Reluctantly, Dani closed her mouth. She wanted to argue that she should be allowed to return home, to fight alongside the Knights she had trained with since she was a kid. To fight with the people she fought alongside during the Salem War. But Hayden was right. It was a nightmare getting from Asylum to this fortress halfway across the country. It wasn't worth it to spirit back and forth across the country when she needed to focus on manifesting her Virtue powers.

"Which of us are returning to Asylum?" Thea asked, leaning casually against her emerald-tipped staff.

"Any of the six of us is powerful enough to help Asylum," Kova intoned, fixing her gaze on Hayden. "We need to prioritize training the Virtues."

Hayden nodded in response, staring at her feet with a pensive expression masking her face.

Apalla's hazel eyes flashed gold, and her frown deepened. "Uh, Hayden, you should probably make a decision sooner rather than later."

Her head snapped up to Apalla. "Crap," she muttered. "Palla, Thea, Jamie. The three of you go to Asylum, temporarily."

"Are you sure?" Jamie's tone bordered on harsh, but Hayden didn't flinch. They were warriors, and warriors didn't falter.

Dani exchanged a look with Ronnie, but the older witch didn't seem concerned based on whatever she read in their auras.

"I need Kelsey here. She can mimic Elliot's powers since the Virtues are susceptible to his Charm Speak until all of them manifest Virtue powers."

"And I'm the demon. They need practice fighting a princess if they are to survive the princes. And Kova has the most experience against the Sins since she killed one. I don't like it," she admitted. "But it's necessary to split up for a few days. After the Virtues learn to fight Kelsey's mind control, we will send Kelsey to Asylum." Hayden met her soulmate's gaze. "Burn them to the ground and come back to me."

Jamie pressed a chaste kiss to Hayden's pink lips. It was light and sweet and full of love, and if they hadn't been surrounded by people, Dani suspected the kiss would have been far more passionate. Ronnie coughed and shifted her weight between her feet, confirming what Dani suspected.

"I wish you'd let me kill him," was all he said before he turned on his heel and led Thea and Apalla toward the side door to the street outside the compound.

"We need to change our training strategy," Hayden observed.

"Two on one?" Emmett offered, waggling his eyebrows.

Axel snorted. "They will hand us our butts, boy."

"So, three on one?" Walker asked nervously.

Mistaking Walker's serious question for a joke, Axel threw his head back and roared with laughter. The younger witch's cheeks burned red, and he ducked his head to hide his gaze behind the curly locks falling into his eyes.

"Nah." Hayden looped her thumbs through the belt loops on her jeans and leaned back on her heels. "I was thinking we can train in a group."

"Magic practice?" Kelsey asked.

"Magic practice." Hayden quirked her head like a cat as she regarded Raphaela. "Charity, you seemed to have caught on to your Virtue powers quickly. Think you can do it again?"

Raphaela didn't speak, only nodded once, closed her eyes, and inhaled deeply through her nose. A halo of yellow light shined around her, and the longer she held it, the brighter it burned.

"Whoa," Mila breathed out. "That's some juice." Air whipped around her as she called upon her element.

"Aye, I feel it, too," Axel agreed.

"What about you?" Dani asked Ronnie. "Does it change your Second Sight?"

"It makes the auras clearer. Like the lines aren't as blurred, or I can decipher the meaning of the aura easier. And I certainly feel the amplification in my water magic."

"Can you feel your Virtue magic?" Ronnie asked her.

"Walker, summon your Virtue power while Raphaela holds the amp," Hayden suggested before Dani could answer, as if she already knew Dani's answer.

Nothing. Dani felt nothing. Her Virtue remained silent. The power amplification she felt was for her elemental magic.

But Walker clearly felt his Virtue amplified, because neon green light wrapped around him like a tree. He dropped like a rock.

Kelsey's air magic wrapped around the witch and gently laid him horizontal on the ground as a green spirit emerged from his body.

"Astral projection." Walker's voice was like a whisper on the wind, yet Dani heard his voice with perfect clarity as though he was speaking directly into her ear. His green astral form stepped away from his physical body, his movements an eerie echo of the way a body moved in the physical realm.

Mila wrinkled her nose. "What's the point of that power? Seems pretty useless."

"Do you ever shut up?" Dani snapped before she could stop herself. "Goddess, you'd think a Virtue wouldn't stoop so low to bully the witches she's cosmically bound to."

"Sheesh, Dani." Kelsey chuckled. "Channeling a bit of Hayden."

Hayden's lips quirked up at the ends, her eyes sparkling with laughter as the only indication that she found Dani's sass amusing.

"Mila." Hayden's eyes didn't move off Walker's astral body. "Any manifestation?"

"No," she grumbled. "I can feel it, but it's not coming out."

"Then focus on your shortcomings rather than tearing others down. You may be Diligence, but that doesn't negate your responsibility to act in accordance with the other Virtues, like Kindness." She stalked over to Walker, reached a hand out, and pushed down on his shoulder, lowering him to the ground from where he floated up a few feet. "Return to your body, Walker."

Silently, he returned to his body, and as his spirit form sank into his abandoned physical body, the neon green glowed around the physical body again, then disappeared. Walker sat up, body and spirit intact.

"Anyone else?"

Emmett shook his head, his arms crossed over his chest. "I can feel it, too. It's just under the surface, but it's not ready to come out."

"Don't worry," Kova reassured him. "It will. Give it time and don't force it. Temperance will reveal Itself when It wishes."

Without warning, Axel's red Patience magic burst to life around him like a supernova. Thankfully, his powers couldn't hypnotize the other Virtues, but Dani could sense his power pressing against her skin, and it felt familiar, like a brotherly hug.

An image of Damien flickered through her mind, and Dani's heart yearned to see her brother. And then she felt something else. The earliest stirrings of something inside her. A magic, ancient, deep, and powerful, that had been slumbering for seven hundred years, beginning to awaken.

"Fight it, Dani," Hayden barked.

The younger witch ground her teeth together. "I'm trying."

"Use your mental shields. Block her out."

Dani had to repress an eye roll. "Way to state the obvious."

The pressure pushing against her mind lessened as Kelsey retracted her magic, and Dani sank to her knees in relief.

Ronnie's hand appeared in front of her, and Dani accepted it, letting the older witch pull her to her feet.

"You did well," she commended. "A month ago, you couldn't resist for more than a few seconds. You withstood Kelsey's mind control for almost five minutes."

"It's still not enough," Dani whined. It was mid-January already. Six months until the Apokalypsis War, and she was nowhere near ready to face a Sin, let alone seven of them.

"Don't underestimate yourself," Kelsey responded with a shake of her head. "You withstood my mind control for five minutes, and I'm stronger than Elliot. He has to speak the commands aloud to control you. I can do it telepathically. I have absolute faith that you will defy his Charm Speak."

"I agree with Kelsey." Hayden fist bumped Dani. "You've come a long way" She smirked wickedly. "It will drive Elliot nuts that you're no longer susceptible to his charms."

"Ew. Why'd you have to say it like that? So gross."

Kelsey covered her laugh with a cough, earning a glare from Hayden. Ronnie laughed under her breath, and Dani wondered what she saw in their auras with her Second Sight.

"Anyhoo, I think it's time we change up our training strategy a bit. Instead of learning to resist Charm Speak, because you will eventually activate your Virtue and receive natural immunity, making all this training kinda unnecessary. So, we're going to focus on *how* to fight the Sins." Hayden sauntered toward Axel to train with him.

"Does that mean..."

Kelsey nodded. "I'm leaving. Asylum needs me more than ever, and I'm sure Hayden would prefer if her soulmate stopped portaling home every other day. Plus, your brother wand calls me like three times a day." She rolled her eyes with every bit of attitude the girl had in her body. "I'm going to kill Apalla for inventing that spell. He's driving me nuts."

Dani laughed at the image in her head. She knew Kelsey wasn't exaggerating, because Damien called her just as many times, if not more, to check in on her training.

Kelsey threw her arms wide and pulled Dani into a tight embrace. "Don't let Hayden run all over you guys. She can be a bit unpredictable. But she means well."

Dani pulled away. "I know." Her eyes flitted to where the Salem Witch worked with Axel, training him to use his hypnosis on a greater demon. As one of the older witches, he adapted to his new Virtue powers quickly, easily learning to hypnotize lesser demons. But every Virtue had to level up their powers to combat enemies as fearsome as the Sins.

"If you ever need to coax her into chilling out, offer her food." Kelsey winked as she tossed her platinum hair over her shoulder. "Especially waffles or chicken tenders or Mexican food. She's been on a taco kick lately."

Dani snorted. "Mexican food is the only food I can cook. Good to know that I'm useful for something."

"Dani. Ronnie." Hayden waved them over to where she had gathered the others in the sparring ring. "New plan guys. I want you to use your Virtue powers, but instead of one-on-one, the seven of you will combine forces to fight me. The goal is to get me into a kill position before I can take down the seven of you."

Mila opened her mouth to argue.

"I'll limit myself to combat. Does that seem fair?"

"Fine," Mila grumbled, crossing her arms over her chest and pursing her lips like a petulant child.

The Virtue of Diligence had made her feelings toward Hayden perfectly clear. Actually, most of them didn't love Hayden. Ronnie and Axel seemed fine with the Salem Witch, but the younger witches, except Raphaela, complained constantly, putting Dani in an uncomfortable position since she was friends with Hayden and still hoping to claim the water representative in her circle someday. But Dani understood their frustration. Hayden was unyielding, grueling, and at times, too harsh. While she was doing her best to train them so they survived the Apokalypsis War, the Virtues saw a powerful witch beating the crap out of them daily. It was hard not to resent her.

"Let's just get this over with," Emmett grumbled.

"Cheer up, kids." Axel unsheathed his battle axe. "It's another opportunity to beat up on Hayden."

"Ready?" She grinned wickedly.

"No," Mila huffed under her breath.

"Begin," Ronnie said.

Black streaked through Dani's vision as Hayden moved faster than any mortal. Her black sword crashed against Axel's axe as he raised it to block.

Colorful light shined around the courtyard as the Virtues who had already manifested their powers called upon their heavenly magic. Purple for Ronnie. Green for Walker. Yellow for Raphaela. And red for Axel.

Axel beamed his red light at Hayden, but she dodged the magic and touched her blade to his side.

"Wound," she declared, then spun away as he swung down at her.

Emmett threw a boulder at her back, but without looking, the witch gracefully avoided it like a prancing ballerina.

Axel swung again, and the two witches exchanged blows. Emmett attempted to help by throwing more rocks, but Hayden dodged all of it with precisely honed reflexes.

A beam of red light blasted at Hayden again, thicker this time as Raphaela's yellow magic amplified Axel's, but Hayden dodged and slid between Axel's legs. Popping up behind him, she pressed her sword into his back.

"Dead."

His red magic disappeared as he shook his head at himself and exited the ring to stand with Kova and watch the fight.

Emmett threw more rocks, which Hayden smashed with her sword. In seconds, she had forced him into a yield position.

"Dead."

Emmett left the ring, and Hayden surged at Raphaela. In a panic, the girl summoned flames to her hands and shot streams at Hayden, but raw magic was useless against the Salem Witch.

The Virtues needed a strategy.

"Dead."

Raphaela left the ring to join Axel and Emmett, her head hung low. The older man patted her lightly on the head as Kova shared words of encouragement. But that wouldn't save the other four in the ring.

Oof. Make that three.

Walker lay on his back, Hayden hovering over him with her sword. In his defense, astral projection left his physical body vulnerable, and because of that, the Virtues had already decided to avoid using his powers in a fight unless absolutely necessary.

"Dead."

Mila shrieked as Hayden rushed her, dropped her sword, and turned to run.

The Salem Witch ceased her pursuit as Diligence leaped over the ring guards and landed in Emmett's arms. Rolling her eyes, she muttered, "Not dead, yet, but the Sins would hunt you just for being a coward."

Gulping, Dani shared a look with Ronnie. Two of them against Hayden. And one without her powers. They were dead.

Black obscured her vision as Hayden's hair flew around them. By some miracle, Dani managed to raise her falchion in time to block Hayden's sword, Nightmare.

Ronnie blasted a hose of water at Hayden, but the Warrior Witch dodged and aimed a strike at Dani. Dani blocked, and Hayden spun to slam her blade against Ronnie's.

Block. Strike. Spin. Stab.

The Salem Witch fought the two women simultaneously.

Water swished around them as Ronnie and Dani combined their elemental magic. Dani aimed a spear of ice at Hayden and shot it with terrifying speed. Hayden caught the spear with her bare hand, pivoted, and rammed the spear into the ground at Dani's feet.

Her eyes widened as she stumbled backward from the shock of the blow. A black blade appeared under Dani's chin, and she jerked away, tumbling to her butt.

"Dead."

Ronnie stabbed at Hayden from behind. The warrior spun, caught Ronnie's wrist with a vice-like grip, and twisted, forcing the blade from Ronnie's grasp. Nightmare leveled with the older witch's heart.

"Dead."

Ronnie merely pursed her lips, displeased with her own performance. As did Dani. That was not a spectacular display of skill from any Virtue. Pathetic. Seven on one. And they lost.

Kova led the other Virtues back into the ring, then offered a hand to Dani, who gratefully accepted.

"And what did we learn from this?" Hayden prompted.

"Um..."

Hayden sighed, shaking her head. Her startling blue eyes found Dani's chocolate brown ones. The blue glimmered with hope that Dani would be wise enough to answer her question.

"Teamwork and strategy. We're fighting as individuals instead of as a unit with a plan. Divided, we're dead. United, we will be victorious."

CHAPTER FIVE

"Accidental" demon Summoning

"Haywire, who gave you the black eye?"

Hayden shot a wild grin at her soulmate, a look of pure exhilaration on her face. "I did," she stated triumphantly.

Jamie raised an eyebrow. "You gave yourself a black eye?"

Apalla snorted from the opposite side of the ring, where she stood with Dani. "She kneed herself in the face as she shimmied through the bars to get into the ring."

Tossing back his head, Jamie roared with laughter. The Son of Fire returned to Salem after dealing with the demonic armies attacking Asylum, and Kelsey returned to the Midwest after having caught the Virtues up on how to repress Charm Speak, more or less... it wasn't an exact science.

"Haywire, I know you're not the best healer in the world, but it's just a bruise. Why haven't you fixed it yet? Or had Dani do it?" He gestured to the Virtue of Chastity.

Dani and Ronnie both possessed healing abilities, but Ronnie admitted she spent little time honing those powers because the sight of wounds made her queasy. Thus, Dani was established as the Virtues' resident healer.

"Because it gives me an edgy look." Hayden waggled her eyebrows.

Dani couldn't stop the snort that came out of her, drawing the attention of three of the most powerful witches in the world.

"You think that's funny?" Hayden asked darkly.

"Uh ..."

A wild grin split Hayden's face. "Dani, I'm messing with you."

"Oh, thank goodness." Dani breathed out a sigh of relief. "I know we're friends and all, but you're freaking terrifying."

Hayden grinned wickedly, her eyes twinkling with mischief. "If you don't terrify people at least a little, then what's the point of being a Princess of Hell?"

Dani snorted out a laugh. She had been around Hayden for years now, but the tension existed between the Virtues and the Salem Witch. While Hayden was all sharp edges and harsh words, the Virtues were softer beings, with Dani falling somewhere in the middle.

"Dani," Hayden said her name. "Are you ready?" She raised an eyebrow as she brandished her sword. "To spar?"

"Oh, yeah." Dani shook herself from her thoughts running and unsheathed her falchion.

"Don't overthink," Hayden advised. "I'm not going all out on you, so fight to the best of your ability. I'll match your skill level."

She nodded, slipping into the fighting stance she had practiced every day since she moved to Asylum to attend the Spellery, and had used countless times in the weeks—no, two months—since she had moved here.

Hayden struck first, sticking true to her word that she would match Dani's skill level. Dani had seen first-hand how *fast* the Salem Witch could move, but Dani was able to track her movements and meet her blow with a block of her blade.

Dani pushed Hayden's blade off her falchion and delivered her own strike, which Hayden caught with ease. The two women danced back and forth, every which way around the ring, exchanging blows and blocking and countering, all without magic. Not that Hayden needed it.

Sweat dripped between Dani's shoulder blades, beading down her spine and soaking her forehead as she toiled, despite the mild weather inside the compound on the mid-winter day. But Hayden didn't break a sweat. In fact, she kept one hand firmly behind her back—and it was her right hand, meaning she was using her nondominant hand to fight Dani.

The realization fueled the fire steaming inside Dani's chest. She had to be better, stronger, quicker if she wanted to survive the Sins. Hayden was greater than the Sins, but Dani was not. And with less than six months until the Apokalypsis War... Dani had a lot to learn despite the months of training. And she hadn't manifested Chastity's powers.

Quickening her steps, Dani charged Hayden with a flurry of strikes, which Hayden caught with ease. Wrenching her arm back, Hayden prepared to stab Dani through the gut, but Dani easily side-stepped and spun around Hayden's back.

Hayden pivoted, swinging her black blade at waist height to cut into Dani's hip. Dani caught the strike with her falchion and held against the pressure Hayden pushed into her blade.

"Hey, Dani?"

Dani paused, looking in Hayden in the crystal blue eye. "Yes?"

Hayden's foot caught Dani around the ankles and knocked her legs out from under her. The Virtue crashed against the cushioned floor of the sparring ring.

"Hey!" Dani protested. "That was dirty fighting."

"The Devil never fights fair." Hayden offered Dani a hand and hauled her to her feet. "And neither do the Sins."

"Aren't we supposed to be better than them?" Ronnie asked calmly, raising one eyebrow. "Why debase ourselves to fight dirty?"

Hayden shrugged. "Who said that's dirty? Sins and Virtues alike are bound by the cosmic rules of the Apokalypsis War, but otherwise, the Sins will fight to win by any means necessary. As long as you're not acting immoral, like using another mortal as a human shield, then all fighting is fair fighting. What I did was nothing compared to how the Sins fight. You have to be prepared for what you're up against."

"This isn't working." Hayden huffed out a breath in frustration.

"Gee, ya think?" Mila snapped as she rose to her feet and brushed the dirt off her clothes. "We're not you. We're not warriors. We're *Virtues*." Slapping her hands on her waist, she emphasized the word.

"Virtues *are* warriors." Hayden rolled her eyes impatiently. "But most of you don't have war experience. It's February. And only four of you have manifested your powers, yet we're five months away from the Blood Moon Eclipse. Normally, all of you have channeled your Virtues by now." She frowned, studying each of the Virtues before catching Kova's eye. "We're lucky the Sins haven't attacked yet. I suspect the wards and our circle dissuades them, and Elliot replacing Asmodeus changes their battle strategy. But we're behind. They're horrible fighters, and at this rate, they'll likely die—"

"Horrible fighters?" Mila's voice rose three octaves. "You're seriously standing here and calling us horrible fighters to our faces." She threw her hands out to the sides. "Ever think it's not on us? That you just suck at teaching?"

The Salem Witch remained calm, raising a single eyebrow. "You done?"

Rising to her full height, Mila threw her bonded sword in the dirt. "No, I'm not done. You saunter in here all high and mighty with a chip on your shoulder, acting like you know everything, when in reality, you're a coward using the rest of us as pawns to sacrifice in your stupid war."

"That's not true," Hayden answered coldly, her words spoken without inflection.

"Really? It's not?" Mila laughed hollowly. "Is that what Harbor Bishop thought when you forfeited her life to save your skin?"

Hayden went deathly still, and the temperature in the room dropped twenty degrees.

"I've heard the stories." Mila looked Jamie in the eye and spat. "It's disgusting how you dote on her when she's the reason your sister is *dead*."

Hayden surged at Diligence in a streak of black. Dani's heart stopped beating in her chest as Ronnie gasped next to her. Black lightning cracked in the air, splitting the sky.

Kova beat Hayden, spooking in front of Mila in a flash of green light before the younger Salem Witch could rip Mila's heart out with her bare hands.

"Maybe it's time for a break," Kova suggested calmly, raising a flat palm in front of Hayden's chest to halt her in her tracks.

Appearing beside his soulmate in a flash of red, Jamie wrapped his muscular arms around Hayden, and she sank into his chest. The effect those two had on each other—it was like Jamie could walk her back from whatever edge she toed. When she overflowed with anger like none other, only the Son of Fire could calm the Princess of Hell.

When she opened her eyes, Hayden merely shrugged and leaped out of the ring. "I could go for some chicken tenders."

Jamie frowned as he flung his arm around his soulmate's shoulders. "You know chickens don't have tenders, right?"

"Ruin my lunch, and I will throat punch you," Hayden warned with a devilish smirk. Pausing, she craned her neck to look over her shoulder at the Virtues. "Well? Aren't you all hungry?"

"Uhhh, weren't you about to pulverize me five seconds ago?" Diligence muttered under her breath loud enough for Dani to hear but based on the evil grin Hayden shot at them, Dani suspected the air carried Milena's whispers to the Salem Witch. "I swear, she's more bipolar than the weather." Despite her grumblings, Milena trudged after the Salem Witch and her circle with the other Virtues in tow.

"I wouldn't complain, if I were you," Walker advised. "I thought you were dead."

"I can't believe she's letting you off the hook for that comment," Dani agreed, regarding Diligence coolly. "I'm glad you're not dead." Dani stepped in front of Mila, stopping her mid-step so they stood nose-to-nose. "But don't ever mention Harbor Bishop again," she added darkly. "Hayden and Jamie aren't the only ones willing to kill for Harbor. All of Asylum stands by them. Harbor was one of our own, and she sacrificed her life to save the world. Don't *ever* diminish her sacrifice by suggesting her life was forfeited by Hayden's choice."

"Chicken tenders sound good," Axel said, stepping between the women to break the tension between the female Virtues. Shrugging his massive shoulders, then hooking his thumbs in his waistband behind his belt buckle, he glanced over his shoulder at Mila. "The witch is a bit insane, but at least she feeds us."

"Why does she assume we know to follow her after she says something like that?" Emmett complained, heading toward the door to the mess hall.

"Because she mentioned chicken nuggets." Ronnie signed, waving for the others to follow. "If she mentions food, especially pancakes, waffles, breakfast burritos, or nuggies, she either isn't too mad or has forgiven us."

"Food has always been her peace offering," Dani said with an amused smile, recalling all her fond memories at the Spellery lunch table with her brother and Hayden. "At least for as long as my brother has known her, which has been since she moved to Asylum."

Twenty minutes later, the Virtues and Hayden's circle gathered around a meal spread across a long table in the compound's mess hall. Per Hayden's insistence, chicken nuggets sat piled on several plates with an array of dipping sauces.

Snatching a handful of chicken tenders from the nearest plate, Hayden gestured for everyone to dig in and casted a side-eyed glare at her soulmate who regarded her with disgust as he drank what appeared to be celery juice. How the Goddess mated a health-nut with someone who ate like Hayden, Dani would never understand.

"We need someone you can fight, who you aren't worried about killing." Hayden announced as she dunked a chicken tender in barbeque sauce—much to the disgust of her soulmate— and shoved the entire nugget in her mouth.

"Babe, I don't think the problem is that they're worried about killing us," Jamie explained. "But rather they aren't worried about us killing them."

Hayden's crystal blue eyes lit up, sending a thrill of excitement and a shiver of dread coursing through Dani.

"Oh, way to go, Jamie," Apalla muttered. "You gave her an idea."

Thea frowned, twisting her staff in her hand so the emerald caught the sunlight. "I thought we were trying to avoid that."

With a snort, Kova said, "When you live for an eternity, you'd be amazed what you think of with the downtime."

"You're right, babe." Hayden trailed a finger down Jamie's arm. "We need to simulate the same emotions they experience when they encounter the Sins."

"Which is what?" Ronnie asked, but the tone in her voice suggested she knew she would regret asking.

"Fear," Jamie said simply, not taking his royal blue eyes off his soulmate. "Consciously, you know we won't kill you, so when you come face to face with the princes, who will kill you, you will freeze. Freezing on the battlefield is a death sentence."

"You need to practice fighting a real enemy that strikes fear in your heart, but in a controlled setting." Her lips twisted into a devilish grin. "And I know just the thing to help us."

"Demons?" Jamie asked, knowing his soulmate well.

"Demons."

But Apalla's frown disagreed. "The Virtues know Jackal and Buddy and some others." A constant stream of demons, who devoted themselves to Hayden in the last war and earned themselves a soul, like Jackal and Buddy, teleported between Salem's compound and Asylum at Hayden's command. She was a mastermind puppeteering a game of chess. "And powerful as they may be, they were created to be pawns in Lilith's army. Their abilities are a shadow compared to that of the Sins."

"No, not *my* demons."

"Oh, Goddess." Kova tilted her head and blew out a breath. "Here we go."

"Zuzu," Hayden crooned.

"Who is Zuzu?" Walker asked in confusion.

"Short for Pazuzu—a greater demon."

The silence was deafening.

A chicken tender slipped from between Dani's fingers and crashed into the plate. A light gasp escaped Raphaela's throat as she stared at the Warrior Witch with wide eyes. The Virtues stared at her with a mix of horror and uncertainty in their wide eyes, except Ronnie, who merely lounged in her seat and studied the air around Hayden.

Hayden's circle barely reacted. Jamie kept his arm thrown around his soulmate's shoulders, Apalla dunked her chicken nuggets into a pile of ketchup. Thea nibbled on her fruits and vegetables with one hand while leisurely stroking the velvety fur on Salem's head as the Yellow Labrador drooled over the chicken nugget in Apalla's hand.

Kova pursed her lips, considering what Hayden was suggesting. "It's not your worst idea."

"Exactly." Hayden beamed.

"Notice how she didn't say it's a good idea." Walker groaned.

"All of Haywire's ideas are bad," Jamie said nonchalantly. "After a while, you learn to roll with them because facing the demon is probably easier than trying to convince her otherwise."

Hayden's grin broadened at what she perceived as praise as Walker gawked at the Nephilim.

Dani forced herself to repress the shudder of horror that threatened to rip through her.

Hayden wrapped her fingers around a blue conch shell charm on her charm bracelet. Light flashed as she transformed the charm into a grimoire the size of a college textbook.

"Greater demons? Are you insane?"

"Demon. As in singular." She waved a hand nonchalantly. "Don't be such a worrywart. The demon and I go way back," Hayden said flippantly, flipping through the grimoire with one hand while she bit off a chunk of chicken from the chicken tender in her other hand.

"There is not enough sage in the world to protect us from the Hell you're about to unleash." Apalla's lips curled into a feral smirk. "Let's do it."

"Again, are you insane?" Diligence shrieked.

Jamie shrugged, unconcerned. "We have sage on hand."

"And if sage doesn't contain the demon?" Ronnie raised an eyebrow.

"Then we're all screwed," Hayden said, shooting a devious wink at Dani. Drawing her silver wand from her jacket sleeve, she flicked it to use a practical magic spell to flip through the pages for her. Turns out she did learn some practical magic in the last two and a half years since the Salem War. Pages turned in a furious flurry. How she could read the pages to know which one to choose was beyond Dani.

"We're all going to Hell." Mila's voice rose two octaves.

"If I go to Hell, at least I'll be with all my friends." Hayden shared a wicked grin with her circle. It was concerning how nonchalant the woman was about messing with Hell.

"Have you no restraint?" Kova sighed, pinching her nose with her thumb and forefinger, but when she raised her head, her ancient green eyes danced with amusement.

Hayden waggled her eyebrows at her mentor. "What's the fun in that?" Her hand shot out, slapping down on a page and stopping the grimoire's furious page flipping. Leaning toward Apalla, she pointed to the page and muttered something indistinguishable to the Priestess.

With a nod, Apalla shot Hayden a calculating grin, which was more unsettling than Hayden's wicked little smirks. Dani's stomach rolled, and she fought the urge to vomit.

Summon a greater demon? Here? In the compound filled with other mortals?

Hayden may be blessed by Heaven, but if she believed the Virtues could contain a greater demon without ensuing carnage, she *was* insane. But they had to. The Sins were worse than the average greater demon.

With a flash of black light, Hayden transfigured the grimoire into a blue conch shell pendant and returned it to her charm bracelet. Blue eyes dancing with mischief, Hayden grinned at the Virtues in a way that made Dani's stomach drop.

Milena puked on the floor between hers and Dani's seats, regurgitating bits of partially digested chicken nuggets.

"Why so uneasy, Diligence?" Jackal asked, swiping a thoroughly licked paw over his feline panther face. Hayden had called in Jackal and Buddy from Asylum for the day since the

Virtues were going to battle the greater demon. While Jackal immediately greeted Dani, Buddy had run toward Salem and tackled her. Ever since, the two immortal dogs frolicked around the courtyard despite the humorous difference in their sizes. The courtyard was starting to get cramped.

"I don't trust demons." Mila stepped away from Jackal, her nose wrinkling in disdain. "All you do is destroy."

In the blink of an eye, the morpher demon shifted from his panther form to a regular cat. "Funny, we say the same thing about you witches." Jackal licked his paw again, then swiped it over his kitten face. "In my service to the princess, she not only defeated the First Eve, but she withstood the oppression of the Supreme Council, who exacerbated the damage inflicted on the witching world. Witches are just as dangerous as demons, depending on their choices." He shrugged his tiny black cat shoulders.

"This will take a while," Hayden shouted from where she huddled with Apalla and Kova at the center of the courtyard. "Y'all should get comfortable."

Grumbling, the other Virtues plopped into the dirt or sprawled in the grass, pulling out their wands to play with magic or send wand messages. But as Dani glanced around the courtyard, she spotted a sight more interesting than what her wand could offer.

Jamie squatted low as he cleaned his broadsword with a whet stone, his back leaning against the wall of the courtyard. It was the first Dani could recall seeing the Nephilim more than ten feet from his soulmate. If she learned one thing in her time at the Spellery—it was rare to see the powerful witches apart, but if you could get one of them alone, it wasn't an opportunity to waste. She had rarely seen one without the other, even when they were children.

Glancing at the other Virtues, she noted they were oblivious to her observation. Moving before she could talk herself out of it, she strode to the wall of the courtyard, drawing her blade.

Squatting beside the Son of Fire, she extended her hand in silent request.

Without stopping the smooth stroke of his hand against his blade, Jamie summoned a second whet stone in a flash of red light.

Without speaking a word, the two witches sharpened their blades in a comfortable silence. Chatter from the other Virtues drifted across the courtyard to Dani's ears, but not a word came from the witches working to summon Pazuzu.

"What weighs on your mind, Dani?" Jamie asked gently, maintaining the comfortable vibes established between him and the younger witch.

"Why do you assume something weighs on me?" she asked, scraping the stone against her falchion.

With an amused smile, Jamie mirrored her action. "Because I can guarantee Damien imparted his wisdom on his little sister." Tucking the whet stone in his back pocket, Jamie stood and sheathed his broadsword, and Dani did the same. "Let me guess, he told you that if you see me and Hayden apart, take the opportunity to talk to us."

Dani shrugged, not meeting his eyes as her cheeks heated. "He said you're rarely not together. It's a chance to get to know you as an individual rather than a couple. I didn't understand at the time why it was so important."

"And now?" He quirked an eyebrow.

"You feed off one another, sometimes it's hard to know where one of you ends and the other begins. It's hard to distinguish your thoughts, your behavior, your motivations. Even though you're soulmates, you're different people and you don't always agree with one another, and I think it's important to know the difference. To know how you handle life when you aren't encompassed by unconditional love, because the rest of us operate without soulmates, yet we're constantly trying to achieve the same level of magic and skill as you two."

"Don't," Jamie advised, a stern edge to his tone. "Hayden will be the first to tell you to not copy her. Don't be like her. It never works out. Be like you but be the best version of yourself. Use Hayden as inspiration, yes, but don't desire to be like her. You cannot achieve being her, just like she cannot achieve the greatness the Creator has fated for you. I'm her soulmate, and even I can't be like her. And I don't want to be. I want to be her other half, filling in the places she needs me to."

Jamie sheathed his sword and leaned against the wall, his eyes boring into Dani's head as she avoided his gaze. Dani took a deep breath, mulling over whether or not to ask the question weighing on her.

"When did you know Hayden was the one?" Dani asked the Nephilim.

A peaceful smile tugged at his lips as he watched his soulmate converse with the other powerful women in her circle. "From the first moment I looked into her eyes in the Athenian Council's courtroom. The day she was put on trial for murdering her father."

"Before you knew she was the Salem Witch?" Dani asked, surprised the Nephilim had fallen in love before he knew how powerful the girl was. A girl with the power of a god.

"Irrevocably. There was something uncanny and demonically, yet angelically, fascinating about her, even standing barefoot in scrubs. She stood there with all the confidence in the world, radiating love. And that's when I knew she was the one. She is Heaven with a twist of Hell. She wears all black, but her heart is like her father's—all angel. And it is all mine."

The way Jamie spoke about her... the love radiating off his person... something stirred inside Dani, the beginnings of her power unfolding inside her chest. He didn't love her because of her power. He didn't want to use it for his own ends. He wanted to protect her so she could run free like the wild witch she was.

And Dani craved that kind of love. Love that, somewhere, deep in her soul, she knew was fated for her.

"Only her soulmate could see the angel in her," Humility said, approaching from behind Dani. If Jamie knew she was approaching and said it anyway, he didn't mind sharing that emotional side of himself. "Unless you have Second Sight to see auras. She would terrify me if I didn't."

"Ha," Jamie barked out a laugh. "If she scares the hell out of you just a little, then you know she's the one. Hayden is wild and reckless. She has the smile of an angel, but the smirk of a demon, and I wouldn't want anyone other than the woman who balances Heaven and Hell so perfectly. She's my yin-yang girl. As for the unconditional love part..."

He hesitated, glancing at his soulmate. Satisfied she was locked in concentration and oblivious to his conversation, he admitted to Ronnie, "The moment I looked into Hayden's eyes for the first time, I fell in love. My heart had always belonged to her—that was just the first time I became aware of it."

Pain twanged through Dani's chest as his words resonated with her. Dani's heart belonged to someone, and her soul, her magic, knew it. But Dani didn't know who. But she wished she had it—the crazy, wild, reckless love of soulmates.

Oblivious to her internal turmoil, Jamie continued, "But she was clueless. In fact, she seemed irritated by my mere presence, and I spent a better part of the next few months trying to irritate her on purpose." With a dazed expression, he placed a palm to his forehead and shook his head. "Goddess, I was such an idiot. I thought if I was irritating, then I controlled when she was irritated with me, which in my head was somehow better than her being annoyed with me as a person. I was so terrified she didn't love me back that I purposely tried to make her not like me."

Dani stared at Jamie in bewilderment. "Guys are idiots."

Tossing his head back, Jamie barked out a merry laugh. "Don't I know it. I know better now, of course. Turns out she was in love with me the whole time, too. Love at first sight." He blew out a gentle sigh, his eyes practically pulsing with hearts. "We weren't seventeen yet, but I think we both knew.... Our bond was that strong. But like the naïve kids we were, we fought our feelings. Futilely, of course, but to your comment about our unconditional love... we denied that part of ourselves for the same reason the Goddess doesn't mark us, doesn't allow the bond to surface until we are seventeen—so we discovered who we were without the other person, and so we can function whether we are surrounded by love or not."

"Like Kova and Hunter," Dani said in a whisper, glancing at the red-haired woman.

Solemn silence descended on them then as the heaviness of being separated from one's soulmate for eternity weighed on them, and that stirring of light inside her dimmed, fading to nothing.

"Alright, Virtues," Hayden shouted from the center of the courtyard, waving the Virtues over. "Let's shake this up like mentos in a soda bottle."

"Do we have to?" Walker asked, his disgruntled tone revealing how excited he was to summon a greater demon.

"Don't fight her." Apalla sighed, shaking her head. "It's easier to go with it." Patting him lightly on the shoulder, she said, "Save your strength for fighting the demon."

"Great," he drew out the word sarcastically, then looked to Dani. "Think you can talk any sense into her? She likes you."

"Not a chance."

Axel strode past, clapping Walker on the back. "Relax, Kindness. This is just practice. I have faith that if something goes south, the Princess of Hell will control the beast." He shrugged. "Plus, with all these powerful witches, at least one of them is bound to subdue this Pazuzu."

"All of us," Apalla corrected, casually braiding her golden hair into a plate. "We're all blessed by the Divine, so even as the mortal in the circle, I can defeat most, but not all greater demons."

"Not all?" Mila questioned snottily.

Unperturbed, Apalla shrugged. "Pazuzu is one of the stronger demons since he was one of the fourteen chief lieutenants in Lucifer's rebellion. He's an evil little bugger."

Mila's jaw dropped open. "What?" she shrieked. "If you can't subdue him then how are *we* supposed to defeat him?"

"Because you're Virtues," Hayden said simply, not looking up from the salt she poured in a circle on the ground. "You're gifted with powers for the express intent to fight demons, unlike the rest of us."

"Unlike the rest of you, who are blessed with sheer, raw magical power," Emmett said with a smile. "Seems like raw power is applicable to any situation, not just fighting demons."

"As are the Virtues," Kova said pointedly. "Your purpose as mortals on this Earth is to fight the Sins, but the Virtues have a holier purpose in the grand scheme of Heaven and Earth."

"Do not underestimate your power," the Heart of Earth added. Thea's emerald eyes swam with untold energy. "It is not a lack of power, but a lack of knowledge of how to wield your magic that is hindering your fight against the Sins."

"Which is why we're summoning Zuzu," Hayden chimed in merrily. "Fighting him will give you experience with your Virtue magic, and maybe you'll learn something about how to wield your powers. Or for those of you who haven't accessed Virtue magic yet, you might manifest." Hayden's crystal blue eyes pierced into Dani's soul as she added the last sentence, but something in her expression made Dani suspect Hayden knew tonight would not be the night Dani uncovered her unique abilities.

"Alright, ready?" Hayden looked at her circle, who nodded in response and assumed their positions. "Virtues?"

"Ready as we will ever be." Axel unsheathed his massive axe and gripped it with both hands.

"No." Mila shook her head, her straight platinum locks shaking behind her. "No, no, no. I'm so *not* ready."

"Eh," Hayden shrugged. "Too bad."

Summoning black light to her hand, she slammed her palm flat against the earth at her feet. A baseball-sized blob of black magic expanded outward. When it was the size of a basketball, the other four shot their elements at the swirling black portal. Golden sunlight mixed with pink magic as Apalla commanded air. White holy flames and red light beamed at the portal from the south. Kova called upon water magic, but her magic remained its usual green that was several shades darker than Thea's earth magic. And silver Spirit joined the others at Hayden channeled Heaven and Hell. As the portal expanded, the magic of the elements rimmed the circle, controlling its expansion and halting it when it was the size of a kitchen table.

Walking between worlds of Shadow and Light,
I call upon demons of darkest night.
Annunaki of blood and bone,
Your Winds of Destruction blown.
Gruesome sight and demonic fright,
Upon your name, I need your blight.
Pierce the Veil to enter mortal realm,
To haunt the witches at their helm.
Pazuzu, the Agony of Mankind,
Leave Hell behind, remove your confines!

The earth shook beneath Dani's feet, forcing her down to a knee. The other Virtues fell or dropped to a knee, except Axel and Emmett, who were sturdier thanks to their bulk.

Mila muttered something about insane witches as she brushed the dirt off her pants with a hand, then staggered to her feet only to fall again.

But Dani's eyes were torn from the struggling Virtues as poison-tipped horns and claw-tipped bat wings crested from the portal as Pazuzu rose from the black hole, his body crouched into an upright fetal position. Once the demon fully emerged, Hayden released her magic. The portal slammed shut, and the demon unfurled itself with a satisfied roar, its limbs popping and cracking.

Pazuzu was the oddest-looking demon Dani had encountered. With a human torso, legs, and arms, the demon resembled a human figure, but larger since he stood ten feet tall. But that was the only normal thing about him. Instead of feet, bird talons dug into the dirt. His hands were normal except he held the left hand down and the right hand up as though his arms were paralyzed in that configuration. And claws curled out of his fingertips. Scales covered his body like a lizard, disappearing under a scarf of fur that floofed out like a poodle's.

Yet his odd and misshapen body wasn't what made Zuzu terrifying—his face was truly grotesque with bulging eyes and wrinkled cheeks hovering over a wrinkled snout like a pug's. Human ears sat at uneven heights on either side of his head, but the tips were pointed. Horns that reminded Dani of a gazelle protruded from his head, the gentle slopes curving into a point so sharp, the light seemed to glint off it. Behind him, four bat wings extended from his back, the leathery materials torn and burned in places. Under the wings, snaked a scorpion's tail with a curved and poisoned point.

Black venom dripped off the tip of the stinger, searing a hole in the ground when it dropped to the earth. Thea scowled at the spot and waved her hand, infusing the earth with her Heart of Earth energy.

"I am Pazuzu of the Annunaki," the demon roared, clacking his claws together as he rose to his full height. "God of the Winds of Destruction and King of the Lilu. Who dares to summon me?"

CHAPTER SIX

ENEMY AT THE GATES

Pazuzu's beady black demon eyes scanned the Virtues, evaluating the threat they posed.

Glancing at the other six and her own trembling hand, Dani realized how truly unintimidating the seven of them were. They were pathetic excuses for warriors.

Reaching the same conclusion as Dani, the greater demon scoffed. "These are the peasants who dare summon me? Mortals of no consequence?" He bristled, his talons digging into the bricks under his feet. "Lamashtu is not here, yet you harmless mortals dared to call upon me?"

"Lamashtu is his nemesis, a rival demoness," Apalla whispered to Dani. "Mortals will call upon him for protection against her. It's the one time he does something good. Not because he cares about the mortals, but out of spite for her."

"Which one is worse?" Dani muttered.

"Worse? Oh, Lamashtu, for sure. Preying on pregnant women and newborn babies is about as evil as it gets. But Pazuzu is far more powerful."

Tossing back his hideous wrinkled face, the greater demon let loose a horrible shriek that tore through Dani's skin and flesh to the bones. "I will peel your flesh from your bones, strip by strip. Your screams will be heard in the depths of Hell as I damn your souls to my father. Agony, will be your master—"

"Yo, Zuzu." Hayden waited for the demon to look at her, his face abhorred at the use of his nickname. "Chill, dude."

"Witchling," he roared in a guttural tone, eliciting an eye roll from Hayden. "You dare assist these mortals in summoning without purpose?"

"First of all," Hayden held up a single finger, "It's 'Princess' to you. You may be Annunaki, but Mesopotamian demons—"

"I am a GOD." His rage echoed off the walls of the compound.

"A weak one," Hayden taunted, eliciting groans from the Virtues.

"Why does she have to antagonize him?" Walker whined.

Hayden continued, unfazed by the interruption. "Mesopotamian demons, even those who served as Lieutenants to dear old Luci, bow to the Princess of Hell." Cheekily, she added, "Don't worry, Zuzu. I won't kill you today."

Blinking at her, the greater demon's taken aback face conveyed what Dani thought may be confusion. It was hard to decipher emotions on a demon's demented face.

Using a pale hand, the Princess of Hell gestured to the seven Virtues. "Let's see how the power of Hell holds against the might of the Virtues." Cutting her piercing blue gaze to the Virtues, Hayden caught Dani's eye, then winked mischievously.

Colorful light flashed, temporarily blinding Dani and the Virtues as Hayden and her circle spooked, abandoning the them.

Alone.

With a greater demon.

Mila's breakfast reappeared as she vomited next to Dani, but she refused to look as bile splashed over her combat boots.

"Did she..." Walker trailed off, spinning in a circle to scan the courtyard.

"Yup," Axel answered, giving his massive battle axe a practice swing. "It's up to us to subdue this beast."

"I can't believe she abandoned us," Mila shrieked before puking again.

"I can," Ronnie responded, unsheathing her weapon as Pazuzu sniffed the spot Hayden disappeared from, apparently just as confused as the Virtues. "It's not Hayden's responsibility to fight the Sins in the final battle. If the seven of us can't defeat a single greater demon, then we're doomed for the Blood Moon Eclipse. Hayden knows that, and she's trying to prepare us."

"By throwing us into a life-threatening situation?"

"Yes," Dani answered with more confidence than she felt. "In the end, it's us against them with no Salem Witch to save us."

"How did past Virtues defeat the Sins?" Emmett asked.

Axel opened his mouth to respond, but his answer was silenced by Pazuzu's horrible shriek that preceded a strike from his scorpion tail.

Reacting purely on instinct, Dani snagged Mila's shirt collar and yanked her as the poisonous tip crashed down where Mila had been hunched over, expelling bile. Chunks of earth flew through the air, dirt spraying as Dani hit the ground, rolling with Mila.

"What are you doing?" Diligence barked at her, pushing Dani off her and scrambling to her feet.

"Uhhh, saving your life?" Dani answered, her response meeting Mila's back.

Ronnie snorted. "That girl is a different kind of Diligence." She offered a hand to Dani while the other Virtues—minus Mila who hid behind one of the pillars of the ring—battled Pazuzu.

It wasn't so much of a battle as it was the Virtues struggling to avoid the greater demon's scorpion's tail as he flapped around, stabbing at the Virtues below him.

"Any ideas?" the older witch asked Dani as they took in the unfolding battle.

Wherever the venom from his stinger splattered on the ground, the earth shriveled up and died. Winds blew violently like the gusts before a storm.

Dani took stock of the Virtues and their respective powers. Walker could astral walk, but those powers wouldn't help in this battle, especially since using his powers rendered his physical body vulnerable. Emmett still hadn't manifested his Virtues powers. Neither had Dani or Mila. Axel's powers of hypnosis may sedate the demon for long enough for them to subdue him completely, but how? Raphaela's amplifying powers were always useful. But they needed a power that could kill the greater demon or send him to Hell.

Dani's thoughts were interrupted by a strange buzzing sound originating from far off.

"What is that?" Dani paused, listening to the wind. "Is that clicking?"

Ronnie squinted, straining to see into the distance as a dark cloud rushed toward them faster than any regular cloud could move.

"Are those..."

Dani seized Ronnie's arm. "Locusts." She pointed at the cloud. "That's a swarm of locusts."

Humility's jaw dropped open. "How does she expect us to fight a swarm of locusts and *that*?" She emphasized the word by stabbing the point of her sword in the direction of Pazuzu.

"I'm not sure the two are mutually exclusive." Dani drew her falchion. "Can you use your Second Sight to identify Pazuzu's weaknesses?"

Ronnie's eyebrows rose on her face. "I never thought of that before. It may take some time to tune into the right frequencies, so if you can cover me for a while, I can try."

Dani sprinted into the fray to join the others fighting Pazuzu. It was terrifying and exhilarating at the same time. Dani had never faced a greater demon before—and from the looks of it, neither had the other Virtues.

Walker blasted wind at the demon's wings, but it didn't faze Pazuzu as he flapped around, his wings beating the air. Duh—Pazuzu was a wind demon.

Since Pazuzu wasn't on the ground, Emmett's and Axel's earth magic wasn't of much help except to throw boulders.

Raphaela's fire magic was ineffective against the demon since demons were generally flame resistant, even if Pazuzu couldn't wield flames himself.

Dani shot a blast of water at Pazuzu's feet, freezing it into a block of ice. Gravity seized hold of the ice block, and Pazuzu's feet crashed to the ground. Leaping at the chance, Emmett summoned green vines from the earth and wrapped them around the demon's arms and legs. Roaring, Pazuzu ripped his arms free, his claws shredding through the plants with ease.

The ice melted at his feet, probably from his inherently high demon body temperature. Zuzu sprung off the ground, flaring his wings to escape the vines winding around him.

If they couldn't hold him for more than a few seconds, how were they supposed to kill him?

Mila's high-pitch scream pierced the air behind Dani.

Whirling around like an idiot, Dani turned her back on Pazuzu. The swarm of locusts had arrived at the compound and engulfed Mila in a cloud of miniature demons.

Before Dani could so much as take a step to help her, a sonic blast of power erupted from where Mila stood. Raw magic detonated, throwing Dani to the ground. The force plowed into the locust demons, rupturing their organs and liquifying their insides. The swarm dropped to the ground like pellets, thumping against the worn stone.

Mila blinked in shock, lowering her arms from where she sheltered her face from the bugs. "What just happened?"

Dani opened her mouth to answer, but a shadow fell over her as a stinger stabbed down at her. Rolling, Dani narrowly avoided the venomous stinger that plowed into the stone she had occupied, obliterating the brick into bits. Pazuzu's tail retracted, then stabbed at Dani as she rolled to her feet.

She swiped her sword through the air in a frantic attempt to save herself. The stinger was half a foot from her face. By sheer luck, her falchion swiped through the tail at the end of a section, where it was thinnest, and ground through the dense muscles and tendons.

The stringer dropped to the ground, saving Dani from certain doom and earning her an enraged roar from the greater demon.

Pazuzu's wings flared open, snapping so forcefully, the wings swatted Axel, who was sneaking up behind the demon, his war axe raised to strike.

The bestial demon gripped the end of his severed tail and spit on it. The raw flesh bubbled and popped, giving form to new flesh as Zuzu regenerated his stinger.

Dani gulped.

How did they kill a demon that could regenerate himself from any wound?

Summoning a javelin of water, she threw it at the demon, and it sank between the scales and scarf of fur, piercing his vulnerable flesh. Another roar ripped from his teeth and Walker blasted him with air magic, toppling him out of the sky.

The Virtues would have to banish him to Hell, but how could they do that? They needed a portal. Hayden could open one because she was a Princess of Hell, but none of the Virtues could walk between dimensions—

Except Walker. He was an Astral Walker, which meant he could walk across realms at will. If he could do that, then could he open a portal to Hell?

A plan unfolded in her head, as Dani visualized the Virtues wielding their specific powers. Was this how Hayden felt all the time? The crafty cunningness and mischief of plotting a devious scheme to banish the greater demon.

"Can the four of you hold him?" Dani asked Axel. "I have an idea."

"Do it." Axel didn't ask what her idea was, whether it was because he trusted Dani or because they didn't have any other options, she didn't know. "We will hold him as long as we can. Whatever you're gonna do, do it fast."

Fighting the voice screaming at her to help her fellow Virtues, she spun on her heel and sprinted across the courtyard. Dani slid to her knees besides the pale-faced Virtue of Diligence who had never seen a day of real battle in her life. "Mila, do you think you can replicate that blast of power?"

Mila nodded, and said without her usual snark, "I'm certainly terrified enough." She hesitated, thinking, then said, "I can feel the power inside me. All I have to do is let it out."

Without wasting another minute, Dani shared her plan with Mila, who, to Dani's surprise, didn't balk. The locusts must have really done her in.

Leaving Mila where she sat, surrounded by piles of dead insects, Dani emerged from behind the pillar of stone and sprinted toward Axel. Before he could charge the greater demon again, Dani slid into his path. Emmett, Walker, and Raphaela would have to hold him off for now.

"Can you hypnotize him?" Dani jabbed a thumb over her shoulder.

"Yea', but I've been holding off until we have a plan. If I use it too early, he could avoid it if I try too many times."

"Good thing I have a plan, then." Dani shared the details in less than a minute, then let the Virtue of Patience join the others. But as Axel leaped into the fray, Dani dragged Walker away by his shirt collar.

Yelping, the older boy spun to strike Dani, but she disarmed him with a flick of her wrist. He really needed to improve his combat skills. Even sweet, little Raphaela could pound him into the ground.

"I need you to open a portal," Dani demanded.

"Wh-what?" Walker blinked at her in surprise. "I can't do that."

"Yes, you can." Dani jabbed a finger into his chest. "When your powers activated, Apalla said you have the power to cross dimensions right?"

"Yes, but that doesn't…" He faltered. "That doesn't mean I can—I can't… how am I supposed to open a portal? And to where?"

"To Hell. We're gonna throw Zuzu in the Pit."

Walker's face turned whiter than a sheet, but with a slight tinge of green as though he was going to be sick.

"I-I-I can't do that! Are you insane? How am I supposed to open a portal? No, no, no. Absolutely not."

"Open it the same way you astral project." Dani gave him a tiny shove in the direction of Pazuzu. "Just figure it out, and we will handle the rest." She sprinted off to inform the others, letting Axel and Emmett battle it out against Pazuzu since they were the most experienced warriors.

Raphaela didn't bat an eye when Dani asked her to amplify Walker's powers as he attempted to open a portal to Hell. The young witch pursed her lips and nodded, never tearing her eyes off the greater demon as it battled their friends.

Dani rejoined Ronnie and filled her in.

"It's a solid plan," Ronnie said. "But Pazuzu can regenerate himself, and he seems sturdy on his feet. Mila's sonic blast might not throw him through the portal depending on how far he is, even if Raphaela amplifies her powers, assuming she can amplify two at once."

"What are you seeing?"

"I can't be positive," Ronnie admitted. "But I think our best shot is if he's in the air. Mila can hit him with a combination of a sonic blast and her air magic. You and I can blast him with hoses of water. Together, we may generate enough force to push him through. It's all subjective to a number of factors falling in our favor."

"Then let's make those factors favor us." Dani sheathed her falchion. She had a feeling it wouldn't help her much now as she sprinted to Raphaela. "Go amplify Walker's powers," Dani told the fire witch. "I'll help the others stall Pazuzu."

The quiet girl ran to where Walker hunkered down. His face contorted in a constipated look as he struggled to open a portal but relaxed as Raphaela's amplifying magic flooded his. Neon green light flared around him as his magic increased thanks to the yellow glow of Raphaela's Charity Virtue.

A neon green orb of light ignited in the air near Walker, but Pazuzu, who battled Axel, didn't notice, probably because he was fighting to not be hacked to pieces. Axel seemed to enjoy cutting off the scorpion's tail, letting it regrow to hack it off again.

Emmett and Axel took turns swinging at Pazuzu, forcing him to pivot one hundred and eighty degrees to face each opponent. But in the air, the demon moved with skilled agility, so it wasn't much of a hindrance. Dani was here to change that.

Casting a blast of water at his feet again, she froze a block of ice around his lower half so gravity pulled him to the ground.

"Axel, now!" Dani shouted.

Ruby light haloed around the Virtue of Patience. Light beamed from his massive hand as he shot Pazuzu in the face with hypnosis. Instantly, the raging growls of the greater demon ceased and his horrifying face relaxed, although it may have made him more gruesome. His leathery-bat wings went limp as his shoulders slumped forward and his upper body swayed, held upright by the block of ice frozen up to his waist.

The blob of neon green expanded in the air, large enough to fit an adult woman. It needed to be much larger before Pazuzu would fit.

Leaving Axel to maintain the hypnosis, Dani sprinted to where Mila cowered, grabbed her by the arm and roughly dragged her to her feet. The older girl followed easily when Dani tugged on her arm, but she shook under Dani's touch.

Positioning her in front of Pazuzu, Dani said, "Don't look at him. Don't think about him. Just close your eyes and summon your magic."

Blessedly, the girl didn't argue but did exactly what Dani said. Teal light haloed around Mila as she summoned her Virtue with ease.

Walker's neon green portal to Hell expanded to full size as Diligence summoned her magic, as though the Virtues fed off one another.

Catching Ronnie's eye, Dani nodded, and both witches summoned water to their hands. Following their example, Emmett summoned a boulder from the ground.

"Can't hold it much longer," Axel grunted.

"You don't have to," Mila answered, her voice strong and clear despite the quivering arms she raised in front of her. Her eyes flared open, and a wave of power rushed from her palms. Unlike the other Virtues, Mila's teal magic didn't infuse the sonic blast of raw power she shot at Pazuzu. The invisible shock wave blasted through the air, and Dani fought to stay on her feet. Thrusting her hand forward, she shot a hose of water at Pazuzu at the same time as Ronnie.

Mila's magic slammed into the greater demon first.

Axel's hypnosis magic died as Mila's shockwave tore through Pazuzu—the greater demon's face sharpened as he regained clarity, but it was too late. Pure power slammed into him, followed by the hoses of water. Combined, the force lifted the demon off his feet and threw him backward. Emmett threw his boulder with so much force, it cracked into two when it collided with Pazuzu's face. The demon tumbled backward through the neon green portal with a roar of rage.

Zuzu sank into the light. Walker released his magic, and the portal slammed shut with a definitive "BOOM."

Unsettling silence fell on their ears.

With the threat gone, the light of the Virtues receded, leaving them alone in the dull, gray courtyard of the compound.

"Not bad but needs improvement."

Dani and the Virtues whirled around.

Hayden leaned a shoulder against the wall of the compound with one ankle crossed over the other, the rest of her circle gathered around her.

Mila scowled at the Warrior Witch but said nothing, her body still shaking from fright. She was probably too emotional to deal with Hayden after facing Pazuzu. Not that Dani blamed her since the Virtue of Chastity herself was absolutely *fuming* at Hayden.

"Good job manifesting and wielding your powers." Hayden nodded approvingly at Mila. "But we need to work on your fear in the field. You are Diligence. Act like it. Your mental game is stronger than the physical one. Don't let fear make you a Sloth. Walker"—she pointed to the Virtue of Kindness, who slumped against Raphaela for support—"same critique. Don't be afraid of your powers. You could have summoned that portal a lot faster if you weren't quaking in your boots. Raphaela and Axel—you two crushed it," the Warrior Witch's praise made the skilled Virtues swell with pride, or perhaps relief that her cutting criticism wasn't directed at them. "Ronnie." Hayden grimaced. "Admittedly, I wasn't sure how your powers were gonna work with that one, but Palla said to let you do your thing. Were you able to see his weaknesses?"

Ronnie nodded stiffly.

"Excellent." Hayden's enthusiastic grin infuriated Dani more. "Way to think on your feet, Dani. But you and Emmett are the weak links right now without your powers. Dani—never turn your back on an enemy, even if it's for another Virtue. Damien would kill you for that one."

Weak links? *Weak links*? Hayden thought they were weak, but did she stop to consider that it was her fault?

"What the heck is wrong with you?" Dani demanded, stomping a foot against the ground. "You summon a greater demon, disappear, and expect us to banish it, only to reappear and berate us for not doing a better job?" Dani stepped forward, her chin raised high. "We aren't all powerful, Hayden. Some of us haven't activated our Virtue magic yet, and instead of helping us and showing us sympathy—"

She said the wrong thing.

"You want my sympathy?" Hayden snapped, her ire turned on Dani for the first time since she spirited Dani from Asylum to Oregon. "Because you're a seventeen-year-old little girl and life is too much for you to handle? Well, get over it." She raised a hand to point at her soulmate. "At sixteen, his twin sacrificed herself to save us. At seventeen, I sacrificed my life, as did Kova when she was hanged in the Salem Witch Trials. You want to know what I was doing at your age?" Hayden stepped into Dani, shoving her nose into her face. "I was fighting a war against the Mother of Demons, and I was losing. I lost my father, my familiar, my mentor, and my mother. I had *nothing* left. I hit rock bottom, and you know what I did?"

Dani didn't respond. She already knew. As an assistant healer, she had witnessed the chaos of the battle's aftermath.

"I found my strength in the Creator and rose on my own two feet. Sympathy won't help you against the Sins. Sympathy won't keep you alive. Sympathy is how you end up dead. And my job is to keep you alive, so no, I won't show you any *sympathy*." She emphasized the word in a mocking tone, but then softened her tone when she said, "You keep thinking you don't deserve this power, Dani, and you're right."

The Virtues opened their mouths to tear into Hayden on their fellow Virtue's behalf, but Hayden raised a hand, silencing them.

"None of you do. And you know what? Neither do I. I don't deserve the power of the Salem Witch, but that's not why I have it. I have it because the Creator chose me, just as It chose each and every one of you as Its champions." Hayden spun on her heel and led Jamie to the door. Wrapping her hand around the door handle, Hayden paused and turned to the Virtues, her piercing blue eyes finding Dani's. "You're warriors now, whether you like it or not. And warriors don't back down and they don't give up. So, pick up your sword and strap on your armor and fight. Because otherwise you will die."

And just like that, all the hot air puffed out of Dani.

Because as mad as she was at Hayden, Dani wanted to survive to see her eighteenth birthday. She wanted to live long enough to see her brother again, to find her true love, to have her own family. And most of all, she wanted to live a long, full life. But that wasn't going to happen if she didn't start acting like the Virtue she was born to be.

CHAPTER SEVEN

HAYDEN'S GAMBIT

"**B**abe, I think I broke him," Hayden said to Jamie as she stared down at Temperance.

"Ughhhh," Emmett groaned, trying and failing to lift himself off the training mat. "Tell me the truth..." He groaned again, rolling to his back. "How bad was that?"

"The truth?" Hayden raised an eyebrow. "You're possibly the worst I have ever trained."

"Thanks for the encouragement." Emmett coughed.

"To be fair, she's only trained the seven of you," Jamie added with a shrug. "So, really, you're also the best she's trained."

Hayden shot him a smirk and waggled her eyebrows like this was all a game and she was playing for both teams.

"Screw this." Mila threw down her weapons. "I'm going back to bed."

"So, that's it?" Hayden called after her. "You're just going to quit?"

"Yup," she said, popping the 'p'.

Apalla snorted, leaning against the wall as she threaded her thumbs through her jean belt loops. "Oh, this outta be good."

Hayden's eyes narrowed on Mila's back, and Dani took a step back, not wanting to be anywhere in Hayden's line of sight for what came next. She idolized Hayden. Had from a young age. But she knew how ruthless the Warrior Witch could be. Hayden Black had the face of an angel, but there was a certain devilish wickedness to her mind.

"Virtues can't quit."

"Watch me." Mila waved a hand in the air.

"You quit, then the Sins can kill you anytime, anywhere, without the Rules of Engagement binding them." Her warning gave Mila pause and she stopped walking away from the sparring ring.

"According to you, we're all terrible fighters, so we're going to die at the hand of the Sins anyway."

"You're not terrible fighters."

"You just said we're the worst you've trained."

"Not because you're bad fighters. Because you're not working together." Hayden hissed through her teeth. "You're a team. You need to start acting like it."

"I thought the whole point of being a Virtue is that we're the opposite of one Sins and we use our Virtue to defeat the Sin," Walker asked studiously.

"Not exactly." Kova leaned against the wall with her arms crossed over her chest and one foot hiked up, so the sole of her combat boot pressed against the vertical surface. "You're all blessed with a unique set of powers meant to counter the Sins, yes. But if you are banking on your magic and battle finesse against the Sins, you're sorely naïve."

"Relying on the magnitude of your power to overcome the Sins is a mistake," Thea agreed. "That is a battle of chance, one in which the odds do not favor the mortals."

"Even Hayden didn't defeat Lilith on her own," Apalla said from where she perched on the pillar of the ring. "We, her circle"—she gestured to herself and the others—"summoned the elemental circle before she ended Lilith's terror."

"It's the *combination* of powers that is so deadly," Jamie emphasized.

"Evil is about separation and division. Good is about unity and oneness. The Sins battle separately," Kova explained. "Each is content to claim their own victory. The Virtues do not. Your magic is designed to complement one another."

"How so?" Dani asked, still ignorant to her powers.

"Raphaela is an amp. She increases the rest of your powers. Axel can hypnotize your enemies while Mila blasts them with her sonic wave." Kova shrugged. "That's only one example."

"Isn't it your job to teach us that?" Mila accused Hayden.

"I'm *trying*." Hayden sighed, her black locks flying behind her as she shook her head. "But I can't force you to work together. I can teach you to fight and be a sparring partner. I can help you harness your magic, but I can't force you to work together. The seven of you must figure that out for yourselves."

"How do we do that?"

"With a leader." Axel answered before Hayden or her circle of witches could.

"But who?" Walker asked hesitantly, clearly hoping it wasn't supposed to be him.

"Not you," Mila snapped.

Jeez. She didn't have to say it out loud.

But Walker sighed in relief.

"Diligence is the obvious choice." She puffed her chest.

Apalla covered her laugh with a cough, but Humility didn't try to cover her laughter.

"No, absolutely not," Ronnie scolded. "You are the worst possible candidate."

"If not me, then who?" Mila rolled her eyes. "One of those block heads?" She gestured to Axel and Emmett, the earth elementals. "Or meek little Raphaela?" She waved at the shy fire elemental. "Give me a break."

"Me." Dani surprised herself, not knowing where the courage came from for her to speak up. Heck, she hadn't intended to speak up.

"You?" Mila asked incredulously. "Don't make me laugh."

"She's right," Ronnie defended her. "I can see it in her aura. Dani is meant to be our leader."

Axel shrugged. "The girl has a good head on her shoulders. You won't hear any argument from me."

"Nor me." Unsurprisingly, Emmett echoed Axel's sentiment. "It was Dani's plan that beat Pazuzu. If she can come up with that on the fly, then I stand behind her leadership."

Raphaela nodded silently, but her eyes and ears missed nothing.

"I don't know," Walker questioned. "Dani is only seventeen. She's the youngest of the Virtues. Shouldn't Axel or Ronnie be the leaders since they're the oldest."

"It's not about age," Ronnie countered. "It's about Spirit. And Dani has the strongest connection of any of us."

Mila snorted. "Yeah, right. She hasn't even manifested her powers yet."

"Chastity is always the youngest and always the last to manifest," Kova said, being the first to interrupt the Virtues since they began this debate.

"And always the leader," Hayden added quietly, her gaze already on Dani when the younger witch looked up.

"Me?" Dani choked. That couldn't possibly be right. What was wrong with her? What possessed Dani to suggest herself as the leader of the Virtues in the first place? It was ludicrous. "No. No, I can't. I'm not a leader. I'm just a fighter. A regular witch."

"A regular witch?" Axel scoffed. "None of us are regular witches."

"I haven't manifested my powers yet," Dani argued. "Why would you want me to be the leader? Regular old me?"

"Yes, you, Dani," Ronnie reiterated. "Chastity is the Virtue of restraint when confronted with the temptation of the Sins. I can see it in your aura—you are the only Virtue who has not succumbed to her opposing Sin at any point in life."

"No." Dani shook her head, her braid whipping behind her. "I can't be... I don't know why I suggested myself.... It slipped out of my mouth. I don't want that kind of power... that kind of responsibility."

"Which is exactly why Chastity always is the leader. Right?" Axel looked at Kova for confirmation, and at her nod, said, "You never crave power. Those who do not seek it are the best suited for it."

"I don't crave it because I can't control all that power," Dani explained. "It's not because I'm virtuous. It is because I have enough power for myself. I can't channel more."

"Yes, you can." Hayden said it as if it were the simplest thing in the world. "Control isn't about your physical abilities. It is your mindset, your mentality, and you have one of the strongest mindsets of the Seven Virtues. The same is true for leadership."

"I don't want to control anyone else. I don't want to tell them what to do." She splayed her hand over her chest. "My mindset is strong because I know I can control myself."

Hayden shrugged. "Then it shouldn't be hard to lead the Virtues."

"And when everything goes wrong?"

"That's the whole point. Everything will go wrong, and when it does, the Virtues need a leader who can maintain her control. I have complete faith in you."

Dani scoffed. "Easy for you to say. How am I supposed to lead if I can't sanchol anything but myself?"

"Control yourself, everything else will follow."

"You don't understand," Dani yelled, balling her hands into fists in frustration. "You're Hayden Black, the Salem Witch. You're never *not* in control."

Hayden went deadly still, as did Jamie. Tension tightened between them as though they were recalling an unpleasant memory. The Salem Witch broke his gaze to address the rest of her circle. "I think it's time to show them exactly how in control of our powers we are. And how this circle operates as one."

"Salem, you stay here, girl."

The Yellow Labrador laid her head over her paws and whimpered, clearly distressed that her witch was leaving her.

Hayden kicked open the side door that exited the courtyard to the street outside Willamette Park and ushered the Virtues out.

Black and silver and white magic sprung to life in the shape of a circular portal. Hayden strode to her portal, then glanced over her shoulder and raised an eyebrow. "Come on. We don't have all year to teach you how to defeat the Sins."

"Oh, great," Mila grumbled, casting a dark look in Dani's direction. "Thanks a lot, Dani. This is gonna be a disaster."

"What is the point of this?" Mila scrunched her nose as she looked over the edge of the state building to the four story drop below.

Orange and yellow and pink painted the city as the sun dipped lower in the sky on the April day, casting long shadows over the city with a quaint, small-town charm. Light glistened off the Willamette River to the west as it bubbled and gurgled, moving in a slow but steady stream.

"You're not working as a team," Hayden responded without looking at Diligence. "You all think I can't possibly understand what it's like to be a poor, weak Virtue because I don't know what it's like to be out of control." Hayden finished rifling through the charms on her bracelet and faced Mila fully. "But I understand it better than anyone. I'm a *demon*, remember? When I was thirteen, I nearly succumbed to my demonic nature and to the darkness Lilith infected me with."

A blast of energy swept out of Hayden, and Dani's stomach churned. She had a sickening feeling that that magic wasn't the magic of Heaven, but of Hell. A demonic calling.

"I survived because my friends did not abandon me. They fought for me and loved me. When you survive hardships together, an unbreakable bond forges. Watch and learn how an unbeatable team works together. This is what the seven of you must achieve if you want to survive to see another year."

A wave of black rose on the horizon. Demons of every shape and size and rank raced toward the Capitol Building. Not Hayden's demons like Buddy and Jackal. Bad demons. Like really bad demons.

That was why Hayden left Salem at home. The Yellow Labrador was nowhere to be seen. Only Jackal and Buddy had accompanied them.

"You summoned an army of demons?" Raphaela snapped, which was very out of character for the shy girl.

Axel scratched his head. "Does seem a tad extreme, Hayden."

"Not at all," Jamie countered. "You won't be fighting today. We are."

"Sit back and watch," Thea advised as she summoned an orb of emerald green magic to surround the Virtues as a protective bubble, kind of like Emmett's shield magic.

"This is insane. *You're* insane," Mila remarked. "How are you *Nephilim*? Everything you do is so twisted."

Hayden shrugged, unfazed by the insult. "I really am an angel, but some jerk stole my halo."

"Yeah, an angel with black wings," Raphaela mumbled under her breath.

Hayden beamed like it was a compliment. "Yes, see, now you're getting it." Holding her arms out to the side in a "T" shape, she fell backward off the Capitol Building into a free fall.

The Virtues gasped, running to peer over the edge.

Hayden rocketed past them as wings of silver Spirit magic flapped at her back, propelling her into the sky. Apparently, those were for more than show.

"Show off," Kova muttered, extending her wings of golden Spirit before launching in the sky to join the other Salem Witch.

"So, they abandoned the three of you here on the ground?" Mila shot at Jamie, challenge dripping from every syllable.

"Yes," Jamie answered in monotone. "Because that is the whole point. You kids keep thinking of yourselves as separate individuals instead of as a whole unit—the Seven Holy Virtues. We function as a circle, and as such, each of us is exactly where the others need us to be. We don't have to be attached at the hip to fight together." He cast her a scathing look. "Watch and see. Our circle fights as one. The Virtues must learn to do the same."

Black bodies blotted out the sun as winged demons of every variety filled the sky, legions upon legions heralding to the call of the Princess of Hell.

Shrieks of bloody murder pierced the air, and Dani covered her ears to keep the drums from shattering. As the screams faded, she instinctively reached for her falchion to unsheathe the blade but stopped short as she watched the circle of witches leap into action.

Dani had seen them fight, but every time, they took her breath away. And based on the other Virtues' expressions, they were as shell-shocked as she had been the first time.

White flames arced in the air as the immortal Nephilim called upon their heavenly abilities. Jamie's broadsword danced with white flames as he stabbed it into demon after demon, not waiting for one to disintegrate before killing the next. If it weren't for the constant stream of holy flames he summoned to dust the demons, he'd be surrounded by a pile of decaying demons.

Beams of sunlight shot from Apalla's palms between shots of flaming arrows. Pink magic danced around her as she protected herself with a swirling tornado of air.

Thea wielded her emerald-tipped staff with unexpected ferocity from the gentle-natured Heart of Earth... had Dani not known her. Vines and ivy grew over the sides of the Capitol Building to wrap around demons and squeeze them to death. Flower buds bloomed as their thorns pierced demons' black hearts.

And then there was Hayden and Kova, both of whom were indescribable, surrounded by personal storms of the elements. It was like they didn't have to consciously direct the magic as they fought. The elements protected them of their own volition while the women fought with their bonded weapons.

And while they all fought separately, somehow, they fought together. Apalla shot an arrow through the eye of a demon behind Jamie before he turned to kill it. Thea summoned vines to squeeze a demon to death before it could swipe Apalla with its claws. They protected one another's backs because they couldn't always see their own.

Sunlight shined through the masses of demons above like rays of heaven smiling down on Earth. And with every demon death, the light grew brighter until finally, the last demon's screech was cut short, and the sounds of battle subsided.

Thea's protective green bubble popped. Jamie strode to the Virtues and offered a hand to Dani. Thea kindly thanked the plants for coming to her aid, then allowed them to recess to the ground. Apalla's personal cyclone dissipated as she dropped to the roof and helped Raphaela to her feet.

Dani did not realize the Virtues dropped to the floor to keep themselves out of harm's way, which was silly since Thea's magic had shielded them.

Kova appeared in a flash of green and helped the men to standing. The tall Nephilim wasn't fazed by Axel's weight, which must have been twice that of Kova's, as she hauled him to his feet with unnatural strength.

Hayden landed with feline-like reflexes beside the rest of her circle and brushed the demon dust off her leather jacket.

"Whatcha think?" She waggled her eyebrows at the awe-struck Virtues.

"That was absolutely frightening," Walker said, shivering, and not from the cold. "You truly are a Princess of Hell."

"The level of destruction... I've never seen anything like it." Emmett shook his head in disbelief.

"Even the Devil admires my work." Hayden grinned. "I think I impressed him on my little excursion to Hell."

"You've been to Hell?" Walker gawked.

"Aren't you half angel?" Ronnie asked skeptically, raising a single eyebrow. "I thought Nephilim were forbidden from entering Hell as mortals."

Hayden shrugged like the rules of the Universe didn't apply to her. "If you obey all the rules, you miss all the fun."

Emmett snorted. "Facing the Devil is fun?"

Hayden grinned, her eyes wild with exhilaration. "It is if you kill half the demons in Hell."

"Hey," Jackal squawked from where he sat curled in a ball atop Buddy's back, basking in the warmth of the blue hellfire burning along the hellhound's hackles.

Hayden rolled her eyes. "Not my demons, Jackal. Just the ones loyal to Uncle Luci."

"Uncle Luci?" Raphaela choked.

Jamie hung his head as he shook it at his soulmate. "Don't ask," he groaned.

Hayden clapped her hands together. "Whelp, now that you've witnessed our little demonstration—"

Hayden froze, then spun in a half circle, glaring into the distance. A blast of power rocketed out of her like a sonic boom.

"Hold on..." Patience held up a hand. "What's that sound?"

Dani didn't hear anything despite straining her ears.

Hayden cursed at the same time Apalla's eyes flashed gold. Then Dani heard it, the distant beat of leathery wings.

Axel cursed under his breath. "Demons. More of them."

"Not just demons," Jamie warned, unsheathing his broadsword and lighting it with white holy flames.

"The Sins," Hayden announced, unsheathing Nightmare.

"What?"

"The Sins. They must have sensed our magic, or the magic of the Virtues. Since you're their antithesis, there's a link between each of you and your respective Sin. They can sense you and you can sense them. And the Sins used the connection to track our location."

"If they can sense us, then why haven't they attacked before? The Rules of Engagement—"

"Because mine and Hayden's wards around the Salem compound prevent them from tracking your exact location as well as keep them out." Staring into the distance, Kova warned, "Get ready."

"If we can track them, why can't I detect their location?" Ronnie asked, her voice level and calm.

"Because the Sins have endured this war countless times as immortal demons. This is your first time as a mortal fighting this war. They've had eons of practice. You have none."

"Doesn't sound like a fair playing field." Ronnie frowned.

"Oh Goddess, I don't think I can do this." Walker held his stomach, looking a little green. "I'm going to be sick." His breaths came in quicker bursts. "No, no, no, I'm so not ready to face Leviathan. Oh my Goddess, I can't breathe." Walker's voice raised an octave as the panic set in.

"Walker," Ronnie reached for the Virtue of Kindness, no doubt seeing the panic in his aura. "Please calm down."

"Calm down? Calm down?" he shrieked. "Can't you see I'm having a panic attack?"

"I don't care if you're panicking," Hayden snapped at Kindness in the least kind way. "Just do it quietly and pull yourself together. If the Sins sense weakness, they'll pull power from your lowered emotions."

Hayden's back went rigid.

"Too late, *Michaelina*," Abaddon taunted from behind the Virtues.

Abaddon wasn't horrific looking like Pazuzu, but something about the Sin struck fear into Dani's heart. Angry red skin the shade of a tomato covered his entire six-foot frame. Black chains crossed his chest in an "X", and black metal shackles tied the chains to his wrists, like the bindings themselves were a physical representation of how the fallen angel chained himself to Sin. Three-inch horns protruded through the dark hair atop his head, and his long, muscular legs streamlined into cloven hooves. The scent of decay filled the air, as though the Sins were rotting from the inside out.

Hayden disappeared faster than the blink of an eye to reappear behind Abaddon. Kicking him in the backside, she shoved him off the top of the Capitol Building and away from the Virtues.

"Draw your weapons."

Dani's was already in hand.

But her blood ran cold. Abaddon had ascended the building to stand alongside his brethren.

The Seven Deadly Sins stood opposite the Seven Heavenly Virtues.

Walker gulped beside Dani. "We're dead."

"Not yet we're not." Dani whipped water through the air so her hose crashed into Elliot and knocked him off the roof.

The other six didn't react, except Belial, who clicked his tongue like a mother hen. "Well, well, well. At long last, we meet again."

How did Dani know he was Belial? How had she known it was Abaddon whom Hayden kicked off the roof?

Must be the link between the Sins and Virtues.

But thing about the Sins—they didn't look like normal demons, except the red-skinned Abaddon. And Leviathan, whose body was warped and demented so his limbs twisted at odd angles, and his face was rearranged so the features were placed grotesquely with one eye where his mouth should be and other in the center of his forehead. His nose was on his cheek and a mouth filled with rows of razor-sharp teeth gaped open from the center of his face. But he was the only monstrous looking one.

The Sins were extremely beautiful, alluring even. Their flawless appearance and the pure power radiating off them... Dani almost desired them, craved them.

The pull toward Evil... that was what truly scared Dani.

Except for Elliot. He was a Sin, but he was confined to his mortal body. The other Sins—Beelzebub, Mammon, Belphegor, and Belial—stood six feet tall, a full foot shorter than the height of a heavenly angel.

Belial and Belphegor—Pride and Sloth—were two halves of the same coin.

Belial wore a perfectly tailored suit, his close-cropped black hair styled to perfection, and his posture exuding confidence and poise, every move, every shift of his weight precise and calculated. His aura exuded classic and sharp, as was fitting of the Sin of Pride.

Belphegor, on the other hand, as the Sin of Sloth, looked like a stoner frat boy going through a mid-college crisis with his hair pulled into a man bun. Belphegor could have been preppy and put-together like Belial, but instead, he achieved a lazy arrogance that came with easily obtained natural good looks, clothed in gray jogger sweats and nothing else.

While Belial and Belphegor sported dark locks, Mammon's golden curls were cropped short but shaggy to achieve that casually messy look that somehow was perfectly styled, too. Mammon exuded wealth from the expensive loafers on his feet to the watch of solid gold—scratch that, *two* watches, one on each wrist. His suit was probably worth more than Dani's house, but the golden earrings in his lobes were kind of hot.

Beelzebub... he was more of a conundrum. Dani expected the Sin of Gluttony to be anything but what he looked like, which was flawless in his cuffed jeans, button up shirt, and sports blazer. He pulled off casual elegance with ease as the sole redhead of the Seven. His copper wire hair fell to his shoulders.

And Dani hated that they all looked so seamless together while the Virtues looked like... absolute disarray.

Hayden and her circle leaped into action.

Each of the Heaven's immortals engaged a fallen angel, leaving the Virtues to fight the rest. Three on seven. Eight, actually, as Apalla threw herself between the Virtues and the Sins.

They could do this. Right?

Dani's stomach dropped out of her as Elliot grinned. She shot a hose of water at Elliot to push him off the top of the Capitol Building. Again.

The other Virtues, except Emmett, glowed with energy as they positioned themselves in a circle, their backs facing one another so the Sins couldn't attack from behind. Raphaela stood inside the circle, her yellow light extending to connect with the other Virtues to amplify their powers.

Dani felt Raphaela's amplification, but only her elemental magic responded. Chastity remained silent.

Kova fought Leviathan while Hayden took on Abaddon, the two worst of the Sins. Jamie battled Belphegor, and Thea was beating the crap out of Belial with her staff and wild vines that spewed wild flower petals everywhere. Despite their immortality and the vast power at their fingertips, Hayden's circle seemed evenly matched with the Sins, neither getting the edge on the other.

Jackal and Buddy sprinted between the Sins, clawing and biting to distract their enemies, but as lesser demons, they were nearly ineffectual against the princes.

Elliot had returned from his plunge off the roof, and he, along with Beelzebub and Mammon, surrounded the Virtues.

Mammon waved his hand, releasing yellow magic the color of pee to slam into the Virtues' weapons. Dani's falchion twisted and curled, folding on itself like an abstract art piece and rendering the hunk of metal useless. Mammon, the Sin of Greed. He could transmute materials, especially metal.

Dropping it, Dani abandoned her metal weapon in favor of the one she was born with—water. With Raphaela's power amplifying her own, Dani summoned a javelin of ice and threw it at Mammon. Her aim struck true, and the ice, as sharp as a sword, sank into his abdomen.

The Sins attacked.

Elliot lunged for her, his rapier in hand, but Dani was anything but defenseless with her water magic. Before he could reach her, she froze his sword in a block of ice. His arm dropped to the ground like an anvil, and Dani slammed her ice-coated knuckles into his face.

Raising a hand, Elliot summoned his elemental magic—air—but Walker teamed up with Dani and counteracted Elliot's attack with ease. Despite his uncertainty with astral projection, Walker was a skilled elemental. All the Virtues were.

Slamming a hand forward, Walker shot air at Elliot's mouth, sealing it shut so he couldn't use Charm Speak. If he wanted to use mind control, he'd have to muster up the power to do it wordlessly, something he had never accomplished before.

It devolved into a battle of the elements.

Dani pivoted, barely avoiding a stream of yellow hellfire as it flew by her head. Mammon. Yellow was the color of Mammon. Greed.

Emmett and Azel fought vehemently against him, but without their weapons, they were at a disadvantage. And Emmett didn't have his Virtue power. Only Axel's hypnosis abilities kept them alive.

Mila and Ronnie weren't fairing much better.

Beelzebub was a siphon. He could steal powers from others, including the magic from witches. But Ronnie and Mila kept him at bay. Ronnie read his aura and picked out his weak spots, then directed Mila to hit Beelzebub with a sonic blast before he could recover enough to siphon their powers. He should have been able to absorb their elemental powers, but Ronnie could see gaps in his aura. And he couldn't absorb Virtue magic because it was the power of Heaven, just like holy flames and Spirit magic. The others battled the Sins, but neither side was winning.

"Walker..." Dani whispered her plan into his ear after he threw up a sound shield with his air magic.

He didn't waste a second to lift Elliot in the air with magic.

Elliot's air magic lashed out of his free hand to counteract, but Dani was quicker and froze him in a block of ice from the neck down. Combining her magic with Walker's, the duo threw Elliot over Axel and Emmett to where Mammon stood.

Lust bowled into Greed like a wrecking ball into a wall, and the two toppled over the edge.

It wouldn't hold them for long but—

Whoa!

Beelzebub's sword sliced down at Dani. The only reason she wasn't split in two was because Axel barely grabbed her shirt scruff in time to pull her backward.

The Sin of Gluttony had abandoned Ronnie and Mila to kill Dani. And he nearly achieved exactly that.

Dani summoned water to her hands to shield herself and Axel, but Beelzebub moved with the speed and agility of a fallen angel. His arm raised overhead, his simple steel sword glinting in the sunlight.

Water solidified into a spear of ice in her hand, and she thrust up. But she was too slow.

Beelzebub's sword swung down at Dani faster than she could strike. But the blow never landed because his sword bounced off a hard wall of orange magic that bubbled around Dani. Orange magic that encased the Virtue in a dome.

Taking advantage of Beelzebub's confusion, Dani summoned another spear of ice and sank it into the Sin's abdomen like she had done to Mammon earlier, then blasted him away from her and off the roof with a hose of water.

Dani whirled around.

"Did you just—"

"Summon a shield?" Emmett stared at his hands, then looked up, a wild grin on his face. "Yeah. Guess we finally know Temperance's power."

"Then use that power to—"

An infernal scream pierced the air.

Flaming broadsword in hand, Jamie charged toward his soulmate, who was crushed under the supernatural strength of Abaddon's hand.

Wasn't that his power? Superior strength beyond that of a normal fallen angel?

Black manacles with dazzling, blood-red gemstones adorning the metal encircled Hayden's wrists as she raged against Abaddon and Belial who held her prisoner. Mammon had abandoned the Virtues and joined the others in fighting the immortal witches.

Ramming her shoulder into Belial, Hayden broke free. Abaddon threw a punch, but the Warrior Witch ducked and slammed a knee into his abdomen. She fought tooth and nail, even with her hands bound.

Why didn't she summon the elements?

Jamie swung his sword at Abaddon's head, intending to dismember him.

Elliot threw himself between the Prince of Wrath and the Nephilim of Fire. Magic billowed around Elliot as his eyes darkened to a shade blacker than the night.

"Freeze."

Jamie froze, his sword raised in the air, poised to strike.

Hayden jerked wildly, trying to launch herself toward her soulmate, but Wrath's preternatural strength held her, his arms like bands of unyielding steel around her waist. Together, Abaddon and Belial wrestled the Warrior Witch to her knees, but she fought like a bucking bronco.

The shackles... they repressed her magic.

Elliot forced Jamie to sink to his knees, his broadsword discarded.

"I would cease your rebellion, Hayden," Elliot sneered, then gestured to the Virtues, who stood back-to-back in an attempt to keep their eyes on the Sins, then to the rest of her circle, who abandoned their weapons under the threat of Elliot's dagger tip pressing into Jamie's jugular.

But Jamie was immortal, why would—

The air rushed out of Dani's lungs.

She recognized that dagger.

A black dagger of frozen hellfire. A weapon that could kill an immortal Nephilim. Even a resurrected one like Jamie. A blade only Hayden Black had ever been known to survive.

Elliot commanded Jamie to his knees, and the Fire Nephilim did as he was told, a victim to Elliot's demon-fueled mind control.

"You know, Hayden," Elliot drawled, "I've been asking myself these past three years, how do I exact my revenge on you?" He traced the tip of the dagger over Jamie's face, getting dangerously close to his royal blue eye. "I wanted nothing more than to see you enslaved to the Dark Mother, a battery source for her magic. And *mine*."

Hayden remained dangerously still, frozen like a statue by the sight of her soulmate at the mercy of the Seven Deadly Sins.

"I must say, I never expected you to be Nephilim. Certainly not the daughter of the reverently feared *Michael*," Elliot mused, dancing closer to Hayden to peer down at her. "Part demon, part angel, and Salem Witch to top it all off. This dagger didn't kill you all those years ago. If not this, then what weapon forged could kill you?"

Evil danced in his dark eyes. "But then I realized… why kill your body, when I can kill your *soul*?" He whirled around and stalked to Jamie. "What is the most torturous form of punishment? After all, I already killed your father—Cain dealt the blow, but I was responsible for entrapping you and your father—and then I realized…"

He pointed the blade at Kova. "Poor Alice, trapped in an endless cycle of heartbreak and death because her and her soulmate are forever separated. A fate Harbor Bishop refused to share." Elliot gripped the front of Jamie's shirt, balling his hand into a fist as he pulled the Nephilim toward him. Hayden stiffened at the sight, her muscles tightly wound. "So, what better way to kill you than to take away the one thing you thought you'd have forever? Your soulmate."

Elliot's vile grin could make a nun swear.

"Say goodbye to Jamie Bishop." Elliot raised the dagger, light glinting off the black blade as he prepared to strike. "Eternity will keep you apart."

"NO!" Hayden screamed, the sound enough to shatter glass.

The desperation in the voice of the Warrior Witch pierced straight to Dani's heart. All her power. All her might. All her sacrifices. And Hayden was about to lose the one thing she had left in her immortal life.

Dani's chest constricted, tightening painfully as a weird burning coursed through her veins, like her blood was boiling. Dani writhed uncontrollably, her fingers clawing at her skin as though she could scrape the heat away. What was this burning? It was like her soul was on fire. Her heart beat erratically, blood pumping through her ears, like her heart would explode out of her chest as she watched the scene unfold.

Elliot's black dagger sailed toward Jamie's chest, the point gleaming with a cold, cruel light. Pain stabbed Dani's heart as if the blade was piercing her own flesh, and the heat scalding her from the inside out evaporated as a baby blue light haloed around her body.

And then it stopped.

Jamie's hands clapped around the flats of the Nephilim-killing dagger, stopping the blade in its path. Glowering up at the Prince of Hell, Jamie surged to his feet and ripped the blade from the Sin's hands, then slammed it into Elliot's gut. The blade sank up to its hilt, black blood spurting from the wound.

"What?" Abaddon barked in rage. "No! Stop him!"

Hayden's crystal blue eyes widened in surprise as she watched her soulmate narrowly escape death, then snapped to Dani and widened further. She moved like lightning.

Abaddon's preternatural strength dissolved to a normal fallen angel's, because Hayden slammed a foot underneath her. Pushing off one foot, the Warrior Witch launched herself into the air with supernatural agility despite the magic-stifling manacles clamped around her wrists.

Kicking into the air, Hayden turned upside down and clapped her hands on either side of Wrath's head. Sailing up and over the prince, she twisted her body, snapping Wrath's neck with a resounding "CRACK."

Before Wrath's red body hit the ground, Hayden's knee slammed into Pride's crotch. The air rushed out of his lungs as he dropped his sword and fell to his knees. Hayden's hand wrapped around the grip of the sword before it hit the ground, and swinging up, she sliced the metal through Pride's neck.

The Sins were dead—temporarily. Like Lilith, the Princes of Hell would regenerate eventually, but long after Hayden and the Virtues fled.

Hayden's piercing blue eyes landed on Dani, widening in surprise. "Dani," she shouted. "Whatever you're doing, don't stop!" Yanking her wrists apart, she broke the chains holding the manacles together, but the shackles still clamped around her wrists. She whirled around to face Elliot who fought her soulmate in a deadly dance despite the blood gushing from his abdomen. "What doesn't kill me better run," she growled, rushing at the Sin of Lust, those magic-dampening shackles still chained her wrists.

Violence for violence was the rule of beasts, and Hayden was a *beast* on the battlefield with and without magic.

But Dani didn't dare move for fear it would disrupt the aura of blue light surrounding her. She didn't even breathe too deeply in case the expansion of her chest suffocated her powers.

Because the blue light... it must have been her Chastity power... but Dani had no idea what it was doing.

Elliot roared commands at Jamie and the rest of Hayden's circle, thrusting his hand at each of them in turn, but whatever he said, his Charm Speak didn't work. The witches remained as unaffected as Hayden and Kova, who were immune to such powers because of their bond with Spirit. But now, the Virtues were immune, because, at long last, Dani had manifested.

Hayden's fist collided with Elliot's nose, and his head snapped back. Spinning around him, she jumped on his back and locked his neck in a choke hold. With Hayden on his back, locking his head in place, the Sin of Lust couldn't wiggle away as Jamie decked in the face over and over again, black blood spurting. The Nephilim had a lot of rage to pound into the traitor witch.

A tingling sensation tickled the back of Dani's neck, making the hairs stand up. Slowly, she craned her neck to stare over her shoulder at the approaching Sin.

Gulping, Dani tried to swallow the fear threatening to consume her. Blue light sputtered around her, faltering for an instant before she wrangled her fear under control. "Hayden!" she cried out.

The Salem Witch's head whipped around so fast, she should have broken her neck. Dani saw Hayden's crystal blue eyes land on Beelzebub and the savageness in them quelled the fear clawing at Dani's throat.

Hayden moved impossibly fast for a witch without magic. Positioning herself between Beelzebub and where Dani crouched against the ground, she used her body as a human shield to protect Dani.

In her mind's eye, Dani could imagine the feral smile Hayden shot Beelzebub, baring her teeth like a predator in warning.

"You do not want to do battle today, Little Warrior," Beelzebub called, his tone mocking as he used the nickname Heaven had endowed on Hayden to rile her up.

Hayden raised her hands, shaking the broken shackles at Beelzebub in a taunt. "Whoever said I needed magic to defeat you, Beelzebub? No witch magic and no demonic magic. Seems like a fair battlefield to me." Her hands curled into fists. "May the better warrior win."

Beelzebub closed his eyes and inhaled a deep breath. "I have lived for hundreds of thousands of—"

Hayden didn't wait for him to finish that sentence. She moved like lightning, stabbing Belial's sword through Beelzebub's stomach before he opened his eyes. Wrenching it out, she swung in a circle and sliced the blade through his neck, decapitating him instantly.

Beelzebub's head fell to the earth, followed by his knees crashing into the ground, then his torso flopped against the dirt. It was temporary, of course. The Sin's blades weren't fatal to themselves, and the Princes of Hell would regenerate with time. Had he not been so prideful—despite his Sin being Gluttony—that battle would have taken longer, but Hayden fought dirty. Dirtier than the Sins.

Spinning on her heel, Hayden's sharp eyes scanned the battlefield, then landed on Dani, who kneeled in the dirt, afraid to move for fear of ceasing the flow of magic. Hayden reached down and hauled Dani to her feet.

"Green remains." She raised Belial's sword to point at the red fallen angel who battled Kova and Jamie while Thea and

Apalla played defense, using their earth and sunlight magics to shelter the Virtues within a ball of green and gold magic. "Can you maintain... this?" She flourished a hand at the air around Dani.

Dani hesitated for a heartbeat, then nodded, steeling her nerves. She wasn't sure what "this" was, but she would let Chastity do the work, if that was what it took to save them.

Hayden bent, grabbed Dani around the legs, then hauled her over her shoulder. Dani's face was level with Hayden's butt as she ran to join the other Nephilim, then Dani was on her feet again, that blue magic hovering around her.

But she was terrifyingly close to Mammon. As in less than ten feet away from him, and though his back was facing her, Dani had to force herself to stay standing. Yet, the proximity of her blue light to Greed seemed to trigger whatever change in his demonic abilities. Chastity's magic was dependent on distance.

Mammon's demonic alchemy faltered as his powers waned, reducing his abilities to the physical ones he was gifted with in the body of a fallen angel. Kova's and Jamie's swords were both discarded on the ground nearby, the metal deformed into an unrecognizable shape from Mammon's alchemical powers. But as Dani's light filled the area, the swords unfolded, the metal returning to its original shape.

Noticing the reversal of his alchemy, Mammon abandoned his fight with Kova and Jamie. He flung his body away from them, away from where Hayden and Dani snuck up on him. Turning, his rage-filled eyes landed on Dani, flickering with understanding.

Hayden rushed him, keeping herself between Greed and Dani. Even Mammon wasn't stupid enough to take on three Nephilim without his Sinful powers. Spinning on his heel, Mammon ran, fleeing from the Salem Witches and the Virtues.

Hayden skidded to a halt, shared a look with Kova and Jamie, then abandoned her pursuit of Greed.

As the last Sin disappeared into the horizon, abandoning the dismembered bodies of his comrades, Dani finally breathed out a breath she had been holding since Elliot nearly killed Jamie. Elliot, whom had escaped while the Nephilim battled the other Sins....

With the expulsion of her breath, the baby blue magic around Dani faded, the light retreating into her skin. The warmth of the magic on her skin dissipated as it retreated, winding into a tightly wound spool in her chest like it wanted to hide from the world.

Chastity was gone. For now.

CHAPTER EIGHT

CAN'T BUY ME LOVE

Uncanny silence blew on the breeze as the Sin of Greed disappeared into the horizon.

"Belphegor and Leviathan?" Hayden asked.

"Temporarily hacked to pieces," Kova replied, scooping up her sword from where she had abandoned it, by which time Thea, Apalla, and the other Virtues had rejoined them.

"Temporarily?" Walker's face was white as a sheet. "What do you mean temporarily? They looked pretty dead to me."

"Fallen angels, like Lilith, can regenerate because they're not only immortal, but nearly invincible," Dani explained.

"Then how do you expect us to kill them?" Raphaela snapped with the most ferocity Dani had witnessed from her. "Shouldn't you restore their souls?"

"I cannot." Hayden shook her head. "Angel souls aren't the same as human souls because angels are celestial beings in immortal bodies. There is no provision for redemption as far as I know. Their choice to rebel against the Creator was final and irreversible."

"Why?"

"Because every fallen angel rebuked the Spirit in their rebellion, which is the unforgivable Sin. They lived in the presence and glory of the Creator always, yet surrendered all of Heaven's Good to gain power. Mortals were not born into the constant presence of the Creator, so we are granted the potential for redemption."

"What about Elliot?" Ronnie eyes narrowed at the Nephilim, no doubt using her Humility Virtue to read their auras. "You can't kill him, but you haven't restored his soul yet. How do we trust you can protect us from him?"

"Pfft." Apalla blew out air.

"Elliot is a child of little concern," Kova dismissed the grievance.

"Of little concern?" Emmett echoed. "We were sitting ducks because of his Charm Speak!"

"Unfortunately, Charm Speak is a suitable ability for Lucifer to gift him," Hayden grumbled. "He always had a way of manipulating others with his words."

"Hayden and I are immune to his abilities," Kova pointed out. "And now that all the Virtue powers are activated, the seven of you are immune to his powers as well because the fullness of Heaven's might will be upon you."

"All I know is that Elliot is the creepiest guy I have ever seen." Mila shuddered and wrapped her arms around her torso. "I don't see the whole 'charm' in his Charm Speak."

"Mind control was a gift from the Creator, and the Creator never revokes Its giftings," Ronnie explained. "Charm Speak is a demonic gifting due to his affiliation with Darkness. So, as long as we activate our heavenly power, we cannot be compelled by his charm."

Apalla snorted. "Some of us were," she said pointedly, earning looks of bewilderment from the Virtues.

"No way..." Ronnie's jaw dropped open.

"Can you believe Hayden actually liked that guy?" Jamie asked, shooting his soulmate a heart-melting smile, but she only glared at him.

"When I was *twelve*."

"Yeah, and you crushed on him when you could have been crushing on me."

Hayden threw her hands up. "To be fair, I was crushing on both of you."

Jamie's grin dropped into a scowl. "Now you tell me? How could you like me and him at the same time?"

"Ugh." Hayden slapped her palm against her forehead. "I can't tell if you're flirting or trying to start a fight."

"I'm with Jamie," Dani blurted out without thinking. "How could you be attracted to him?"

Hayden and Jamie turned to her with wide eyes, and a heavy blush crept up her neck.

Then Hayden threw her head back, her black locks floating on the breeze, and laughed. "Dani, you're not wrong. Sometimes, I want to go back in time and punch myself in the face."

Jamie howled with laughter, his ocean blue eyes dancing with love as he stared into Hayden's magnetic blues.

"You're laughing?" Mila accused. "We almost died at the hands of the Sins, and you're laughing?"

Radiating confidence, Hayden shrugged, unconcerned that she and Jamie faced their literal end. "If we died, we would just rise from the dead. We do it all the time."

Dani's mouth opened of its own accord, but when Hayden's electric blue eyes sliced into her, Dani snapped it shut. It dawned on her, how truly frightened Hayden was. She was terrified of losing Jamie, but the others didn't know about the Nephilim killing blade. The jokes, the banter... it was all a cover.

Dani's eyes darted to Hayden's hands, then Jamie's, but all she saw were their regular weapons. The dagger was gone, but Hayden held it earlier... Hayden didn't want the Virtues to know how much Elliot had scared her today. She didn't want the Virtues to see her, the Salem Witch, the most powerful witch to ever exist, scared.

Because if she was afraid, then how were they supposed to face the Sins and win?

"Maybe you can't die, but we can," Emmett fumed.

"I think you will find the human spirit is a hard thing to kill," Hayden said, cleaning the blood from her blade, her hands still bound by the magic-dampening chains.

"There are at least thirteen ways that could have gone better," Emmett accused. "Literally. I'm counting them right now. You morons—"

Hayden surged forward, shadows wrapping around her as though they would spirit her across time and space, but the shackles blocked her spooking ability. Even without her powers, Hayden moved like a wraith in the night, her hand appearing wrapped around Emmett's jugular as she lifted him off his feet.

"Now may be a good time to remind you... all the Sins can kill you, but I can kill the most efficiently." She cocked her head, darkness dancing in her eyes. "Or maybe I will make it the least efficient and draw it out ever so slowly."

"Hayden, that's enough." Jamie spooked in a flash of red, pulling his soulmate off the Virtue. "What do we say?"

"Maturity is knowing you can beat somebody's butt but don't," she grumbled reluctantly.

"Good girl," he cooed. He glanced at the Virtues. "But she's not wrong."

Hayden cleared her throat as she straightened her spine, still hiding the terror Dani knew was buried deep inside. "Things did not go as planned, but after an encounter with all seven Sins, none of you are dead, so today is a win."

"A win?" Emmett scoffed. "You consider us almost dying before the war to be a 'win'?" He scrunched his fingers in the air quote symbols.

"Careful, Tempy," Jamie warned, his voice deep and fierce as fire flashed in his eyes. "Every single one of you is alive right now because of her."

Hayden breathed out a ragged sigh, the emotions from almost losing her soulmate clearing draining her. "Listen, kids—"

"Kids?" Axel scoffed. "I'm older than you."

All the Virtues were shaken, obvious by the tension between them and Hayden's circle.

"That's not how I see it," Hayden snapped. "How many of you have fought in a war and won?"

None of the Virtues raised their hands, not even Dani, but Hayden didn't forget. She raised Nightmare, pointing the blade at Dani from across the circle.

"Dani is the only one of you who has fought in a war against Hell and survived. They say innocence is the first casualty of war. Do you know why? Because we need power to win, and power demands pain and sacrifice. I doomed myself to an eternity on Earth to save a world full of pathetic witches like you. So yes, in comparison to the life we live and the fact that Jamie and I are immortal, you are *children*." Hayden practically hissed the last word.

Axel simpered down, raising his hands in surrender.

"As I was saying," Hayden continued, a steely edge to her voice in comparison to when she was trying to be comforting earlier. "War can take everything you have and destroy it." The Virtues looked down in defeat. "But it can give you everything from nothing. Whether you let it break you or not... the choice is yours. Push your fears aside, for they will get you nowhere. When fear knocks, let faith answer the door."

Hayden spun on her heel to leave, her circle flanking her, but Diligence just couldn't leave it at that.

"If you're so powerful, why don't you face the Sins alone?" Mila taunted.

Hayden froze, her hands curling into fists at her sides. Jamie threw his arms around her, squeezing her tight to his chest, whispering into her ear. The two most dangerous witches in the world. In a fight, they were lethal, but with one another, they melted. Whatever he said, Apalla must have used air magic to prevent the others from hearing because Dani couldn't hear them. Hayden nodded slowly, responded to whatever Jamie said, then stepped out of his embrace to face the Virtues.

She stared Diligence in the eye as she asked softly, "Do you honestly think I couldn't kill every last one of them on my own?"

Walker gulped, a stricken look of fear twisting his face, and Mila paled a shade.

"Let me be perfectly clear. I am the deadliest piece on the board. You do not want to fight against me, girl. You will want me fighting by your side in this War. There is one Sin that I cannot physically harm because of a deal I made with the Devil." She stepped into Mila, her calmness more frightening than her rage.

Damien always told Dani to be afraid of the calmest person in the room. *You can tell by how a person quietly holds their anger inside if they are dangerous. The calmest witch is always the most dangerous.* Years after her brother said those words to her, Dani understood. He was talking about Hayden.

"But here's the thing. I won't do that. Do you know why? Because the Creator told me not to. It is not my place to kill the Sins. Humanity—represented within the seven of you—must scrounge up the courage to *want* to beat them." Hayden Black's voice cut like a frigid winter blizzard, her tongue sharper than a knife's edge. "Did you know that as an immortal Nephilim with the power of Spirit, I can reach into your soul and rip away your Virtue and endow it on someone else? I could choose another mortal to wield Diligence, but I will not. Because the Creator chose you for a reason, and I am not better than the Creator. And neither are you. So, you will fight this war, if it is the last thing you do. And I will fight alongside you, doing my absolute best to make sure you see the other side of this war.

"But if you want to walk away, if you want to turn your back on the Creator, then fine. That is your prerogative. But me? I will follow the Creator. And if that's not convincing, then fight because whether you do or don't, the Sins will seek you and kill you. Fight because you don't want to die quietly. The choices you face may not be the choices you want, but they are choices nonetheless. You can walk away, or you can stand and resist. I don't know if you kids pray but now is a good time to start conversing with your Creator."

And with that, Hayden Black turned on her heel one last time. Flicking her wrists, she flung black magic into the air—or she would have if the shackles around her wrists weren't preventing her from using her angelic magic.

"Thea," she growled, and the Heart of Earth slammed the butt of her staff into the ground. Green magic sparked in the air, forming a portal that Hayden stormed through.

"Go to Hell!" Mila spat at her.

"Been there. Done that. The Devil asked me not to come back."

Without looking back, she stalked into the mass of swirling green magic, her loyal circle following without question. And this time, Hayden didn't check to make sure all the Virtues made it through the portal.

Dani knew, after today, they were on their own. Hayden would no longer hold their hands as the Virtues learned to master their gifts, just like Kova let Hayden sink or swim on her own. Life was about to get bitter and grim and grueling.

Dani was the first to follow, ignoring the hateful glares from her fellow Virtues.

"Dani," Hayden called from where she leaned against the frame of the door. "Mind stepping in here with me?" She turned on her heel and strode into the Salem, Oregon Athenian Council's chambers.

Dani gulped, trying to swallow despite the sudden dryness in her throat. Today had not been pretty, and Hayden did not end on a good note with the Virtues. Not that Dani blamed her, but she didn't know where this left her with her possibly tentative position as the water witch in Hayden's circle.

Guess it was time to find out.

Following her inside, Dani found Hayden's entire circle, assembled around the table. Hayden strode to the head of the table, then sat, kicking her worn and dirty combat boots up on the table. She gestured to the empty seat for Dani, then steepled her fingers, studying Dani over her hands.

"So, Dani," Hayden drawled. "What are your thoughts about today?"

"M-m-my thoughts?" Dani stammered. "You wanna know what I think? I mean, I don't think... I'm not a military expert..."

"Just speak the truth," Apalla encouraged, her gentler nature soothing compared to Hayden's harsh, militaristic demeanor.

Upon hearing her best friend speak, Hayden seemed to realize how on edge she made Dani and relaxed her posture to be more welcoming.

"The truth?" Dani realized her eyes were wide and frightened. She probably looked like a doe in headlights. "Well..." She cleared her voice, trying to instill some confidence in herself. "Well, it didn't seem like... it's just that..."

Hayden raised an eyebrow.

"Jamie almost died," Dani blurted out, then clamped her lips shut.

Hayden tore her piercing blue eyes away from Dani to glance at her soulmate, relief seizing her features. Jamie met her gaze, then gently reached out to grab one of her hands and tugged on it. Bringing it to his lips, he pressed a kiss to the back of her hand.

"It was close today," Jamie admitted.

"If you go, I go, too, Angel Boy," Hayden said, staring lovingly into his eyes. Stirring herself, she tore her gaze away from him, and Dani sensed it was a significant effort for her. "But he didn't, and do you know why my soulmate is alive and sitting next to me, Dani?"

"Because you killed Wrath and Pride temporarily and incapacitated Elliot?"

"Okay, technically, you're right, but that's not what I'm getting at." Hayden grinned wickedly as she dropped her feet from the table. "You."

"What about me?" Dani asked in surprise.

"You're the reason Jamie is alive."

"W-w-what? But I didn't do anything."

"That's one way to phrase it." Jamie grinned, leaning back in his chair.

Hayden stood, bracing both hands on the table as she stared Dani down, her crystal blue eyes glimmering with intrigue. "Dani, you're a Null."

"A what?"

"A Null," Apalla began, "is a witch with the power to cancel out other witches' powers. An extremely rare magical ability."

"From my knowledge, there has not been a Null in three thousand years," Thea said in her melodic, ethereal voice.

"And you're more powerful than the last one," Apalla finished.

"What? How is that possible? I'm the weakest Virtue. I haven't manifested my Virtue yet." Her head spun. Wait, didn't she manifest earlier? Ugh. Her head hurt.

"That's the beauty of it, Dani." Jamie grinned. "*That* is your Virtue."

"You are Chastity," Hayden explained. "You nullify demonic magic." She grinned wickedly. "Think about it. Chastity is about refraining from immorality. Hell is immoral at its core. Chastity overcomes sin by canceling Evil's powers."

"I'm... I'm... I nullified Hell magic?"

Hayden Black grinned wickedly. "Oh, yes. And you will do it again."

"Again," Hayden commanded.

"I can't," Dani screamed in frustration.

"Yes, you can, Dani," Hayden practically growled. "You're not even trying, you're—"

Kova's hand landed on Hayden's shoulder. "Maybe I should take it from here. You're a little intense."

Hayden frowned. "I think you meant tense."

"I know what I said. You need to ease up, kid. You're not the best teacher yet. Give it a few more centuries."

Hayden glowered at her, then muttered, "Understatement of my existence." She wrenched her shoulder from Kova's grasp to stalk to the other end of the ring.

A month had passed since Dani manifested Chastity's nullifying powers against the Sins, and Hayden drilled the Virtues harder than ever, especially Dani, fearful the Sins would attack at any moment. Being one month closer to the Apokalypsis War had everyone on edge. Months of training had passed, and while most of the Virtues had improved tremendously, it wasn't enough. Not nearly enough. But Dani was the worst. An absolute failure.

Because she hadn't manifested nullifying powers since that night. Not a flicker of the powder blue light that surrounded her as she switched off the powers of Hell.

Jamie strode to the ring and tossed his arm around Hayden's shoulder, pressing a light kiss on her cheek. "Don't mind her, Dani. Haywire is a touch overdramatic."

With an exaggerated eye roll, Hayden attempted to shove him away, but he wrapped his arm tighter around her, dragging her in for another kiss.

Dani's heart swelled.

Those two were so in love, it was nauseating, but Dani found herself craving what they had. True love. And according to Jamie, it had been love at first sight. Dani didn't even ask for that. She just wanted the real thing.

Her eyes darted to where Kova stood, watching the immortal soulmates with a sorrowful smile. Then again, sometimes love wasn't enough. Kova found the right guy, time and time again, but somehow, it was never the right timing.

"I know what you're thinking," Kova said softly, her hunter green eyes darting to Dani. "And the answer is that love is *always* enough. In the last three centuries, I have never run out of love. And while seventeen years apart from my soulmate are torture every time, I find myself choosing more and more people to love, and my heart only grows. That's the thing about love—you can never run out. The more you love, the more love you have to give."

"Aren't you angry at the Creator? For never reincarnating Hunter into an immortal?"

"Angry?" Kova barked out a laugh. "Of course I get angry, but over the years, I've seen the miracles the Creator has performed. I watched Hayden master the elements in less than five years, I saw the Heart of Earth manifest into a human body, I've seen her soul returned to the Mother of Demons. And over these centuries, I have spoken intimately with our Creator, and I know It has a reason and a season for everything, even when I cannot see it." Sorrow filled her hunter green eyes. "I do not know why John has not been reincarnated into an immortal body yet, but I know the Lord and Lady have a better plan than I could comprehend. It is called faith, and through it, all things are possible. If it weren't for John's last life as Hunter Black, I might not have raised Hayden as my own. My daughter, Ariel, passed centuries ago, and while Hayden could never replace Ariel, she is the closest I have come to having a daughter in the last three centuries."

Without thinking, Dani asked, "What if Hunter was reincarnated as one of Hayden and Jamie's children?"

The wrestling Nephilim paused in their playful fighting as Hayden prepared to flip Jamie over her shoulder. Her jaw slackened, falling open slightly, as Jamie's eyes widened in shock. His eyes shot to Kova who glared menacingly at the boy married to the girl who was basically her daughter. Releasing Hayden, he jumped away from her, throwing his hands up placatingly.

Kova howled with laughter at the Nephilim of Fire, shaking her head. "I wasn't glaring at you for that reason, Jamie. I'm glaring at you because you better be the father of my soulmate for his next reincarnation."

"Now that's just weird, when you say it like that," Kelsey said from where she leaned against the corner of the ring with Apalla. The witch of terror had portaled to Salem earlier in the week to help with training and something about logistics for the upcoming war, which sounded like a super boring conversation that Dani was glad she wasn't part of.

But Hayden continued to stare at Dani in shock, then she whirled on her heel to face Apalla, her mouth gaping open, but no words coming out.

With a sigh, Apalla shook her head, her golden locks flying on a magical breeze. "You know I can't tell you either way, Hayden."

A whimper escaped Hayden as she turned to Kova, pain swimming in her piercing blue eyes. Dani had not realized how much damage her words would inflict. Stupid. She needed to think before she spoke.

"It will not happen any time soon, kid," Kova spoke softly. "He has been born into this world, and this time, I pray I get more than twenty-seven fractured years with him. I want a full lifetime."

"Why don't we take a break, Haywire?" Jamie asked, wrapping a protective arm around the invincible witch who was breaking down silently in the middle of the ring.

In a flash of red, he spooked them away, leaving Dani with Kova, Apalla, Kelsey, and Thea.

"I... I didn't mean to make her so upset," Dani said, her heart fracturing.

"It's not your fault, Dani," Kova said reassuringly. "We know Harbor will be reincarnated as their daughter, but I don't think it crossed her mind that Hunter could come into this world as an immortal, and certainly not that she may be the mother who could bring it about. At nineteen and twenty, children aren't part of Hayden's and Jamie's plans yet. In the life of immortals, they're extremely young, so they're waiting to have kids. But now, Hayden may speed her plans up by a few decades." Kova chuckled to herself at the thought. "But enough about that, let's focus on your training."

But Dani couldn't let it go. Talk of soulmates made something stir in her chest. Something she hadn't felt since that terrible day when the fate of the world rested on her shoulders and she didn't know it.

"I don't think the thoughts are completely exclusive from one another," Dani said, her mind churning. "When my nullifying powers manifested, Elliot was about to kill Jamie and Hayden was bound by those manacles. The way she cried out for him... when I looked at them, I knew it was true love, and I couldn't bear for Hayden to lose that."

"And that's when it happened?"

"And that's when it happened," Dani confirmed.

Kova smiled warmly. "Like I said, Dani, love never runs out. What you felt was the undying love between soulmates. You tuned into that frequency, like tuning into magic, and love is the strongest power in the Universe, especially the love from the Creator. You were touched by bottomless love, and it triggered your powers."

"But I don't know how to tap into that energy again," Dani admitted hopelessly. "It's not like I have that kind of relationship with someone for me to tune into."

"There is so much more to love than romantic relationships," Thea said. "I do not love other humans the way mortals do, but I love all the creatures who walk my planet and the plants that thrive on Earth. It is an unending love that always fills me."

"So, I should tune into the love of Earth?" Dani asked uncertainly.

"While that is an option, it is not what I meant." Thea smiled sagely as she brushed her box braids over her shoulder. "You must find the unending love unique to you."

"What is yours?" Dani asked Apalla.

Her lips pulled into a brilliant smile, and her tanned Native American skin seemed to glow brighter. "Self-love. I didn't always have it, but when Hayden helped me find my confidence, it was like falling in love with myself. I realized I loved who I was, and I wouldn't want to be anyone else." She spread her arms wide. "The Creator made me, and if It loves me, why should anybody else's opinion influence how I see myself?"

"Okay, so maybe that's the key for me, too? Self-love?"

Apalla's eyes flashed with golden light, and she shared a look with Kelsey, seemingly communicating without a word. Dani hated when they did that. Which was often.

"Unlikely," Kelsey drawled, leaning against the wall. "Every soul faces a challenge in their life that forces them to choose between love and the lack thereof. Thea—is, well, Thea. Apalla had to find her love of self. I had to choose the love of friendship when all I had ever known was tyranny. Harbor chose sisterly love. Kova..." Kelsey trailed off.

Kova smiled tightly. "Let's go with 'it's complicated'."

Kelsey nodded. "It's complicated. But Hayden, she had to choose her love for the world over her love for herself and desire to do what was best for her soul." Kelsey glanced at Kova, and Dani suspected Kova's history as the Salem Witch in 1692 Salem, Massachusetts brought about a similar decision.

"None of those sound right," Dani admitted. "Actually, nothing about those *feels* right."

Kova's hand landed on Dani's shoulder, giving it a reassuring squeeze. "Stop trying to force it. Take some time off training to focus less on the physical outcome of your powers and more on what your soul needs internally. Until you can call upon your powers from the love within, you can always tap into the love between us." Kova gestured to the other three women standing with her and then at the Virtues scattered around the courtyard, training various battle tactics with the Salem Knights.

Disheartened, Dani nodded and exited the training ring, knowing she could never compare to the four powerful witches she abandoned in the ring. Their gazes burned into her back as she exited the courtyard to go to her room, and a silent tear rolled down her cheek.

Dani Sanchez was a failure, and she would doom them all.

"You're a bit tense."

"Am I?" Dani bit out with excessive snark at the Virtue of Humility.

Ronnie merely raised an eyebrow at her.

Sighing, Dani scrubbed her hands over her face. "I'm sorry. I'm in a mood."

"Clearly. The question is *why* are you in a mood."

Mila snorted as she strode to Ronnie's side. "Probably because it's been over a month, and Dani can't summon her nullifying powers." Mila glanced Dani once over, disdain written all over her face. "If me and my sisters die because you're too weak to—"

"Enough, Milena." Ronnie's cold tone brooked no argument from the younger witch. "Dani is a Virtue. She is one of us. We need to work together like Hayden said, and your attitude is anything but unifying. It's divisive."

At least Mila had the good graces to look ashamed, her cheeks staining red before she sulked away.

Ronnie stared after her, shook her head once. "That girl has issues, I tell you."

Dani raised a flat hand. "Nah, I'm good. I don't want to see everything you do."

That earned a tight smile from Ronnie. "Neither do I."

A comfortable silence fell upon the women as they watched their fellow Virtues train with soldiers in the courtyard. Hayden and her circle were nowhere to be seen, probably sequestered away with the Athenian Council, cooking up war plans. With the War a little over a month away, the Warrior Witch was spending more and more time scheming, leaving the Virtues to train amongst themselves. Dani suspected it was intentional. If the Virtues couldn't figure out how to bond and work as one cohesive unit on their own, then Hayden wouldn't be of any help. She had trained them in combat and magic. It was their job to figure out how to apply her lessons.

Which would be significantly easier if Dani could muster even a whisper of Chastity's nullifying power. But nothing had arisen since the day Elliot nearly killed Jamie.

Sighing, she unsheathed her falchion and signaled Ronnie to follow her to the center of the courtyard.

"Virtues!" she called them to attention, beckoning them to abandon their training and join her and Ronnie. She was their leader. She should start acting like it. Some followed orders more willingly than others—namely Mila as the soldier who begrudgingly followed orders—but they assembled as asked by their leader.

It was unbelievable that Dani was their leader, but here she was leading... sorta.

"We need to work as a team."

Mila rolled her eyes as she crossed her arms over her chest. "Do you ever not sound like Hayden's echo?"

Dani's cheeks flushed red with embarrassment. Was that how the Virtues viewed her? As a wannabe Hayden? It would make sense. Dani put Hayden on a pedestal since before she befriended the Salem Witch. She so badly wanted to be like her with her warrior spirit and fierce nature. But Dani wasn't her. And her strengths weren't the same. Yet, Hayden seemed confident in Dani's ability to lead the Virtues.

"Shove off, Mila," Emmett snapped. "Only an idiot would ignore the Warrior Witch's advice." His eyes met Dani's, and he nodded once in encouragement to continue.

"Right, so the thing is, we've been training together for six months now, but we're not working as one cohesive unit—not like Hayden and her circle." They were such a well-oiled machine that they read each other's minds. "So, I wand called my brother." Apalla's recent spell invention to level up wand messages to virtual calls to mimic human cell phone technology was an absolute game changer. "He said Hayden and her circle became so harmonized because they didn't just train together, but they solved problems together, even menial ones. They were only teenagers, and though the fate of the world rested on her shoulders, Hayden faced real teenage problems like bullying and family and insane grandmothers trying to kill her."

"Literally," Raphaela muttered under her breath.

"What are you getting at?" Axel asked, his burly arms crossed over his barrel chest.

Dani licked her lips and wiped her palms on her jeans. "I think we need team bonding beyond combat training."

The Virtues considered her, and Dani celebrated a silent win that they didn't immediately shoot down her idea.

Emmett was the first to answer. "I'm game," he said with a shrug.

"Agreed." Ronnie's eagle-eyes didn't miss a thing as she studied the other Virtues as they answered.

"I think it's worth the shot," Axel agreed.

Raphaela merely nodded. She wasn't particularly loquacious.

Walker fidgeted uncomfortably, uncertain with the proposal. "I don't know... what do you have in mind?"

"An escape room." Dani wiped her hands on her jeans as more sweat accumulated on her palms.

Walker perked up, his face brightening as he exclaimed, "Really? I love escape rooms. That's a brilliant idea for team bonding."

Dani nodded, hoping the relief didn't show on her face. The Virtues turned to stare at Mila for an answer.

Mila rolled her eyes. "Fine."

An hour later, Dani and the Virtues stood in a circle at the center of the courtyard with a crystal orb of labradorite—a crystal known for its ability to help a witch see through illusions—placed in the middle of them. The Knights had dispersed for the rest of the day, leaving the Virtues with Apalla to toil away under the heat of midday.

"You all remember the safe word?"

"Labradorite," they echoed back to her.

Apalla merely nodded. "Then let's get started." Without closing her eyes, she tipped her head to stare into the blinding rays of the sun, her palms facing up to absorb its rays. Must be a perk of being a Daughter of Apollo.

One hand raised in the air to the sun as she pointed the other at the orb. Sunlight beamed from the sky above into her hand, making her body glow light a miniature sun, then another beam of light shot from her hand into the orb.

Magic of illusion, magic of light,
Magic of the sun, hear our plight.
Darkness grows and tensions are tight,

Help these Virtues find their might.
As daughter of the sun,
I call upon illusion's fun,
Cast my glamour,
This very hour.
My mind's eye sees the illusion to be,
As I will, so mote it be.

Golden magic exploded from the orb and domed over the Virtues like glitter raining from the sky. As Apalla's magic fell around them, it solidified into the illusion of a room.

A room in a magical school.

Dani repressed an eye roll. The room looked exactly like the Spellery's library, where Apalla practically lived, even now as the High Priestess. That girl loved academics way too much.

"Whoa," Walker breathed out the word and spun in a circle slowly. "This is incredible. I've never seen a more expansive collection of magical text."

Awe etched across all the Virtues' faces. Evan Mila ogled the shelves stacked two stories high and the stairs leading to the annex above that only the head librarian, Mrs. Wright, and other notable witches and professors, were allowed to access.

"This is even bigger than the library in L.A.," Mila agreed. "And that was for human books. This is all *magic*."

Their awe-struck reactions gave Dani pause. She never considered how spoiled she was to attend St. Salem's Spellery and learn magic from the best professors in the world. It had been the status quo for her. A guarantee since childhood. But the other Virtues weren't from Asylum. They weren't even from the Midwest, so they'd never seen the world Kova had built for all of witchkind.

"We should start looking for clues." Walker browsed the stacks. "Escape rooms usually have hidden clues or ciphers or a puzzle."

Dani frowned but followed suit as the Virtues spread out to browse for clues. Dani walked down an aisle, brushing her hand along the shelf, remembering her days spent in the library mastering the theoretical study of her element.

Dani smacked into a hard wall of air and rebounded, falling on her butt. She had reached the end of the escape room where Apalla surrounded them with a hard wall of air. The illusion carried further, though, making the aisle appear to continue like it would if they were at the Spellery. Sighing, Dani turned around and headed to see what the others found.

Which was nothing.

"It's too complicated, even for Walker, the brainiac."

Walker rubbed the back of his head. "Human escape rooms aren't normally this hard. I can solve them in ten minutes or so. We've been in this one for at least thirty."

"So, what? Apalla made it impossible?" Raphaela asked, casting a glance around the room.

Discussion broke out between the Virtues. Thankfully, nobody was arguing, not even Mila, but nobody had any good ideas, either. Dani tuned out the conversation as she stared out the window to the sun shining beyond. Apalla's sunlight.

Hadn't Damien told Dani countless times that Hayden and her circle were holed up in the library searching for some answer or another? Of course, Damien never stepped foot in the library since he was allergic to learning, but... what if Apalla didn't choose the library out of nostalgia or familiarity? What if she chose it because that was where the circle bonded?

"It's not a human escape room," Dani blurted out, then spun slowly in a circle. "Apalla didn't model it based on a human escape room," she repeated, "because she designed it for a team of witches. We can't beat it by splitting up and looking for clues. We have to find them together."

"If it's not meant for humans, then who is to say there are clues?" Ronnie questioned, always the observant one of the Virtues.

"Then how do we get out?" Walker asked, his brow twisting in confusion.

"Oh!" Raphaela gasped, her yellow light surrounding her as she called upon Charity. "I get it."

"There are no clues." Emmett held up his hand, letting his powdery orange magic dance around his palm. "Because we have *magic*."

"But how are we supposed to work together to use our magic?" Mila threw her hands in the air. "Each of us has magic specific to counter our opposing Sin."

Dani shook her head. "I think that's the point. We have to stop thinking of ourselves as separate, because we're not. The previous Virtues didn't defeat the Sins by facing them one on one, but by combining their magic."

"Wouldn't it make sense to start there?" Ronnie asked rhetorically.

"Yes," Dani agreed. "But against what? What do we use our magic on?"

Walker snapped his fingers. "The orb."

"What?" the other six asked simultaneously.

"We have to find the orb using our magic, without saying the name of the crystal out loud. I think Apalla added it as an extra layer of difficulty."

"But how do we do that?" Axel asked, eyeing the room warily.

"I have no idea," Walker admitted.

"I think I do." Dani strode to the center of the room to the table Hayden and her friends had always occupied. "The orb is physically here. We must break through the illusion to find it."

The Virtues gathered around the table.

"Walker, I think your powers will be key. You can open doors, walk through dimensions. So, you should be able to walk through this glamour. Raphaela, you can amplify his powers, or any of the rest of ours. Ronnie, you can see through facades. You'll be Walker's guide to where the orb is."

"What about the rest of us?" Axel asked.

"I have an idea," Ronnie interjected before Dani could answer, much to Dani's relief because she didn't have an answer. "Mila, your shockwave could disrupt the magic behind the illusion or at least disturb the light waves for me to spot the orb. And Axel, if you would be so kind... if I open my mind to you, I think you could use your hypnosis to lull me into a trance that allows me to see through the glamour more easily."

Emmett met Dani's eyes. "What about us?"

Dani shrugged. "I'll let you know what I come up with for a shield. Nullifying would kill the illusion before we solve the escape room."

Axel moved behind Ronnie and placed a hand on either side of her head. Red light hovered around him as he called upon his hypnosis magic, and Ronnie's eyes relaxed, the lines around her eyes smoothing out as she fell into a light meditation, her purple magic haloing around her and gently mixing with Axel's red glow.

"Mila, shockwave, please," Ronnie asked, her voice soft and mellow.

Raw energy exploded from Diligence, sweeping through the Virtues but leaving them unaffected.

"Again."

Mila repeated the blast of magic.

"Again."

Over and over the women repeated the blast of magic and Ronnie's eyes sweeping over an area of the library until—

"There!" Ronnie pointed to a spot at the top of a stack in the furthest, darkest corner of a shelf. "The orb is hanging in the air, but it's glamoured by the appearance of the bookshelf."

"How do I get up there?" Walker craned his neck to look up.

"Emmett." Dani pointed to him. "It's not Virtue magic, but can you raise him up with earth magic?"

Emmett and Walker strode down the aisle until they stood at the end of the bookshelf under where Ronnie identified the orb to be located.

Calling upon his earth magic, Emmett easily lifted Walker into the sky on a pillar of stone until Kindness stood chest-height with the top shelf.

Neon green light haloed around him, amplified by the beam of yellow light from Raphaela's Virtue power. Walker stretched a glowing hand forward and his appendage passed *through* the bookshelf and books as if he were a ghost grasping empty air.

But it wasn't empty.

Clasped in Walker's was a polished orb of blue labradorite.

Golden glitter exploded around them and crashed to the ground, shattering the illusion of the library. Apalla's grin greeted them as her magic dispelled.

But she wasn't alone. Hayden's entire circle stood behind her with stupid happy grins on their faces.

"Congratulations, Virtues. You're finally working like a team." Pride radiated from Hayden, and love warmed Dani's heart. Love she hadn't known she craved.

Something swelled inside her chest, like a cord unraveling from a tightly wound spool. A spool of magic.

Chastity magic.

Dani tunneled down inside her, reaching out a hand to grab hold of the end of that spool and tug. Dani's Chastity magic was part of her, and though she accessed the power only once, she instinctively reached for it. And finally, at long last, it reached back.

CHAPTER NINE

IN HARM'S WAY

Alarms blared through the compound.

Evening had fallen, and the compound's alarm system jolted Dani from her post-dinner nap.

If Hayden was testing them with another drill—

The door to Dani's room flew open, revealing Ronnie standing the door frame, her face sheet white. "The Sins."

Dani launched to her feet, seized her falchion from where it leaned against her desk, and flew out the door, nipping at Ronnie's heels as they raced to the courtyard.

Hell reigned supreme.

The Seven Deadly Sins waged war on the Knights, only deterred by the might of Hayden's circle and the feeble attempts of the Virtues to repel them.

"How did they penetrate the wards?" Dani demanded.

A nearby Knight answered, "We think Hayden's shackles were imbued with Hell magic to absorb her magic in the wards."

Dani cursed under her breath as she scanned the courtyard.

Emmett's orange shield encircled him and Mila as the Virtue of Diligence blasted out sonic wave after sonic wave of pure energy, repelling droves of minor demons.

Hayden, Jamie, Thea, and Kova each held their own against a Sin, but that left three more to wreak havoc on the mortals.

Raphaela and Apalla teamed up, with Raphaela's amplifying powers swelling Apalla's sunlight. Demons despised sunlight, and Mammon cowered from the concentrated beams of light.

Axel, Emmett, and Walker fought Abaddon. The boys were a fearsome team with Walker opening and closing portals like doors to jump across the battlefield. Emmett's shield protected them against Wrath's magical and physical attacks, since one strike from Abaddon could kill a Virtue. And Axel was Patience incarnate, the antithesis of Wrath. His powers of hypnosis, while temporary, were vital to subduing Abaddon by entrancing him, if only for a moment for Walker to land a blow and draw black blood from the red-skinned demon.

One Sin remained unengaged… Elliot.

Dani shared a look with Ronnie. The women charged together, sprinting to where several Knights rushed Elliot. The Knights were mortal and vulnerable to his Charm Speak, but with the final Virtue power—Chastity—activated, the Virtues were immune thanks to the heavenly magic enshrouding them constantly.

"Stop!" Elliot commanded them with mind control. The witches froze at his Charm Speak.

Water lashed out of Ronnie as she summoned her element.

Dani leaped between two Knights, flying at Elliot.

Her heavier falchion smashed down on his rapier, making his thin blade quiver under the force. She aimed a kick at his knee, and bone cracked under her steel toe.

Elliot's knee collapsed under him, and he crashed to the ground, catching himself with his hands at the last second. His rapier rolled away from him, and Dani kicked the blade out of his reach. The Charm Speak holding the Knights released, and the Salem Knights fled as the Virtues entered the fray.

Dark blue magic pooled in Elliot's hand as he yanked his arm back, preparing to blast her.

Black hair engulfed Dani's vision as Hayden spooked between her and Dani. Hayden's back blocked Dani from seeing what happened, but dark blue magic flashed between the Sin and the Salem Witch.

Turning, Hayden winked at Dani, then disappeared in a flash, leaving Elliot laying the dirt, knocked unconscious.

How did she do that? How did she spook with the shackles on?

Dani caught Ronnie's gaze, but the older woman offered her a shrug, unsure of what happened either. Dani scanned the courtyard for where Hayden went.

Belial, whom Hayden had been fighting when Dani first entered the courtyard, was slowly clamoring to his feet. Hayden must have knocked him unconscious, too.

But why?

The Salem Witch appeared behind Beelzebub as he battled her soulmate. Silent communication passed between the soulmates. What was she up to?

Beelzebub possessed siphon power. Any magic Hayden or Jamie threw at him would fuel his magic more. Heavenly magic like the Virtues' powers or Jamie's white fire was so holy that it couldn't be absorbed by a being as dark as a Prince of Hell, and it clearly provoked Beelzebub.

Another stream of white flames blasted the Sin in the face. Beelzebub clearly wasn't used to fighting opponents blessed with heavenly magic, because he didn't summon hellfire to block the searing flames.

"What?" Jamie jeered from where he stood feet out of Beelzebub's reach. "Too afraid of holy flames to blast me with hellfire?"

"You want hellfire, boy?" Beelzebub roared. "I'll show you hellfire."

Orange flames sparked in both palms. The Sin lunged for Jamie, both hands blazing.

Hayden wedged herself between the Prince of Hell and her soulmate faster than Beelzebub could react. Gluttony's hands slammed against her shackles, and Hell's magic sank into the metal. Orange magic blasted from the manacles, hitting Beelzebub square in the chest and knocking him onto his back.

Hayden didn't check if the Sin of Gluttony was unconscious before spooking to the next Sin.

Elliot groaned from behind Dani. Whirling around, Dani raised her sword, but Ronnie slammed the hilt of her sword against Elliot's head, knocking him out again.

"That won't last long."

"I don't think it has to." Dani pointed to where Hayden stood on the roof of the compound's corner watchtower.

Hayden raised a hand in the air. Her wrist caught on Abaddon's serrated sword before he could land a blow. Red light sparked as the toothed-edges of his blade glanced off the shackle wrapped around her wrist. But that light... It was sparks from metal scraping metal. The shackles glowed red, the rubies dazzling brighter as magic absorbed into the metal.

The shackles.

Hayden was trying to break the shackles that had bound her powers for the last month.

Hayden's foot collided with Abaddon's chest. Her kick sent him spinning off the edge of the tower.

"She's breaking the shackles," Ronnie observed.

"I don't understand."

"I think I do. The Sins put the shackles on her, right? The shackles are imbued with the Sins' powers. So, she needs the essence of each of Sin to break the shackles."

Belphegor abandoned his battle to appear on the rooftop behind Hayden. His foot slammed into her back before she could react. The strength of the fallen angel combined with the angle of the roof sent the Salem Witch stumbling forward a step to careen over the edge of the tower. Hayden dropped in a free fall to the earth.

Ronnie gasped, covering her hands with her mouth.

But Hayden would catch herself like she always did. She had air magic, she—

The shackles... she couldn't use her air magic.

Hayden was going to splat against the ground. She was going to die. Could she resurrect if those manacles were on her wrists?

Dani lunged forward. She would never make it time, but she had to try.

And then Jamie was there, catching Hayden in his arms just feet before she shattered against the cement.

Dani stumbled to a stop and pressed a hand to her chest where her heart hammered too fast.

"You know, I'm really sick of watching you get thrown off the tops of buildings," Jamie said to his soulmate.

"Eh. After the first time, I haven't been too concerned."

"How often does that happen?" Walker asked, an incredulous look on his face.

Jamie and Hayden shared a look.

"A fair bit, actually," Jamie responded.

"But I can't die," Hayden pointed out.

The Virtues gawked at Hayden.

And then the battle crashed into motion again.

Hayden spooked in front of Mammon, and Apalla's beams of sunlight receded. Mammon reared upright. Yellow magic haloed around him as he directed his powers to transmute Hayden's sword. Right before the beam of his yellow magic smashed into Nightmare, Hayden dropped the sword and thrust both hands into Mammon's Sinful magic. The shackles absorbed his power, and beams of sunlight burst from Apalla's hands. Hayden was gone in a flash.

"The shackles absorb magic, not just repress it," Dani observed. "If she absorbs a piece of each Sin's magic, then the shackles unlock."

"And each time she absorbs demonic magic, the shackles lose their powers. That's how she can spook." Ronnie slammed her sword hilt against Elliot's head before he could awaken. But Abaddon and Belphegor were awake and raging. Jamie had Belphegor contained, more or less, but Abaddon…

"Ronnie." Dani pointed to where Apalla and Raphaela lay unconscious at Abaddon's feet. Mammon stood beside him, a menacing smile twisted his pink lips, causing adrenaline to rush through Dani's veins. What did the Sins do to the women?

"Let's move."

Ronnie slid between Mammon and the unconscious girls, summoning a wall of ice twelve inches thick. Mammon's sword glanced off the crystalline wall. The Sin of Greed's power was alchemy. He could transmute her sword if he got too close. She had to rely on her elemental and Virtue magics to survive Mammon. And Dani would have to survive Abaddon and keep Apalla and Raphaela alive until they recovered.

Panic bubbled up in her throat, drowning out any thought other than the thought of facing the red-skinned Sin of Wrath prowling toward her.

Chastity. She needed Chastity's nullifying power. If she could summon that blue light, she could defeat Abaddon. He may be a fallen angel, but Abaddon relied upon his preternatural strength, making him sloppy in combat, which is why Hayden could beat him despite his thousands of years of experience.

And if Hayden could beat him. Then Dani could, too. She had to keep telling herself that. If she could believe it, then maybe Chastity would answer her.

But dread welled inside her as Abaddon reached her, drowning out any feelings of love she might have felt to access Chastity.

Abaddon's sword met Dani's falchion as she swung, her strike precise despite the anxiety plaguing her. Her teeth vibrated inside her head as Abaddon countered the attack and slammed his sword down on hers from overhead.

His strength... it was devastating.

But Dani didn't need to beat him. Just survive until Hayden freed herself of the shackles.

Wrath and Chastity fought bitterly, losing themselves to a dance of blades and strength and magic. Blue water swirled around Dani, but no matter how hard she tried, Chastity's blue light evaded her as her thoughts splintered between her magic and dodging Abaddon's strikes while delivering blows of her own. She stepped and struck, countered and blocked with sword and sorcery.

Her falchion sailed toward him, then, at the last minute, she twisted her wrist and stabbed the blade through Abaddon's foot, earning a roar of anger from the Sin. Definitely anger, not pain, because Abaddon ripped his foot away from the blade, letting it slice from the middle of his foot to the edge. Red magic glowed as the flesh stitched itself together.

Dani pulled the hilt of her falchion, but the blade was embedded in the hard-packed dirt. Abaddon reared back. Dani yanked again, fear setting in as she realized she was doomed if she couldn't get her sword free. Water magic surged around her to blast the Sin with a hose. Any other Sin would have been thrown away from Dani, but with Abaddon's physical strength, all he had to do was dig his heels in and withstand the pressure.

She yanked the sword again, still blasting Abaddon with water magic.

A red hand shot from the water hose and slammed her sword further into the ground. Dani stumbled backward, tripping on Raphaela's arm, but caught herself before she tumbled to the ground. Her water magic faltered, and Abaddon threw his larger body at her.

Wrath's fist smashed into Dani's cheek and bone fractured from the blow before she crashed to the ground. Dani's head bounced off the hard packed dirt, her vision blurring black at the edges. Her eyes closed against her will, but the thought of laying vulnerable beside the other witches, being at the mercy of a Sin, catapulted through her head. With tremendous effort, Chastity peeled her eyelids open, but Abaddon wasn't there.

Instead, she watched sideways as the Salem Witch and Jamie battled Leviathan vehemently. Seemed he had caught onto what Hayden was doing, and the Sin of Envy purposefully didn't use his demonic magic. The three were consumed with provoking it out of him

The elements. Dani still had the elements, even if Chastity wouldn't answer her. She peeled herself off the ground, her head ringing. Her sword, she needed her sword. Dani turned in a circle, her movements sluggish as her vision blurred.

Through the haze, her gaze landed on Apalla and Raphaela who were still unconscious. Was blood dripping from Apalla's head? Oh Goddess, Dani didn't notice their injuries before.

Injuries that were minor compared to the Sin of Wrath hovering over them, his serrated blade gripped in both hands as he raised it overhead. Abaddon's sword plunged downward, aimed at Raphaela's heart.

Without thinking, Dani threw herself between Raphaela and Abaddon. Water solidified into an ice wall between her and the Sin. Her water magic saved her life as the element froze around Abaddon's sword before it could pierce Raphaela.

Rage burned in Abaddon's eyes, and red hellfire burned through Dani's ice wall. Dani's falchion protruded from the earth, out of reach.

Hayden. They needed Hayden. Or Kova, or Jamie, or—

Hayden absorbed a blast of Leviathan's Envy magic into her shackles. Green magic exploded between the Prince and Princess of Hell like a volcano of vomit, and both were thrown backward. Hayden's back slammed into the brick path, and the

Salem Witch didn't move. Jamie hovered over his soulmate, protecting her with a ring of holy flames as the other Sins charged. Kova met them with the force of the elements.

Dani was on her own.

Abaddon's serrated knife swung down at her.

Dani's life flashed before her eyes, but the serrated sword screeched to a halt as Axel's battle Axe blocked the Sin's strike.

Barely.

Dani sagged with relief, her vision blurring as Axel stepped between her and Abaddon to shelter her and the unconscious witches. Mila had joined Ronnie, using her sonic blast to repel Mammon moments before he killed the Virtue of Humility.

"I've faced bullies like you before," Axel growled. "You may possess physical strength, but it reflects the truth of what you lack—moral strength."

Abaddon tossed his head back and laughed humorlessly. "Foolish mortal. I do not lack strength." He flexed, making his red muscles bulge, the veins popping against the sinewy flesh. "I am strength incarnate. No mortal can withstand my strength."

Dani blinked rapidly, trying to stay awake, stay alert against the darkness threatening to swallow her. But she fell backward, catching herself with her forearms braced against the cold, hard dirt. She reached for Raphaela with her free hand, but fell short, her hand splashing into the puddle of blood pooling under the girl.

Axel would protect Dani, Dani just needed to get to Raphaela. Raphaela couldn't die. She couldn't. Dani had water magic. She could heal her. She could save her if she could reach the Virtue of Charity.

"Physically, perhaps." Axel squared off against the Sin, his own red magic haloing around him. "But where I come from, strong men do not seek to harm others. Strong men protect. They do not prey on people smaller or weaker than them. Yet, you seek to kill these women, these witches, because they are a threat to your so-called *strength*."

Dani crawled toward Raphaela, inch by inch, digging her fingernails into the ground, drawing blood as she shredded her cuticles. Water magic answered her call, healing her despite the fog in her brain, like her element worked on her behalf without conscious direction from her.

Dani reached the other Virtue and forced herself upright before pulling Raphaela into her lap. Red blood smeared over Dani's clothes, but she hardly noticed as she fought the darkness threatening to pull her under.

"Is that what you are doing?" Abaddon sneered. "*Protecting* them?"

"Yes," Axel growled.

A concentrated shot of red magic blasted from Axel to wrap around Abaddon like a snake. His fiery eyes simmered down as the taut muscles in his face relaxed, the hypnosis magic of Patience seizing hold.

Axel lifted his axe overhead, then thrust it forward. Light glinted off the sharpened axe as it whistled through the air, then sank into Abaddon's red chest. A gaping hole opened as the axe arced downward, slicing the Sin open from collarbone to abdominals.

Despite the darkness clouding her vision, Dani stared into the abyss that was Abaddon's chest. Empty blackness stared back at her. Because that was what the Sins were.

Empty. Hollow.

Water magic surrounded Dani, the element rising from the ground, tracing rivers over her skin as it wound its way to her head. As the element touched her, the darkness waned from her vision and clarity returned to her brain.

The fog lessened, and Dani slammed a palm against the earth, summoning more water from the depths. The element rose to meet her command. Fuzziness plagued Dani, but she had enough faculties to direct water to heal Raphaela without knowing the girl's injuries.

She sensed energy return to the Virtue of Charity before Dani lost her grip on the water magic, her head still aching from the blow of Abaddon's fist. She must not be as healed as she thought.

No, that wasn't it.

Beelzebub appeared beside Abaddon, his orange magic haloing around the two Sins.

No!

Beelzebub siphoned Dani's elemental magic. She cut the flow of power so he couldn't drain her and swell himself up with magic. The Prince couldn't siphon heavenly magic, so he couldn't—

Axel's red magic disappeared from where it had wrapped around Abaddon. But Beelzebub cannot claim Heaven's magic for himself.

The Sin of Gluttony chuckled darkly. "I may not be able to siphon your powers, Patience, but I can siphon your life force."

The hypnotized daze melted off Abaddon's face as Axel's red magic returned to him. Two Sins. Axel opposed two Sins.

Dani reached for her magic, fighting against the fear and panic clawing at her chest. Chastity. She needed Chastity. If she could nullify the Sins' powers, then Axel might stand a chance. Blue magic rose in her chest as Dani stretched a shaky hand into the depths of her powers. But brain fog made it hard for her to grasp hold of her Virtue.

Abaddon's fierce eyes burned with fury as the hypnosis washed away completely. With flaming eyes, Wrath reached up, grasped Axel's war axe, and dislodged it from his chest.

She stretched her fingers, frantically reaching for Chastity's life-saving power. Red magic flared around Axel as he called upon the power of Patience. Blue magic flickered around her. She almost had it. Chastity flared as her heart hammered harder in her chest.

Abaddon's arm swung. Crimson blood sprayed in an arc as the battle axe sank into Axel's chest. Red magic billowed out of Axel's body as his soul separated from his physical vessel.

Abaddon's blood-stained hand reached for the Virtue, a vicious, victorious sneer on his face. If he touched Axel's soul…

"HAYDEN!" Dani heard herself scream, but it was like she was in a bubble and heard everything as though the sound waves were traveling through water.

It was useless. Hayden was unconscious. She needed Kova or Jamie or…

"ANYONE! HELP!" Her scream was half a sob.

Black flashed in her peripheral as Hayden leaped into the air, jumping clear over Dani where she sheltered Raphaela, and into the mist of red magic billowing into the air.

Silver, black, and white magic mingled with red as the magic of Patience absorbed into Hayden's body before Abaddon could steal the Virtue.

Hayden slammed a palm against Abaddon's chest, her wrist free of the demonic shackle, and he crumbled to the ground under the intense shot of hypnosis Hayden plunged into him.

Beelzebub swung a fist at her, but she caught it with her bare hand and twisted, snapping his wrist. Red magic shot from her hand so forcefully, Beelzebub flew across the courtyard and slammed into a brick wall. Debris rained down on his as he crumpled to the ground.

Grabbing Abaddon by the chains, she lifted his massive body with ease, then spun in a circle like a professional discus thrower and tossed him at Elliot, who was clamoring to his feet on top of the compound's tower steeple.

His black eyes widened a second before Abaddon crashed into him.

Lightning struck.

Kova appeared in a flash of green. "The other four are dispatched."

"Where?"

"The bottom of the ocean."

"Good." The word was a growl on Hayden's lips before she disappeared in a swath of shadows and reappeared on top of the tower like the grim reaper given form.

She seized Elliot by the throat, then tossed him from the top of the fourth story. Gesturing to Kova and Jamie to deal with him, she spooked with Abaddon, probably to drop him into the ocean.

Before Elliot could peel himself off the ground, Jamie was on top of him, hammering his fist into Elliot's face. Relentlessly. Black blood splashed over his knuckles, but Jamie didn't stop.

Thea had to summon her vines to wrap around Jamie and pull him off the Sin of Lust, who was alive despite the beating thanks to his demonic magic.

A swirling green portal opened, and Apalla summoned a cyclone of air to throw the Sin through the portal. Kova's magic slammed shut behind him, ending the battle.

A short, but brutal battle.

Melancholy fell on the courtyard.

Dani gasped as Hayden's face appeared in front of hers. Hayden's pale hands landed on Dani's tan cheeks as she inspected Dani for wounds.

Deciding Dani was whole, she pressed two fingers to Raphaela's neck to check her pulse, then snapped the fingers of her other hand to draw the attention of a field medic who rushed over with a gurney.

"Dani," Hayden said softly, but Dani couldn't focus her gaze on the Salem Witch, not with all the blood... "Dani," Hayden's voice was gentle, the gentlest it had ever been, "I need to you release Raphaela. She will be okay, but I need you to let her go."

Dani's gaze turned away from the body lying in a puddle of blood and dropped to the warm girl in her lap.

"Can you do that for me?"

Dani nodded, though the movement didn't seem to be a conscious thought, like her mind was operating separately from her physical body. Hayden peeled back Dani's fingers from where they clamped around Raphaela, prying the Virtue of Charity out of Dani's arms to place her on the gurney.

Raphaela would be okay. She would be okay.

But Axel...

Dani vomited. Bile burned her throat as her breakfast reappeared. A cool hand pressed against her forehead as another brushed back her curly brown hair while she vomited again. The cold brought some relief, but an uncomfortable warmth heated Dani's face, then spread down to her entire body.

Dani had failed him. She failed them all.

She failed to summon her magic.

And Axel was dead because of it.

CHAPTER TEN

NIGHTMARES & DAYDREAMS

Eerie silence haunted the night, only broken by the sound of Dani's combat boots scuffing lightly over the concrete sidewalk as she landed in a crouch outside the walls of the compound. Swathed in the shadows of the wall, Dani slowly rose to her feet, then paused with her back pressed against the stone as the Knight patrolling above her paused, flashing a light at the ground outside the compound that missed illuminating Dani by mere inches.

She didn't dare breathe for fear it would be visible in the chill of the night. Salem, Oregon was warm—warmer than Asylum, Wisconsin—but a certain cold sucked the warmth from the air in the wake of the battle with the Sins. A battle that left the Virtues and the Salem Knights reeling. That left a hollow chasm gaping in Dani's chest.

Water. She needed water. She needed the river and its cleansing element. She needed to dive under the surface and let the currents wash away the trauma and tragedy of the day.

Only when the light withdrew did Dani release the breath she had been holding. With a glance at the Knight patrolling the wall above her, Dani turned on her heel and burst into a sprint in the opposite direction. She needed air. She needed space from the suffocating walls of the compound trapping her within. Where they were *supposed* to be safe. But today proved the compound wasn't safe. Hayden and Kova restored the wards, but the Sins proved they could kill the Virtues with ease.

The only thing standing in their way was one of their own—Hayden Black. If Hayden hadn't been knocked unconscious, the Sins would not have grasped the upper hand, and Axel wouldn't have—

It was like an anvil smashed into her chest, and Dani skidded to a halt.

It was her fault. It was all her fault. She was supposed to be their leader, yet she failed when it mattered most. And her failures cost Axel his life.

Why was she so incompetent?

None of the others struggled to manifest their Virtue powers. Dani's took *months* to surface. And once it did, her powers were unreliable at best and nonexistent at worst.

What was wrong with Dani? What was wrong with her powers? Why did Chastity not want to help her? Did Chastity not want her anymore?

A feeling she couldn't identify squeezed her chest, threatening to suffocate her.

No.

No. If she stopped now, she would become a victim of her own emotions. No. She couldn't break down here. Riverfront City Park wasn't far.

So, she ran, forcing herself to put one foot in front of the other. Blood rushed in her ears, drowning out the noise of her light footfalls. Focusing on her breath, she ignored the burn in her legs, pushing harder, running faster to reach her destination.

The streets flew by, the storefronts and apartment buildings blurring together in the dim light of the streetlamps. It was a straight shot from Wilson Park where the compound was located to Riverfront City Park. No turns, no stopping for cars or streetlights at this time of night. Not at three in the morning—the witching hour. Few people were out and about at this hour, and those who were either witches like Dani, or up to no good. But Dani didn't stop to think about that. After the day she had, she wasn't afraid of any mortals who might lurk in the shadows. No, she was afraid of the Sins who came for her during the day.

Sidewalk faded to grass as Dani entered the park, but she didn't slow her run as she approached the river. Fire burned brighter inside her, heating her body from the inside out. Her skin must have been scalding, but she didn't stop running. As her foot landed inches from the edge of the grass where the ground met the water, Dani brought her feet together and her arms over her head. Pushing with all the strength in her exhausted, sore legs, she dove into the river and beneath its rushing waves.

Channeling the power of her element, Dani sank beneath the surface, down, down, down, until her feet landed in the squishy sand of the riverbed.

The frigid water caressed her skin, relieving some of the heat consuming her from within. Opening her mouth, Dani let it fill with water, then screamed at the top of her lungs, expelling all the oxygen inside her. The viscosity of the water dulled the sound, absorbing her scream so no one would hear, and when the oxygen finally ran out, Dani sucked in a shaky breath. Being a water elemental, she knew she could breathe underwater, but she had never attempted it before. That was how desperate she was to escape the burdens of the Salem compound. Only the natural waters offered her any comfort.

Perhaps she would stay beneath the river forever and live among the curious fish swimming past her in schools, where it was unlikely she would be responsible for the death of another.

Oh, Goddess, *Axel.*

Beneath the waves, hidden from the others, hidden from Hayden, Dani broke down and cried and cried and cried, letting the turmoil that chewed at her from the inside manifest as hot tears washed away by the cool water of the river.

This was the breaking point Hayden had warned her about.

Axel was *dead*, because Dani couldn't summon her Chastity powers. All the other Virtues, even Mila, accessed theirs and displayed full control. But Dani was useless, utterly hopeless. Why did she manifest her null powers when Elliot was about to kill Jamie, but not before Abaddon killed Axel? What was *wrong* with her?

Contemplating the dead and her miserable lack of power, not to mention questioning why the Goddess would choose *her*, why Hayden would offer her a place in her circle, Dani laid on her back in the river bed, allowing herself to sink into the sand that molded around her body.

She so badly wanted to be like Hayden, the witch she idolized, but being around Hayden, the most powerful witch to walk the earth, was a stark reminder of her own shortcomings. She could never be like Hayden.

Maybe that is not who you are meant to be, a gentle voice floated through her mind, and Dani rocketed upright—or tried too against the resistance of the water. Spinning in the sand, she squinted her eyes in search of someone in the water with her. Sensing nothing, Dani relaxed into the sand once more but kept her magic alert. But something in her gut told her that she was all alone out here.

Just her... and Spirit...

A peaceful calm washed over her, and Dani breathed.

After what felt like eternity and not enough time, Dani kicked off the bottom of the river bed and swam upward, moving her arms and legs in long, sweeping strokes. With her power over water, Dani could easily command the element to bring her to the surface, but she wanted to feel her limbs move in mighty strokes. The movement soothed her as she reluctantly left her bubble of solitude for the pressures and burdens of the mortal world.

As her head broke the surface, a bitter cold wind swept over the surface of the river, biting into Dani's wet skin and hair. Treading water, she scanned the city that remained quiet at this time of night. Lights glimmered in the distance, the only indication of any life in the city.

Reluctantly, Dani swam to the edge of the river and wrenched her soaking wet body from the water. The pool at the compound wasn't the same as the fresh water in nature. Only nature could truly soothe a witch's soul. But it was late. Probably four a.m., and Dani needed to return before anybody realized she was missing. After the battle against the Sins, she couldn't imagine the panic that would ensue if someone discovered her empty bed.

A cold breeze cut through the park, chilling Dani to the bone. Shivering, she mentally called upon her element and drained the water from her clothing to return it to the river. Dry again, she wrapped her leather jacket tighter around her torso.

With one last glance at the river and a resigned sigh, Dani turned away from the river, then stopped dead at the sight of a glowing woman standing in the middle of the park.

"Hello, Daniella."

Stumbling backward, Dani's foot caught on something, and she tumbled into the dirt. Landing with an "oof" on her back, she lost any shred of dignity she might have had. Pushing to her elbows, Dani stared up at an impossibly beautiful woman with hair like strands of gold that tumbled to her hips in flowing waves. A fitted gown of white spun cotton covered her from neck to ankle, but it wasn't prudish on her. Somehow, it seemed ravishing on her angelic frame. But her purple and white eyes were striking beyond comparison.

Dani had seen Gabriel before, but from a distance, and the way Hayden described the eyes of the archangels... if it hadn't been for the elegant white wings protruding from the woman's spine, Dani would have recognized her as an archangel from her eyes—purple irises wrapped around an entirely white pupil.

It was uncanny yet mesmerizing at the same time, and Dani found herself wanting to reach out to touch the woman.

"You know who I am?"

The angel smiled, revealing white pearl teeth behind her lips. "Of course, I know who you are, Daniella. You are the vessel for the Virtue of Chastity. But I knew you long before you were born on this mortal Earth. I knew you when your soul was conceived by our loving Mother and Father. But you would not remember me, not when you are living in this mortal body." Extending a hand, the angel wrapped her fingers around Dani's wrist and pulled her to her feet. An electrifying sensation zapped through her body at the contact, like power filled her cells, but the feeling faded as the woman dropped her hand to spread her arms wide. "I am Jophiel, the Archangel of Beauty and Light."

Archangel of Light? Hayden never mentioned that. In fact, nobody had. Since the Salem War, the Spellery made Zola's *Angels* course mandatory for all students. As one of the seven main archangels who interacted with humanity, Jophiel was a primary figure studied in the class, but nobody had mentioned she was the Archangel of Light. Only Beauty had been accredited to her. Surely Hayden knew this.

"The Salem Witch is well aware of my title and duties," Jophiel declared. Angels must be able to read mortals' minds. Is that why Hayden seemed to always know what Dani was thinking? "But it is not her place to share my secrets with humanity."

"Then why tell me?" Dani didn't miss the part where the angel clearly didn't broach Dani's thought about Hayden's secret abilities.

"Because you are no ordinary mortal, for you hold a special place in my heart, Daniella."

"Why?" Dani asked dumbly. Shaking herself, she quickly added, "I mean, I'm not like this uber beautiful girl. I'm not feminine and girly and—"

Jophiel raised a flat palm, halting Dani's word vomit. "There is more to beauty than one's outward appearance. My beauty is not as shallow as mortal appearance, for it is so much more than that. I represent the beauty of Heaven and all of Creation. And as I said, I am not just the Angel of Beauty, but the Archangel of Light." Folding her hands over her stomach, Jophiel cocked her head, studying Dani, and asked, "Do you know why beauty and light go hand in hand, Daniella?"

The young Virtue shook her head dumbly.

"Because beauty can only be seen in the light. Darkness can disguise all kinds of unpleasant things. It is why Evil prefers the Darkness, for it can hide. But in the light, all is revealed, and Evil cannot hide its ugliness." Raising a perfect hand, Jophiel cupped Dani's cheek. The electrifying sensation buzzed through Dani's head. "And you have a soul of such beauty and light, Daniella. There is no darkness in you."

Dani's lip quivered with emotion. How could Jophiel think that? Look at what Dani caused today. It was her fault so much chaos and destruction rained down on the witches of Salem. It was her fault Axel was—

She choked at the thought, squeezing her eyes shut and hiding her face from the angel. If Dani had summoned her nullifying powers... If she wasn't so ridiculously weak... If she was more like Hayden—

"While I love my niece dearly, Hayden is the last person a Virtue should aspire to be."

Dani whipped her head up so fast, her neck cracked. Mind whirling, Dani struggled to comprehend what Jophiel was saying. Angels weren't... Gabriel and Michael called one another brother, but it didn't mean genetically... Hayden and Jamie weren't related.

Smiling, Jophiel said, "Yes, Hayden is my niece because Gabriel is my twin brother, and she is soul-bonded to my nephew. Gabriel and I are the only twins in the Angelic Choirs, which is why his mortal children were born as twins."

"But how? Angels can't be... Can they?"

"Only Gabriel and I are related by what you consider genetics. Angels are made of light and spirit. When the great Creator formed us, It mixed our angelic souls, exchanging the light that constructs our divine nature, so we shared light. Where soulmates are two souls who fit perfectly together because they were made from the same light, Gabriel and I did not come from the same soul material, but rather we possess a piece of one another. We were made in one another's image to reflect the balance and divine nature of the God and Goddess."

"So, you're the only two archangels who are actually siblings. So, the Kensingtons..."

"Are cousins to the Bishops, yes."

"If Gabriel had twins, why didn't you?"

"Who is to say I did not birth twins?" Jophiel winked a beautiful purple eye. "Hayden was not the only Nephilim child hidden for her mortal safety. But my children would not be related to Michael's, for we are not the same. Nor would Gabriel's nor my children be related to the children of another angel of a different choir."

"Choir?" Dani asked. "What is a choir?"

"The choirs are the rank of angels. Archangels are one of the nine choirs of angels. Virtues are another. Seraphim are the highest of choirs."

"Wait, did you say..."

"Yes." Jophiel smiled kindly. "Virtues is the name of a choir of angels, just as it is a name for the entities you bear to fight the Sins."

"What makes the Seraphim the highest choir? And where do Virtues and Archangels fall in the ranks?"

"You have an inquisitive mind, young Chastity, much like the Salem Witch you look up to so much, but different. You are more controlled, less wild." Dani blushed at the comparison. "It is a compliment." Jophiel leaned in to whisper, "Michael's daughter is too unruly for most angels. I love her dearly, but your soul is better suited than hers to the angels. But to answer your questions, Seraphim are the caretakers and protectors of the Throne of the Creator, which makes their purpose the highest of all tasks. Virtues are the second rank of the middle choirs, for they wield raw power in the form of the physical elements of your mortal world and perform what humans and witches perceive as miracles. Archangels are the eighth choir, and one of the closest to the mortal realm. We travel regularly between the physical and cosmic worlds to enact the will of the Creator, which is why we are the angels commonly known to bear mortal children. Virtues and Archangels frequently travel across *dimensions*." Jophiel emphasized the word, her purple eyes widening slightly as though she shared a secret that Dani should understand.

"I have so many more questions."

"I know you do, my sweet child, and they will all be answered in time, but that is not why I am here." Jophiel smiled. "The Lord and Lady have a message for you."

"I thought Gabriel was the Messenger Archangel."

"He is, but this message is more in my realm of expertise. Or *dimension*." There was that word again, and Jophiel said it with more emphasis this time. "For it is a reminder that the Creator's love for you is infinite. It has no end, no borders, and therefore, Its love is everlasting. The Creator loves you unconditionally and limitlessly."

Tears poured from Dani's eyes as the sincerity of the message, touched her soul in a way no other words could.

"Why send you all this way to tell me this?"

"Because you are lost, dear child. You believe you are without love, and you are suffering for it. But you do not need more love. All the love you could possibly need is already inside you. All you have to do is accept it, Daniella. Do not allow your perception of isolation prevent you from meeting Chastity, for the Virtue is part of you as surely as your brown eyes. Love is the means by which you will win this war, for it is the means by which you will wield Chastity."

"I don't understand."

"No, but you will." Jophiel smiled in a knowing way that reminded her of Hayden when she heard the whispers of Spirit. "Lust is the primal, base desire of a savage animal. Love is the genuine respect and deeper emotional and spiritual connection between two beings of light. Chastity is the self-control to prevent oneself from falling to the temptations of lust in all its forms."

"Chastity is the opposite of Lust, as all the Virtues are the opposites of the Sins."

"Are they?" Jophiel raised a skeptical eyebrow. "Are they opposites? Or are they means by which to subdue the Sins? *Love* is the opposite of Lust. Chastity is the ability to control Lust so Love reigns supreme. Love cannot thrive without Chastity, and Chastity has no purpose without Love. Pray on it, Daniella, and Spirit will give you answers." She pressed a gentle hand to Dani's cheek. "Now, return home. This little interaction is bound to call to demons due to our angelic energy consolidated in one place. Hurry along before the demons come. But if they do, help is not far away."

Jophiel gestured to the path behind Dani. Following her hand, Dani glanced over her shoulder into the darkness, but when she turned around, the beautiful angel was gone and had taken her heavenly light with her.

A cold shiver wracked Dani's body and it had nothing to do with the temperature and everything to do with realizing how very alone out here she was in the middle of the city in the dead of night. Jophiel was right. What was Dani thinking, coming out here by herself? She needed to return to the compound.

Tucking her hands under her armpits, she pulled her jacket tighter to her body as though it would protect her from the monsters lurking in the night.

No sooner had she taken a step toward the pathway home—the path steeped in shadows—than she heard a clicking sound.

Oh no. No, no, no, no, no.

Dani *hated* spider demons. Not because she was afraid of them, but their legs freaked her out.

Air whooshed as she unsheathed her falchion in time for a spider demon to scuttle from the shadows at the edge of the park.

Summoning water to her hand, Dani froze it into a spear of ice. Dani threw the weapon at the spider demon, but it scurried out of the way and the ice shattered against the concrete.

Those eight legs helped the spider move too quickly for Dani's liking. Besides the fact that spider demons were poisonous, she hated spiders in general. But the river was nearby, containing gallons of her element, and no humans around to see.

A wave rose from the river and crashed on the spider from overhead. Dani unleashed the ice in her veins and froze the bulbous backside of the spider. Before it could so much as squeal, Dani sliced her falchion through its head, severing the appendage from the body that had too many. Dani released the water, and the body fell to the ground with a thump and decayed into black dust.

Scowling at the carcass, Dani spun on her heel to march down the sidewalk and return home but came to an abrupt stop.

A dozen spider demons stood between her and the sidewalk, pinning her between them and the river with no route to escape on foot or call for backup from the compound.

These demons were smaller than the one Dani just killed which meant... the first one was their mother. And based on how they hissed, they thirsted for her blood.

Swallowing, she raised her falchion.

The legs. Oh, Goddess. Too many legs. Dani fought the urge to gag as a hundred legs jerked in rapid movements. Twelve spiders as tall as Dani's knee, raced toward her, snapping their chelicerae with venom-tipped fangs.

Six of them leaped at her at once. Dani threw up a wall of ice, encasing the six in her element. The other six scurried around her magical attack—one climbed over the wall and shot a web of sticky black silk at her. Dodging the webbed attack, Dani sliced her falchion through its front two legs so it fell from the ice block, then she cut her blade through its neck, killing it instantly. Two move dove at her, but Dani stabbed her sword through one and skewered the other with a spear of ice.

Spinning, she kicked a fourth so she could kill the fifth. The sixth demon flew at her, but Dani ducked and stabbed up, cutting the demon in half. Dani approached the spider struggling to roll off its back and stabbed it through the heart.

Before melting the wall of ice, Dani willed her element to stab six daggers of ice through the hearts of the spider demons imprisoned in her ice. As the demons decayed, she released her hold on the element.

But as the water dropped away, it revealed a line of brimstone demons assembled where the spider demons had emerged.

Where were all these demons coming from?

Twenty brimstone demons glowered at her, blue hellfire burning between the horns atop their heads.

Gripping her falchion so tight that her knuckles went white, Dani slipped into her combat stance and summoned water from the river.

Not waiting for them to attack, she shot hoses of water at three brimstones, knocking them off their feet. Spurred by her attack, the waist-high demons charged her, their little legs struggling to cover the distance between them and her.

Though brimstones were a step above spider demons in their intelligence and powers, they were small and slow compared to Dani.

More water blasted a row of brimstones off their feet, buying Dani a few more precious seconds. Freezing the water into three daggers, Dani used her magic to throw the daggers at the brimstones. Two of them hit their mark, sinking into the demons' vulnerable eye sockets. A spear of ice blasted through another demon, eviscerating it.

And then the first row of the three brimstones were upon her. Dani met the first's claws with the back of her falchion. Holding his strike, she spun on one foot and kicked the second brimstone in the face. The third got a blast of water that froze around its head. With its top too heavy for its bottom, the brimstone tipped over, his little arms and legs flailing.

Ripping her falchion free from the first brimstone, she spun and stabbed her sword through the eye of the one she kicked. Without missing a beat, she stabbed the first one. But as the two disintegrated into ash, four more took their place. At least the one with its head frozen served as a block, forcing them to go around to get to Dani.

More ice daggers flew through the air as Dani spun and struck, kicked and stabbed. Over and over, she drove her falchion through a brimstone's eye, only to have another replace it. She didn't have time to attempt calling upon Chastity. It was all she could do to cut down the little buggers before they overwhelmed her with their sheer numbers.

Claws raked over her thigh, and Dani gasp in pain as her flesh tore open. Staggering, she managed to keep herself upright and shoot a hose of water at the demon, blasting it away from her. Before she could inspect her wound, another brimstone slashed its claws at her. Stabbing it in the eye, Dani pressed her free hand to her thigh, and when she pulled it away, it was damp with red blood.

Crap.

She would have to heal the wound, but that meant she couldn't wield water to fight. Well, she could, but she wasn't as good at psychically commanding the elements as Hayden.

Water from the river flowed around her hand, and she pressed it to her thigh, bringing instant relief to the swollen, angry skin.

Keeping her palm firmly pressed against her leg, she stabbed another brimstone in the eye, then a second demon before hitting a third one with a water whip. It wasn't as strong as normal, but it sent the small demon spinning, giving her time to finish healing her thigh.

Six of the annoying little demons remained, but they charged her simultaneously. Kicking the first one in the chest, Dani shoved it into another brimstone. A wave of water from the river slammed down on the third, freezing its arms and legs at its sides so Dani could stab it through the eye.

Four left.

A whip of water wrapped around the neck of the fourth one, yanking it away from Dani so she could block a strike of claws from the fifth one, sever its arm, then stab it through the eye so it exploded into a cloud of dust. Still holding the other demon by its neck, she killed it with her falchion.

Two left.

The demons rushed her from opposite directions, and Dani suppressed an eye roll. Smarter than spiders, brimstones still weren't all that bright, so they attacked in large numbers.

Side stepping at the last minute, Dani leaped out of the way to let the two brimstones ram into one another. As the demons tumbled to the ground in a tangle of limbs, Dani leaped forward. Her falchion sailed through the eye socket of the demon on the bottom, then as she swiped up, she sank her blade into the slate of the final demon's throat. Yanking the sword with all her might while pushing on the demon's back with her foot, she forced the blade through its neck, and it exploded to ash.

The Virtue was finally alone.

Silence fell on Dani's ears, only interrupted by the sound of her heavy breathing and the light scraping of black demon dust as the breeze blew it over the concrete.

A slow clap sounded from behind Dani.

She spun in a half circle.

Hayden Black emerged from the shadows, stepping into the soft glow of the flickering street lamp. For once she wasn't with her soulmate, and Dani wondered if Jamie knew about her midnight adventures.

"How long have you been there?"

Hayden grinned, crossing her arms over her chest and leaning back on her heels. "The whole time."

"You saw the whole thing?" Dani asked with accusation in her tone. "Why didn't you help me?

Hayden shrugged. "You didn't need it."

Dani's mouth gaped open. "Didn't need it?" She scoffed. "Did you miss when the spider demon nearly bit me? Or when that brimstone demon clawed me? Or—"

A misty fog rolled across the black lawn, bringing an unnatural chill with it.

Hayden went deadly still, her sharp eyes missing nothing.

"What is that?" Dani breathed out the words in a whisper.

And then she felt it.

That cold dread crawling down her spine. A warning.

A Sin was nearby.

Hayden growled, the sound low and reverberating through her chest, echoing with her unfathomable power. "Abaddon."

Fear shot through Dani to seize her heart in its tight, cold grip, and she became suddenly aware that she and Hayden were alone out here. Dani never faced a Sin without the other Virtues…. She never faced a Sin without the power of Hayden's full circle behind her. Let alone Abaddon, the leader and most dangerous of the Sins.

While Dani quaked with fear, Hayden was a wall of unyielding steel. Confidence exuded from her, not a trace of fear to be detected.

Do not be afraid, Dani, Hayden's voice sang in the wind. *The Creator's power is within you, and It will not fail. We shall make the Darkness tremble.* Her voice roared through Dani's mind like a mighty lion.

Chastity stirred inside Dani, nudging her gently like a loyal familiar nuzzling against its witch, and she was comforted by the warmth that spread through her chest, down her arms, and to her fingertips, where the power of Chastity hummed.

But the soft, baby blue light that glowed around her during the first battle with the Sins eluded her. Her power was within her grasp, buzzing below the surface of her skin, but despite her will, the magic would not break free of her physical vessel.

Fear clawed at her throat. Without her nullifying powers, Abaddon was at full strength, and while a warrior at heart, Dani was a mere mortal compared to a fallen angel... and against that kind of power—

Dark power erupted from the shadowy abyss like a sonic wave, bringing with it the rotten scent of decay that tainted the air wherever the Sins infested the earth.

Bile rose in her throat, and Dani fought not to gag on the putrid scent. Bent over with her hands on her knees, she would have been eviscerated by Abaddon's power had it not been for the wall of silver Spirit surrounding the angel-touched women.

"Dani." Hayden's voice was sharper than a blade's edge. "I can spook us out of here. But Abaddon knows that. It's a test, to see if we will run from a fight with him. To see if you're ready."

"Because if I'm not..."

"Because if you're not, the Sins will view it as a weakness." Hayden's candor cut like glass. "Not just weakness. Worse. They will perceive it as though *I* do not think you are capable."

"And if you don't think a Virtue is capable of defeating a Sin, then Heaven doesn't. If Heaven doesn't have faith in the Virtues, then the Sins have nothing to fear and will attack us before the Blood Moon Lunar Eclipse."

Hayden nodded sharply, conflict contorting her face. "I will not throw you into this battle if you are not ready, but you need to know the consequences before you make a decision."

"You want me to decide?" Dani asked skeptically. "I can't..." She sucked in a deep breath. "I can't summon my Virtue power. I can't nullify his powers."

"You must decide, Dani. I may be the Salem Witch, but you're the leader of the Virtues. If we flee, they will attack the Virtues again. But if we face them and win..."

"They'll likely leave us alone until the Eclipse."

The wall of silver Spirit shimmered around them. Hayden nodded. "This is your war, so you must decide. As for your powers..." She shrugged nonchalantly, as if the lack of magic wasn't a terrifying thought. "I faced Lilith without any magic while she was fully powered, yet I defeated her." Those crystal blue eyes bored into Dani's with unwavering certainty. "What makes you think we need to nullify Hell's magic to defeat Abaddon? It was the Archangel *Michael* who expelled him from Heaven the first time."

Straightening from her bent position, Dani squared her shoulders, and with more confidence than she felt, she said, "Let's fight."

With a wicked grin that was terrifying to enemies and encouraging to Dani, Hayden snapped her fingers, dissolving the wall of Spirit.

"Hello, Abaddon," Hayden drawled in that casual tone of hers that was more menacing than when she growled. "To what do we owe the pleasure?"

Shadows undulated as they reluctantly shed away from the Sin, revealing his naked, toned torso painted an angry red. His signature black chains crossed over his chest in an X, unnaturally silent as the links clashed against one another.

An eerie silence suffused the entire park, screaming at her to run. Swallowing the urge to shrink, Dani raised her chin as she focused her gaze on the Sin.

"*Nephilim.*" He spat on the ground, then his hellish eyes cut to Dani, and it took all her willpower to not retreat a step from his flaming gaze. "*Virtue.*" A hiss slipped from his throat.

"You killed Axel," Dani shot at him without thinking. Once the words escaped her lips, she couldn't find it in herself to regret them, even under the scrutiny of Abaddon's murderous gaze. Axel's death was like a stinging brand, the wound raw and blistered.

"Sins and Virtues cannot engage one another again within three days of an engagement," Hayden stated matter-of-factly, leaning back on her heels.

Steam billowed from Abaddon's red nostrils. "Incorrect, Nephilim. We engage as often as we deem necessary. The Rules of Engagement only apply to battles to the death."

"Which is why you planned to capture Dani." Again, Hayden spoke with a disturbing level of calmness, but alarm zinged down Dani's spine.

He could do that?

"Then perhaps the child should have wisdom to not wander in the night."

"Who said I was wandering?" Again, Dani spoke with more conviction than she felt.

Abaddon regarded her the way a human would a gnat. Like he might swat her.

Hayden stepped in between them, severing Abaddon's line of sight and saving Dani from the intensity of his gaze.

"Regardless, leave Abaddon. Perhaps the Virtues can only wallop your butt thrice..." Dani could hear the devious grin on her lips as Hayden said, "But I am under no such limitations. My father's magic pumps through my veins."

The air heated around them as Abaddon's anger unfurled. "Your *sire* did not defeat me on his own. He required the help of a Virtue. You are no such match for me alone, *Nephilim.*"

"Good thing I have the help of a Virtue." Tossing her head back, her black locks shaking as they turned silver from root to end, Hayden cackled like an evil witch. "Haven't you heard, Abaddon? I'm more powerful than my father. And Dani is more powerful than any previous Chastity reincarnation. With nullifying powers like that... well." She clucked her tongue. "You'll be powerless."

Was it Dani's imagination, or did the red of Abaddon's skin pale a shade?

"A null who cannot access her powers?"

"Can't she?" Dani couldn't see Hayden's face, but she imagined she quirked an eyebrow, silver Spirit rising around her as the shadows slinked closer. "Shall we find out?"

Panic rushed through Dani. She couldn't access her Chastity powers. She had told Hayden as much. She—

Hayden was gone, disappeared into the shadows, leaving Dani and Abaddon alone in the park.

Oh, *crap.*

CHAPTER ELEVEN

Vulnerable Virtues

*D*istract him. Hayden's voice commanded in her mind.

How? Dani thought back in earnest, but she didn't receive a response. Did that trick work in reverse if Dani didn't have telepathy?

He can't kill you. Did Hayden hear her, or did she know Dani would be clueless. *By attacking you first, Abaddon forfeited his immunity. You can inflict fatal damage on him, but he can't mortally wound you.*

Abaddon's serrated sword arced through the air, slicing an inch above Dani's head as she ducked. She stared at the ancient Prince of Hell with wide eyes, her brain scrambling to catch up. Abaddon didn't get the memo that he couldn't fatally wound her.

Wrath didn't give her a second of reprieve, stabbing at her with his hideous sword again. Dodging, Dani ducked under his arm, swinging as she spun until her falchion met resistance. Throwing her weight into it, she dug the blade deeper into his red, angry flesh until he roared, his forked tongue writhing in the air.

Striking out with his hooved foot, Abaddon kicked her in the rear, sending her sprawling behind him. Stumbling over uneven ground, Dani struggled to right herself, but the toe of her combat boot caught, and she crashed to the ground. A jagged stone crashed against her wrist, and her grasp flew open. The smell of coppery blood stung Dani's nostrils from the gash running the length of her forearm from wrist to elbow.

The massive body of the Sin of Wrath flew through the air, Abaddon's serrated sword held high, ready to stab Dani.

Shoving away from the pile of rocks she landed on, she rolled over the grassy field, barely missing Abaddon's hoof as it crashed into the ground, leaving a crater in the dirt where her chest had been.

Yeah, he definitely missed the memo about not killing her.

Where was Hayden?

Her sword... Dani needed her sword, it... it was on the other side of Abaddon... while Dani lay in the dirt.

Snorting out a huff of steam, Abaddon pivoted on his hoof to stare her down like a bull at a matador.

She was *so* screwed.

"I am going to kill you, little girl." Anger flashed in his eyes as they landed on her, like the mere sight of her irritated his demons. "And there will be no one to mourn you. No Virtues, for they shall all be dead, too. No Salem Witch and her circle because they do not care about you—you're merely a pawn to them. Do you understand me? *No one.*"

And that's when Dani understood. All that hatred, all that anger inside Abaddon wasn't about her. It was directed at her, but he didn't hate Daniella Sanchez. He didn't know Dani Sanchez, otherwise he would know she had a brother. And he would know Damien would mourn his sister until the end of time. But he didn't mention Damien, because he didn't know the Virtues personally. He didn't know the details and nuances of their lives.

They were all the same to him. There was no difference between Chastity now and the Chastity of seven hundred years ago or six thousand years ago. All he saw was a mortal with the power to oppose him, and it angered him. The thought of a mortal witch being his demise... it enraged him beyond comprehension.

Because he was a Sin... he wasn't capable of love.

But Dani was. Isn't that what Jophiel said to her?

Abaddon may not see Dani's worth. He could try to undermine her confidence and break her spirit before he broke her body, but in his blind rage, he was oblivious to the facts that would allow Dani to defeat him and the other Sins. Dani didn't have Humility's power, but she could see through his lies.

Maybe the Virtues wouldn't miss her. Maybe she really was a burden on Hayden's circle. But Damien would *always* love her. And it was that feeling that seized hold of her heart and pushed her to reach for her special magic—the power of Chastity.

Baby blue light illuminated around Dani like an aura as warmth spread from her heart to the rest of her body, coursing through her veins like the blood pumping through her until it warmed even the tips of her fingers.

Abaddon's eyes, narrowed in hatred, widened as the light burst to life like a beacon.

Staggering backward, Abaddon released an involuntary gasp as Dani's nullifying power hit him. The unadulterated anger in his eyes lessened under the pale blue light of Chastity as Hell's hold retreated. Even the crimson tinge of his skin lightened a few shades.

Surging to her feet, Dani summoned water to her hands before Chastity's nullifying powers wore off. Thrusting her hands forward, she commanded the water to freeze Abaddon in a cage of ice.

Opening his mouth, Abaddon roared, clearly trying to enact some magic, but nothing happened.

Dani sprinted around Abaddon, giving him a wide berth despite the ice entrapping him, and dove for her sword. As soon as it was in her hand, she spun around to face him, slipping into the battle stance she honed over the years training at the Spellery and perfected these past months under the Warrior Witch's diligent supervision.

The pale blue light haloing her body had disappeared, and with it, so did her Sin-cicle. Why did Chastity do that? Why didn't it maintain the magic?

Because of the panic drowning out the love in your heart.

Touche, Dani telepathically said to the voice in her head that she was convinced was her brain going insane.

"You will pay for that, Chastity, and for all the meddlesome trickery in your past lives." The brutal red returned to Abaddon's skin, a stark reminder that he was out for her blood.

As he stomped toward her, Dani tightened her grip on her falchion and sent a prayer up to whoever may be listening to help her survive this encounter.

That nasty serrated blade sliced through the air with impossible speed, but not as fast as Hayden. Swaying backward, Dani cleared the range of the blade while bringing her own up to block, just in case. But Abaddon didn't stop. As soon as the first strike was complete, he swung his sword for another, then another, backing Dani up one step each time. He was herding her where he wanted. Or playing with her—Dani wasn't sure.

As he raised his blade to strike again, Dani prepared herself. She would *not* yield another step to him. Reality slowed as Abaddon struck again, but instead of dodging the attack, Dani pressed into it.

Blocking his sword with her bonded falchion, Dani threw the blade backward, then spun into Abaddon to bash the pommel of her sword against his sternum. Spinning out before he could react, Dani watched Abaddon stumble from the force of her blow, though she suspected it was more from surprise than anything given his super strength. She would not be able to pull that move off again.

Abaddon stepped back into the darkness swarming the stone wall lining the estate. Shadows writhed, peeling away as crystal blue eyes appeared over Abaddon's shoulder. Hayden's black sword was barely visible in the darkness. Hayden, dressed in her usual black, with her midnight hair, was barely visible if not for her piercing blue eyes and porcelain skin.

But Abaddon was oblivious to the presence of the Salem Witch as he stabbed down at Dani. Distracted by Hayden's unexpected reappearance, Dani barely raised her falchion in time to block, the blade deflecting Abaddon's hefty sword. Barely. The serrated edge brushed past Dani's shoulder as Abaddon recovered control of his sword.

A roar of pain ripped from Abaddon's throat as Hayden sliced her blade behind him, and the Sin crashed to his knees. She must have severed his Achilles' tendons.

Reacting on instinct, Dani stabbed. The wide razor tip of her falchion pierced Abaddon's heart, and black blood spurted from the wound, dribbling down his muscular chest.

Axel's face flashed through Dani's vision. The last face Axel made as Abaddon used Axel's axe to cut open his chest. As that fatal moment clouded Dani's mind, anguish burned her heart.

The falchion twisted in her hand. Without thinking, Dani ripped her blade from his heart while pressing down on the hilt so the blade sliced down his chest, drawing a line of black blood.

Slapping her hand over the gaping wound, Hayden's palm flashed with heavenly white light.

Abaddon bellowed with a mix of wrath and agony.

Snaking her arm around Abaddon, Hayden's sharpened nails sank into Abaddon's fleshy jugular, biting into the sinewy muscles hard enough to draw demon blood. Twisting, Hayden lifted the massive Sin into the air like he didn't weigh any more than a foam finger.

A wicked grin twisted her mouth. "You might have taken one of Heaven's today, Abaddon," Hayden growled, her eyes flashing silver. The sound alone sent a shiver racing down Dani's spine, and she could have sworn Abaddon quaked in fear of the Princess of Hell. In a disturbingly soft voice, Hayden whispered, "But you made a grave mistake coming after Chastity tonight. And you will pay for it with your life. Enjoy the next few weeks. Because you will be the first casualty during the Blood Moon Eclipse. And I cannot wait to burn you to ashes with my father's holy flames."

Tossing him away like a ragdoll, Hayden summoned her signature silver flames to her hand in a silent threat. Dust billowed around Abaddon's red body as he slammed into the ground. Groaning—the Sin actually groaned—Abaddon pushed to his hands and knees, his red biceps shaking.

What did Hayden do to him?

Silver flames erupted in a semi-circle around the Deadly Sin. Lurching, Abaddon recoiled, and shadows enveloped his body. With a final enraged glare that promised retribution, he disappeared into the darkness.

Breathing out a heavy breath she didn't know she was holding, Dani stumbled backward until her back slammed into the cold metal of a streetlamp. Weight crashed down on her shoulders, and she slumped forward.

"What the hell just happened?" she muttered breathily. "What the *hell* just happened?" she shouted.

Her falchion slipped from her hand and clattered against the stone under her feet. She survived hand to hand combat against a Sin... against a literal fallen angel... the Deadly Sin of Wrath. And she survived. Not only did she survive, but she wounded him. Stabbed him in the heart and twisted the knife. Of course, it would heal in a matter of minutes...

"It won't heal," Hayden said, and Dani again wondered if the Salem Witch could read her thoughts. "I infused Spirit magic with white lotus flower and angel's trumpet—it's an herb poisonous to mortals, angels, and demons alike. Every blade made in Heaven is forged with both white lotus and angel's trumpet, thus every Angel Blade is a death sentence to a demon." Hayden squatted in front of Dani, retrieving her falchion from where it laid on the brick. "The wound you inflicted is permanent. The trinity of angel's trumpet, white lotus, and Spirit magic will keep the wound open perpetually, bleeding constantly to weaken him. His body will continuously attempt to heal, expending magic, but will never seal the wound, slowly weakening him until the final battle. Do you know what that means, Dani?"

Hayden pushed to standing, scrutinizing the falchion as she twisted it in her hand before sliding it into the sheath on Dani's hip. "It means he will be weak. Weaker than any Sin when the Blood Moon Eclipse begins. We may be down a Virtue. But Abaddon is down a Sin. His Sin. It would be a miracle if he can wield the full powers of Wrath, because his angelic powers and strength will deteriorate by then, all thanks to you and your sword fighting."

Swallowing the lump in her throat, Dani forced herself to respond, shaking her head. "No, that wasn't me. Yes, I mean, I stabbed him, but you're the one who—"

"Don't diminish your accomplishments, Daniella," Hayden reminded her fiercely. "Do not discredit your abilities. You held your own against a Sin. Against a Prince of Hell. Do you have any idea how incredible that is?"

Oh Goddess, she might be sick. "I'm trying not to think about it."

"Then don't," the dark princess advised. "Thinking about it is a mortal thing to do. Thinking about it is what creates fear inside you. But your spirit is not afraid. Rest in knowing your spirit is one of courage and strength, Dani. That is why you're the leader of the Virtues."

A groan escaped the teenager's lips. "Don't remind me."

"You cannot deny your responsibilities as the head of the Virtues, nor can you deny that you are the leader. Your spirit knows the truth. And you were so excited to be part of my circle,

Dani. Excited to be a Virtue. I saw it in your soul—you asked for a purpose from the Creator, and It gave you one." Searching her face, Hayden asked, "So why do you fight so adamantly against your role as the leader?"

"Because I'm weak," Dani admitted before she could stop herself. Averting her gaze, she stared at the brick in shame, studying the few blades of grass pushing through the cracks at her feet. "Because as much as I want to be strong and powerful, I'm not and never will be." She blew out a ragged breath, then ran a hand through her curly, voluminous hair. "I wanted to be like you, you know. You were the most intimidating person I had ever met, and even as a kid, you were so confident in yourself. I looked at you, and I saw the kind of witch I wanted to be. You were so fearless and smart and tough, and I tried to be all those things, but it was all a mask. And underneath that mask... there's nothing virtuous about me. I'm not patient like Axel or kind like Walker. At the end of the day, I'm a pathetic, scared little girl who has no idea what she is doing, and my incompetence got Axel killed."

"You're wrong about yourself." Hayden raised a finger. "One, you're not pathetic. And okay, you're scared." Hayden shrugged her leather-clad shoulders. "Who isn't?"

"You aren't," Dani insisted.

Hayden barked out a sharp laugh. "Dani, I'm an immortal Nephilim with the power of five elements and a Princess of Hell. Of course, I'm not scared. Anymore. Do you have any idea how many times I was afraid during my Trials?" Placing her hands on Dani's shoulders, Hayden stooped to look into Dani's eyes. "Do you have any how utterly terrified I was when Elliot nearly killed Jamie? I was shaken for *days* afterward. You can't tell me it didn't show. I hid it from the others, but you know me better than that. Believe me, Dani, it's not your incompetence that's getting people killed. It's mine. It's me who must do better, not you."

The Salem Witch breathed out a sharp sigh, looking at the sky with what might have been regret before snapping her piercing blue gaze to Dani's soft brown one. "And so what if you don't possess all the traits of the Virtues? You think I'm patient or humble? Definitely not. I'm a literal demon, dude. I'm like the absolute opposite of a Virtue. But you know what, the Creator chose me as Its champion. The all-powerful God and Goddess of the Universe chose something tainted by demons and used it to save the world. But let me tell you, it wasn't easy. Five deadly Trials were anything but easy. They stripped away every weakness inside of me. But it was more than that. With every Trial, I began to understand who I was, and even better, I envisioned who I wanted to be at the end of my Trials. There is power in accepting who you are in this moment. Knowing both your strengths and weaknesses is a virtue. But never let that impede your vision of who you want to be. Acknowledge both persons but set your sights on what is greater." She gave Dani's shoulders a reassuring squeeze before letting go.

"What if I can't become the Virtue I'm supposed to be."

"You can," Hayden said it without hesitation, without doubt. "You can do anything through the Creator, who strengthens you. You were not merely born to be a leader, Dani. You were chosen by your fellow Virtues. And that is a far greater weight. Do not bear it lightly."

"But I messed up today. Big time. I'm afraid, Hayden," Dani admitted. "I'm freaking terrified, because I can't keep fighting like this. I'm not you. I'm not the Warrior Witch, so how am I supposed to lead the Virtues in a war that I'm not convinced I can survive?"

"Breathe, Dani. Breathe." Hayden placed both hands on Dani's shoulders. "Breathe through the fear, and you will walk through the fire unburned. I promise you, you will make it out of this war alive."

"How do you know?" Dani asked, choking on a sob.

"Because Death happens to be an old friend. And this war is not meant to be your end. It is your chance to bring virtue into this world."

"Were you scared? When you faced Lilith?"

Hayden's lips pulled into a tight smile. "Terrified."

"Did you know you were going to die?"

"I did," Hayden said simply. "I prayed I was wrong and that my Trial would trigger before midnight, but I knew going into it that I was Nephilim, which meant I had the power to resurrect. And if I did, I would be a Master of Spirit and could save my mother and defeat Lilith for eternity."

"How did you face her, knowing you were going to die? I mean, what normal person does that?"

"First of all, I like to think that I'm not normal." Hayden shot Dani a cheeky smile, crossing her arms over her chest. "Second, I didn't want to die. I faced her because if I didn't, she would either kill or enslave everyone I loved."

"Then how aren't you afraid of this war? I get that you won't die, but what if we lose? You'll have to live under the reign of the Sins for the next seven hundred years."

"Nothing scares me anymore, Dani. Once you meet the Creator face to face, you understand that everything unfolds exactly as It intends. All the forces of Darkness cannot overcome what the Creator has ordained. And it has ordained *you*, Daniella Sanchez. The Sins cannot win. It is when were are at our lowest points in life, when we truly hit rock bottom, that we can rise once again, stronger than ever, using the solid foundation beneath us." Hayden squeezed Dani's shoulder in a big sister kind of way. The Salem Witch frowned, glancing around as if remembering where the two witches were. "But that doesn't mean you should be out in Salem in the middle of the night." She sighed. "Did you learn anything from this excursion? Besides proving you can fend off a Sin?"

"Um..."

"Never greet a stranger in the night, Dani. In the dark hours, you never know who is a demon."

With a wink, she summoned the shadows to swallow them whole.

Hayden shoved a spoonful of what must have been a sample of every food on her plate into her mouth and let out a moan. "That's not cooking, that's sorcery." Swallowing, she scooped up another spoonful. "Angel Boy, you cook better than my dad."

"If it keeps *you* from cooking, I'll make dinner every day."

"Deal."

Kova chuckled from where she lounged in her chair, her boots kicked up onto the table. "That's the exact deal I made with your father when we got married."

Jamie scowled. "What is with the Salem Witch and the inability to cook."

"We're too busy trying to save the world to learn domestic skills."

"That may be true for me," Hayden said between bites of food. Was she even chewing? "But you've had three hundred years to master the culinary arts."

Kova rolled her eyes and held up her palms appeasingly. "Okay. John forbade me from cooking a meal for us after I accidentally set a chicken on fire."

The table fell silent, staring at her.

"Was it—"

"Yes, Hayden, it was still alive."

Jamie and Apalla roared with laughter as Hayden shot mashed potatoes out of her nose.

"I snuffed the flames immediately. It didn't feel a thing."

Tears streamed down the Warrior Witch's cheeks. "Did you still cook it? It was only on fire a little bit."

Kova scowled. "Of course not." Crossing her arms over her chest, the older Salem Witch pouted, then grumbled, "I broke its neck, *then* cooked it."

Hayden hit the ground, having fallen from her seat from laughing so hard.

"Is this what you're like when you're not beating the crap out of us?" Walker asked, glancing between the crazy witches.

"Yup."

"Oh, totally."

"Actually, we're usually much worse."

"When you're immortal, you have to take your joy where you can find it," Kova advised. "Our lives are infinitely more complicated than a normal witch's, but when you're mortal, it's more meaningful to savor the moments, because a lifetime can pass before you realize."

"Is that why we're gathered here?" Raphaela gestured to the spread of food that the Virtues, except for Dani, hadn't touched. "To savor our last days because we're likely going to die in the war in a few weeks?"

"No," Thea responded, her melodious tone a soothing balm compared to the harsh boldness of the immortal Nephilims'. "We gathered here to partake in fellowship."

"I don't understand," Mila admitted, looking uncomfortable in her seat, like she wanted to understand, but couldn't wrap her mind around why we would all share a meal. "What is the point of fellowship?"

"It's about connection," Apalla supplied, but for once, she wasn't speaking the textbook answer Dani was so accustomed to from the High Priestess but rather, she spoke from experience. "It's to honor our shared experience and foster a sense of belonging. Every person in this room was destined to be here by the power of the Creator."

"We are all connected." Thea continued where Apalla left off. "Fellowship is an opportunity to share our joys, our sorrows, our grievances and give support and comfort where needed. In doing so, we foster a sense of belonging and connectedness. It is a reminder that, especially in the face of impending war, we are not alone."

"Who wants to share first?" Apalla asked innocently.

Uncomfortable silence suffocated the room.

Crystal blue eyes pierced Dani's soul, and she fought not to flinch under the weight of Hayden's gaze. She was the leader. She should go first. She knew she should go first...

Inhaling a deep breath, Dani steeled herself to share a part of herself raw and innocent and vulnerable, then maybe, just maybe, the others would open up, too.

"You all think I follow Hayden around like a puppy dog."

"You kinda do," Mila pointed out, though it wasn't unkind.

"And you probably think it's because I'm an Asylumnite following her out of blind devotion." Hayden's blue eyes searched Dani's chocolate ones. If she knew what Dani was going to say, she betrayed nothing. "Or because my brother and her are friends, or you think I'm attached to my childhood hero, but that's not it."

Inhaling a shaky breath, Dani let her eyelids shut to give herself a reprieve before they fluttered open. Wood scraped against tile as she stood and pushed her chair back.

"The reason I admire you so much, Hayden, is because the first time I met you, you seemed so brave and strong and fearless. Tasked with the insurmountable, you never flinched in the face of danger. Demons didn't scare you like they did everyone else. *Lilith* didn't scare you. You laughed in the face of danger because you were so sure of yourself, like you knew nothing could defeat you, and I so badly wanted to believe that about myself."

Turning around in her chair, Dani slowly peeled off her sweatshirt, then her short-sleeve t-shirt, exposing her sports bra and the bare skin of her back where a gruesome scar ravaged the skin.

"When I was seven, I was attacked by a hellhound." Dani shook her head. "To this day, I have no idea how I survived. All I know is that I manifested my powers that day—I didn't use water magic against the hellhound. I found out the next day when I was taking a shower, so I don't know how I stopped it. By the time my parents found me, it was too late for the healers to mend the wound completely. To this day, magic can't heal these scars."

With effort, Dani turned around, her cheeks burning red, to face the Virtues. "I so badly want to be like you, Hayden, because I want to be strong. I think I'm Chastity because I don't want to control other people—I want to control myself and protect myself and the people I love, and I saw the same desire in you. I never wanted to be afraid of another demon again."

"Chastity was with you that day," Kova answered softly. "It manifested for you to save your life when you couldn't."

"What?" Dani straightened in her chair.

"Hellhounds don't stop attacking unless they're called off," Jamie spoke quietly. "If Chastity nullified its Hell powers... it would have been enough for the beast to flee... in fear of *you*."

Dani was dumbfounded... her whole life... she hadn't known. How did she not realize she was Chastity? Why didn't the Virtue reveal itself to her? Even as a child... she wasn't as weak as she had thought...

"Don't desire to be like me, Dani," Hayden said kindly. "If you want demons to fear you, they already do. You are all the things you want to be. You are strong and brave and fearless." Tears of pride welled in her eyes. "Do you not remember the Salem War?" Her long black locks rippled as she shook her head. "When all was lost and everyone thought I was dead, one person stood against Elliot. You leaped into danger without regard for the consequences because you knew in your soul that it was the right thing to do. If that isn't fearless, then I don't know what is."

Pressing her lips together, Dani fought the tears, but when Hayden spooked beside her, she unfolded into her arms and let the tears flow. Holding Dani to her chest, Hayden pressed a kiss to the top of Dani's head and gently rocked them back and forth.

"I'm sorry, Dani," Mila said, her face strained with emotion. "For judging you without knowing your story." Closing her eyes, she shook her head. "That story... was harrowing. I guess we all should have tried to get to know one another sooner. Maybe then we would have understood each other better and worked better as a team."

"I think that makes it your turn to share, Milena," Ronnie said kindly, but the color drained from Mila's face as she visibly gulped.

"Okay. Okay... yeah, I can do that." Hesitantly, she began, "I know you all think I'm this shallow queen bee, a stuck-up brat from L.A." Diligence looked like someone kicked her dog. Her face tinged green as she worked up the courage to speak. "But I wasn't always like that. You all grew up in these cozy little towns or cities with close-knit witch communities. L.A. isn't like that. When my parents died..." she shifted in her chair and focused on playing with the tassels on the chair cushion. Dani hadn't known Mila parents were deceased. "When my parents died, my sisters and I didn't have any support. I suppose the reason I am the vessel for Diligence is because I had to be so on top of everything, keeping my sisters and I together as we went from foster home to foster home." She blew out a single hollow laugh. "It's like everyone thinks foster kids are either these messed up kids or meek little flowers. They're not. Foster life is hard, and it's even harder when those foster parents are horrendous like the ones in L.A., and worse, we were witches living with humans. After those kids beat the crap out of Camila,"—one of Mila's younger sisters who lived at the compound but kept to herself—"I became the queen bee so nobody would touch my sisters. I became the bully so nobody would bully us." Straightening her shoulders, she tossed her platinum hair behind her back.

"Why didn't you leave?" Walker asked kindly. "You had magic. You could have gone anywhere."

"No, I didn't." Mila's eyes cast off to the side. "My parents never told me about Asylum and the Spellery. Had I known, I would have moved us there in a heartbeat." Her toned held an edge of resentment, but not for the Virtues... for her parents.

"Why didn't they tell you?" Jamie asked, placing his forearms on the wooden table and leaning forward.

"L.A. is all about the glamor," Mila explained. "St. Salem's isn't glamorous, so parents don't send their kids there. How would sending their kids to the Midwest to study magic make them more elite than anybody else? Unless you're from an ethereal bloodline, you're irrelevant. The celestial descendants walk all over us lesser bloodline unless we learn magic, which isn't an option. L.A. parents don't teach much magic, either. It distracts from elitist politics. Knowledge gets forgotten with every passing generation, and nobody cares to fix it."

Hayden's sharp gaze fixated on Kova's as they held one of their telepathic conversations. Rumors is Asylum told that Hayden had her own experiences with haughty ethereal bloodline witches.

Descended from Elijah Black, the Nephilim son of the Archangel of Death, Azriel, the Black family's blood had been diluted over the last ten centuries, but Hayden Black didn't share a drop of their blood. Her adoptive father, Hunter Black, was actually her half-uncle who gave her his last name. Michael, the Warrior Archangel, was her biological sire. Not that Elizabeth Black had known that when she disowned Hayden from the House of Black.

As Hayden scratched Salem behind the ears, Dani got the distinct impression that these ethereal bloodline witches would be making significant changes to L.A. once the Sins were renounced. And she would likely recruit Mila's help to do so.

Thea placed a gentle hand on the older girl's arm. "I am sorry for what you endured during your adolescence. But you do not need to be queen bee here. Here, you are one of us, as are your sisters."

"I suppose it's our turn to apologize, Mila. I can only speak for myself, but I did view you as a shallow snob, and frankly, I didn't understand why the Virtue of Diligence chose you, but now I do," Dani sympathized. "Thank you for sharing that piece of yourself with us."

"Emmett, please save me from this embarrassment and share your story," Mila begged the Virtue sitting across from her.

Tilting his head back, the Virtue of Temperance blew out a breath, steeling himself before leveling his face with them. Rubbing his jaw, he pondered his next words.

"I'm embarrassed to admit this, but... in my youth, I wasn't what I would consider a virtuous man. In my teenage years especially, I was a bully. And not every so often. I was cruel. I ruled the school, and nobody messed with me or my boys. It helped that I was a witch in a mortal town in the south. I was popular, a football player, Prom King—everything a young man could want, yet I wasn't the one thing the Creator wanted me to be. Instead I was a terror to the people around me. It wasn't until years later, when my younger sister was tormented mercilessly by the younger sisters of the stuck-up queen bees I hung out with that I realized the consequences of my actions on the kids around me. I brought Evil and hatred into the lives of so many other young people. I suppose I look at the Apokalypsis War as my way of leveling the field against Evil, to repent for my hand in bringing Evil into the lives of others."

Dani didn't know what to say. She had never been bullied, and any bullying at St. Salem's was handled swiftly... by Hayden. Maybe because everyone had magic, but... her gaze landed on Apalla's as her hazel eyes flashed with golden light, and she remembered...

Damien had told her about Hayden's first year in Asylum. Before Apalla was ousted as a Daughter of Apollo, Kelsey was the reigning queen bee at the Spellery and she tortured Apalla using mind magic. Unbeknownst to anyone, Apalla had more magic than Kelsey, but the Prophetess never lifted a wand against the other air witch because Kelsey didn't bully her with magic, she harassed her mentally to the point that Apalla hid herself and her magic.

But years after the fact, Kelsey completely turned herself around, defied her heinous grandmother, and became a close, trusted friend of the Salem Witch and her inner circle. Redemption had called Kelsey's name, and she seized it for herself.

Apalla winked a hazel eye at Dani, and Dani was certain the Prophetess knew what Dani would say before she did.

Opening her mouth, she let the words out, not quite sure where they came from, but it had to be from a source other than herself. "Redemption is offered to each of us, Emmett. Because redemption isn't for the sinless, it's for the imperfect mortals that we are. Whether we're witches or humans or angels or demons, we're flawed, which means we fail ourselves, others, and the Creator. But redemption means we have the opportunity to free ourselves from sin, and who if not us, the Heavenly Virtues, will redeem the Virtues against the Sins? You can't change what has been done, but you can move on and change the future. For the better. And we will help you do it."

Meeting the Prophetess's eyes again, Dani was greeted with a subtle smile and another wink. Relief sagged her shoulders. She said the right thing. Yet, she couldn't recall exactly what she had said. Hopefully it was good.

"I'm not meek and timid like all of you think I am," Raphaela blurted out, not waiting for any prompting. "Charity is bold and forthcoming, but... but after years of being told I'm too much... I wanted a fresh start. I've given myself to so many people so many times, only to be cast aside like useless trash.

And I couldn't take it anymore. I was afraid... I was afraid if I opened myself up to you guys, you'd do the same, and then I couldn't run away. I'd be stuck with you for seven months, feeling like I was unwanted." She twisted a strand of thick black hair around her fingers. "But I suppose... I suppose that was silly of me, looking back. If there was any group of people I should have shared myself with, it is you all." She squared her shoulders. "But I will not be weak when we face the Sins. I will be strong and ruthless, because that's who I am."

Jamie snorted. "You don't say?" When the Virtues regarded him with skepticism, he said, "What? Have you guys sparred her in the ring?" He waggled a finger at her. "Raphaela he does *not* hold back. Seriously, she dislocated my shoulder during training."

"How did I miss that?" Dani asked. As the resident healer, she would have been the one to set his shoulder.

Kova, Hayden, and Apalla burst out in laughter.

"Because instead of asking you to heal it, he 'took a bathroom break'"—Hayden formed air quotes—"and asked me to reset it."

Tears streamed down Apalla's cheeks from laughing so hard. "The fact that he asked *you* of all people..."

"You are a terrible healer," Thea agreed.

"The absolute worst," Kova said between gasps of air as she tried to control her laughter. "No one should ask Hayden for a healing unless they're desperate."

"He was desperate that none of you knew sweet, little Raphaela wrecked him."

"It was one time." Jamie rolled his eyes at his soulmate. "I should never have asked you to heal me. I should have shoved it back into place myself," he grumbled under his breath. "Walker, please save me from this embarrassment."

"I got you, bro." But after glancing around the table at his fellow Virtues, the Virtue of Kindness looked at his lap, his cheeks tinging red in shame. "Honestly, I'm not sure why I'm the Virtue of Kindness. I've been anything but kind in my life." Tears dripped from his eyes to stain his blue jeans. "And I'm so ashamed of what I've done." Silence permeated the room as the witches waited for Walker to take a deep breath and say, "Not only did I ruin a friendship, but I wrecked a relationship." He covered his eyes as he said. "I loved her since before her and Charles started dating. I was too scared to tell her about my feelings. Charles was my best friend since childhood, but it killed me every time I saw him with her. He knew I had a crush on Elena when we were younger, but in college, he thought I was over her. I wasn't... and after they got together... I..." He scrubbed his hand over his face. "I stole her from him. I seduced her so, for one night, she chose me, but when you lay with the Devil, you get short changed. She told him what we did, out of guilt, and it ended my friendship with Charles. I was naïve to believe she'd want me. I was a fool... she left me in the dust, too. All because I was envious of my friend instead of being happy for the man who was like a brother to me."

Walker lowered his face in shame, unable to look his fellow Virtues in the eyes. Black light flashed at his placemat, depositing a box of tissues in front of him. Seizing hold of them, he dabbed at his eyes, then wiped his nose, sniffling to stop the sobs.

"I suppose this is the ultimate atonement, then," Dani said, breaking the silence. A subtle nod from Hayden reinforced Dani's confidence in taking the lead. "Defeating Leviathan will devastate and conquer Evil in such a way to lessen the power of Envy over mortals everywhere. You might have been a victim of Leviathan's power once, but not anymore. Now, you have the power to defeat him. Because you're not the same person you once were, and it's okay to forgive yourself. Actually, I think the Creator would want you to. You've known Envy, you knew the Sin intimately, and because of that, you're a stronger warrior against the Sins. You overcame it once, and with the power of an angel inside you, you will defeat him for good."

Sniffling, Walker wiped his nose with another tissue. "Thanks, Dani. I hope you're right."

"I know I am." Dani's confidence in her fellow Virtues outweighed her confidence in herself, but as each of the Virtues bared their souls, she felt more and more like the leader she was supposed to be.

Every eye turned to Ronnie, but she merely smiled. "I think you all know the vulnerable parts of me as I have shared bits and pieces with you individually. As you all know, I have trust issues, for I have always been able to see past mortals' facades to the truth of their souls hidden underneath masked exteriors. It has made me jaded and skeptical. But with you, I have seen virtuousness that is rare in the world. And being able to see your auras, I am the only one of the seven who has been able to connect with my fellow Virtues. There is nothing for me to share."

"Why isn't Humility the leader?" Dani asked. "If you can connect with us so easily, wouldn't it be more likely we'd follow you into war?"

"No," Hayden answered. "Chastity never lusts for power, which is the cornerstone of a virtuous leader. Chastity is the virtue of control, and through it, one can repel the other Sins, Pride included." She shrugged. "Among other reasons."

"What about you?" Emmett asked Hayden boldly. "If we all have to share our secrets and expose ourselves and our vulnerabilities to one another, then why don't you?"

Jamie snorted from the bench he shared with Hayden, their bodies pressed against one another like they were two parts of the same flesh.

"Hayden doesn't have any vulnerabilities," Apalla mused, but the flash of gold in her eyes then the wink at Hayden suggested something remained unsaid between the best friends.

Straightening on the bench, Hayden asked, "What do you guys want to know?"

The six Virtues exchanged a look. Shrugging, Ronnie sank in her seat. If anybody didn't need to ask a question, it was her. She probably could read the answers to her questions in Hayden's aura.

"Do you hate us?" Raphaela blurted out the question, breaking the silence. No so shy after all.

By the way the others blinked at her, they were surprised by her boldness as well. Hayden's crystal blue eyes widened in surprise as her sudden outburst, then her lips twisted into a smile of what appeared to be pride for the Virtue.

"Hate you?" Hayden breathed out a hollow laugh. "Raphaela, I could never hate you—any of you. I know I've been hard on you these past months, and I know I'm not the easiest person to get along with—"

Every witch in her circle guffawed, to which she rolled her eyes in response.

"And I'm definitely not the best teacher. But those are *my* shortcomings. Not a reflection of the six of you. The reason I'm unyielding with your training is because my teachers were the same with me." She looked pointedly at each witch in her circle, who smiled mischievously. "In the end, I thanked them for their brutality. Because it kept me *alive*. Because of them, I mastered the elements against all odds. The hardship, the struggle, the suffering... it is why I defeated Evil time and time again, and it's why the six of you have survived seven months against the Sins, and why you will survive the Apokalypsis War. So, no, Raphaela, I do not hate you. I *love* each and every one of you. Even though your bickering is insufferable, you all love each other, too. And love is the most powerful force in the Universe. It is the love between you that will defeat the Princes of Hell. Once and for all."

CHAPTER TWELVE

THE REVELATION

"We're all going to die tomorrow."

Uncomfortable silence hung in the air.

Even Hayden remained quiet, leaning against the window sill, staring out the rain-splattered window into the darkness beyond, her lips pursed in a pensive look and her leather-clad arms crossed over her chest. The witch was as still as a statue, even as her soulmate watched her with a worried expression, his eyes never leaving her.

When she didn't say anything, the Virtues muttered amongst themselves and their friends. It wasn't just Virtues and Hayden's circle in the Council room. Knights, the Athenian Council of Salem, and other high-ranking officials were gathered, along with the Virtues' personal friends who traveled all this way to stand at their sides as they prepared to die in an unavoidable war. Except for Dani. Her parents weren't warriors, and Damien was Air Representative of the Asylum Athenian Council. Asylum was without their High Priestess with Apalla and Kova portaling between the hidden witch town and the compound in Salem, so Damien had to stay in Asylum during their absence.

Leaning against the North wall of the fortress, Kova mirrored Hayden's position, but with Thea standing at her side, Kova's silent statue-like posture seemed less foreboding. Yet, the teenage Heart of Earth remained mysteriously quiet.

Apalla mimicked Jamie. Perching on the edge of a nearby table, the Priestess of Asylum methodically fletched her arrows, filling her quiver one by one while keep an eye trained on the two earth witches. But Dani didn't miss the golden light flashing in the Prophetess's eyes as she channeled her powers as a Daughter of Apollo.

What did Hayden's circle know that the rest of them didn't?

Dani had lived around them long enough in Asylum to detect when they were hiding something.

Tearing her gaze from Hayden's stock-still statuesque frame, Dani surveyed the rest of the room. The other Virtues were oblivious to what Dani suspected.

Yet unease hung in the air.

Mila and her near identical sisters huddled in a circle, giggling about something Dani would likely find ridiculous. One of the girls held a magazine in her hand, flipping through the pages as they looked at celebrities. Was it Dani's imagination, or did Mila seem uninterested in the magazine? Mila might have been an annoying, spoiled brat. But she was diligent, especially when it came to raising her two little sisters. She didn't do everything right, but she tried.

Walker and his older brother, Preston, occupied the comfy armchairs in the corner, sipping tea and talking quietly. They were nothing compared to the ruckus aroused by Emmett and his burly man of a father. But it was hard to be annoyed by the boisterous men as they wrestled and joked with the Knights in an attempt to keep their minds off the impending doom.

Like Dani, Ronnie didn't have any family who could travel to Salem, so her best friend since childhood, Paul, portaled in. Despite being raised in Salem together amongst countless witch families, Paul and Ronnie had formed a bond. It wasn't romantic in nature, but their friendship had prevailed, even when Ronnie ventured away from home to travel the country and Paul stayed to become a Knight in New York City. There was kinship there that Dani couldn't explain, but it reminded her of the way Apalla and Hayden interacted—like they brought the best out in one another.

Dani's heart panged with sadness. She wanted that. She wanted love like Hayden's and friendship like Ronnie's. As much as she envied those things, she reminded herself of the cost. Ronnie barely had any friends because long before she could see auras as Humility, she could read people and their intentions. After years of encountering vile people with horrible motives, Ronnie became jaded. But being around the Virtues changed something inside her. She had opened up these part months, especially to Dani, and a kinship had formed between the women.

Huddled around a table in the corner by a window, Raphaela held hands with her mother and father as they prayed and whispered in tongues. Dani couldn't hear them, but she knew Raphaela was firm in her faith. Interesting that her Virtue, Charity, coincided with Raphael, the archangel who expelled Mammon from Heaven and the angel for whom she was named. It was hard to picture Raphaela driving a sword through the heart of Mammon, but if she was going to survive tomorrow, she'd have to. Or at least hold her own until Hayden could kill the Lord of Fools. Which was probably what they were praying incessantly for.

Silently, Dani sent up a prayer for the girl, for them all, a plea for the Goddess to protect their mortal lives when fighting beasts of unimaginable strength.

Mila wasn't wrong necessarily.... The odds that any of the Virtues would survive tomorrow was abysmally nonexistent. And Hayden's solemn demeanor didn't raise any spirits.

Settling into a chair around the massive table that the Council normally conducted business at, Dani kept her eyes trained on the Nephilim, watching for any sign that might reveal what plagued the women. What felt like long hours passed, but, in reality, minutes ticked by while the Salem Witches starred out the rain-splattered windows.

A sinking feeling in her gut said it had everything to do with the Virtues. Something they weren't telling them, and Dani prayed Apalla hadn't seen Dani's demise in a vision.

At long last, the unbreakable Salem Witch stirred from her post at the window, the movement capturing the attention of the entire room, but Hayden's eyes glossed over everyone, even her soulmate, as she sought Kova's hunter green ones. As the Salem Witches locked eyes, understanding passed between them, and they nodded simultaneously.

"Thea?" Hayden asked the question in a single word.

"It is time," the teenage witch advised sagely, her melodious voice ancient compared to her youthful face.

Prowling to the head of the table, the seat that belonged to the High Priest or Priestess, Hayden dismissed the Knights with a wave of her hand. "Get some rest, warriors." She pinned the Athenian Council with a look that brooked no argument. "Council, if you would not mind, I wish to speak with the Virtues privately."

"Of course." The High Priestess of Salem bowed, then motioned for the other six Council members to exit the room before she did, closing the door soundly behind her.

Flanking her, Jamie stood on her right side as she lowered herself into the chair, lounging in it like nothing in the world fazed her. Yet her eyes were sharp, alert, as she carefully examined each of the remaining Virtues. The rest of her circle followed suit, with Kova flanking her left side, and Dani had to wonder if they planned these things in advance, or if they were so magically attuned to one another that it came naturally.

Leaning forward, Hayden placed her elbows on the table and gestured at the Virtues. "Sit," she commanded, steepling her fingers in front of her face.

Wordlessly, the others followed her orders. Dani was already sitting. Nervous energy filled the room as each of the Virtues fidgeted in their seats.

Hayden's gaze fell on them heavy and dark, but then her mask fell, revealing exhaustion as she rubbed her face with her hands. "Now I know how you must have felt during my Trials," Hayden muttered to Kova before facing the Virtues once more, a shameful expression marring the terrifying beauty of her face.

"The burden of the immortal is a heavy one, dear Davina," Kova used the name Leyla gave Hayden at birth. Davina Michaelson Nightfall, renamed to Hayden Huntleigh Black by her adoptive father.

"Yeah, yeah. I know." Hayden rolled her crystal blue eyes without looking at her mentor. "Really incentivizing for us to stay here for eternity."

"I think that's the point," Jamie muttered from beside her, but he tugged on her hand, pulling it closer to him so he could twist his fingers with hers.

As though her soulmate's touch gave her the strength she needed, she finally announced, "Those of us with the knowledge and wisdom of Spirit at our disposal have been concealing the truth regarding the nature of your souls."

Silence.

And then angry shouts erupted from five of the Virtues. Chaos tore through the chamber as others joined the shouting match, each voice struggling to be heard over the din of voices raging through the room. Some tried to calm others, while others fueled the fury pulsing through the atmosphere.

But betrayal was like a hot knife to Dani's heart as she stared at Hayden, at the witch she had looked up to and admired for so many years, and let the truth sink in. The truth that Hayden was a puppet master pulling their strings. She didn't care for them. She didn't love them. She didn't love Dani.... Not like Dani had believed she did. Otherwise, how could she keep a secret regarding the *nature of their souls*?

"*You what?*" The words rolled off Dani's tongue like an unrestrained growl of a feral dog. Heat spread across Dani's face and torso as blood pumped through her ears and red tinged her vision. A clatter sounded behind Dani as she surged to her feet to slam her palms against the table top, toppling her chair.

Hayden flinched at the anger in Dani's voice, then shot a look at Kova. "This is why I argued with Spirit to let me tell them."

The older witch's only response was a pained expression.

Rubbing a hand along her spine, Jamie stooped to whisper something in Hayden's ear. Nodding once, she lifted her chin and faced the Virtues with unyielding solidarity.

"I will preface this by saying I did not want to hide this information from you, but Spirit insisted we should. And one does not argue with Spirit."

Kova snorted.

Shooting her a dark look, Hayden rolled her eyes. "Okay, I do argue with Spirit—*a lot*—but it's not like I win any of those arguments."

"What is your point?" Mila snapped. With a dismissive wave of her hand, she said, "I don't care what your relationship with Spirit is. I want to know what you've been hiding from us."

The other Virtues nodded in agreement, muttering something about the oppressive Salem Witch. But Dani watched Hayden carefully, catching every gesture, every movement of the powerful witch, down to the emotion swimming in her eyes. Dani didn't have to be an empath to know the regret exuding from Hayden's aura, but based on the lack of response from Ronnie, Dani bet that the older woman saw the same emotions in Hayden that Dani did.

"My point, Milena, is that Spirit is wise beyond our comprehension, and it was by the directive of the Creator's Spirit that I did not disclose the entire truth of the essence of a Virtue." She blew an exasperated sigh out from between her teeth. "Remember how I said the Virtues choose a mortal vessel every seven hundred years?"

"Yes."

Dani's stomach dropped. Was Chastity tied to her mortal vessel only? Was their bond not soul-deep like she thought? No, that couldn't be it—even now, she felt Chastity wrapped around her soul and her magic like a cozy blanket on a cold winter day.

"Well..." Hayden drew out the word as she rubbed her neck. "Your Virtues didn't exactly choose you for the first time..." She looked directly at Dani when she said the next part. "There's a reason your elemental magic has always been stronger than other witches. This isn't the first time you've been a Virtue."

Dani blinked. "Wait, what? I've been a Virtue before? As in a previous life?" She glanced around at the other Virtues seat at the table as they stared at her. "What about the others?"

"More like you've been a Virtue in all of your lives." Hayden grimaced. "Since the first Apokalypsis War against Lucifer and the other fallen angels. Not only do the Virtues choose a mortal host every seven hundred years, but they choose the mortal host their soul is born into. As a soul, each of you is bound to a Virtue for eternity."

Her jaw hit the floor.

Hayden frowned up at Kova, quirking her head as she listened to a voice unheard by Dani.

But the other Virtues stared, dumbfounded, as though they were stuck in a comatose state of disbelief. Dani could relate. Them being angels... it was unfathomable, and yet, part of Dani's soul knew it to be true. But a bigger part of her was incensed. How long had they known? How long had they been hiding this catastrophic secret from the Virtues?

"Sorta..." The Spirit-blessed Nephilim corrected herself as she listened to Spirit. "My father and the other Archangels drove Lucifer and the Seven from Heaven, but they didn't do it alone. The Virtues assisted the Archangels, which is why each of the seven Archangels who fought the Sins are depicted alongside a specific Virtue. At the time of the Fall, the Virtues weren't just spiritual entities. They were physical beings, responsible for maintaining balance and cosmic order and gifted with impressive control over the elements, even by angelic standards. Which is why your water magic, Dani, has always been stronger than an average witch. It's why you can call storms. It is why Raphaela's fire magic is unparalleled by anyone outside of my circle. The Seven Heavenly Virtues originated as exactly that—seven angels of the Virtue rank."

"But I'm not an angel... I... I can't be," Dani protested, glancing around at the other Virtues' stricken faces. Twisting her torso, she stared over her shoulder to see if angelic wings protruded from her back, but empty air greeted her. Disappointed, she faced the Salem Witch and her silent companions.

Sorrow clouded Hayden's crystal blue gaze. "Because you're not anymore."

"What?" Mila demanded. "How could I have been an angel thousands of years ago but be mortal now? Isn't it supposed to go the opposite way?" Jumping to her feet, Mila waved her hands at the Salem Witch. "You went from mortal to immortal. And what do you mean 'seven angels of the Virtue rank'?"

"There are more than seven angels in the Virtue Rank," Hayden answered. She scratched the back of her head. "There's actually a ton of them." Glancing up at Kova again, she asked, "There's like, what, seventy-seven thousand or something?"

Shrugging, Kova said, "Sounds about right, although I've never asked Spirit outright, and I never counted during my excursions to the other side."

"Why us seven?" Emmett asked, then flinched. "Us six and Axel?"

The Salem Witches exchanged a look, something passing between them that Dani couldn't describe through the haze of her rage tinging the edges of her vision red.

"It's your choice," Hayden said, answering a silent question from Kova. "Seems like a bad idea for me to call Her given my demon blood." Hayden shrugged.

Sighing, Kova ran a hand through her spiky red hair and dropped her head to stare at the floor. Despite the angry tension between the Virtues and the Salem Witches, silence permeated the air as though every soul inherently understood the weight of this conversation without knowing the topic. Blowing out a ragged breath, Kova lifted her head as her green eyes turned silver, and her red hair faded to the same color.

Her voice resounded through the room like the roar of many waters, entirely ethereal in nature. "Perhaps it would be pertinent for you to speak with the One for whom you sacrificed it all."

Hayden spooked in the blink of an eye, appearing to stand behind Kova as wings of golden Spirit protruded from her back. The younger Salem Witch altered her features to match Kova's, but instead of gold wings, Hayden's appeared silver. Pressing her hands through the golden wings, Hayden placed her hands on Kova's back, and a resounding boom thundered through the air as the elements called a divine storm.

Lightning coursed from the sky, the silvery-blue element striking Kova in the chest as she flung her arms wide. The force of the element threw Hayden backward, slamming her against the wall. Lightning sparked off her as she crumpled to the ground, but as soon as she hit the floor, she bounced upright. The same couldn't be said for the rest of her circle, who struggled to their feet.

But Hayden was in motion, guiding Kova to sit in the chair at the head of the table while her head tilted back, the lightning zapping over her skin and *through* her body.

The golden wings protruding from her back turned silver as Hayden chanted a spell:

Darkened night and vibrant moon,

Spirit, mind, and body commune.
East, South, West, and North,
By these elements, I call Goddess forth.
Mother above, I call to you,
Help us heal these opened wounds.
Earth below and sky above,
Darkened night filled with love.
As above, so below. As within, so without.
As the Universe, so the soul.
Spirit of Greatness, Lady of the Divine, Creator of All,
Answer Your chosen one's most reverent call.
Consume this holy vessel with Your might,
Illuminate the Salem Witch with Heaven's light.
This circle is cast, Her light unbroken,
So mote it be, the Goddess's magic has spoken.

Dani's bones shivered from the rush of power filling Hayden's words. This wasn't practical magic. Not the kind the Spellery taught. Yet it was beyond the elements. An elemental storm filled the room, threatening to destroy them with its might as it transformed Kova. With skin glowing silver with the light of the moon, her body quaked, as though it could barely contain the power shooting into her from a light beaming from Heaven above. Her short, spiky hair grew rapidly before Dani's eyes. Thick, luscious locks extended to her waist, brushing over the chair, and Dani imagined that must be the way the Goddess wore Her hair—the same as Hayden did now and the depictions of Alice Parker from centuries past showed.

Kova's head snapped forward, her eyes landing on Dani. Silver orbs pulsed with untold power, and Dani gasped as she realized her eyes were not Kova's marked by the Goddess.

Those eyes belonged to the Goddess.

"Holy..." Emmett breathed out. "Are... are you..."

"Sit, children." Kova gestured to the Virtues, but her mannerisms were off. Because it wasn't Kova. It was the

Goddess. "There is much to discuss, and My dearest Alice cannot channel My essence for long."

Her voice was different than when Kova first spoke. It had sounded like a thousand voices overlapping, but now... it sounded like the purest, cleanest sound that spoke all of life into existence.

"I know you have many questions."

Hayden was a silent shadow behind her, a dutiful guardian channeling the power of Spirit to protect her Goddess. A bubble of silver light surrounded them, protecting Her from the outside world and the forces of Darkness that sought to harm the Goddess through Kova's vulnerable body.

"You wonder why I chose you six along with your brother, Axel, to be My champions."

"Yes," Dani said, her voice coming out sturdier than she felt under the all-seeing gaze of the Goddess.

"The first war between the Sins and My angels wreaked much carnage and destruction upon Heaven and Earth. Not all Virtue angels fought so valiantly against the Fallen. Seven, in particular, selflessly sacrificed themselves in the original Apokalypsis War. Seven who honored Heaven above the others."

"But why Virtues? Why not the Archangels? Why us?" Dani whispered the last question. "Why me?" It had been hard to come to terms with her identity as a witch holding the Virtue of Chastity in the mortal realm, but accepting that she was an angel? It was incomprehensible. Even Hayden, the most powerful being on earth, was only half angel. How could Dani be a full-blooded angel? She wasn't more powerful than Hayden.

"I'm more powerful than my father, too," Hayden whispered, as though she feared he might hear. "Michael is the strongest of the Archangels, yes, but he does not wield the power of Spirit. Those of us who accept the full power of the fifth element channel the Spirit of the Creator, a power not granted to full-blooded angels as it would compile too much power in an immortal heavenly creature, one who does not possess any mortal weaknesses. And yes, immortal Nephilim possess mortal weaknesses."

"The Sins were too powerful, too ruthless. It took two of our angels to expel one of them," Jamie explained. "But as powerful as angels are, their powers are limited."

"A fact My son has yet to learn all these millennia later," Goddess intoned, her voice sad, and gleaming teardrops that resembled crystals dripped from her silver eyes. "Lucifer fell because his pride led him to believe he was more powerful than Me and My other half. What he fails to realize even now is that since the inception of time, I have always maintained balance. Angels, as cosmic immortals who do not undergo cycles of death and rebirth but remain un-aging and eternal, must be limited in their powers."

"But Hayden isn't limited," Dani argued.

"Yes, I am," Hayden answered quietly. "I am forever confined to the boundaries of the mortal realm. Yes, I can cross the Veil as I please, but I cannot enter the Garden of Eden." She glanced between Kova and Jamie. "If not for eternity, then close to it."

Goddess nodded, Her silver hair swirling around Her waist from the motion. "Hayden's powers are balanced by her eternal connection to Earth. But angels do not have such restrictions, so I limited the amount of power a single heavenly creature could hold."

"But when the princes fell and invited Evil into their physical forms with the sole intent to gain more power, their bodies and consciousnesses were perverted, deformed in such a way that Evil infused them with more power than an angel of Heaven could possess."

"That's why it took an Archangel and a Virtue to cast each Sin from Heaven," Dani surmised.

"Yes. Each choir or rank of angels is dedicated to a particular purpose—"

"I know about the nine choirs," Dani interrupted Hayden. "Jophiel told me about them."

Hayden's eyebrows flew into her silver hairline. "Jophiel visited you here on Earth? When did that happen?"

Dani shrugged, but didn't deign to answer.

Hayden cast a glare at the ceiling instead of at Kova as if she knew the God and Goddess would see it. "Seriously, you didn't tell me about that?"

Returning her glare with a motherly smile, Goddess reached up a hand to pat her chosen daughter on the head. "As much as Spirit speaks to you, you do not need to know the happenings surrounding every child of Mine."

Crossing her arms over her chest, Hayden grumbled something about being left in the dark despite her access to all the information in the Universe.

"My point about the nine choirs," Goddess started, shooting a pointed look at a pouting Hayden, "is that each has a specific purpose. Responsible for governing the laws of the natural world and ensuring cosmic order, the Virtues are the strongholds for maintaining balance within the Universe, including the balance between the Kingdoms of Light and Darkness."

"I know all of this," Dani groaned, plunging her hands into her hair to grab at her scalp. But the other Virtues remained attentive. All of this was new information to them.

"What does this have to do with us having once been an angel but not anymore?" Walker asked inquisitively.

"Everything," Goddess emphasized. "Archangels have their own purpose in protecting humanity."

Kova-Goddess stood from her chair and moved across the room to stand in front of Dani, cupping her black palms around Dani's cheeks, her silver eyes glimmering with love and adoration. "You, my dearest Daniella, you were the youngest, and the strongest of the Virtues. So in every reincarnation, you have always been the youngest and your power has been the last to manifest, but it has always been the pivotal weapon in the war against Evil because you were the one to lead the Virtues against the Sins. You were the first to shed your divinity so your soul could assume a mortal vessel worthy for Me to imbue with more power."

"I forfeited my angelic nature to become mortal for more power?" Dani cried out. "But my Virtue is Chastity. I am supposed to represent the opposite of lusting for power."

Kova-Goddess pressed a kiss to Dani's forehead and calmness washed over her frantic soul. "I refused to give the Virtue angels more power as it would throw the cosmos out of balance. If you had relinquished your angelic nature for power, you would be among the fallen angels, but you did not fall for power, my child. You made a heavenly sacrifice to assume mortality to gain more power in exchange for more vulnerabilities to maintain cosmic balance. This was the only way I could grant My children power to face the Seven Deadly Sins. In doing so, you agreed to reincarnate every seven hundred years to battle the Sins and thwart their evil from manifesting untamed to torment humanity. It was your great love for Me and for humanity that inspired the other six to follow suit. Thus, making you their elected leader."

"What do our souls do for the seven hundred years between wars?" Dani gestured at the other Virtues.

"As a Virtue, you live amongst the angels, but as a human soul, you live amongst the mortals. You are one of the few who belong to both realms. The longer you rest in the Garden amongst your angel peers and your loving mortal families, the stronger your Virtue powers become until too much power is concentrated in a single soul and you must reincarnate.

"But the same is true for the Sins. The source of their power comes from Hell, so the longer they dwell in the depths of the Pit, the stronger they become until they can cross dimensions into the mortal realm. Their bloodlust and rebellion calls to you, and the Virtues within you awaken, and the Apokalypsis War is fought anew. After your mortal life ends, you return to the Garden to rest. And the cycle renews again.

"You are the Holy Virtues, because you were the seven to sacrifice yourselves for the pursuit of the Kingdom of Light. You are holy beyond all other Virtues. Find it in your souls to forgive My children"—she gestured to Hayden and the body She possessed—"and to forgive Me for keeping you in the dark as to the truth of your souls. It was not for nefarious means, nor to keep you ignorant, but to ease your transition into this world, for it is no easy task for an immortal soul to enter the mortal realm, but it is more insurmountable for an angelic soul to separate from the Heavens.

"But I must depart, my darling Virtues. If I stay longer, it will exact an inexorable toll on Alice's body. The Salem Witch was conceived by My intrusion on a mortal woman's body once. It does not do to siphon more power into a witch who already possesses such a blessing."

Goddess's silver moon eyes caught the gaze of each Virtue, one by one. "I love you, My children, more than you could possibly know. I know you struggle with accepting the lack of transparency but know that I did it to protect your souls. It is no easy task for an immortal soul to endure the mortal realm, and knowing your origins will exact a heavy toll on your mortal lives in the years to come. I hid this secret from you to lessen the burden of the Virtue on your soul. Forgive me and know that I am with you always."

"Davina," Goddess held a hand to Hayden. "Ground her magic."

Hayden's hand touched Kova's, and power blasted through the room. It was all Dani could do to keep from falling to the floor. As the pressure faded with the heavenly magic, Dani straightened her spine despite its protesting.

Kova's hair magically receded, growing in reverse until her hair was short, red, and spiky. A glimpse of hunter green irises flashed before Kova's eyes rolled into the back of her head, and she collapsed. Catching her before her head smacked the arm rest, Hayden kept a hand firmly grasping the one Goddess had offered.

Gold and green magic wafted from Kova into Hayden, and Hayden swelled with power until she released a blast of black lightning that decimated a hole in the stone ceiling. Debris rained down on the Salem Witches, but was discarded to either side as elemental magic protected them. As more magic pumped from Kova into Hayden, she released it into the sky, serving as a conduit for the Goddess's power coursing through Kova's body. After another twenty strikes, Hayden finally released Kova's hand, but the older woman remained unconscious.

Kneeling in front of the chair, Jamie checked the woman's vitals, then gripped her hand and eased some of the golden magic haloing around her into his body to release the magic in the form of holy flames. Thea did the same, channeling green magic through her body and out her feet into the earth. Only Apalla, the sole mortal of the circle, remained a healthy distance from Kova to avoid the overwhelming concentration of magical energy.

Knowing the experienced immortals would take care of the Nephilim of Earth, Dani tore her eyes from the woman who had channeled the Goddess, a feat not accomplished since Eve, if the legends were to be believed. Hot rage filled her veins, boiling her blood and heating her face. Red tinged the world around her as she trained her angry gaze on the witch responsible for this disaster.

"You knew," Dani accused, thrusting a finger in Hayden's direction. "You knew we are angels, and you didn't tell us."

Hayden flinched and rubbed the back of her neck. "In my defense, I didn't know right away, and I was sworn to secrecy."

"Why?" Dani demanded, crossing her arms over her chest.

"Because, like Goddess said, knowing of your divine nature would make living as a mortal unbearable. You would constantly seek the angelic realms and the nature you know to be your birthright. It would cause chaos and pain. In remaining ignorant, you were able to find joy in your mortal life."

"Sounds like a load of crap to me," Mila bit out. "You've been lying to us for *months*."

"Technically," Hayden held up both pointer fingers, "I omitted telling you something you didn't know you were missing."

Dani's eyes nearly rolled out of her head. "A lie by omission is no lesser than an outright lie."

"You never outright asked me a question. I simply didn't bring it up."

"Why didn't you bring it up?" Ronnie snapped. For Mila to be angsty was one thing... but if Ronnie was biting back at Hayden, the older witch was truly furious at the turn of events, and Dani felt vindicated in her fury despite the encounter with the Goddess.

"Spirit gave me a direct command."

"And you can't fight it? You can't go against it?" Dani challenged. "Don't you have free will like any other mortal soul?"

"I can," she admitted reluctantly.

"Then why didn't you."

"Just because we can ignore the Creator doesn't mean we should."

Kova groaned, stirring where she slumped in the chair. Lunging for her, Jamie helped the Salem Witch sit up, but as soon as he let her go, her body went limp. Reaching for her again, he lifted the woman as though she weighed no more than a doll. After exchanging a look with his soulmate in which they had one of their classic silent conversations, he spooked in a flash of red light.

"Will she be alright?" Walked inquired, staring at the spot Jamie disappeared from.

"Yes." Hayden hesitated, following Walker's gaze. "Even for an immortal Nephilim, it is overwhelming to contain the Goddess's essence for any amount of time. To be the mouthpiece of the Creator is a daunting task, but one Kova deemed necessary for you to commune with Her."

"Won't Spirit revive her?" Emmett asked.

Hayden had once explained Spirit magic as an endless source of all energy in the Universe. Surely it was the same for Kova?

Again, Hayden hesitated. "It's the opposite, actually. Kova channeled so much Spirit magic at once that her body and soul are trying to drain it. So, no, Spirit won't revive her. She has to release the magic to a normal amount."

"I thought Spirit magic was infinite," Walker asked quietly.

"It is," Hayden agreed. "But we are not. The Salem Witch is a conduit for Spirit magic. The Goddess *is* Spirit magic."

"And what exactly was the point of all that?" Mila waved at the chair the Goddess had sat in. "Besides the Goddess herself answering our questions because you apparently *don't* know everything."

To her credit, Hayden didn't attempt to argue with her. Instead, she looked Mila dead in the eye. Shadows rimmed her blue eyes as exhaustion tugged at her. "The point was for you to understand your soul's purpose. The point was for Goddess, for whom your souls sacrificed your divinity, to encourage you before you enter war against such magnificent Evil. To know Who and what you are fighting for. The point was for your souls to settle with the knowledge of your angelic nature so you can wield your full power against the Sins tomorrow." Hayden's crystal blue gaze pierced to Dani's soul as she said, "For *all* of you to wield *all* of your power."

With boiling blood, heated by that last sentence, Dani growled, "Screw you." Spinning on her heel, Dani gestured at

Hayden with an unruly sign and stormed out the door, leaving the other Virtues to make their own choice on how they wanted to deal with the Salem Witch. But as heat pumped through her body, Dani couldn't stand to look at Hayden.

She would *never* forgive her.

CHAPTER THIRTEEN

HAND FROM THE COSMOS

Knuckles rapped against Dani's door, which swung open before she could unfold herself from under the pile of blankets she had burrowed into on her bed.

Leaning against the door frame was none other than Hayden Black.

"May I come in?" she asked, raising a single eyebrow.

Dani shrugged, the pile of blankets shifting with the motion. "I don't see why not. You do whatever you want anyway."

Sighing heavily, Hayden let her head fall forward as she strode into the room and settled on the bed next to Dani. Elbows on her knees, the Salem Witch leaned forward and held her head in her hands. It was then Dani remembered… Hayden wasn't yet twenty years old. Tomorrow was her twentieth birthday, and for the second time in her life, she would wage a war on her birthday.

It was easy to forget that Hayden was a couple years older than Dani, that the young witch had carried the weight of the world on her shoulders for the better part of five years before her Salem War… for the last three years, too. While Dani had been in school, mourning her mundane life, Hayden had yet again sacrificed her days to seek out the Virtues and ready the witches for the next war.

But it didn't absolve Hayden of lying to her.

Blowing out a breath, Hayden lifted her head from her hands and twisted to stare Dani in the eye. Those crystal blue eyes pierced down to the depths of her soul, and Dani wondered if she would ever not be struck by the magnificence of their color.

"I'm sorry, Dani," Hayden said unflinchingly.

Oh. Oh, wow.

Dani sat up straighter.

Hayden Black was not someone who said those two words often. Not because she was stubborn or arrogant—although she definitely was those things—but because she was rarely wrong, and she knew it. If she was apologizing, she truly felt regret over her actions.

"I really am." Folding her hands together, she placed them in her lap. "I'm used to the other Virtues begrudging me, but I hated the betrayal in your eyes tonight. I can't fix things, but I want you to know I don't relish keeping secrets from you."

"You could have told me. You *should* have told me." Dani barked out, but her tone lost some of its bite from earlier.

As her lips twisted into an easy grin, the older witch snorted out a laugh, shaking her head slightly so her black locks rustled around her.

"Are you seriously laughing at me right now?" Dani's voice raised an octave as her rage reignited.

"No, no." Hayden patted her leg. "I'm not laughing at you. It's just when you said that right now, it reminded me of someone."

"Who?"

"Me," she said with a smug grin, then sank into the blankets littering Dani's bed until her back rested against the wall. "After my Earth Trial, when I discovered Kova's hidden identity as Alice Parker, I was livid. I absolutely lost it on my friends, on the Council, on everyone who kept the conspiracy a secret from me. Then I stormed off on my own."

"Yeah, yeah, I get it," Dani mumbled. "I should have kept my anger in check."

Hayden's eyes flew open. "Oh, yeah, that's probably the advice I should be giving you. But to be honest, I was going to say you handled it better than I did. I hit them like a nuclear bomb." She snorted out another laugh, then wiped a hand over her face. "Goddess, yeah, you are way more in control than I ever was. Water elemental versus fire witch, I suppose."

"If you know how much it hurts, then why did you lie to us?" Dani threw her hands in the air.

"Because I've learned since then." Hayden's knowing smile faded as she traveled into her thoughts. After a long pause, she finally said. "Have you ever prayed to the Creator and not gotten a response?"

Shrugging, Dani said, "All the time. Why?"

"And when you don't get a response, does it seem like the Creator was listening anyway? Doesn't the Universe weave life in such a way that it yields your best good?"

Dani blinked. "I guess always." She had never considered it before, but now that Hayden mentioned it, life had a funny way of working out when all seemed lost.

"When you didn't receive an answer right away, you probably felt hurt or let down, right? But when things came to fruition, you were thankful. Maybe it didn't work out like you planned, but it probably worked out better because God and Goddess *always* know better. You probably weren't too upset anymore It didn't give you an answer earlier."

"Yeah, that's probably true," Dani admitted sheepishly.

"Was the Creator was lying to you by not supplying answers to your prayers right away?"

And it hit Dani full in the face... what Hayden was getting at. "No."

"So, doesn't it make sense that I wasn't intending to lie to you by not mentioning a random fact none of you suspected?"

"I suppose so," Dani conceded begrudgingly. Her logic made sense, but it didn't soothe the wound of betrayal digging into Dani's back. "But I don't always feel heard by the Creator."

"You're telling me." She blew out a haggard breath. "You have no idea how many times I felt that way during my Trials. Thank Goddess those are done." Hayden's hand landed on Dani's shoulder, bringing a comforting warmth with it. "Look, I'm not condoning lying or lies by omission. What I'm getting at is that Spirit had a reason for not explaining Itself fully to you at the beginning. While I don't know all the reasons Spirit makes decisions, I do know one of those reasons is a very good one—the longer you know about your divine nature, the harder it is to endure a mortal life. Believe me"—sorrow clouded those crystal blue eyes—"I speak from experience."

Tense silence filled the room as the Asylum witches fell into a sorrowful state.

"It wasn't the lie that hurt," Dani said softly, then blew out a breath. "Logically, I know you weren't... you weren't choosing secrets over our friendship, but..."

"But it feels like I neglected our friendship and betrayed you by not sharing a secret that pertained to you." Hayden nodded, her black locks rippling from the movement. "That's how I felt when I learned the truth about Kova. Nothing hurt worse than Jamie keeping that secret from me. I am sorry, Dani. But I can't go back in time to fix things. All we can do is continue forging forward." Clapping a hand on Dani's back, she finished with, "I hope you can find it within yourself to forgive me, because it may not seem like it to you, but I do value our friendship. I've been hard on you these last seven months—harder than I've been on the others—because I worry about you the most. Don't get me wrong, I want the others to survive this war. But if I had to choose between one of them and you, I'd choose you every time."

An emotion Dani couldn't place swelled inside her heart. How she had admitted to Hayden that sometimes she didn't feel seen or heard by the Creator—it was the opposite of that. It felt like the Goddess was acknowledging Her love for Dani using Her favorite vessel—the Salem Witch. It was silly to put all her emphasis on the opinion of one person. Hayden would say so herself. Yet it filled Dani with a sense of purpose and an intuition in her gut said she would survive tomorrow, if only because she had a guardian angel in Hayden Black.

Clapping her hands and rubbing them together, Hayden said, "You coming to the courtyard or what?"

Dani's face twisted in bewilderment. "The courtyard?"

"One final lesson before the Apokalypsis War." Hayden rose from the bed and opened the door. "I promise, you guys will like this one."

Hayden led Dani into the courtyard, where her circle and the other five Virtues assembled.

"Good. You're all here."

Mila raised a questioning eyebrow but for once remained quiet. She had grown these last seven months, and whether she knew it or not, she had Hayden to thank for that.

The Salem Witch had a rare talent for ticking people off while simultaneously inspiring them to become the best versions of themselves.

"Hate to break it to you, but with our track record, I doubt you can teach us anything tonight and expect us to master it before the Blood Moon Eclipse tomorrow morning," Emmett intoned, eliciting a devious grin from Hayden.

It was near midnight. Twenty-four hours until the Apokalypsis War.

"Actually, I think you will find this skill easy to master. Powerful, but easy." Striding to the center of the courtyard, she gestured in a circle. "Spread out," she commanded the Virtues, waiting until each took their place to form a six-pointed star.

"The Star of David," Apalla muttered from behind Dani. "With Hayden in the center as the seventh point. It's a powerful symbol of protection."

Dani could hear the calculated frown that probably marred Kelsey's face as she responded, "And with Hayden's birth name being Davina, derived from David, I'm willing to bet she knows something we don't, yet again."

Kelsey must have portaled in after Dani stormed out of the Council chamber.

"Probably," Apalla agreed. "But I think it's simpler than that. Hayden understands the power of symbolism. And the Star of David represents the connection between the Creator and humanity. Ancient texts theorize it represents the connection between the Creator and the Seven Holy Virtues."

Dani stilled at that. Symbolism was more than a sign that held meaning for mortals. It was magic in its rawest form. Symbols stored power, so much so that the Spellery used simple sigil magic to conjure food in the dining hall. If Hayden assembled the Virtues in a specific symbol, and—

Dani did a double take.

Hayden's hair shimmered like silver fire as the strands floated on the breeze, but her normally crystal blue eyes had melted into a molten silver. The Mark of the Goddess.

The Shield of David didn't just represent divine protection—it represented the six directions of the Universe—up, down, right, left, inward, and outward—with the Creator at the center, symbolizing the omnipresence of God and Goddess. With Hayden at the center, bearing the Mark of the Goddess...

Hayden wasn't just teaching them a new spell. She formed the Shield of David to bless and protect the Virtues before the war tomorrow. To evoke the powers of Heaven.

She was calling the angels.

"Recall that I mentioned Virtue Angels are distinguished by their impressive control of the elements. Which is why your elemental magic is stronger than other witches. Virtue angels govern the elements of nature," Hayden's silver eyes danced with anticipation, "including storms."

"*Merkaba*," Ronnie whispered in awe. "You're connecting our bodies to Spirit in the higher realm."

"What?" Mila whipped her head between Ronnie and Hayden. "What does that mean?"

"It means she's connecting us to the angelic powers we once had," Dani answered, surprising herself. How did she know that? "Our powers won't be as strong as if we were actually angels because our mortal vessels can't channel that much power without burning the bridge between our souls and mortal bodies but—"

"But your mortal bodies allow you to channel both the angelic power *and* Virtue power," Hayden finished for her.

"As angels, you would possess raw, angelic magic, but you could not channel the unique powers of the Virtues gifted to you on earth. Dani would not be a null, Ronnie couldn't see auras, and so on. But as witches—"

"We have access to both powers," Dani finished for Kova. "Because we need diversity in power, not raw magic like the Salem Witch. It's our Virtue powers that ultimately defeat the Sins in every Apokalypsis War. Not our angelic powers. That's why we became mortal."

A twinge of sympathy mixed with pity crossed Hayden's face, but she masked it quickly. "Because of your original angelic nature, the six of you can call upon storms individually, but together, your powers magnify each other beyond the sum of your parts."

"Like a circle?" Dani asked.

Hayden nodded. "Exactly like a circle."

"Together..." Dani glanced at her brethren Virtues. "How will a storm help us fight the Sins?"

"Storms are the elements made manifest," Kova explained, pushing away from where she leaned against the courtyard wall. "Elements are the basic building blocks of the Universe.

Part of what makes the Salem Witch so powerful isn't the use of each element separately, but the synergy of combining them."

"Storms are a manifestation of holy energy." Hayden pointed to the sky. "While it might not necessarily help you kill the Sins like a sword to the heart, summoning a storm of divine power will weaken the Sin's demonic power, making them vulnerable by weakening their immortal bodies."

Hayden grinned wickedly. "But it gets better. Since the Sins' bodies are fallen angels, they contain the building blocks of energy that Heaven used to form their bodies..."

Ronnie gasped as understanding dawned on her, but Dani didn't follow. Isn't that why the Sins were so much stronger than them? Why was Hayden talking like it was a weakness?

"Care to share, Ronnie?" Hayden gestured for the older witch to speak.

Lowering her hands from where they covered her mouth, she relaxed her widened eyes. "The storm can steal energy from their bodies, sapping them of their angelic strength."

Hayden grinned maniacally as she pointed her dual-toned dagger at Humility. "You asked how the past Virtues defeated the Sins? This is how."

"How vulnerable will this make them?" Walker asked, his eyes sharp and calculating as he took in this new information.

"Practically mortal," Kova answered.

A sharp intake of breath sounded around the courtyard as the Virtues gasped simultaneously.

"If you do it right," Hayden as a caveat, shrugging her shoulders.

"Why would you wait until the day before the war to tell us this?" Mila demanded. "We should have been practicing for *months*."

"Because like all things in the Universe, nature requires *balance*," Thea said. "There is a limit on how many times you can jointly summon a divine storm to weaken the Sins."

Emmett's eyes shot to Hayden. "How many times?"

She raised three fingers in response.

"And what if we don't get it right?" Walker asked uncertainly.

"You will," Hayden announced with unwavering certainty, her silver hair and eyes adding to her air of authority. "Because you're calling a storm to drain *me*."

"Wh-what?" Ronnie stammered. "But won't that drain you for the war tomorrow?"

Shrugging nonchalantly, like she wasn't the least bit concerned, Hayden said, "Eh. Kova will hold the power of Spirit for me, so you will only drain my demonic energy. Once she gives Spirit back to me, I'll bounce right back. Perks of being a Spirit-touched witch. Anyhoo, let's do this!

"Ronnie, Mila, Raphaela—the three of you form one triangle." Hayden pointed at each of them with her amulet athame. "Emmett, Walker, and Dani—the three of you form another triangle. It doesn't have to be any specific three. You can have any arrangement of the six of you, all that matters is that you connect your magic with the witches one over from you instead of the witches right next to you. This forms two opposite triangles superimposed on one another. A six-sided start. The Shield of David."

"Okay, but how do we form the triangles?" Raphaela asked, glancing between Dani and Walker uncertainly.

"With our Virtue magic," Dani answered, looking to Hayden for confirmation.

"Exactly. Extend your magic like you would with the elements to sense the world around you. Virtuous calls to virtuous. You will find one another, and when you do, let your magic take control. Your souls know what to do, even if your mortal minds don't."

Doing as Hayden instructed, Dani pushed out a thread of magic. It felt like the warmth she had come to associate with Chastity. Trailing the magic through the air, she sought her fellow Virtues. When her magic brushed against Ronnie's, it pulled in that direction, but with a gentle hand, Dani guided it past the Virtue of Humility to Temperance.

As Dani's power connected with Emmett's, a beam of light sparked between them, illuminating one side of a triangle. Another beam of light appeared as Emmett and Walker connected, then two more as Ronnie connected to both Mila and Raphaela. Pushing Chastity in the opposite direction—which was strange as Dani had never separated her magic to flow in two directions—she stretched invisible magic fingers for Walker's Virtue. Angelic power connected, snapping together in the form of a band of light.

Wings of powder-blue-colored Spirit emerged from the muscles along Dani's spine, just like the wings of an angel. Tears welled in her eyes, but for once, these weren't tears of grief—they were tears of *joy*. Wings. She had wings. Something about it felt so natural, so right, so *ancient*. Her soul was so light, she felt like she could fly.

"Wings," Mila marveled, twisting her neck to stare at the teal wings pumping the air behind her. "We have wings."

"Whoa," Emmett breathed out, staring over his shoulder at his orange wings.

"We really were angels," Raphaela exclaimed, tears welling in her eyes. "We were the Virtues in another life."

"No," Dani said. "We were the Virtues in *every* life."

"Call the storm, Virtuous Ones," Thea called from outside the Shield of David. "Push your power into the sky and call upon the Lord and Lady for their divine might, for it is your birthright. Let it brew in the sky instead of within you."

"All of us?" Mila asked.

Shrugging, Dani said, "I don't see why not. We're all Virtues."

Nodding, Emmett agreed. "On the count of three. One. Two. Three!"

Dani thrust her power into the sky, pulling the magic of the other Virtues with her. Chastity mingled with Kindness and Temperance as their magic surged toward the Heavens. But it didn't make it there. Because angelic magic beamed down from above. It wasn't visible, yet Dani could sense it in her mind's eye, like she could see it but not really see it.

Storm clouds brewed above the compound, blown in by a strange wind. But that strange wind didn't stop. Rushing faster and faster, it twisted in a circle around the Virtues in the courtyard. Dust kicked in the air, swirling with the wind until a cyclone spun around them.

Electricity charged the air, making Dani's hair stand on end. Thunder rumbled overhead as the elements and angelic power swirled together. Ground quaked under Dani's feet, but she remained upright, unaffected by the motion of the earth.

Pellets of water rained down from the storm clouds in sheets, but not a drop touched Dani. The Salem Witches could have commanded the water to do the same, but both women allowed the rain to soak them to the bone.

A silver thread of light beamed between Hayden and Kova as the younger witch transferred her infinite power to Kova. No, it was more like she handed her access to Spirit to Kova for safe keeping, isolating it from her demonic nature. As she did so, darkness fell over her face and shadows swarmed around the Princess of Hell.

"Don't worry," Hayden said, her voice lower than before. "I'm not evil. More of my demon blood manifests when Spirit isn't present to cancel it out, but I'm in complete control." Squaring her shoulders, she cleared her throat. "Now, hit me with it."

"Which of us does it?" Raphaela asked with wide eyes, glancing at each of the other Virtues in turn.

"Any one of you can." Hayden shrugged casually, but her sharp eyes never left Dani's face.

"Me," Dani declared more confidently than she felt. She was the leader of the Virtues, whether by choice or by fate, but it was her responsibility. "I'll conduct the magic."

Tilting her head back, Hayden offered herself for sacrifice.

Tunneling into the pool of power wrapped in a neat spool inside her chest, Dani called out to Chastity. And the moment she connected with the Virtue, she wondered why she ever struggled to begin with. They were one and the same. They weren't separate, but of the same essence. Chastity chose her soul because Dani was inherently in control of her magic and never gave into the temptation for power, for she was the Goddess's Judge against Evil.

Tugging on the thread of power, she fed it into the storm in the sky, feeling the angelic essence vibrating down the connecting thread. It responded so easily to her, like an eager puppy. As she turned her thoughts on Hayden, the divine storm seemed to know exactly what she wanted it to do. Striking a bolt of blue lightning into Hayden's chest, it seized control of her powers—her demonic powers. Shadows drained from her, fleeing for their survival. The darkness in her face washed away to reveal pale, clammy skin. Her lips tinged blue, and her lustrous black hair turned matted and dull as the power leached from her.

Gasping, the Warrior Witch dropped to her knees, then fell face-first into the dirt. Jamie started toward her but caught himself. Clenching his jaw in what was visibly a struggle, he forced himself to step back and ground his hands against the wall of the compound. Whatever Hayden was going through, it was a different kind of torture to make her soulmate watch.

Power pumped from Hayden into the sky above, illuminating the storm clouds with flashes of lightning.

Dani's eyes snapped to Kova's hunter green ones. "Is she..."

"She's drained," Kova confirmed. "You can release the storm." Then, shrugging, she added, "Or keep it brewing to get payback at her for lying to you."

"You lied to us, too," Walker pointed out.

"Eh." Kova shrugged. "I'm not the demon being drained by a divine storm."

Rolling her eyes, Dani made the decision. "Cut the storm." Although part of her did want to sustain it to torture the Warrior Witch longer. "Ronnie, Mila, Raphaela—call your magic."

The light connecting the three Virtues in a triangle of power blinked out of existence as they retracted their power. The tornado swirling around them lessened to a strong wind and rain stopped pouring in sheets to be replaced by a light mist.

"Walker, Emmett—break the connection."

Tearing her power away from the sky, Dani called Chastity to her, feeling warmth return like an embrace from an old friend. As their triangle of light broke, the power slammed into Dani's chest, nearly throwing her backward, and she had to take a step to keep from falling.

Walker slammed to the ground from the force of his power returning, and Emmett dropped to a knee, breathing in large lungfuls of air.

Darkened clouds vanished from the sky, taking the raindrops with them. The electricity charging the air evaporated as though it were never there to begin with, and the winds halted their assault until a soft July summer breeze blew through the courtyard.

As the remnants of her angelic power seeped into Dani's body, coiling into the spool holding her magic inside, the sky cleared and the last of the storm dissipated until the moon winked at them from between big, puffy white clouds.

Groaning, Hayden flopped to her back, her limbs thrown away from her, so she sprawled spread-eagle in the dirt. "I had forgotten what it was like to not have Spirit magic." She blew a strand of pitch-black hair from her face. "That sucked." Flapping an arm in the air, she said to Kova, "Hit me with it."

The strand of silver thread reappeared between the Salem Witches as Kova transferred the power of Spirit to Its rightful heir. As the silver light absorbed into Hayden's body, life returned to her. Dani couldn't read auras like Ronnie, but as a witch, she could sense the strength of the energy.

Black lightning crackled over her pale skin, but instead of spazzing, the Warrior Witch relished in it. Placing her hands flat on the ground to either side of her head, Hayden rolled back onto her palms, then kicked up into the air and landed lightly on her feet.

Bouncing upright, the Salem Witch spun around, grinning at the Virtues like a maniac. "Now *that* is what I call an elemental storm," she hollered, high-fiving each of the Virtues, then cackled madly. "I knew you'd get it on your first try, and with us"—she gestured to her circle—"the angels have stacked the odds in our favor."

"We shall make the Darkness tremble," Kova agreed, her voice layered with the power of Spirit.

"And kill the princes," Jamie added darkly. "The Sins may still exist, but they will never hold another immortal vessel."

"What about Elliot?" Dani asked. Her counterpart wasn't a fallen angel—Kova guaranteed that over three centuries ago. "Elliot might be a Prince of Hell, but you refused to kill him during the Salem War."

Hayden exchanged a look with Kova and Jamie, like they had held this conversation before. Striding to Dani's side to clap a hand on her shoulder. Pausing, she cocked her head to the side, staring off into space in the way she did when she was listening to Spirit. "I sense Elliot will meet a different fate than his brethren." She shot a glance at Apalla before rolling her eyes. "Not that anybody will confirm it."

Unfazed, Apalla shrugged her shoulders, not deigning to reply.

"Spirit will guide you and the other Virtues. Tomorrow will come and bring what it will bring. Don't think about Elliot's mortality. That's for Heaven to reconcile. Anyhoooo," she drew out the word, indicating a change of subject as she tossed her arm around Dani's shoulders. "I totally forgot to mention that I wanted to make amends to you about the whole not telling you that you were an angel like thousands of years ago. Sooooo," she drew out the word as she spun Dani in a half circle, "I called a friend to help me out."

"Damien!" If it weren't for Hayden's hands holding her up like bands of steel, Dani would have fallen to her knees right then and there as uncontrollable sobs seized control of her. "Damien." She reached for him but staggered as she tried to step forward.

In a flash of black light, Dani reappeared in front of her older brother, then threw herself at him, not caring if he was ready or not. But, of course, he caught her. He would always catch her. He was her big brother, her protector, and her best friend.

Sobbing, Dani buried her face in the crook of his neck, and his gentle hand patted the back of her head.

"Hey there, little sis. I've missed you."

His warmth seeped into her, the warm protection of a big brother. She wasn't alone. In all these months, that's how she had felt—alone. Sure, Hayden had been her friend and her trainer, but Hayden was wrapped up in all the Virtues and had a soulmate and a circle to watch over and Knights to prepare to lead into battle. And the other Virtues were good to her—well, Mila wasn't great at first, but she had come around—but their families and friends had moved to Salem with them. But Damien was a Representative on the Athenian Council, which left Dani alone these past seven months.

"Come on, Dani." Damien wrapped an arm around her shoulder and pulled her toward the dormitories. "You have a lot to fill me in on before we go to war tomorrow."

"We?" Dani asked, sniffling so snot didn't drip from her nose as she tried to stifle her sobs.

Damien scoffed. "As if I would let my little sister battle the Seven Deadly Sins alone? Girl, please. I'm the only one allowed to beat up on you. If Elliot wants to get to you, he has to face me. Wouldn't be the first time." Damien scowled at the thought of his once-friend now turned demon prince.

"I'm so glad you're here." Dani squealed, wrapping him in a hug. "I have so much to tell you."

Flicking his wand, Damien opened the door to Dani's room, then strode inside and settled in the desk chair. "Well, start talking. We don't have all night. How crazy has it been with Hayden? Be brutally honest. I will absolutely hold this over her for the rest of my life." Mischief danced in his chocolate brown eyes. Eyes identical to hers.

"That girl is mega powerful," Dani said. "But oh, my Goddess, is she freaking *nuts*."

Damien snorted, then kicked the other rolling chair over to her. "You better sit down."

Dani did as he said and dove into the story of everything that happened since she arrived in Salem. She talked about the other Virtues and training with them, the uneasy dynamic between them and Hayden and how it put Dani in a strange position. She told him about the powers of each Virtue and the lack of her control over her powers. Damien narrowed his eyes, his lips pursed but kept quiet. Despite her better judgement, Dani even told him about the battle where the Sins cuffed Hayden and nearly killed Jamie, how Chastity's null saved the Nephilim's immortal life. Letting him hold her, she cried through the battle that ended with Axel's demise.

For some reason, though, she didn't tell Damien about her encounter with Jophiel... it seemed too personal to share, even with her brother. But she dared to tell him how she battled Abaddon and held her own, resulting in a brutal blow to his angelic body. He clearly wasn't pleased that Hayden left Dani alone with a Sin, but he didn't say anything, indicating Hayden already told him. Damien was anything but subtle, especially when freaking out.

When she told him about her angelic nature, Damien sighed, removed his glasses, and rubbed the bridge of his nose.

Shock speared through her chest. "You knew." It wasn't a question.

Returning his glasses to his face, Damien grimaced, then met her gaze. "No, but I suspected."

"You knew and you didn't tell me," Dani accused.

"I didn't know for sure," he corrected her. "If I told you and was wrong, what then? I pieced it together based on breadcrumbs Apalla trailed, which in hindsight, was probably intentional. I'm not sure if her and Hayden discussed it, or if Apalla knew because of her visions as a Daughter of Apollo, but I suspect she gave me just enough information to draw my own conclusions, knowing I would panic less about Hayden spiriting you here to Salem."

"I can't believe this," Dani grumbled, crossing her arms over her chest. "First Hayden, now you. What else aren't you guys telling me."

Damien rolled his eyes at her dramatics. "Goddess, Dani, seriously? You need to chill. So what if Hayden kept a secret from you? Do you have *any* idea how many times that girl outright lied to my face or hid the truth from me? And we're still friends."

"And you still trust her?"

"With my life," he answered without hesitation. "She never kept me in the dark to hurt me. It was typically for my safety or hers. I can't tell you how to handle your friendship with her. That's on both of you. But I didn't tell you because I was afraid I was wrong and didn't want to mislead my kid sister to believe she's the mortal incarnation of a Virtue Angel only for her to discover that I'm an idiot. So what if you are? Does it change anything?"

When he waited for an answer, Dani begrudgingly admitted, "No, not really. But I had a right to know."

"I don't disagree. And honestly, I thought Hayden would have told you sooner."

"She's insane, you know that?"

"Oh, abso-freaking-lutely."

"But I wouldn't want anybody else to lead me into war against all the Evil in existence."

"If anyone can keep you alive, it's her," Damien admitted, and Dani saw the sincerity in his eyes. He truly believed Hayden hid this massive secret for Dani's own good, and if Damien trusted her after all of her screw ups... Dani felt her heart softening toward the Warrior Witch.

"I thought you two might be chatting like the insufferable gossips you are."

Dani's heart leaped from her chest from the shock of Hayden materializing from the shadows.

Taking a pillow off Dani's bed, Damien threw it at the Salem Witch, who let it hit her in the face without so much as flinching. *"Don't do that."*

Grinning, Hayden retrieved the pillow and returned it to Dani's bed. "Sorry, I shouldn't have assumed you would have remembered my bad habits in the time we've spent apart, Damien."

Rolling his eyes, Damien slapped his hands on his hips. "Girl, don't even start with me. We are about to go to war tomorrow against six Princes of Hell and an evil wannabe."

Hayden and Dani shared a twisted look.

"Um, Elliot is a Prince of Hell, Damien," Dani pointed out.

Raising an eyebrow at her, he dared her to fight him. "As if." He scoffed. "Elliot can think he is a prince, but that boy was just a pitiful air witch, no better than the rest of us. Pfft. As if he could compare to a princess." He flourished a hand at Hayden.

"Or a Virtue." Hayden copied him but flourished her hand at Dani. "You know I can't harm him directly."

"Which means I have to," Dani said softly, causing regret to twinge Hayden's features.

"I'm sorry," she muttered. "He's the only one I can't kill."

"Don't be," Dani waved her off as she slumped onto the bed. "I don't think the problem is killing him."

"I'm sorry, *what*?" Damien asked. "Dani, you have to kill him."

"I agree with Dani," Hayden said. "I don't think she should kill him."

Mouth agape, Damien whipped his head between the two black-haired witches in disbelief. "But he's a Sin!"

"He's mortal, Damien," Dani challenged. "He was a witch, just like Lilith was once human, and Hayden didn't kill her."

"That's different," Damien argued. "Hayden is... she's Hayden. You're you."

"You don't think I can do it?" Dani accused, surging to her feet, her hands balled into fists.

Damien scoffed. "Do you have the power of Spirit?"

"No."

"Then you can't strip Elliot of his powers like Hayden did to that old hag."

Pinching the bridge of her nose, Hayden complained, "I *so* did not see this coming." Splaying her palms, she stepped between the siblings. "Look, I didn't come here to start a fight between you two." Placing a sympathetic hand on Damien's shoulder, she waited for his chocolate gaze to meet hers. "Damien, as much as I respect your need to protect your little sister and envy Dani for having a big brother to protect her, *she* is the Virtue of Chastity, not you. Ultimately, it is her decision how to deal with Elliot. All we can do is be there to protect her."

Conceding to the Salem Witch with an exaggerated eye roll, Damien shoved off her hand. "Yeah, yeah. You know, since you became immortal and got full access to Spirit, arguing with you hasn't been as much fun."

Snorting in response, Hayden shoved Damien playfully. "I let you win sometimes." Sobering, she addressed Dani. "There's something we need to discuss before tomorrow."

"Uh oh," Dani groaned. "Why do I get the feeling that I'm not gonna like this?"

"It's not life-shattering," Hayden promised with a small smile. "But seeing as you, Chastity, are the leader of the Virtues, it's imperative that you lead us into battle tomorrow."

Dani's jaw dropped as she openly gawked at the Salem Witch. "Are you insane? I'm the leader of the Virtues, but that doesn't mean I have the authority to lead you and your circle and an *army*. I never even served as an officer in the Knights' ranks."

"Neither had Hayden when she led our armies against Lilith's Island," Jamie responded after he spooked into the room. He nodded to Damien once, then said to Hayden, "Babe, when you're done here, the Athenian Council wants to talk to you."

"Give me ten minutes."

After pressing a light kiss to his soulmate's cheek, the older Nephilim fist-bumped Dani and disappeared in a flash of red light.

"See." Dani flapped her arms. "The Athenian Council wants to talk to you about war plans. Not me."

"Relax, Dani," the other witch advised. "Take a deep breath. I will command the Knights in battle tactics. But I want you to take point against the Sins. When we enter the portal, you are the first one through, followed by the other five Virtues. My circle and I will follow."

"Why does it matter? Why can't you walk through first."

"Political maneuvering," her brother answered, sliding his glasses up his nose. "It's not about whether you're actually leading or not—it's about the Sins perceiving you as the leader."

"Exactly," Hayden agreed. "If I walk in front of you, it appears like I'm leading the Virtues, but as of tomorrow, I will use the power of Spirit to harness Patience, one of the Virtues who follows *you*."

"If you don't take point, the Sins will think the Virtues are weaker than in past Wars. They'll perceive you as needing Hayden's protection, and therefore, you aren't much of a threat to them."

"I'm not as much of a threat to them as she is," Dani said pointedly.

"True." Hayden shrugged as though it didn't matter. "But if they aren't concerned with you, then they'll focus on me. And if I'm busy fighting all the Sins at once—"

"Then you can't kill them," Dani surmised, reaching the conclusion the older witches had been leading her to. "If the Sins are busy fighting the Virtues, then you and your circle have more maneuverability to kill them."

"Precisely. But here's the thing, Dani—I don't want them to just perceive you as the leader of the Virtues. I want them to know you're a threat. Because you are." Mischief sparked in her eyes as she grabbed Dani's shoulders. "You are the key to defeating the Sins and killing their angelic vessels. There is a reason Chastity's powers manifested as a null this time. There is a reason I am alive during *your* era."

Hayden released her shoulders, and it all came crashing down on her.

"I'm not you, Hayden," Dani said quietly, fighting the hot tears welling in her eyes, threatening to spill over. "I'm not the Warrior Witch. I'm not a beautiful, terrifying witch with endless power who walks through Hell like she owns the place because she literally does." She lifted her gaze to meet Hayden's. "I'm just some kid. I'm barely an adult at seventeen, and I'm the youngest of the Virtues. I'm not fit to lead. I'm not sure I'll survive tomorrow. I don't terrify the Sins, not like you do. As much as I want to be you—and I've tried, Hayden, I've really tried to be like you, because since I met you, I wanted to be like you—I'm not."

Hayden opened her mouth to respond, but Damien beat her to it.

"Good." Damien looked at Hayden. "Don't get me wrong, Hays, I love you, but I am *so* glad my sister isn't you. No offense." He grimaced.

Shrugging, Hayden seems completely unoffended. "None taken. It is chaos being me."

"Sis, there's a reason Hayden's the Salem Witch and you're not. And there's a reason you're a Virtue and Hayden isn't. The Creator doesn't make mistakes. The Goddess chose Hayden as the Salem Witch because the Creator had a perfect plan. And It chose you as Chastity because only your soul can fulfill the task. In like, what, eight years, Hayden has never defeated Elliot." Damien threw his hands up in surrender. "Don't kill me, Hays, but seriously, you *could* beat him in combat while blindfolded, but you've never actually beat him."

She pursed her lips, contemplating his words and seemingly having a silent argument with herself, which probably meant she was communing with Spirit. "Actually, Damien makes a good point. After the Salem War, Spirit told me that it wasn't my place to defeat Elliot. But now I wonder if it wasn't my place, or if it wasn't within my skillset."

"Not touching that one," Damien threw out. "But I do know the Creator would never choose you for Chastity if you weren't capable of beating Elliot. I still think you should kill him—"

"Damien," Hayden growled in warning.

Throwing his hands up in surrender, he said, "I'm just saying. But whatever you decide to do, Goddess chose you for a reason. You *will* beat him tomorrow, I'm sure of it. And I'll be there to help you."

Lightning flashed through Hayden's eyes, and Dani glanced out the window to see if a storm was brewing, but the weather was calm. The lightning must have been Hayden's power. Why?

"I think Damien's onto something, kid," she said from where she leaned a hip against Dani's dresser. "If we're being honest, water was the hardest element for me to master. The fighting aspect was a breeze because it was my third element, but the spiritual stuff... not so much. It took me like a year and a half to pass my Water Trial while the other elements took a year max. Granted, I would be a fire elemental if I wasn't the Salem Witch—ya know, Princess of Hell and Daughter of Michael and all—which makes water my opposite element, but our elemental magic is often determined by our personalities. If you, Chastity, are a water elemental, and are the opposite of Elliot, Lust, then something about *you* is Lust's kryptonite."

"Yeah, magic that is completely unreliable in a fight."

Hayden shrugged. "Not all power comes from magic, Dani. During my Trials, my decisions were more impactful than the magic I wielded. Choices won my Trials, not magic, and choices defeated Lilith. Remember when I offered you the water witch position in my circle? I didn't know you were a Virtue, so that's not why I offered you the position."

"It's not?"

"No," Hayden shook her head, sending her black locks flying behind her like a halo. "I chose you because of how you confronted Elliot when you could have cowered. Instead, you swallowed fear and defied Evil to its face."

"You say all that, but I still don't know what I'm doing. I didn't even think back then. I was a kid acting on instinct." Dani blew out an exasperated sigh. "The Sins will take one look at me tomorrow and know I'm scared. Elliot included."

"No, they're won't," Hayden said confidently.

"And how do I convince the Sins that they're more afraid of me than I am of them?"

"Simple. Let the monsters see you smile." Hayden tossed a wicked smile to the Sanchez siblings. "Imagine how terrifying you'll be when you look Evil in the face and grin like you have all the power in the world. Because you do."

Something inside Dani's chest stirred awake at those words.

Chastity, is that you? Dani asked.

No verbal response came, not like how Spirit spoke to Hayden, but Dani got the distinct impression that Chastity was with her, and this time, her Virtue would not return to its slumber.

Damien frowned, his hands braced on his hips. "It's concerning how much time the two of you have spent together in the last seven months."

"Oh, you have no idea." Hayden grinned wildly, then cut her gaze over to Dani's. Squatting in front of her, she placed a steady hand on Dani's knee. "I know you're not ready to forgive me yet, and that's okay. Hate me if you must but know everything I've done in the last three years has been to keep you safe and to prepare you so you survive this war."

"You want my forgiveness?" Dani whispered. "Then tell me the truth. How many times have I survived the Apokalypsis War? How many times have the other Virtues survived?"

"It's not a simple statistic," Hayden warned. "The answer is convoluted. Dependent on other factors."

"Tell me."

Sighing, Hayden dropped her hand from Dani's knee to rub the back of her neck as she dropped her face to the floor. Before answering, she met Dani's gaze again, the crystal blue filled with a steely determination as she admitted, "You have never survived the Apokalypsis War."

"What?" Damien shrieked, jumping to his feet. "Dani... No... No, that can't be right." Grabbing Hayden by her shoulders, he hauled her to her feet and shook her. "Hayden, you must be wrong. Spirit must be—"

"Spirit is never wrong," Dani cut him off, but kept her eyes focused on Hayden. "I suspected as much."

Pulling free of Damien's grasp, Hayden met the Virtue's gaze. "The reason you never survive is because you're the leader. You always sacrificed yourself to ensure the Sins were defeated or to save the life of another Virtue. It's a noble way to die." Something flashed in Hayden's eyes. An unreadable expression on her face, but Dani sensed Hayden saw something in Dani that reminded her of herself.

Squatting in front of Dani again, she gripped the younger girl by both cheeks. "But every life before this, in every Apokalypsis War before this one, you never had *me*. It was no accident that the Blood Moon Eclipse coincides with my birthday, nor is it coincidence that three immortal Nephilim—two of whom are Salem Witches—the Heart of Earth, and a Daughter of Apollo are alive today to fight alongside you. We will not just defeat the Sins, Dani." Her crystal blue eyes that Dani loved so much sparkled with light. "We will kill the Princes of Hell."

Dani wanted to believe her so badly, her soul ached. But in every life, Dani died. Died before she had the chance to live.

"You *will* survive tomorrow, Dani." Hayden rose to both feet and unhooked her longsword from her waist. "Because you will use Nightmare to fight the Sins."

She placed the black leather sheath across Dani's lap, but the Virtue couldn't move, frozen by shock.

"Nightmare is an angelic weapon. Once the blade of Lucifer himself, it is an Archangel Blade. Besides Spirit, which I will wield tomorrow, Nightmare is one of the only weapons on Earth that can kill a fallen angel." Hayden tapped a finger under Dani's chin. "So, kill them, Dani. Kill them all. Become their nightmare."

CHAPTER FOURTEEN

UNITY OF HELL

"Coffee?" Dani offered.

Of all the things in the world, that one word made the Warrior Witch shudder. "Nooooo." She backed away a step, keeping her hands up as though they would protect her from the evil pot of coffee Dani held.

The Virtue raised a questioning eyebrow.

"I tried the stuff once when I was younger," Hayden explained. "Nearly destroyed my house with the elements, my magic was so hyped up."

"Yikes." Dani took a sip of her black coffee.

"Tell me about it. I didn't stop shaking for like three days. Took forever to clean my house."

"I was referring to the fact that you can't have coffee for the rest of your life."

Hayden threw her head back and laughed the most carefree laugh Dani had heard from her in the last seven months.

"Maybe you should have a cup," Dani suggested. "Blow up the Sins."

"As much as I love the way your mind works," laughter shimmered in her crystal blue eyes, "I knocked myself unconscious for like a day." Sobering, she scanned Dani from head to toe. "How are you feeling?"

"Honestly?" Dani leaned against the coffee station in the Council's private chambers. "Weirdly... calm."

The door to the chamber flew open and in stormed a haggard looking Kova, followed by a snickering Jamie.

"Coffee?" Hayden offered innocently, earning a glare from the other Salem Witch. "Who peed in your cereal?"

"Do you have any idea how annoying your father-in-law is?" the elder witch demanded. She waggled a finger at Hayden, then at Jamie. "From now on, you two are dealing with him. There are three of us, I do *not* have to be the one to summon him." Flopping down on the couch, she grunted out, "I'm the Uriel-only Nephilim. Got it?"

"*How* did Gabriel pee in your cereal?" Dani asked, biting back the laughter threatening to bubble out of her as she shared a devious smile with Hayden.

"Dad decided on violence today."

"What does that mean?" Dani asked, looking to Hayden to translate.

Popping up from the sofa, Kova glared at the snickering Nephilim. "It means Gabriel finally got retribution for the time I summoned him seventeen times in a row." She flopped back down on the couch.

"You summoned him *seventeen times*?" Dani choked. She couldn't imagine summoning an angel once let alone—

What was Dani thinking? She *was* an angel.

"It was a Trial thing," Hayden supplied. "I suspect Gabriel has been waiting for the opportunity to prank Kova in return."

"No one bothered me this much when I was dead," Kova grumbled.

"You weren't dead," Hayden replied flippantly. "Your body 'mysteriously disappeared'." She made air quotes with her fingers. "And the angels knew exactly where you were, so they could have bothered you anytime. What did Gabriel make you do?" She pressed her water glass to her lips.

"Don't you dare," the red-haired witch warned Jamie.

"He made her wear a cowboy hat and ride a bull—"

Hayden spit out her water.

"Jamie—" Kova warned.

"Seventeen times."

Hayden choked on her laughter, and Dani nearly spit out her coffee, but managed to swallow the steaming liquid.

Kova lurched to her feet and pinned Hayden with a glare. "None of this would have happened if it weren't for your crazy ideas."

Dani opened her mouth to ask what crazy idea Hayden brewed up this time, but snapped it shut when the door swung open and the other Virtues filed into the room, buzzing with chatter.

"At least you got your dose of humor for the day before we head to war," Jamie muttered to Dani. "Doing okay, kid?" the Nephilim asked her. She nodded in response. "Good." He bumped a fist against her shoulder. "You've got this." Pausing, he swallowed roughly, as though he was choking. His next words appeared to be a physical struggle. "My sister was a water elemental... I never wanted... Hayden wouldn't dare give you my sister's spot if Harbor herself didn't bless you." He swallowed again, looking at the floor. "You're a lot like her. I think she would have liked you, if you had more time to get to know one another before she... before she passed. I think... I think she will be with you today—out there on the battlefield. I... I'm glad it's you. I've never viewed anyone else as worthy of taking my sister's place, but if anyone could live up to Harbor, I see it in you—the same spirit that was inside her."

Not trusting herself to speak around the emotion clogging her throat, Dani nodded at the Nephilim. But he seemed to understand her wordlessness. After reciprocating her nod, he stalked to the head of the table where Hayden stood flanking the head chair.

"Dani," she waved the Virtue over. "Take a seat, won't you?" She gestured to the head seat.

Sucking in a breath, Dani steeled her nerves and assumed her rightful place at the head of the table. To her surprise, none of the Virtues balked, not even Mila. Instead, they waited for her... to lead them.

"We're about to go to war," Dani said dumbly. Ugh, what was wrong with her? They knew that. She cleared her throat. "A war our souls have fought before and not just survived but *won*. And we will win today. We are the Holy Virtues, hand-picked by Goddess herself, the Almighty Creator. It would not have chosen us if It did not know with absolutely certainty that we would bring Heaven victory."

Emmett thumped a fist against the table twice in agreement, then cried out with a cheer. The other Virtues followed suit, rallying their spirits for the fight to come.

"Remember, the Sins can't engage us until the Blood Moon Eclipse starts," Dani clarified. "Nor can we attack them. We're arriving early to give ourselves time to implement the first part of the plan. Is everybody clear on our tasks?" Dani waited for each of the Virtues to nod. Their movements were curt and abrupt, the seriousness of the situation, the fate of their lives and the world, weighing on their shoulders.

But they had fought this war before and won. They would taste victory today whilst the Sins choked on defeat.

"Raphaela, stay close to me. With you amplifying my powers, we can render more of the Sins magicless. Remember, don't let the lesser demons distract you. Let the Knights handle the pawns. We're the only weapons against the Sins. They're our focus. We take them out, their ranks crumble without leadership. Any questions?"

The faces of hardened warriors stared back at her.

"And what of Elliot?" Hayden asked softly from beside her.

Dani hesitated. "Kill him if you must, if he attacks you, but don't seek him out. I'd prefer to leave him for last, without the influence of the other Sins, but I won't sacrifice our own to do so."

Hayden's nod of approval was curt, but something flashed in her eyes as she pursed her lips. Dani wondered if Hayden would ever forgive him for what he did to her and her family. Understandably, she blamed him for her father's death, and based on the look on Kova's face, the Earth Nephilim felt the same. Sorrow and regret plague them, as though they blamed themselves. But Dani couldn't dwell on that...

She still didn't know how to handle Elliot, but she prayed the Goddess would help her when the time came. Until then, she was trying not to die.

"No one dies today. You are the lights that illuminate the dark." Hayden raised her glass of water in toast to the Virtues. "To the divine spark in each of you." She smirked that wicked smile of hers. "May it inspire a bit of mischievousness within."

"Let's go kill some fallen angels."

"Ready, kid?" Hayden asked.

"Ready." Dani nodded.

"Unsheath Nightmare," she instructed, gesturing to her sword tied to Dani's hip. "Walk into this war with your weapon drawn." She turned to stand behind the Virtues, then paused and glanced over her shoulder. "Oh, and Dani? I don't say it enough, but... I'm proud of you."

A portal of black and silver magic burst to life mere feet in front of Dani, and with one glance back at her fellow Virtues, Dani stepped into the magic.

The other side of the portal was worse than Dani expected. Barren.

The land was utterly barren. Deprived of life.

Sensing the Virtues flanking her, Dani continued forward despite the voice screaming at her to turn around. The scent or mildew and decay stung her nose, more putrid and concentrated than ever. That meant one thing.

The Sins were here.

Striding up the sloping hill, Dani navigated the rocky terrain until she peaked of the hill overseeing a valley of death. In the center of the barren bowl of sand and dirt, stood the Seven Deadly Sins, lined in the order of their Fall—Wrath, Gluttony, Greed, Envy, Sloth Lust, Pride.

Black, beady eyes snapped to her as she crested the peak, darkness and hatred stewing in their inky depths. As the Virtues flanked her and the Knights edged the valley, the Sins' surveyed the threat amassed against them.

Belphegor threw back his head and laughed, but Elliot pursed his lips as he narrowed his eyes in Hayden's direction. The other Sins underestimated the Salem Witch's cunningness, but Elliot knew her conniving nature first hand, and he knew she wasn't afraid to play dirty.

He said something to the other Sins, but Belphegor and Belial, who stood next to him, barely acknowledged the words. Yet Abaddon, who stood at the opposite end of the line, flicked his eyes to Elliot and matched his frown. The others did not give credence to Elliot, but Abaddon was the leader of the Seven, the one who led them in the Fall, and he had a mind of his own to calculate and manipulate while the others only reveled in the darkness of their Sins.

Abaddon's eyes narrowed at the black sword grasped in Dani's hand, then flicked to Hayden who stood with complete confidence despite her weapons harmlessly miniaturized on her charm bracelet.

Always the troublemaker, Hayden shot him a cheeky smile.

"Afraid for the witchling's life, I see," Abaddon growled, inclining his head toward Nightmare. His voice stained the valley with a mocking boldness. "Otherwise, princess"—he sneered—"you would not have lent Lucifer's Angel Blade to Chastity and leave yourself defenseless."

"It's not Lucifer's blade," Hayden snapped, her eyes flashing silver. "Nightmare chose *me*. Only one virtuous in Spirit could dream to wield her." A cruel smile twisted her lips. "And who said I'm defenseless?"

Something about the way she spoke the threat sent a shiver through Dani.

"Enough of this," Belial growled, shooting a glare at Abaddon, his disdain seething across the valley. "We are not here to banter with a Princess of Hell." He gestured a perfectly manicured hand at the sky, where the moon shined with full brightness. "We are here to battle under the Blood Moon Eclipse for the right to own the world for the next seven centuries." Breathing in sharply through his nose, Belial closed his eyes. "I can smell the fear from these weaklings. I can taste victory this time, brothers."

"Oh, about that." Hayden snapped her fingers.

Light flashed in Dani's peripherals as the immortal witches spooked to stand at the four cardinal directions. Thea stood opposite the Virtues, a statue representing the North with her earth magic. Kova took the west as the water representative in place of Harbor, and Hayden spooked Apalla to the east while her soulmate stayed with the Virtues on the south end of the circle.

Three portals burst to life at the other three cardinal points. Kova's and Thea's portals pulsed with power, every shade of green swirling in their magical depths while Hayden's menacing black portal struck fear into the hearts of demons, the black broken by strands of shimmering silver and purple, like her aura.

Armies burst forth from the portals. Witch Knights and soul-filled demons marched through. Across from the Virtues, Thea's portal deposited an army lead by Silas, her Shaman friend, at the Northern point of the valley. Knights upon

Knights with faces Dani didn't recognize flooded out of the swirling green portal. They must have been the friends and allies Hayden and Jamie forged relationships with in the last two years while away from Asylum. That's why they were traveling the world—to amass an army greater than the one that protected Asylum during the Salem War.

In the west, Kova opened a portal for another army, led by Mareena Bishop, who wore a savage scowl as she commanded the Blairsville Knights and then some. Mareena and her father must have used their extensive connections to draw in witches from around the country. The Bishop name held such weight that they could convince others to deploy their armies for the most brutal war of the epoch.

But it was the black portal in the east that brought hope to Dani's heart and instilled courage she didn't know she needed. Kelsey Kensington strode through the portal like she owned the place, peering down her nose at the Sins in disdain as though they were nothing but disgusting cockroaches she was about to crush under her foot.

Beside her stood a woman identical to Hayden with pale skin and midnight black hair, but several years older. Leyla had stopped aging at thirty-three. The mother and daughter could have been twins if it weren't for the eyes—Hayden inherited her piercing blue eyes from her father, Michael, while Leyla bore lavender irises and looked as brutal as her savage daughter as she led the Asylum Knights through the portal.

"Enough," Leviathan's guttural voice cut through the clanging of the armies. "We cannot engage the Virtues until the Blood Moon Eclipse begins," he twisted his distorted neck to stare up at the moon, "but this war begins NOW." Leviathan raised a thick, misshapen leg, then stomped it into the ground. A crater formed under his angelic strength and—

No.

That wasn't a crater. It was a *portal*.

A portal to Hell.

And at the rate it was expanding under the feet of the Sins, it would consume the valley before the Eclipse was complete. The earth shook violently. An unending mass of black bodies erupted from the portal like lava from a volcano. Dani craned her neck to stare at the sky, but the flapping demons filled the sky, blotting out the light of the moon. Terrestrial-bound demons tore through the portal to assemble around the Sins like a barrier.

The Virtues would have to fight their way through countless demons before they could engage the Sins. And the flood of demons into the mortal world wasn't slowing. At this rate, Hell would be emptied of its soldiers.

"Mom, can you shut the portal?"

Hayden used air magic to funnel their conversation to the Virtues and the rest of her circle.

Leyla sheathed her sword and summoned purple hellfire to her hands. "If I can get near it, yes."

"Kelsey—"

"You don't even have to ask. I'll guard her back."

Hayden nodded. "Jackal, Buddy—you're with Kelsey."

Salem remained in Asylum, much to the Labrador's irritation, but the Warrior Witch was not risking her familiar in another war against Evil. Dani couldn't blame her.

In a flash of black, Hayden disappeared from the eastern point of the valley to reappear next to Dani and stared up at the sky, glaring through the layers of demons as though she could see the moon through their corporeal bodies.

"Change of plans. We can't kill Leviathan until Mom closes the portal."

"What?" Walker asked in alarm. "Why not?"

"Because the portal won't seal after we kill him. The Sin of Envy will fuse with the portal and keep it open to haunt us."

Walker visibly paled. He was the Virtue opposite Envy. He would have to fight for his life without dealing a death blow.

"Dani," she dared a glance at the water witch, a twinge of regret twisting her features, "Jamie will protect Walker instead of you."

"I've got this. Chastity is with me." In response, the Virtue stirred inside her chest and feelings of love flooded her body.

"Get ready," Hayden announced to the Virtues, her gaze fixated on the sky above. "In three, two, one—"

Magic beyond belief rippled through Dani.

It was like the very air she breathed was liquid sunlight, filling her entire being with light and magic. And love. So much love. Power flooded her veins and blue light haloed around her as angelic wings of Virtue magic condensed at her spine. The wings were made of light, but they felt as physical as the wings of an immortal angel, as though she could fly.

And with the thought, her feet lifted off the ground.

As she rose in the air, her wings flapped as though they had done it a thousand times in her previous lifetimes. Because they *did*. She was once an angel, and angels had wings. She didn't need to practice or think—she just flew, guided by instinct and muscle memory. The other Virtues had discovered the same truth, rising into the air alongside Dani.

"Wings," Mila marveled, twisting her neck to stare at the teal wings pumping the air behind her. "We have wings."

Abaddon sneered at the Virtues. Elliot whipped his head from the Virtues to the other Sins, but the Princes of Hell didn't spare him a glance as they unsheathed their weapons. Apparently, nobody informed him of the Virtues' angelic roots.

"Time to level up," Abaddon drawled, nodding at Leviathan. The coldness in his voice tightened Dani's veins.

Leviathan's mangled body twisted, the skin swelling. Boils the size of baseballs bubbled from his skin, then burst, oozing dark liquid as Leviathan's body expanded. Pus dripped off the Sin, and his skin peeled back to reveal black scales with a green hue. His twisted neck thickened and elongated into a serpentine appendage.

As the scales shuddered and rippled, Leviathan's monstrous body contorted, expanding until he was the size of a house. His arms, twisted to awkward angles, slammed into the ground as he shifted to all fours. Fangs the size of Dani's leg protruded from his mouth, overhanging his bottom lip. Beady greenish-black eyes peered down at the witches as Leviathan transformed into a wingless dragon. Opening his massive jaws, Leviathan reared back and loosed a guttural roar, revealing three rows of fangs that reeked of death and decay.

"Holy crap," Emmett breathed from beside Dani.

Walker looked like he was about to puke.

"You won't fight him alone," Dani assured him fiercely. "Hayden—" Her name was a question on Dani's lips.

"Do it!" she shouted as black lightning tore out of her. Seven bolts blasted the Sins, buying Dani and the Virtues time.

"Form the *merkaba*," Dani commanded, seizing hold of Walker's and Mila's hands. "We can summon the storm here and direct it at the Sins."

Ronnie, Emmett, and Raphaela joined hands, the light of the Virtues overlapping to form a continuum of color. Beams of light connected the three as their Virtue magic bonded. Blue, teal, and green light beams formed a triangle between Dani, Mila, and Walker.

The Shield of David was formed.

Chastity and Diligence and Temperance frolicked lovingly together as their light beams surged toward the Heavens, accompanied by the other three Virtues. Angelic magic beamed down from the sky, but unlike during their practice session, this magic was visible—a searing white light that obliterated the demons in its way.

Gray storm clouds brewed above the valley. A strange but powerful wind whipped through the air, but didn't disturb the Virtues or their allies. Sand swirled, kicked up by the cyclone dropping from the heavens.

Earth quaked under their feet, but the Virtues stood strong while the Sins shook. Elliot dropped to his knees. Even Abaddon took a step to steady himself. Electricity crackled, and Dani's hair floated on the air from the free electrons. Thunder clapped overhead as Virtue elements met angelic power. Rain poured from the storm clouds in rivers, drenching the Sins.

Mammon sneered at the sky as if he took the rain to be a personal offence.

Unlike before, Dani didn't need to tunnel into her Chastity power. Chastity was right there, at the surface, waiting and eager for Dani to command the Virtue against the Sins. Dani and Chastity were one and the same, bound together for eternity.

The Goddess's Judge against Evil.

Angelic power vibrated through her body and down the beam of light. The sky responded to her, the divine storm striking a bolt of lightning so large, it swallowed the Seven deadly Sins whole. Heaven's power surged, tearing into the Sin's demonic powers. Darkness peeled away from the Sins as the Virtue's divine storm drained their demonic power.

Abaddon's red skin lightened to a dark shade of pink. Elliot blinked his eyes, brown irises flashing for the briefest of seconds. Belial, the Proud, dropped to a knee, inhaling a shaky breath. Mammon, Belphegor, and Beelzebub remained standing, but the normal lustrous glow of their tan skin faded, and was it Dani, or did their faces look less devastatingly handsome? Leviathan's immense body shrank as the power was sucked from him like a leech. He was as large as a house but based on the low growl that tore from his throat and through those terrifying teeth, Leviathan felt the lack of power.

"Draining them won't last forever," Hayden warned, white light glowing around her right hand like she held the soul of an angel within her fist. But Dani didn't have time to question it. The Sins were weakened.

"Virtues," Dani called out. "Give them hell!"

A war cry rose from the ranks of witches on the ground as they charged, the wave of witches crashing into the masses of demons assembled in the valley.

Flapping furiously, Dani surged forward on air waves that seemed to flow exactly how she wished them. Water magic sloshed around her as she glowed with blue light, Nightmare in hand.

Leading the Virtues, Dani crashed against the wall of demons that rose to meet her before she could dive at the Sins. Lesser demons sacrificed themselves to save the Princes of Hell in their weakened states. And Dani lost herself to the blood and magic of battle. Lost to the claws and swords and terror. But Dani could not stop as demon after demon flooded toward her. Wielding Nightmare like an extension of herself, Dani slaughtered demon after demon as she struggled toward the Sins. Cowards, hiding behind their pawns instead of facing her.

Chaos reigned supreme.

But Chastity was with her.

Any time a demon got within five feet of her, the demonic power leached from its body. Twirling Nightmare or wielding water, Dani eviscerated each demon into black ash. Wings of blue light kept her aloft, moving her with a mere thought, helping her to duck and dodge with preternatural agility she never possessed on the ground.

Lightning danced in the sky, obliterating hordes of demons as Knights fought with unyielding ferocity. Blades clanged and claws slashed. Magic shot through the air, and the elements waged war against the forces of Darkness.

White flames arced in the sky, clearing a path through the flood of demons to the Sins below. Dani's eyes snapped to Elliot's, locking gazes instantly as he glowered at the halo of blue light surrounding her. Her Virtue. Abandoning his battle with a random Knight, Elliot disappeared into the throng of demons. Hayden could not kill him, but Dani made no such deal with the Devil, and with her powers nullifying the ones he gained by descending to a Prince of Hell, she could. And he knew it.

Tucking in her wings, Dani dropped to the ground, and flared them at the last minute to avoid shattering against the earth.

If it were possible, the battles on the ground were worse than in the sky. The other Virtues had dropped to the ground to battle the Sins, using their wings to fly as needed.

Spinning in a circle, Dani assessed the battlefield. Jamie and Thea helped Walker against Leviathan at the opposite end of the valley. They must have lured him away from Leyla and Kelsey so the Princess of Hell could shut the portal. Thankfully, demons weren't pouring through the hellmouth.

But Apalla and Raphaela teamed up against Mammon, like in the previous battles, to shoot beams of sunlight at the prince. Emmett held his own against Beelzebub, but his blood-stained and torn clothes suggested things weren't going well.

Kova and Ronnie battled Belial, and with the Humility's help, Kova seemed to be gaining the upper hand. But as Dani watched the insanity of battle unfolding around her—not only the war against the Sins, but the Knights battling the lesser demons—the situation changed. Sins swapped opponents or Virtues did, never fighting one opponent for too long.

Elliot was nowhere to be seen, but the other six Sins kept the Virtues and Hayden's circle busy. This war... it was Hell on Earth...

Closest to Dani, Mila battled Belphegor, the Sin of Sloth. A sonic blast of power rocketed from the Virtue of Diligence, blasting into Belphegor. Mila's powers shook the demon to his core. The leather band tying his hair back in a bun had come undone, so his wavy black locks framed his face. His grey sweats were stained and torn from the battle, and sand covered his torso. But as Mila forced him to a knee, the girl trembled. If anyone needed help, it was her.

Rushing forward, Dani called upon the power of Chastity and the water magic that answered so easily. Fifty feet from Mila and Belphegor, she saw the devil's trap.

Raising her hands to deliver another sonic shock of magic, Mila stepped forward into the radius of his time magic.

"Mila!" Dani cried out in warning, but it was too late.

Belphegor surged to his feet and closed the gap between the Virtue and Sin, trapping Mila in his time magic.

Pushing harder and pumping her arms, Dani ran like she had never run before. Angel wings pumped at her back, using the air currents to propel her forward. Belphegor couldn't hold the time freeze forever. Sex seconds. Five. Four.

The Sin of Sloth raised a single hand, protracting his claws. Three. Two.

If Dani could reach Mila before he—

Belphegor's clawed hand plunged into Mila's chest as he released the magic suspending her in time.

Pain rippled through her body as she released a scream that curdled Dani's blood.

Wrenching his fist from her chest, Belphegor withdrew her beating heart, and Mila dropped to the ground in a heap. Scarlet liquid puddled under her body.

Oh, Goddess. How could one body contain so much blood?

Dani spun in a circle, looking for Hayden, looking for another Virtue, looking for anyone in desperation. "KOVA," Dani screamed, her throat burning from how loud she strained her voice box. "Diligence." She thrust a finger at Mila's fallen body surrounded by a puddle of blood. Teal light tore away from Mila as her soul left this realm for the Virtue to hover in the air above the fallen witch.

Abandoning her fight, Kova's head snapped toward where Dani pointed. Sharp green eyes widened at the sight, but the centuries-old witch didn't miss a beat, spooking in a flash of dark green light.

Grinning vindictively, Sloth bared his fangs and reached a clawed hand toward the Virtue's soul. Dani's stomach turned at the thought of what the touch of a Sin would do to a Virtue's unprotected soul.

Rematerializing in front of Sloth, Kova unleashed a blast of gold lightning that threw the Sin with the force of a bomb. Nodding to Dani, Kova leaped into the mist of Diligence hovering in the air. As golden Spirit magic mixed with the Virtue, just like it had when Hayden bonded with Patience, Kova bonded with Diligence, keeping the Virtue alive and its power relevant in this battle against the Sins.

"You okay?"

When Dani nodded, the Salem Witch tore after Belphegor, leaving Mila's lifeless body in a puddle of crimson blood.

Carnage. Carnage surrounded her.

Dani sprinted the remaining distance between her and Mila and slid to her knees beside the fallen Virtue. Mila's blood sloshed over Dani's torn and stained jeans.

Cold blue eyes stared lifelessly at Dani. Dani reached a hand under Mila's body and hauled her up, clutching Mila to her chest.

Mila. Oh, Goddess. Mila's sisters.

Dani's blood ran cold, her body numb to the heat of battle blazing around her as she rocked back and forth. Water magic swirled around the two Virtues, draining the red blood from their clothes and cleaning Mila's hair to return it to its usual pristine blonde.

Get up, a rough male voice demanded, one Dani did not recognize. *Rise, Daniella. Fight!*

Snapping her head up, Dani searched for the origin of the foreign voice, but the only male around was Abaddon.

The Sin of Wrath charged her.

Fear and anger pierced her heart. How *dare* he interrupt her mourning.

Gently laying Mila's body on the dried earth, Dani rose to her feet. Abaddon had the might of Wrath and the powers that came with it. But Dani had Chastity.

And Chastity latched onto the love in Dani's heart, the love she had for Mila despite Diligence's flaws, the love she knew Mila had for her sisters and the things she did for that love. Love powered Chastity's nullifying power until Dani glowed brighter than a bonfire.

Water whipped at her command, ready to defend its witch against the Sin of Wrath.

A mix of nullifying magic and water plowed toward Wrath and before he could dodge the magical assault, Dani's magic hit him with full force. Abaddon's size visually shrank as his Wrath powers subsided further, already depleted from the divine storm, leaving him with uninflated muscles. He had the speed, strength, and agility of a fallen angel, but at least one hit from him wouldn't pulverize Dani. Unlike last time, Dani wasn't protected by the laws that prevented him from engaging her in mortal battle.

Abaddon sought her blood.

Dani surged at him, her wings propelling her forward as she threw an ice dagger. Dodging her water attack, Abaddon smoothly side-stepped her and rammed an elbow into her spine.

Sand slipped under her feet as she struggled to get her footing. When she steadied herself, she realized Abaddon was only just keeping up with her whereas before, he would have annihilated her already.

For the Sin of Wrath, he sure had a lot of patience as he watched her with those anger-filled eyes. He didn't want to kill her when she had defiance in her heart. He wanted to break her until she was defenseless and terrified, begging for her life.

But Dani would never. She would never give him the satisfaction. If she was going to die, then she would take him with her. And Chastity was with her, pushing that nullifying blue light into his body.

They were equally matched...

"I've waited seven hundred years for this, *Daniella*." Abaddon licked his lips as though he could taste her scent on the air. "To watch the light leave your eyes as I rid you from this world, from *my* world. I cannot fight the angels directly, but you and little *Michaelina* will be more than enough vengeance this time. They so hate it when you die."

He was a lunatic. Dani had no idea what he was talking about, except the part about him killing her. Not gonna happen.

The wound Dani and Hayden had inflicted on his chest oozed black blood and what looked like demonic pus. Hayden dealt a fatal blow to Abaddon, and though he wasn't dead yet, Dani could use it to her advantage.

Raising Nightmare again, Dani rushed Wrath, never tearing her gaze away from his vile smile. His serrated blade swung at her, and she ducked. She stabbed at his abdomen, but the serrated sword caught Nightmare on one of its grooves.

Pulling it free before he could twist the sword and disarm her, Dani sliced at him again and again, but every time she struck, Nightmare clanged against metal. Water swirled around her, freezing in a shield of ice around her blade as she blocked attacks from Abaddon.

Daggers of ice shot at him as Nightmare struck, but the ice shattered harmlessly against his impenetrable skin. Impenetrable except for the stab wound on his chest. As Dani battled Wrath, the leader of the Sins, she slowed. Her ineffective blasts of water were weaker, and Nightmare no longer whistled through the air with the speed and intensity of before.

But she had to keep fighting. If she stopped fighting, she was dead. And Chastity hadn't given up yet, still pulsing around the Sin and Virtue with blue light, nullifying any Hell magic that neared Dani.

An ice dagger sank into the wound on his chest, eliciting a furious roar from the Sin. Dani stabbed Nightmare at his chest, angling the angel's blade to pierce his black heart and end him once and for all.

Before Nightmare could strike its target, Abaddon caught it on his serrated blade and twisted, wrenching the obsidian Angel Blade from Dani's hand and sending it flying.

Dani stared in horror as Nightmare smashed into the ground fifty feet from where she now stood defenseless before the Sin of Wrath.

A foot slammed into her chest, knocking the wind from her lungs, and Dani sailed backward until her back slammed into the ground. Wheezing, she attempted to suck in air to relieve her burning lungs, but the muscles in her chest constricted. Finally, sweet, blessed air filled her lungs.

If it weren't for her Chastity powers, Abaddon's wound, and the Virtues' divine storm, that kick would have killed Dani. Her ribs must have cracked, based on the unbelievable pain rocking through her.

Abaddon's angry red body appeared in her blurred vision as he stood over her. With his serrated blade raised overhead, Abaddon grinned down at the Virtue of Chastity.

This was it. This was the end. Dani would die without taking out even one of the Sins.

"Remind Michael this would end if he fought me himself." Abaddon's gruesome smile grew wider. "*Michaelina* is next. Immortal or not, she will die, and her body will burn beside yours, *Daniella*. One day, I will steal you both, for all eternity."

Abaddon's serrated sword sailed toward her throat.

CHAPTER FIFTEEN

A LIGHT IN THE DARK

Abaddon's serrated sword sailed toward her throat.

Blood splattered across Dani's face as a blade struck home.

Black blood.

Blinking through the confusion, Dani's eyes settled on the flaming sword protruding from Abaddon's heart, to match the fatal wound Dani and Hayden dealt the Sin the night Dani battled him.

Dani stared at Hayden, her heart not daring to beat as she tried to breathe. Hayden saved her life by an inch.

Extending a hand to her, Hayden said, "Why must you fight Abaddon in every Apokalypsis War?"

"I do?" Dani's face twisted in confusion.

Hauling Dani to her feet, Hayden shrugged. "My father told me when I borrowed his sword." She raised the flaming silver sword. "*Flame of Death*. Cool name, huh?" She waggled her eyebrows. "It can burn away the darkest of Evil, incinerating demons upon contact" She pursed her lips. "I probably should have thought about that before I touched it. Eh, oh well. Turned out fine."

Dani stared at the sword with wide eyes, pressing a hand to her abdomen. Tearing her gaze from the magnificent sword was an effort, but necessary as she used water magic to heal the wounds peppering her body.

"Abaddon—" His body... it was gone. Where he had fallen laid a pile of black ash, slowly dispersing as the wind gusted around them. And the entity of the Sin... it had returned to Hell when its mortal vessel was vanquished.

"One down, five to go. Ope—" Hayden pointed over Dani's shoulder to where Jamie stabbed a staff tipped with a deadly spear made of what looked like a sharpened blue crystal into Belial's black heart. "Make that four."

The illusionary powers of the Sin of Pride shattered like glass, and a chunk of black demons around Belial disappeared. Purple hellfire turned to steam as Ronnie doused it with holy water they had blessed before the battle. White holy flames flickered to life as Jamie ignited Belial's corpse with heavenly fire.

"Belial always was the most worthless of the Sins." Hayden laughed at her own joke. "Pun not intended. Gabriel renounced him from Heaven. Belial induced nightmares and make fears come to life, but Empyrean, Gabriel's speared staff, is his nightmare—a stark reminder of his worthlessness compared to the might of Heaven. It's no surprise the Ronnie and Jamie renounced him so quickly."

"Your parents' angelic blades..." Dani scanned the battlefield for Kova until she found the curved golden sword in her hand as she fought Leviathan. Uriel's sickled blade after which early humans modeled their harvesting blades.

"Archangel Blades are fatal to angels... especially fallen ones." Hayden's dark smile should have sent a chill through Dani, but instead, relief coursed through her.

Dani had been so wrapped up in her own fight that she didn't notice earlier when Kova repelled Belphegor with her mother's sickle blade, *Shuhadaku*. No wonder the Sin of Sloth hightailed it away from the Nephilim of Earth after she blasted him with magic.

Hayden pointed across the valley, "Emmett needs our help."

"What about the others?"

"Thea can hold her own against Belphegor, and Raphaela is amplifying Apalla's sunlight powers against Mammon. My demons are giving Elliot one heck of a fight. But Emmett is alone against Beelzebub, and with Gluttony's siphon powers, I'm not sure how much longer Temperance can hold on."

Black light swallowed Dani whole before her combat boots slammed into the ground next to Emmett, who shined with an orange glow as he maintained a shield against Beelzebub. But with each passing second, the shield shrank.

A bolt of black lighting thundered from the sky, smashing into Beelzebub so hard, a crater formed under his body.

Hayden smirked. "I *love* doing that." A smaller bolt of silver lightning shot into Emmett as Hayden transferred Spirit magic to him to rejuvenate his lost energy. "Any ideas?"

Emmett shook his head, clamoring to his feet. "You're the one with that sword." He gestured to Flame of Death. "Can't we just stab him?"

"Great idea. Why didn't I think of that?" Hayden rolled her eyes sarcastically. "Flame of Death may be an Angel Blade, but Beelzebub can siphon the magic out of it before I can get close enough to kill him."

Beelzebub climbed out of the small crater in the sand, his jeans torn and burnt and his sport coat ripped at the shoulder. His coppery hair frizzled at the ends as Hayden hit him with another, smaller lightning bolt that stopped him in his tracks. But as soon as the lightning coursed through him and grounded into the earth, he took another step toward them, a heinous smile twisting his lips. Lightning couldn't stall him forever.

"What archangel helped Temperance defeat him in Heaven?"

"Azriel, the Archangel of Death." Hayden hesitated. "And my father's ancestor. The celestial of House Black."

"Beelzebub is the Sin of Gluttony," Emmett reminded them. "He siphons power from *everything*. The more magic we throw at him, the stronger he becomes."

"Exactly," Dani declared triumphantly. "Beelzebub swells himself with magic and power, right? Azriel, who represents death and lacks the power of life, teamed up with Temperance, who by definition represents moderation and self-restraint, to defeat the Sin of Gluttony."

"Why can't he siphon your lightning bolts?"

"Spirit magic," Hayden answered simply, hitting the Sin with another one. "Sins can't absorb powers from the Spirit." As soon as her lightning hit him, Beelzebub shook off the electrical shock and took another step toward the trio.

"Hayden's our Azriel, right? She's basically death walking."

"Um, thanks?" She didn't bother to look at the Virtues as she threw another bolt at Gluttony.

"I fail to see how this helps?" Emmett threw his hands in the air. "Even lightning isn't killing him. With my shield up, I can only attack with earth magic, but he just siphons it."

"But he can't siphon holy magic. He can't siphon your shield."

"We still can't kill him," Emmett pointed out.

"We don't need elemental magic."

"Ohhhh," Hayden drew out the word and nodded her head furiously. "I get it."

"You can shield our blades," Dani explained. "That's the whole point of your power—it protects us from being siphoned, so we can attack with Nightmare and Flame of Death."

"Oh," Emmett breathed out, his eyes widening. "Oh."

"Oh, good," Hayden chimed in off-handedly. "Jamie and Thea skewered Belphegor."

Dani glanced past Hayden to see Jamie rip Empyrean from Belphegor's naked chest and kick his dead fallen angel body to the ground. Emerald green magic danced in the air as Thea recalled her magic from where it held Belphegor's body so Jamie could stab him.

"Three down," Dani said.

"Three to go," Hayden added.

"Four." Emmett frowned. "Four to go."

Hayden shared a look with Dani. "If she decides to kill Elliot."

Emmett opened his mouth to argue, but Hayden didn't give him the opportunity. "I'll spook us closer to Beelzebub. As soon as I do, throw up a shield around yourself, Emmett," Hayden commanded. Then wrap a shield around each of our swords. If you can't hold both—"

"Shield Hayden's," Dani interjected. Hayden opened her mouth to refute, but Dani said, "You have a better chance of killing him, and we both know it. Shield Flame of Death, and I'll use Chastity to nullify his powers."

Emmett cracked his neck. "Let's do it."

Hayden spooked. An instant later, they appeared ten yards from Beelzebub. Orange light burst to life as Emmett threw a shield around himself and around Michael's sword. Orange light flickered around Nightmare, then faltered. Emmett's fear filled eyes met Dani's.

Splitting his magic three ways was too much. They were lucky he could maintain the shield around Flame of Death.

Hayden launched into action.

"Don't worry about it," Dani shouted before spinning on her heel and half-sprinting, half-flying after the Warrior Witch who was slamming her father's longsword down on Beelzebub's head.

Moving with the strength and agility of a fallen angel, Beelzebub blocked her attack and countered. The Warrior Witch wasn't even breathing hard as she dodged and counterattacked.

Beelzebub slammed his sword against Michael's so hard that a tremor raced down the length of the blade. Fear ripped through Dani as Emmett's orange shield flickered around Flame of Death.

Normally, Hayden would have the advantage with her ability to summon the five elements, but only black lightning and white holy flames surrounded her since Beelzebub could siphon the other elements.

But he couldn't siphon Chastity.

If the shield dropped, not only would Hayden's powers would be useless against a Sin who could absorb the energy and use it for himself, but Flame of Death would be vulnerable.

Before Dani could try to summon her nullifying power, Hayden knocked Beelzebub to his knees. As she lunged in for the kill, he released a roar that resonated with the might of Hell. Twisting, he surged to his feet, swinging his arm as he did so. Catching Hayden by surprise, he backhanded her so hard, she flew a hundred yards, slammed into the ground, then skidded another ten.

Limbs twisted at odd angels, broken from the force of the landing. Enough force to break the bones of a demon princess.

Beelzebub's malicious grin greeted Dani. The divine storm had worn off. The Sins had reclaimed their full strength.

She nearly stopped breathing from the panic clawing her chest. Beelzebub was the one she feared most. More than Abaddon. Because Beelzebub could steal their life forces, the magic that made them witches. The magic bestowed on them for the sole purpose of defeating the Sins. And if he stripped that away, what was left?

Love, an ethereal, otherworldly voice seemed to answer. *My love. And My love never fails.*

Beelzebub stepped toward Dani, and with self-control she didn't know she possessed, she rooted her feet instead of fleeing. Raising another hand with a viciously triumphant smile, Beelzebub took another step toward her. Orange light appeared around Nightmare as Emmett summoned a shield for her.

Behind Beelzebub, Hayden summoned water magic to heal her body, but she would never make it in time to save Dani—too many bones were broken. Twisted at an unnatural angle, her neck looked broken, but her immortality rooted her to this plane. She felt every ounce of pain, and it was etched on her face.

The Sin of Gluttony was only steps away.

Dani was on her own.

And the love you have for Me and My creation. So much of it that you sacrifice yourself in every life to save My children.

Chastity stirred inside her chest.

And for once, she wasn't afraid.

Another step. Beelzebub reached for her.

If the Goddess deemed her worthy of Her love, enough that She spoke words directly into Dani's head, then Dani was virtuous enough to wield Chastity. Calling on the love the Goddess spoke of, Dani thrust a metaphysical hand into her chest, grabbed the spool of magic with a fist and dragged it to the surface.

Blue, nullifying light exploded with the force of a waterfall and crashed into Beelzebub. Stumbling under the force of her Virtue, Beelzebub crumpled on himself but remained upright.

But then Dani heard it—the laughter. He was *laughing* at her.

"Chastity is strong within you, *girl*," he sneered the word at her. "Strong enough to make Abaddon fear you." His gruesome scowl deepened as he stepped toward her again. "But Abaddon was a *fool*." Another step. "You might nullify my siphon." A clawed hand reached up, stretching for her. Two steps away. "But you are human. You are *weak*. What is a mere mortal against the strength of an angel?"

Beelzebub stepped toward her, his movements lazy as those he were bored with the battle. Dani reacted on sheer instinct driven by fear.

He was right. She nullified his powers—her saving grace right now—by clinging to the love of the Goddess, but if he touched her, if he grabbed hold of her, he could tear her in half.

Dani was *so* dead.

Dodging under his arm, Dani spun, her wings steering her and she sliced Nightmare at his ribs, but it glanced off the metal sword that was suddenly there.

He moved *so fast*.

Light flashed as his sword stabbed toward her neck. Throwing herself out of the way, Dani wasn't sure how she avoided his strike. Tripping over a rock, she lost her footing, then stumbled to the ground.

Metal surged at her, and she barely raised Nightmare in time to stop the attack. Metal clashed against metal in a resounding ring, and Dani buckled under the weight of his strike, her arms quivering as they fought gravity and the weight of an angel's strength.

Full strength.... When Dani fought against Abaddon in previous battles, he was weakened by Hayden's magic or by the balancing laws of the Apokalypsis War.

Beelzebub's preppy boat shoe appeared in her vision. Throwing herself backward, she avoided getting her nose shattered, but in doing so, she laid on her back, her upper body resting on her elbows.

Nightmare was still clutched in her hands, but as Beelzebub raised his sword over his head, still surrounded by her blue cloud of Chastity sapping him of his siphon powers, Dani knew her Virtue couldn't save her now.

This was it. This was how she died. Like in every Apokalypsis War before this one.

Dani was tempted to close her eyes, but the flash of crystal blue eyes stopped her.

Red light crashed into Beelzebub's body. Gluttony's face slackened and his tongue rolled out of his mouth as Patience's hypnotizing power paralyzed him. Dani leaped to her feet, swinging Nightmare. The obsidian blade arced through the air as Dani sliced her Angel Blade through Beelzebub's neck, severing his head from his shoulders. Before his head hit the ground, she stabbed Nightmare through his heart. Black blood squirted from his chest cavity, splattering Dani, but she couldn't care less as her legs gave out beneath her. Collapsing, she breathed out the air trapped in her lungs by fear.

This was the second time Hayden saved Dani from certain death. Hayden was the queen in this game of chess, Dani was the pawn used as bait. But at least this time, Dani dealt the killing blow.

"Who is next?" Emmett asked their war leader as she stared between the final battles being waged in the valley.

"I am," said an all too familiar voice.

Dani rocketed to her feet to find Elliot prowling toward them, his black eyes glinting with malicious intent as every bit of darkness in him raged at the light inside of her.

No, no, no. She was so not ready to deal with him yet.

"Emmett—help the others against Leviathan. But don't kill him yet. We need to seal the portal." Hayden pivoted. "Dani—Mammon can transmute blades before we can stab him. He can't transmute Apalla's sunlight, but sunlight won't kill him. Use Chastity to nullify his alchemical powers so somebody can stab him. I'll handle Elliot."

"But Elliot is Lust, and you can't harm him. I should stay and fight him."

"No," Hayden said adamantly, her crystal blue gaze searching Dani's brown one. "You're not in the headspace to make that decision right now, and I can't get near Mammon without him transmuting Flame of Death. If you nullify, one of us can kill him." Her eyes flicked to where Jamie battled the Sins, and Dani understood how painful it must have been for

Hayden to restrain herself to fight here instead of alongside her soulmate.

Blue light haloed around Dani at the thought, causing Hayden to smirk. "Go. You've got this."

With a light shove from Hayden and a final glance at a glowering Elliot, Dani turned on her heel and sprinted toward Apalla and Raphaela.

Unyielding sunlight blinded her, doubled by the rays bouncing off Mammon's perfectly polished golden watches. She blinked the spots from her eyes as she slid to a halt between the Prophetess and Charity.

"Have you tried using your fire magic from afar?" Dani asked Raphaela. When she shook her head no, she asked the same about Apalla's air magic.

"No. Sunlight repels him, but air can't kill him. I didn't see any point in needlessly wasting energy until someone with an Angel Blade arrived."

"Nightmare is an Angel Blade. I just need to get within range."

Apalla clicked her tongue. "Not gonna be easy. You can nullify his alchemy, but he's as strong as Beelzebub, and I'm not sure how you didn't die fighting him now that the divine storm wore off."

"Hey," Dani whined in protest. But she wasn't wrong. They needed a better plan.

"HAYDEN," Kova screamed from where she battled Leviathan. The hilt of Uriel's sickled Angel Blade protruded from a rock and Leviathan's monstrous body separated Kova from her mother's blade. Golden lightning sparked around Kova and Jamie as she relied on the power of the elements to repel Leviathan, but neither Nephilim could spook to retrieve her blade as they wielded holy flames to protect Emmett, Walker, and Ronnie from the hellfire spewing from the demonic dragon's mouth.

There went their plan.

Abandoning her fight with Elliot, Hayden spooked to *Shuhadaku* and retrieved it. As soon as the Angel Blade was in Kova's hand, Hayden stepped into the hellfire and released a counter-stream of white flames.

Crap. Crap! If Hayden was battling Leviathan with the others, then nobody engaged Elliot. He would come for Dani.

She had to end Mammon. Now.

"I can weaken his physical form by leaching his strength through the earth." Thea appeared out of nowhere, her long box braids swinging around her waist as she moved. "You must nullify his demonic powers and stab him."

"I'll distract him with sunlight," Apalla said, blasting another beam at the fallen angel. "Raphaela, can you amplify both me and Dani?"

"If you were both standing here, yes, but not if you're separated by distance."

"That's okay," Dani said as she illuminated with baby blue light. "I don't need it." Chastity was answering her command now, easier than ever. Maybe it was because she encountered the Goddess last night, or maybe it was because she finally understood what it was like to love someone as much as Goddess loved her and Dani loved the Goddess. But either way, she could do this. With the others fighting alongside her, she could kill Mammon.

"When you hit him with Chastity, I'll drain his strength," Thea explained. "Go!" She pushed Dani toward the Sin of Greed.

Flying toward the smirking demon prince on wings of blue Spirit, Dani wondered when she lost her mind? But knew it hinged entirely on Hayden's influence.

Raising a clawed hand, Mammon pointed a twisted finger at Nightmare. The metal shook in Dani's hand

Oh, heck to the no! Hayden would kill Dani if Nightmare was transmuted on her watch.

Chastity's blue magic shot forward like a beam of light and rammed into the Sin with the force to make the fallen angel stumble. Writhing vines shot from the earth to coil around his legs. Thornes stabbed into his flesh, drawing inky black blood to stain his hand-tailored suit. A howl tore from his lips as the thorns grew, then pulsed with emerald green light. Color drained from Mammon's deceptively beautiful face and his movements slowed. The lustrous hue of his golden locks dimmed, as though the gold had lost its value.

Reaching the Sin of Greed, Dani struck out with Nightmare, but Mammon caught it easily. Despite his sluggish movements, he was as fast as a normal witch. Yet thanks to Thea's Heart of Earth abilities, his strength waned to less than a fallen angel's such that when his sword clanged against Nightmare, Dani's teeth didn't rattle in her head like they had with Beelzebub.

Sunlight beamed into his eyes, blinding him for Dani to spin around his back and cut a jagged line diagonally over his angelic flesh, earning her a scream of pain.

Lashing out in a flurry of strikes, Dani rushed to sink her blade into the Prince of Hell, but he matched her stroke for stroke. As she stepped in to slice a shallow cut over his ribs, Mammon howled in pain, then shoved her roughly. With the strength of a mortal man, it was enough to topple the smaller woman.

Slicing down with his sword, Greed hacked at the vines ensnaring him. Horrifyingly, some of his ethereal glow returned to his skin, his golden curls shining with a lustrous gleam.

"No!" Thea screamed with pain, as though the blow was delivered to her body.

Surging to her feet, Dani called upon her water. Hayden said Dani's elemental powers were more profound than other witches because she was once a Virtue angel. Well, she was still a Virtue, and even in this barren wasteland of a battlefield, the element heralded her call.

Water splashed around her like ocean waves, listening to the command of her magic. Thrusting a hand forward, Dani shot the water at Mammon, who was busy hacking at the vines to regain his strength.

It was time to end this.

Water rushed over him with unyielding force. Keeping the water engulfing his whole body, Dani willed his lower half to freeze in a block of ice. Running forward, Nightmare in hand, she released the magic holding the liquid water, and the element splashed away from Mammon.

Spluttering, Greed gasped in air.

But it was too late.

Nightmare's black blade plunged into Greed's black heart, and Dani watched the shock slap him across the face before he stilled. Water soaked the ground as the block of ice melted, so Mammon was held up by the blade clutched in Dani's hand.

Kicking him off her blade, Dani watched with sick satisfaction. White flames shot from behind her to eviscerate the Sin of Greed to dust to be blown away on Apalla's wind.

Spinning around, Dani found Raphaela gawking at white holy flames burning in her cupped palms.

"You're an amplifier." Apalla beamed like a proud big sister. "Instead of amplifying everyone else's powers, you finally amplified your own. By accepting all of yourself and revealing your true nature to your fellow Virtues, you connected with your divine nature, which allowed you to summon holy flames."

"Would have been nice if those had manifested earlier," Raphaela muttered, then, watching Mammon's body finish burning to ash, she frowned. "That was a lot easier than I expected."

"That's because you're finally working together," Apalla intoned. "Whereas before, you all tried to combat the Sins on your own."

"I suspect the Sins have an advantage in remembering every previous war." Thea stared sadly at where her vines were hacked to bits. "They've come to know you and your ways in countless lifetimes while you remember nothing of your previous lives. By working together and fusing your magic, you become unpredictable, which allows you to obtain victory. Two remain. The most difficult to subdue."

Thea was right. The Sins were dead. The princes, once fallen angels, were now ash scattered on the wind. All of them except the King of Monsters and the one who was born mortal.

Elliot.

Who was coming for Dani's head.

Hayden... where was Hayden?

Dani spun around, frantically searching the battlefield. Surely a demon as weak and measly as Elliot hadn't defeated the Warrior Witch?

Air rushed from her lungs as Dani spotted the witch dressed in black fighting Leviathan with her father's Angel Blade.

Elliot's murderous gaze cut into her with nothing and no one standing between them. Nobody was coming to save her this time. It was just Dani and Elliot. The showdown that was always meant to be. The one that had been interrupted three years ago.

This time, Dani would not need saving.

"Go," Dani instructed Apalla and Raphaela, who exchanged an uncertain look. "Help the others. This fight is mine."

Elliot prowled toward her, his rapier dripping with scarlet blood. Fury gripped her heart at the sight, but it was nothing compared to the evil wafting from Elliot's aura. She didn't need Ronnie's powers to see the energy in his being.

Never in her life did Dani feel such intense hatred directed at her, not even from Lilith. Not that Lilith had known who Dani was, but it was widely known she despised mortals, the very thing she once was. Elliot may be more evil than her, which was remarkable and unsettling all at once.

"Ready for a rematch?" Elliot's guttural tone growled at her, his voice less than human.

"Believe me, Elliot," she brandished her sword, "it won't be much of a match."

Because looking at Elliot, she finally understood. She understood the source of her powers. She understood why her and Elliot were opposites. Elliot was a lost boy who refused the love of the Creator, and in his search for worldly love, he felt victim to Lust. But Chastity came from the Divine Mother, and Goddess was the embodiment of love. Dani had felt it the other night when Kova channeled the Goddess. Love, the purest energy of all, filled her. It was why she came to Earth. It was why she fought the Sins time and time again. And it was why she would win.

She didn't need to defeat him in combat—although she was confident she could—all she needed was love and the power of Chastity within her to render him powerless.

Reaching into her chest, Dani grasped hold of it—the love inside her, the love she felt for her brother, for her family, for her friends, for Hayden, for the Virtues... for the Goddess—and she let it fill her.

Powder blue light haloed around her, stretching in every direction as the power of Chastity flowed through her, more powerful than ever, even without Raphaela amplifying her.

Elliot's rapier sailed at her throat, but Dani dodged with ease, stepping into the witch to deliver a solid punch to his sternum. Her nullifying magic enveloped him, sucking the Hell magic from his body so her punch knocked the wind from his mortal lungs. Spinning around his back, she landed a solid kick to his tailbone, sending him sprawling into the mud. Lifting him by the shirt-collar, Dani pivoted and rammed her knee into his nose. Bone crushed under the force of her blow with a sickening crunch, and dark red blood flowed from his nose.

It was working!

Chastity's nulling was counteracting the powers of Hell that sustained his demonic nature. A rattling cough seized hold of his chest, shaking the Sin of Lust until he expelled blood from his lungs, redder than the blood from his nose.

Chastity... Her nullification was killing him. His mortal body couldn't survive without Hell magic... but why?

It didn't matter. Dani had to kill him. She had to end this war and the suffering he had caused. She had to kill him and banish Lust to the fiery depths of Hell where it belonged.

Leveling Nightmare to his throat, Dani prepared to deal the death blow.

Elliot raised his head, his palms splayed and coated with red blood—*mortal* blood...

She couldn't do it—she couldn't kill him.

Just like Hayden couldn't kill Lilith because she saw what nobody else could—Lilith was human once. And so was Elliot... before demons killed his family and framed it on witches—

That was it!

Dani didn't need to kill Elliot. She needed to resurrect his humanity—if he had any left.

He does, Hayden's voice answered in Dani's head though the Warrior Witch was on the other side of the canyon, battling Leviathan. *If you're ready, I can return his soul to his body by pulling it from the depths of Hell.*

The Sin of Lust surged at her, the point of his rapier poised to skewer her, but Dani side-stepped him gracefully. Spinning on the ball of her foot, she rammed her foot in his spine, sending him stumbling. Water rose at her command. Spraying it at him like a hose, Dani willed the water to surround him as Chastity engulfed him from head to toe.

Frantically, Elliot waved an arm to call upon his element of air, but Dani's water magic was faster. Solidifying around his arm, the water turned to ice. Willing the chill to enter her element, Dani wrapped the water around Elliot's entire body, leaving his head uncovered. With the might of a waterfall, the water forced him to his knees, then froze in an instant.

Ready!

Appearing in a flash of black light like death incarnate, Hayden surged toward the Prince of Hell to place her right hand on his heart and her left on the crown of his forehead.

Molten silver kissed her features as the Mark of the Goddess illuminated her. And while Dani couldn't see the Spirit magic at work, she knew Hayden reached her hand into the depths of Hell, as only a demonic princess could do, and seized hold of Elliot's soul. In a flash of silver light, Hayden returned his spirit to his mortal body, and his scream pierced the air. The heat of the magic melted Dani's ice from around him, and the water drained into the dry sand.

Wrenching away from him, Hayden stumbled backward and let him fall forward. His hands caught him before he face-planted into the dirt. Groaning, the Sin of Lust pushed himself upright, but remained on his knees.

Gasping, Dani stepped backward.

His eyes... they weren't black.... His irises were brown, like when he was a normal witch.

"You returned his soul. Like with Lilith."

"Yes," Hayden said the word quietly, staring at Elliot with suspicion as she summoned her father's sword to her hand, as though she didn't trust him even with a soul.

"No," Elliot gasped out the word as he clutched a hand over his heart. "No, no, no, no! You have to kill me. Hayden, please, kill me!"

"No. I've restored your soul, Elliot, and there is no escaping it. May you feel the full weight of the horror of your actions," Hayden growled, not an ounce of mercy in her tone.

"You don't understand." Elliot dug his hands into the dirt in front of him, panting for breath. "I feel *all* of it. Every sin." Tears welled in his eyes and poured down his cheeks. "And I regret it *all*." His brown eyes landed on Dani. "Kill me, Dani. Please," he begged her.

"You made your bed, Elliot," Dani answered, but a tinge of... something—unease maybe—twisted her gut.

"I can't," he cried out. "Please, I will take the punishment for it all, but not in this body."

Hayden's spine went ramrod straight as though lightning had struck her. And Dani sensed it... she sensed his desires shift as his soul was restored. His desire, his lust for power and vengeance gave way to desperation... desperation for redemption.

"I died." Elliot gasped out a breath. "My mortal body died while my soul was separated. Lucifer used necromancy to resurrect me. My body is kept alive with Hell magic. I cannot live without it, and my soul will return to *him*."

Dani looked to Hayden in alarm, but the Warrior Witch had gone sheet white. It was on Dani's shoulders.

"The Devil will not claim another soul, today." Dani kneeled before Elliot and placed a hand on his shoulder. "Repent, Elliot. Forgive yourself for what you've done and reform your soul before you pass on."

"I've done so many terrible things." Elliot shook his head, tears dripping from his eyes to soak into the dirt below. "Unforgivable things. The worst of them to you, Hayden. I'm not worthy of forgiveness. Your father... Hunter is dead because of me."

"Cain killed him," Hayden countered.

"But if I didn't side with Lilith, if I didn't fight with her against you, your father would have escaped before Cain intercepted you. Countless lives could have been spared if it wasn't for my spiteful choices."

"And countless lives could have been saved if it weren't for my shortcomings." Hayden blinked rapidly as tears welled in her eyes. "We're both to blame."

Elliot's arms gave out beneath him, and his torso would have tumbled into the dirt if it weren't for Dani holding him upright. "I have no one to blame but myself. There doesn't exist a soul that I've haunted as much as I tortured yours. I've caused you such pain, Hayden. I—" His voice broke. "I can never hope to absolve myself of the guilt."

"Well, too bad, Elliot Fox. You have to forgive yourself." Tears dripped from the Warrior Witch's crystal blue eyes. "I forgive you, Elliot." Hayden's stony exterior cracked as she hiccupped out a sob. "You are forgiven by me and the Mother and Father above. For all your sins against me and against humanity, for your repentance. I cannot save your mortal life, but if you wish, I can ease your passing."

The Prince of Hell, with his soul returned, reached out a hand, and Hayden kneeled in the dirt, accepting his offering. Gripping his hand tightly in hers, but keeping her father's sword drawn in her other, Hayden muttered a spell of death:

Bound by magic, Hell, and fear,
A soul imprisoned by Sin lives here.
With mortal body it does not belong,
Spirit above, help right this wrong.
Seize this soul and cross the Veil,
While body decays under coffin nail.
Break the chains enslaving this soul,
Divine Creator we give you control!
Virtue's victory has been won,
Death and darkness are overcome!

As the words passed Hayden's lips, Elliot's body glowed with radiant white light. Summoning it, Hayden gathered his soul in her palm and gripped it in her clenched fist, his immortal spirit at the mercy of the woman he had tormented unceasingly.

Lifting her enclosed fist to the sky, the Warrior Witch opened her hand to release twinkling balls of silver light. As they escaped her palm, the specs of light drifted upward, glittering against the night sky like stars illuminating the heavens until eventually they faded as Elliot's soul crossed into the Beyond.

"Dani." The Warrior Witch tugged on Dani's torn and burnt shirt sleeve, urging her to turn around. "Leviathan." She gestured with her father's sword to where the other Virtues, minus Mila, battled the Sin of Envy.

More like struggled.

The Virtues couldn't get near him to land a blow, only shoot magic at him from afar. Even Jamie and Kova were repelled by the angry green hellfire burning around his body. Holy flames arced through the air to counteract the hellfire, and Kova wielded Diligence's sonic blast, yet the Nephilim couldn't gain the upper hand.

"Do you think you can call upon Chastity power again?"

Dani searched her heart for the compassion she just experienced, the ache she suffered on behalf of Elliot, a young witch whose soul was corrupted too easily by the Darkness. Chastity rose to meet her magical touch, enraged by the injustice Lust had dealt against the world.

"Get me close to him."

CHAPTER SIXTEEN

THE HOLY VIRTUES

Black light surrounded the witches as Hayden spooked them into the middle of the fight. But it wasn't where Dani expected. Instead of taking them to Leviathan, Hayden spooked to her mother.

"What's taking so long?" she demanded.

"I can't close the portal while demons are coming through," Leyla grunted. "And I can't stop them crossing the portal and close it at the same time." A killer bee demon surged through the portal as Leyla attempted to close it.

"Kelsey—"

She shook her head as she stabbed a brimstone demon. "I tried. My magic won't penetrate the portal. With angelic blood, my magic won't cross dimensions. That or Leviathan's power is countering mine."

Hayden's blue gaze snapped to Dani's. "Can you concentrate your Chastity magic to affect the portal without compromising mine and my mom's magic?"

Hesitating, Dani bit her lip and glanced at the swirling portal that reminded her of vomit. Nasty green envy as monstrous as the fallen angel who commanded it.

"Dani?" Hayden snapped.

"Yes." Dani straightened her shoulders. She had fought Abaddon, not once, but twice, and survived, then killed Mammon with her own two hands after killing Beelzebub with Hayden's help. If she could do that, then she could direct Chastity to close the portal.

"I'll push my magic into the portal to repel the demons," Hayden explained. "You push your magic at Leviathan's power keeping the portal open. Together, you and my mom can close it. Okay?"

Dani nodded, glancing at Leyla, whose brow was coated in a sheen of sweat as she struggled to hold her magic. She was exhausted from stifling the flow of demons entering this world. Dani wasn't sure if Leyla could close the portal on her own.

"Why can't you seal it while Leyla repels the demons?"

No sooner had the words left Dani's mouth than a pterodactyl demon soared through the mouth of the juniper-colored portal.

"That's why." Hayden pointed a finger at the demon and shot off a tongue of holy flames to incinerate the pterodactyl. "Every time a demon crosses the portal, it renews the portal to its full size. It will be easier for me to repel the demons and for Mom to close the portal." She flinched. "I am admittedly poor at that kind of magic. Ripping open a portal to Hell—no problem. Closing it—I'm a better healer."

Leviathan released an unruly roar. Hayden started forward, but stopped herself, flinching at the sight.

Dani whirled around.

Jamie must have stabbed Leviathan in the leg with Gabriel's staff, but it wasn't enough to kill him, and the Prince of Hell threw Jamie hard enough to knock him unconscious when he hit the ground.

Electricity vibrated over Hayden's skin as she physically restrained herself from rushing to her soulmate's side. The love between them... the self-control and will power it must have required for Hayden to act in obedience to her responsibilities rather than act according to what she wanted… Love blossomed inside Dani's chest.

Blue light haloed around her again, and as Chastity filled every fiber of her being, she knew with absolute certainty that she could close Leviathan's portal.

"Let's do this."

Whirling on her heel, Hayden shot black magic into the portal with the force of a tsunami. Stumbling backward, Dani struggled to regain her footing on the shaking earth. Shaking from the power Hayden pumped against the portal as Hell fought vehemently against her magic.

Leyla gasped, her spine arcing painfully as Hayden zapped her with Spirit magic. As the energy absorbed into her, she fell forward again, her spine loose, and threw her hands out. Pastel purple magic flowed from her palms to wrap around the edges of the portal.

Focusing her attention inward, Dani sought the spool of Chastity magic housed in her chest, and, ever so carefully, she grabbed a single strand and pulled to unravel the magic. Threading the powder blue magic toward the portal, Dani carefully spun the magic into a tight coil so she could pass it between Hayden and Leyla without hindering their demonic magic. As Chastity approached the portal, a dark force pushed against Dani.

Oh, Leviathan did *not* think he could overcome her Virtue magic. It didn't matter if he was a fallen angel. Dani was a null that chastened Hell magic, and Hell would choke on her power.

Thrusting her magic forward like pushing knife into a gut, Chastity overcame the resistance and plunged into the portal. The color of Leviathan's magic dulled. As Dani's pastel blue magic mingled with Leyla's lilac magic, the swirling of the portal slowed, and color faded.

Unwinding more power from the magical spool inside her, Dani fed more magic into the portal, faster and faster until the juniper green stopped swirling. Leyla's magic ate at the portal from the edges, reducing the diameter as she shrank the portal.

A shriek pierced the air. Dani squeezed her eyes shut for half a second before flaring them open. Faster. They needed to go faster. The other Virtues needed her.

Energy seared her from the inside.

Come on, Chastity, Dani pleaded with herself, with the magic inside her. *More*. She could do this. She had to do this. *Love. Think about love.*

Squeezing her eyes shut, she recalled the memories she witnessed mere minutes ago. The love with which Hayden treated Elliot, despite years of hatred between them. Hayden had forgiven him and blessed his repentance so he may find peace on the other side of the Veil. If that wasn't the love of the Creator channeling through her, Dani didn't know what was.

Magic flared inside her chest to the point of painful, and when she opened her eyes, Dani found her blue magic glowing brighter than before.

"Almost there," Leyla grunted.

Pastel blue and purple magic mixed effortlessly, chewing away at the nasty portal. As their magic unraveled Leviathan's portal, they left behind a shimmering residue on the barren patch of earth. The portal was shrinking. Where it had been the size of a house before, now it stretched three feet in diameter.

Dani pushed with all her might, channeling all the love she could muster into closing this portal and saving the world. Saving the ones she loved. She pushed and pushed and pushed until there was nothing left to give.

Flaring bright like a shooting star, her magic surged one final time to obliterate the last of Leviathan's magic.

With a resounding "BOOM", Leviathan's juniper-colored portal slammed shut, releasing a shockwave of power that would have thrown Dani across the valley had it not been for the shield of Spirit magic Hayden manifested around the three women and Kelsey.

A roar echoed from Leviathan as the trio of witches ceased the havoc of his Hell magic, but Dani didn't dare seek out the fallen angel as she huddled behind Hayden who stood as an unyielding pillar against the Hell magic. The overwhelming pressure pushing against Dani evaporated abruptly.

Leyla collapsed, her black hair sprawling over the sand where the portal once was as she ceased the flow of magic.

Catching herself from falling by bracing her hands on her knees, Dani sucked in a rattly breath. Power zapped into her as Hayden infused her with Spirit, and strength like none other filled her, renewing the life inside her and pouring power into the well of magic inside her chest.

Hayden's face appeared in front of hers.

"How are you holding up?"

"Better now." Dani glanced at Leyla, who lay unconscious. "What about her?"

Hayden didn't glance at her mother as she zapped her with Spirit magic. "Kelsey will get my mom out of here. You and I aren't done." Hayden pointed over Dani's shoulder. "We have a Sin to kill."

Whirling around, the Virtue of Chastity spied her fellow Virtues fighting for their lives against the king of monsters.

Holding a hand out to Hayden, Dani didn't peel her eyes off Leviathan as ruthless determination filled her. Chastity responded with eagerness, ready to nullify the last Sin and claim victory in this war.

"No one else dies today," Dani said.

"No one else dies today," Hayden echoed, taking her hand and spooking them across the valley to join the other Virtues fighting the dragon monster the size of a titan.

Releasing Dani's hand, Hayden rushed to her soulmate's side to check on him after Leviathan had knocked him out cold. Didn't matter if he was immortal and would recover—soulmates couldn't bear to see one another harmed. Luckily,

Jamie was on his feet again, blasting balls of white holy flames at the Sin.

"Now can we kill him?" Walker shouted.

Flame of Death appeared in Hayden's hand again, eliciting a bestial roar from the monster. He recognized a blade that could kill him.

"Now we kill him," Hayden agreed.

"I'm not so sure about that." Jamie shook his head. "We have to stab him in his heart—"

"But we can't find it," Kova cut him off. "It's hidden somewhere in that beast of a body of his. He moves its location to avoid our attacks. Ronnie can see it in his energy field."

As Leviathan's gruesome howl faded, every soulless demon snapped to attention. Demons abandoned their fights against the Knights to flock toward Leviathan. Throwing themselves over the King Monster, demons willingly sacrificed themselves as demon shield. What demons didn't throw themselves between Hayden and the demon prince, attacked the Virtues.

Gold and black lightning mixed with white holy flames, and beams of golden sunlight and green earth magic blasted the demons.

"And now we have to fight through that before we can stab the monster." Kova glanced up at the Blood Moon. "We don't have much time left. If we don't banish him or kill him, Envy will have free reign in the world for the next seven hundred years."

Hayden cursed under her breath. "Spirit isn't speaking to me."

"Me neither," Kova agreed.

As her eyes landed on Dani, they widened with a shock of understanding. Hayden grabbed her by the shoulders, pulling her attention from the winged serpent. "Dani, when Kova channeled the Goddess, you mentioned you spoke with Jophiel—what did she say?"

"What? What do you mean?" Dani's brain was blank. Why did her conversation with Jophiel matter in the middle of a battle between Heaven and Hell? "What does Jophiel have to do with anything?"

"Because Jophiel was the archangel who defeated Leviathan with the help of Kindness. Archangels don't travel to the mortal realm because they feel like it. She had a reason."

"I-I-I don't know." Dani wracked her brain for any mention of Leviathan. "She didn't mention his name."

"She must have said something," Hayden insisted.

"Hayden!" Jamie shouted from where he and Kova battled the King of Serpents.

Her head swiveled on her shoulders, took in the situation, then cursed. "Dani, figure it out. You can do this."

The next second, Hayden's hands disappeared from Dani's shoulders as she rushed Leviathan with lightning speed.

Green hellfire blasted from his jaws, the heat so intense that Dani could feel it from over a hundred yards away. The Princess of Hell remained unaffected by the fire, but the force of his magic halted her approach. The Nephilim of Heaven could not land a blow on the King of Monsters.

"Just be thankful he's using his mouth to blow flames."

"What do you mean?" Dani asked Ronnie.

Lifting her hand, she pointed at what must have been different parts of his aura. "Leviathan can open portals to Hell right? Because he himself *is* a portal to Hell. His mouth is literally that—a Hellmouth. A portal to the abyss that would swallow us whole."

"Why hasn't he used it then?"

"If he does, we all end up in Hell, but so does he. And he doesn't want to be trapped there." She shrugged. "And I'm assuming Hell with Hayden would be worse for him than it would be for her."

Dani snorted.

No. No. No. Now was not the time to laugh.

She needed to focus. She needed to find a way to defeat Leviathan before he opened a Hellmouth and sucked them into another dimension—

Oh Goddess—that was it!

Jophiel did not visit Dani just because she found favor with the young water elemental—she passed along vital information. Maybe she didn't mention Leviathan, but she did talk about dimensions. Why couldn't the angels talk outright instead of in code?

So demons cannot interpret what we know. Only beings of light can interpret the coded words of an angel. Goddess's voice echoed in Dani's head, and she wondered what prompted the Goddess to speak to her sometimes and not others.

Dani's hand clamped around Ronnie's forearm. "Can you see where his heart is?"

She shook her head, sending her brunette braid whipping behind her as half her hair was torn from the plait. "I'm not fast enough to keep up with where he moves it. Every time I track it down, it has moved to the next location."

"What if I hit him with Chastity and nullify his powers? Can he move it?"

Ronnie's sharp eyes dashed to the beast's body before cutting back to Dani's. "I don't think so."

Nodding, Dani wordlessly grabbed the older witch by the hand and dragged her unceremoniously to where the other three crouched behind a boulder.

"We are hiding here, cowering while the Nephilim fight our battle," Emmett growled as the females joined them.

"It's not like we can get close to him," Raphaela pointed out.

"Let's summon a divine storm and drain him," Emmett suggested.

"We can't." Dani jabbed a thumb over her shoulder. "There's only five of us. We need six to form *Merkaba*. And Hayden and Kova are a little busy."

"They're not getting near Leviathan either." Walker peered around the boulder. "The ladies are putting everything they have into shielding us from the demon pawns and trying to obliterate the shield of demons protecting Leviathan. Jamie is guarding their backs."

"But you heard Kova," Emmett insisted, pointing up at the moon hanging low in the sky. "If we don't renounce Leviathan before the end of the Eclipse, he earns free reign in the world. We have to beat him. Or die trying." Sighing, he shook his head. "If I summon a shield around me—"

"It won't matter," Ronnie dismissed him. "You'll never get through the wall of demons."

"No, but Walker can." Dani looked at the Virtue of Kindness. "You can astral project. Walk through dimensions—walk through a wall of demons without touching them."

His eyes widened and his lips parted in surprise.

"And leave his body vulnerable to attack?" Raphaela scoffed. "We've avoided that in every battle for a reason, Dani."

"Now we don't have a choice," Dani fired back. "Mila is dead. And we're next if we don't try." Her brown eyes searched Walker's. "Ultimately, it's your call."

"Like you said before. It's my turn to deal Envy a devastating blow." He didn't hesitate. "What's your plan?"

"Emmett will stay here and shield yours and Raphaela's bodies."

"Raphaela will amplify Walker's and Ronnie's powers," Dani explained. "I'm going out there"—she pointed to where the Nephilim battled furiously against the forces of Hell—"to blast Leviathan with my nullifying power. Once I blast him, his heart should stop moving, and Ronnie can pinpoint its location. Walker, you can hear us when we speak to your body, right?" He nodded in confirmation. "Then Ronnie can direct you to his heart." Spinning Nightmare in her hand, Dani offered the pommel to the Virtue of Kindness. "Nightmare is an angel's blade. It will kill him as easily as the Flame of Death.

Since it's an Angel Blade, I think it will transfer dimensions with you."

"You *think*?" Emmett echoed skeptically. "What if it doesn't?"

"Then we're all dead," she responded callously.

"Fair point."

"I'm willing to try." Walker's eyes were filled with steel as he laid down next to Raphaela, Nightmare held firmly in his grasp, and closed his eyes.

Inhaling through his nose, the Virtue of Kindness called upon his power and a lime green glow emitted from him, then vanished as he projected into the astral world, bringing Nightmare with him. Dani breathed out a sigh of relief. He did it. He was astral walking, and he brought the Angel Blade with him as his neon green specter rushed across the field.

Dani prayed the demonic spirits could not sense him.

"Go," Emmett commanded her as he summoned a shield around them, the orb of magic pulsing with a faint orange tinge.

Surging to her feet, Dani sprinted around the boulder to follow Walker . Pumping her arms hard, she pushed herself, her legs screaming in protest. Blisters on her feet tore open as her combat boots dug into the sand.

Hayden gasped in surprise. "Dani."

The water witch thought Hayden would tell her that she shouldn't be here, that she should be hiding, sheltered behind the boulder with the other Virtues, but then she smiled a wicked smirk. "I'm assuming you figured it out?"

Nodding once she said, "Blast the demons attacking us. Let them protect Leviathan if they want. But I'll need you to clear a path through them so I can hit him with my power. You'll know when."

The battle-hardened witch regarded her quizzically, but didn't ask, just trusted as she called back her power and joined it with Kova's to blast away the attacking demons.

Putrid, rotten magic brushed against Dani's skin as Leviathan's energy washed over her, attempting to instill its Sin into her. But Dani's soul was not weak, but strong and dignified, especially against the Sins.

Disgust seized hold of Dani at the touch of the Sin as it tried to evoke jealousy in her heart. It preyed on her desire to have what Hayden and Jamie had. To possess such unending love. But the thing about love... Sin couldn't corrupt it. It was pure in all its forms... down to the Virtue of Chastity.

Blue magic haloed around her, stronger than the times she called it before. Those magical wings sprouted from her back and pumped, raising her into the air. Up, up, up, she went until she soared in the sky above Leviathan's head.

Black magic smashed into the wall of demons protecting the crown of Leviathan's head, decimating the lesser demons until they were nothing but ash on the wind. Other demons surged toward Leviathan to replace their fallen brethren and protect their king, but Dani was faster. *Chastity* was faster.

Virtuous magic hammered down on Leviathan's head.

The feelings of Envy trying to wash over her recoiled. Demons scurried to throw themselves between Leviathan and Dani's magic, but Heaven's power threw them backward before they could touch her beam of blue light.

Black and golden lightning danced around her as the Salem Witches sheltered her from demonic attacks. Flames of white flickered at the edge of her vision, but she felt the heat of Jamie's fire on her back, protecting her from her foes.

Chastity flooded Leviathan's grotesque body, pumping into him like a waterfall, and Dani felt it—Chastity cancelled his Hell magic, paralyzing his heart.

Now, Ronnie! Now! She screamed to herself as her arms shook from the effort of holding her nullifying magic. Her wings faltered, and she dipped in the sky before catching herself again, but she didn't let go of her stream of magic.

Silver lightning sparked against her skin as Hayden fueled her magic with Spirit, bringing reprieve to Dani's aching limbs. Her wings beat against the air in powerful strokes as Hayden pumped a constant stream of Spirit magic into Dani while fighting the onslaught of evil.

Daring a glance at the ground, Dani nearly fell out of the sky at the sight below her.

Walker's green spirit ran past Hayden's circle toward Leviathan, Nightmare in hand. Walker's astral form leaped through the wall of demons, passing harmlessly through them.

"Dani!" Hayden screamed her name, pulling her attention away from Walker.

No!

In her worry for Walker, Dani nearly released the Chastity magic nullifying Leviathan. Throwing a fresh wave of power into her light beam, Dani pushed with all her might until she felt him recoil.

Vibrant green light shined from below, and Dani tracked Walker's movements while keeping one eye on her magic. She wouldn't be so foolish as to forget it again.

Walker sprinted under Leviathan's scaled belly, running the entire length of him.

Where was his heart located?

Every step Walker took sent a shock of fear coursing through Dani, but she remained steadfast, holding her magic and pumping her wings.

Skidding to a halt, Walker unfurled his bright green wings. Pounding them against the air, he sailed upward with Nightmare grasped in his hands. Using his elemental powers, Walker surged up with the Angel Blade.

The green light of Kindness coated the blade as he stabbed it between Leviathan's scales on his underside.

The serpent's shriek punctured the air, and Dani abandoned magic to cover her ears before they ruptured. Folding in her wings, Dani dropped to the ground. Before she hit the sand, Jamie caught her in his muscular arms and spooked in a flash of red.

Hayden threw up a wall of silver Spirit to accompany Kova's golden light protecting the witches from demonic attack as Leviathan stomped and bucked and swung his serpentine neck. Lesser demons fled in a panic as they realized their leader was inches from death.

Reeling, Leviathan struggled to stay on his four legs, but black blood poured like a waterfall from the brutal wound Walker inflicted on his underbelly.

With one final step, Leviathan's knee buckled underneath him, and he tumbled until his chest slammed into the ground, shaking it like a quake, followed by his elongated neck.

A dark shadow fell over the witches as Leviathan's head dropped toward the ground, threatening to crush them, but Hayden stood her ground. Fangs the size of Dani's legs pierced the dirt inches in front of Hayden.

The Serpent Monster was slain.

And silence remained.

Demons scattered like bugs until none remained, their black forms retreating to only the Devil knew where, but the witches in the valley were too exhausted to give chase, even the immortal ones.

Leviathan's carcass lay before them, slowly decaying into ash as the warm palette of the sun's rays kissed the land and the red tinge of the Blood Moon Eclipse disappeared as the moon hid behind the earth. Dawn broke over Salem.

Wings of Spirit disappeared from the Virtues' backs as the amplification of their Virtue magic dissipated with the morning light.

The Apokalypsis War was finished. At least for this lifetime.

White flames sparked to life, licking Leviathan's obscene corpse to devour it faster.

Dani finally breathed in a real breath, filled with the crisp morning air. As her heartbeat returned to a normal rate, she surveyed the carnage around her until her eyes landed on Mila's body.

Mila. Milena Wardwell.

Five of the seven.

It was impossible to believe.

Never in the history of the Apokalypsis War had so many Virtues survived. And never had they killed the fallen princes. But today, they killed six, banishing all Seven Deadly Sins to Hell until they clawed their way into this world. But never again would a Sins possess the body of an immortal.

And the world was safer because of it.

"We survived."

Dani looked up at her fellow Virtues. They survived.

Hayden and her circle remained silent, allowing the Virtues to work through the aftermath.

Morbid laughter bubbled out of Raphaela, and she collapsed into the dirt. "We survived," she repeated, tears streaming down her face.

Ronnie stared at the sunrise, an indescribable peace mixed with sorrow claiming her features, and Dani wondered what she saw with that mystical sight of hers.

"We survived," Emmett echoed, placing a hand on Walker's shoulder. "But our brother and sister did not." He nodded pointedly to Walker, who still stared at Mila's cold body.

"Are they—" Dani stopped, licked her lips, then looked Hayden in the eye. "Are they okay?"

Her smile was bittersweet. "They are at peace in the Garden. Both of them. Speaking of which…"

Hayden intertwined her fingers with Kova's. Red light haloed around Hayden as teal light manifested around Kova, both of them donning silver hair and eyes. The light traveled from their auras to their combined hands, and the women gently raised their clasped hands to the sky.

Balls of twinkling red and teal light floated toward as the witches released the Virtues from their Spirit magic.

"Blessed be," the Salem Witches whispered simultaneously.

"Dani?" a familiar voice shouted, interrupting her inner thoughts of mourning. "Dani?" His voice got shriller as he searched frantically for his sister.

Bursting between Hayden and Jamie, Damien stumbled to a halt at the sight of his sister on her knees in the dirt.

Tears sprang to his eyes as he dove at her, pulling her into the most bone-crushing hug of her life. "Thank the Goddess, you're okay." Hot tears fell on her shoulder as Damien buried his face in her neck. "Thank you, thank you, thank you," he muttered over and over.

Pulling back, he gripped her face with both hands and scanned her for injuries. Not that he would find any—she had healed them, and Spirit's touch seemed to heal wounds as quickly as they were received.

Hauling her to her feet, he scanned the rest of her body, then spun her around to check her back. "You're not hurt?" He spun her to face him. "You're alive." His lip quivered with emotion. "My baby sister killed the Sins. All seven of them."

"It wasn't me," Dani argued, gesturing to the other Virtues. "We all fought against the Sins. Together."

"But you led us, Dani," Ronnie emphasized. "It was your idea that killed Leviathan, we just followed our leader."

"Thank you for trusting me." Dani smiled at them and received genuine, though exhausted, smiles in return.

"I think our past lives were wise to choose you as our leader, Chastity." Emmett inclined his head. "It took real bravery to do what you did. I just wish Axel and Mila were here to see it."

Silence fell over the valley, the sun shining brightly on the horizon and illuminating their world, casting long shadows over the ground as they mourned their fallen brother and sister.

"So, what now?" Ronnie asked, staring at Leviathan's burning body turning to ash under the power of holy flames. "Is that it? The war is over, and we go our separate ways?"

Hayden's lips quirked to one side in a mischievous smile. "Now, Ronnie"—she threw an arm around Humility's shoulders—"begins the next chapter of your life."

"But what is that chapter?" Walker looked to Hayden like a lost puppy dog. The Virtues had spent the last seven months struggling to survive. With the Sins gone and the Apokalypsis War over... they felt... lost.

And yet... Dani felt the guiding hand of Chastity urging her toward greater. Or was the Goddess acting through her Virtue? Either way, this life was far from over, and Dani couldn't wait to discover her next adventure.

"That's the beauty of the Creator," Hayden said with a wink. "Free will dictates that you decide what you do next." The Salem Witch looked to the Heavens above, letting her hair and eyes transform into a molten silver. The Mark of the Goddess. A small smile tilted the corners of her lips as she said to the sky, "But Fate guarantees you'll always end up exactly where you're supposed to be."

"And where is that?" Emmett frowned, then cast a glance at Walker, who stared at Mila's cold corpse. "How do we move on from this?"

Kova placed a reassuring hand on his shoulder while Thea moved to Walker's side, humming a melodious tune. Magic wafted off the Heart of Earth as she used her powers to lull Walker into a deep sleep. Lowering him to the ground, she met Hayden's eyes, nodded once, and spooked with Kindness in a flash of green light.

"Mourn," Kova answered Emmett. "Don't try to move on prematurely. Mourn your losses, recover from battle. But allow Spirit to fill you." Golden light poured from Kova's hand into Emmett's body as she filled him with the life-giving element, and he seemed to sag into her with relief.

Emerald green light flashed as Thea reappeared, her box braids swinging behind her. With a nod at the Virtues, Thea accepted Emmett into her arms and spooked with him, leaving the female Virtues standing alone.

"Where did they take the guys?" Raphaela asked, wrapping her arms around herself for comfort.

"Back to the compound," Apalla answered. "To rest." She shrugged. "Some Virtues take the War harder than others."

Kelsey shrugged. "You'd be surprised how resilient a woman's heart can be."

"Should we return to the compound, too?" Ronnie asked, exhaustion lacing her voice despite her sharp eyes.

"If you want," Jamie answered. "We will take you wherever you wish to go."

"I'm not sure where I should wish to go." Raphaela hugged herself tighter. "I left everything I knew behind to move here to fight this war, and suddenly, it's over. I don't know what to do, or where to go. I need someone to tell me." She looked at Hayden, desperation written across the poor woman's face.

"I cannot tell you where you're meant to go, Raphaela. Spirit wants you to figure that out for yourselves." A kind smile flitted across Hayden's lips. "You do not need to make any decisions now. Like Kova said, rest, recover from this war. Then decide where you want life to lead you. But Dani," Hayden's crystal blue gaze landed on the Virtue of Chastity, "if you feel so inclined"—she gestured to herself and her circle—"I would be honored if you joined my circle as the water elemental. That is, if you've forgiven me for keeping secrets."

"Promise you'll never do it again?"

Hayden snorted at the same time as Kova. Jamie scoffed, and Apalla outright laughed. Kelsey rolled her eyes.

"Not likely," Hayden said, sharing a look with Kova. "Salem Witches keep more secrets than you could imagine. But I can promise I will share with you whatever secrets Spirit allows. How does that sound?"

Slowly, a smile crept across Dani's lips. "Sounds like Fate guaranteed exactly where I'm supposed to be."

"How do you feel about that one, Damien?" Jamie asked, clapping a hand on his shoulder.

Burying his head in his hands, he dramatically cried, "Oh, kill me now. I can't take the two of them together for the rest of my life."

"You should try dealing with Hayden for the rest of eternity," Jamie retorted.

"You're stuck with me, Angel Boy, whether you like it or not." Pushing up to her tippy-toes, Hayden pressed a kiss to his cheek, and something pulled inside Dani's heart.

To this day, she craved the kind of love those two had. The kind of unconditional love only soulmates could experience.

As though she could read Dani's thoughts, Hayden's crystal blue eyes cut to Dani's, and with a wink, she said, "Don't worry, Dani. If you don't find him in this life, he's up there"—she waved a hand at the heavens—"waiting for you. But in the meantime, there's so much life to live."

CHAPTER SEVENTEEN

HEAVEN'S GATES

Seventy-seven years.

Seventy-seven years after the Apokalypsis War, Dani Sanchez lay on her death bed as a crone witch at the age of ninety-four.

Every breath was a shaky, painful rasp, yet Dani clung to life. Her elemental magic ran out long ago without life force to fuel her powers, but the magic of her Virtue remained fully intact. Even now, Chastity gently caressed her soul, soothing the pain as best as it could, for the Creator's gifts were irrevocable.

But Dani was not long for this world. She was ready to go. Perhaps she was waiting on the slim possibility of saying goodbye to the last of her friends. The ones who disappeared decades ago.

Her beloved brother, Damien, passed a few years ago. Kova was immortal, but she said goodbye earlier, along with many of Dani's mortal friends. Apalla was alive at the age of ninety-seven, but as a Prophetess, her lifespan extended beyond a normal mortal's. But the Virtues did not extend the lives of their hosts, evident by the fact that Dani was the last of the five who survived the war.

Even her husband, Dakota, had passed seven years prior.

Ah, Dakota. They had lived a happy life together with their four children. Children who were now grown and had children and grandchildren of their own, all of whom filled Dani's hospital room at Mother Mary's in Asylum. They traveled from across the world to be with her during her final days.

And they were wonderful days full of love and light and laughter. Dani could not have asked for a better ending to her life than to be surrounded by the family that loved her so greatly. The family that was strewn across the room, asleep in various chairs and roll-away cots, and some on sleeping bags on the floor.

Dani smiled to herself as she glanced at her granddaughter, Danielle, who was named after her. Danielle's hand gripped Dani's despite the soft snoring coming from under the pile of black hair atop her head. They always had a special bond, the two of them, and Dani was so grateful that her granddaughter had brought her children to say goodbye.

But one person was missing..

Perhaps that was why Dani waited to cross the Veil. She could sense Death lingering, waiting for her final breath to pass her lips, but Dani was not afraid, for she had faced far worse than Death all those years ago when she led the Virtues to victory against the Sins. The greatest victory achieved in the history of the Apokalypsis War.

The shadows in the hospital room grew darker despite the moonlight filtering through the window. She had asked the healers to keep the blinds open so she could see the moon every night—the symbol of their Goddess.

But the supernatural darkness was a result of magic. Chastity nudged her soul.

Everything went still. Silence suffused the room. The only noise came from Dani's raspy breaths, but her family remained frozen in time.

Shadows gathered in the far corner where a section of floor space was carved out from the sleeping bodies littering the room.

And that was where she appeared.

Hayden Black emerged from the shadows.

She looked exactly like Dani remembered. Black clothes and long hair as dark as night. Pale skin that rivaled the moonlight, and piercing blue eyes that saw straight to your soul. And a face that couldn't be older than thirty-three years old.

A friendly smile warmed her face when her gaze met Dani's.

"Hello, old friend," Hayden greeted her warmly, then fully stepped out of the shadows.

Shock slapped Dani across the face.

Hayden was not alone.

Her soulmate, Jamie Bishop, followed her closely, but holding each of her hands was a child. One boy and one girl. And in Jamie's arms, he held a bundle of blankets.

This was why the soulmates had gone into hiding decades ago. They finally decided to expand their family. Their immortal family. The children were fully Nephilim—a quarter angel from Gabriel and a quarter angel from Michael. Chastity could sense the power flooding their veins.

The family approached Dani, walking on hardened air to avoid treading on Dani's sleeping family.

"Hello, Dani," Hayden spoke softly, a tone the Warrior Witch reserved for her friends and family. But the woman was different. She had always been made of hardened steel, forged in the fires of the Trials, but she seemed softer now. Dani glanced at the children. Hayden was a mother now. In the amount of time Dani had been a great-grandmother, Hayden had become a mother. "It's been too long, my friend."

With effort, Dani sat upright. Jamie stretched a hand to help her, but Dani waved him off. She could manage for this. For these final moments.

The Crone surveyed the children clinging to Hayden's side. They were young—no older than seven or eight. Twins.

The boy was the more reserved of the two, hiding behind his mother's leg, but Dani could make out his golden bronze hair and royal blue eyes. He was a near replica of Jamie, and Chastity told Dani of the power of fire surrounding the boy, strong beyond a normal witch's even at such a young age.

But the girl—she was more curious than her brother and did not hide behind her mother's leg but faced Dani fully, her ocean blue eyes meeting Dani's.

A gasp escaped Dani, and her gaze shot to Hayden, who smiled knowingly.

"Dani, I would like you to meet my children." Gently pulling her son out from behind her, Hayden urged him to say hello. "This is Mikael, named in honor of my heavenly father."

Mikael waved. "Hello, Dani," he said confidently, but Dani could tell he did not understand why they were visiting this strange, elderly woman.

"And this is Haven," Hayden said, nudging her daughter forward. Haven did not need much incentive.

Cocking her head, she stepped toward Dani and after a brief hesitation, she climbed onto the bed. Her long black hair framed her tanned face in stark contrast to the brightness of her eyes.

"I know you," she said gently, gazing at Dani. "From my previous life." Haven looked to her mother for approval, and when Hayden nodded, Haven returned her gaze to Dani. "I do not remember my past life, but the Creator allows me glimpses into certain truths. You assumed the element of water in my mother's circle after my previous life passed away. I do not know what state I left the world in when I died, and my parents will not tell me—"

"It is not for us to tell you yet, Haven."

The young girl rolled her eyes at her mother, and it looked so much like Hayden that Dani had to laugh.

"You have the sass of your mother and Harbor combined," Dani commented, making the little girl beam with pride.

But Jamie rolled his eyes. "Yeah, and I'm the one who has to deal with attitude from both of them."

Hayden grinned maniacally and waggled her eyebrows. "Oh, you love it and you know it."

Clearing her throat pointedly, Haven silenced her parents. "Thank you for the role you played in maintaining the circle after my passing and for fighting alongside my parents during the Salem and Apokalypsis Wars to do what I could not." Haven pressed her small hand against Dani's wrinkled cheek. "The ways of water are strong within you. Chastity chose you for the purity of your soul, and it will remain with you beyond the Veil, as will your bond with the element of water."

And with that, the child climbed off the bed and returned to her mother's side, but her blue eyes, swimming with emotion, did not leave Dani. Haven Bishop-Black was an empath in this life, the same as she was in her past life as Harbor Bishop.

Jamie transferred the bundle of blankets into Hayden's arms, and then she stepped forward and eased herself onto the bed next to Dani.

"I'm sorry we kept you waiting. I know you are in pain, and I do not wish to prolong your suffering. We would have come sooner, but my littlest one was not yet ready to spook, and since we are in hiding, we did not dare risk traveling by other means. But now that he is a few weeks old, we felt safe spooking with him." Hayden carefully transferred her baby into her arms. "This is Everest, the reincarnation of my father, Hunter." Hayden winked a crystal blue eye. "As you predicted so many years ago. I wonder if we were mistaken to not test your magical abilities for True Sight."

Dani released a rasping laugh. "I think that is a stretch, although I find satisfaction in knowing I predicted the future.

Had I known, I would have teased Apalla relentlessly while I had years left."

The soulmates laughed in response, and it was life-giving to hear their laughter after so many decades.

Everest opened his tiny eyes, and Dani caught a glimpse of his hunter green orbs before his lids drooped closed, and he snuggled into the blankets, completely at ease in her arms.

"He's strong," Dani said. She made to hand the boy to Hayden before her arms gave out, but a burst of pure, unyielding energy flooded her chest and filled her veins. A slight gasp escaped her lips at the shock of power.

A sly smile twisted Hayden's lips.

"I should have imbued you with Spirit sooner. But after so many years, I have forgotten that mortals do not have the magical nor physical strength of Nephilim."

"I must admit," Dani began, gazing at the precious boy in her arms, "I had forgotten the power of the Salem Witch after all these decades. You've been in hiding a long time, Hayden."

Hayden's smile turned bittersweet, and a look of what might have been regret flashed across Jamie's features.

"It is not easy for immortal Nephilim to get pregnant. We tried for many years before the twins were finally conceived. With Everest, we tried again right away, but it took seven years to conceive again."

"That doesn't explain the decades before the twins were conceived."

Tossing back her head, Hayden roared with laughter, but the world around them remained undisturbed, as though the family and Dani were removed from time. Mischief glinted in Hayden's eyes, and Chastity nudged Dani. There was always more to the story when it came to the woman who wielded Spirit.

"We've only been in hiding for three decades," Jamie pointed out.

"And the children are eight. If you started trying fifteen years ago, what of the fifteen years before that?"

The couple shared a look, communicating silently in a way only soulmates could.

"The Order of Saint Michael," Hayden whispered reverently. "I knew when we retreated into hiding that the world would fall out of balance, even with the Sins defeated. In the years following the Apokalypsis War, we hunted demons, but the Wars unleashed trillions and trillions of demons. We made a dent, but it wasn't enough, even with the help of my loyal demons. Without me and Jamie on the front lines, demons would overrun the world with their evil."

"But you wanted a family."

"But we wanted a family," she echoed, her tone hallow. "So, I communed with my father, Michael, and he gave us his blessing to step away—temporarily, of course—and he told me of the ways of the ancient witches who honored him as the Warrior Archangel."

"The Order of Saint Michael?"

"The Order is a network of witches throughout the world dedicated to ridding the world of evil. They are Knights of the highest caliber, organized into legions in strategic locations where the most concentrated populations of demons haunt—typically cities. Jamie and I spent decades reviving the Order, recruiting witches, and training them to assume Michael's mantle."

"When the Order could sustain itself, we retreated into hiding," Jamie added. "Even then, there have been times of dire need that the Order has called upon us."

"But the Order has fought Evil on your behalf while you started your family," Dani concluded.

"Yes." Hayden nodded. "I know it was selfish of us. We could have waited until we killed more of the demons, but—"

"It's not selfish, Hayden," Dani interrupted in her gravelly voice. "I have lived as many years as you, but because I am mortal and my time on this Earth is finite, I have a deeper appreciation for time. The time will never be just right. Evil will never be completely defeated, not while our souls reside in this world. Delaying your family would not have defeated more evil but would have given Evil what it wants—to steal your joy. I think you were wise to establish the Order. The safety of the world does not fall on your shoulders alone. It belongs to all of us. I was always eager to fight for our world. And there are plenty of others like me and you who will fight for this world."

"We will," Mikael and Haven said in unison, drawing the eyes of their mother and her old friend.

"Mikael and I weren't born into this world without reason," Haven said in a melodiously sweet voice.

"The Creator has a purpose for our lives," Mikael added with confidence.

But pain flickered through Hayden's and Jamie's expressions as they shared a look. Those were not the words a parent wanted to hear, especially not from the mouths of their young children.

"May I remind you that a certain witch was tasked with the impossible at a young age, yet prevailed against all odds," Dani said with a pointed look to Hayden, who sighed out a heavy breathe.

Strain tugged at Hayden's ageless features. "I remember my Trials well, but I do not wish for my children to endure such suffering."

Dani's smile was heart-wrenching as she gestured around the room. "It gets harder with each life born into your family. It will not be an easy path forward, but it never is for those destined for such a great purpose as the Lord's and Lady's."

"We know," the mother and father said in unison.

"Which is why Mikael and Haven will be staying here, in Asylum."

Dani's eyes widened in shock as her gaze slid to Hayden's.

"Our visit was timed for more than one reason, Daniella. We have been training the twins since they were three, like Jamie and Harbor, but with Everest..."

"Kova agreed to train the twins while we remain in hiding," Jamie finished for her. "And it's best if Everest grows up separate from her, so they do not bond prematurely."

"The children will grow up separately, too?" Dani asked, her heart breaking for the family being torn apart. When would Hayden be allowed to live in peace with her family together?

"Not exactly." Hayden's grin was nothing short of mischievous. "Kids, do you want to show Dani your special powers?"

Blue light flashed, followed by red as the children spooked, disappearing from where they stood to reappear on the other side of Dani's bed.

Their matching grins were identical to Hayden's, and Dani released a groan. "Oh Jamie, you have your hands full with these three mischief makers."

Rolling his royal blue eyes, he released a groan. "Don't I know it."

"Aww, babe, you know you're stuck with us." Hayden winked a twinkling blue eye. "The kids know how to find us, even with the extensive protections I've wrapped around our secret home. And my mother is here in Asylum. She visits plenty, especially to see the baby." She nodded at Everest swaddled in blankets in Dani's arms, held aloft by the power of Spirit that Hayden steadily trickled into her body. "I refuse to let our family be separated. My children will not grow up the way I did. The Devil may seek vengeance against me, but I've walked through Hell, and I have nothing to fear from the Darkness, for it should fear the Spirit."

Silver flames danced in her midnight black hair and silver light encircled her pupils in the mark of the Goddess.

There it was—that spark of Heaven and unrelenting power. The power of the Creator flowing through her.

"Hayden," Dani's voice came out as a whisper. "Your powers of Spirit—is that what it's like in the Garden?" She gestured to the silver magic surrounding the Salem Witch as she felt her life force fading, remaining in her body only by Hayden's power. "Is it always so magnificent?"

"It's this and so much *more*," she said as she took Everest from Dani's arms and handed him to her soulmate. "It's indescribable, and the Creator... It's ineffable. Beyond mortal words." Her warm but pale hand landed on Dani's old wrinkled one. "It will be complete and utter peace for all eternity. And *love*. So much love, for you will reside with the Creator, forever."

As Hayden's words passed her lips, Amara appeared beside the Salem Witch. If she was visible to Jamie and the kids, they did not let on, but Hayden knew. As Master of Death and a vessel of Spirit, she sensed Amara before Dani.

"James, why don't you take the kids to my mother's house? I will return soon." Hayden's eyes didn't leave Dani's as Spirit magic filtered into her.

Two flashes of red light and a single flash of blue light illuminated the room as the family disappeared, but the witch dressed in black remained alongside Amara, who appeared as a little girl with lusciously tanned skin, candy apple red hair, and jade green eyes.

"Hello, Daniella Sanchez."

"Hello, Amara," Dani said, her voice raspier than before, as though the mere presence of Death expedited the departure of Dani's soul. "It has been many years, but I always knew we would meet face to face again," she said with a warm smile. "Are you finally here to release me from my pain?"

"I am," Death spoke, and the two simple words seemed so solemn coming from the mouth of the little girl.

Hayden's hand clasped Dani's. "And I will be with you every step of the way—if you wish, that is."

"What fool turns away the company of an old friend as she crosses the Veil? I would be honored to have a Master of Death walk alongside me in my journey to the Garden."

Amara smiled what was a completely unhinged smile on the face of a child as she extended a tiny hand to the old crone.

With one last look around the room at her beloved family, Dani placed her free hand in Amara's, and the world went white.

Painlessly, Dani's soul separated from her body, but she felt the hands of her companions touching her soul while blinded by purifying light.

Then sight returned to her eyes—or her soul, for everything was made of light here.

Dani glanced down at her body clothed in a white linen dress. Her attire was not surprising, but Dani did not expect to find her soul like that of Dani's young, lithe thirty-year-old self. Lucious black hair tumbled down to her elbows in loose curls, and the dark pigment of her Hispanic heritage returned to her tanned skin, which glowed with life.

Recovering from her shock at her magical de-aging, Dani glanced at the immortals beside her. Amara remained unchanged in her child form, and Hayden looked the same as in the mortal world, except instead of her usual black garments, she donned white linen pants and shirt. Her usual knowing smile brushed over her lips.

"I was surprised to find our permanent heavenly age is thirty-three here when I died for the first time, too."

"That's why you aged after your Resurrection, but never a day past thirty-three," Dani stated. She had always wondered... but Hayden and the other immortal Nephilim never deemed it necessary to explain their eternal youth and the mystery behind their aging and lack thereof.

"The mysteries of my age are meaningless compared to what awaits you, Daniella." Spinning her finger in the air, the Salem Witch gestured for Dani to turn. "Turn around."

Her heart beating faster, Dani whirled around.

Two elegant gates of simple design stood at erect attention, imposing to demons and welcoming to the souls who call it home. The gates glistened with silver and gold, the colors intermingling to create a luminescent, pearly light that radiated off the metal-like bars. Each gate was adorned with a flat, circular disk—a silver moon embellished the golden gate while a golden sun hung from the silver gate in perfect balance to one another as the Gates of the Garden of Eden demonstrated the balance and glory of the Divine Masculine and the Divine Feminine.

"Home." Hayden sighed from behind Dani, a certain longingness detectable in her breath, as though a heavy burden weighed on her chest. And Dani understood the longing for the Gates to open for her like the arms of a parent welcoming their prodigal child.

"Home," Amara echoed, her expression twisted into a pained apology as she glanced at the Salem Witch, but when she met Dani's gaze, she added, "Home for those of us who accept our mortality. Life within the Garden is pure, Dani, purer than the mortal world could hope to achieve. I am sorry your human life ended, but I am honored to introduce you, and every soul who crosses the Veil, to the Kingdom that rules us."

Licking her lips, Dani hesitated. "Am I worthy?" she questioned, her voice small.

Warmth wrapped around her shoulders. "Are you worthy?" Hayden quirked an eyebrow. "No, not even close." Dani's heart plummeted in her stomach. She had been a Virtue. One of Heaven's seven chosen warriors, once an angel of Heaven, and that wasn't enough to secure her home in Eden. "But neither am I," Hayden continued, shooting a longing look at the Gates. "No mortal soul can achieve the wonder and glory of divine purity required to save our souls... so it's a good thing the Creator, in Its infinite wisdom, chooses us not because of our worthiness, but because of Its love for us."

"What if I wasn't a Virtue?" Dani asked meekly, fear clutching her chest as she thought of the fates of her friends and family, the ones who had departed before her and those who remained in the mortal realm.

"You should know by now, Daniella, that I do not abandon My children, whether they are blessed with a Virtue or not," said a woman's voice, more ethereal and magnificent than any voice in the mortal realm.

An impossibly beautiful woman with black skin that glittered like stars twinkling in the night sky appeared in front of Dani, and Hayden stepped backward, bowing in reverence. The woman's face was young—thirty-three like everything on this side of the Veil—but radiated endless power and love. Straight silver hair fell past her shoulders, stopping at her waist, shining with the shimmering glow of a full moon. But her eyes were striking, more so than an angel's. Shining silver orbs lacked a pupil but held the wisdom of countless lifetimes, and Dani released a light gasp. Hayden's hair and eyes turned silver during a Trial or when she channeled the full power of the Salem Witch.

It was truly the mark of the Goddess.

"Goddess," she breathed the name.

She smiled, her teeth like beautiful white pearls against her night-sky skin. "Hello Daniella, I have missed you so."

Hot tears prickled Dani's eyes as memories flooded her soul. "I remember you from when I was made. You were the first thing I opened my eyes to.... You told me..." She hiccupped as she stifled her sobs. "Before I entered this new life, you shared your love with me, so I knew when I sought the mortal realm that my gift was love. It would always be love."

"Yes, Daniella. While your Virtue, which clings to your soul, is Chastity, My special gift to you has been and always will be unconditional love. Lust, while not the most powerful of the Seven Deadly Sins, is the most manipulative. Many great men and women have resisted pride and anger only to mistake lust for love. Lust is the most natural of the sins, making the line between it and love blur through the hazy vision of a physical mind and body. Only the soul can recognize true love. I believe it is why Chastity chose you as It's vessel, for it knew the gift of the Spirit that I bestowed on your soul."

A fresh round of tears wetted Dani's eyes as her bottom lip quivered with emotion, and part of her wondered how it was possible for a body of light to cry, but part of her didn't question it.

"But I messed up so many times. My friends... they died because of me." Dani tore her gaze away from the Goddess to stare at her feet in shame.

A black hand cupped her chin and gently forced Dani to raise her head. "Yes, you did. But you have given to Me all your burdens and sins and traumas just as you have allowed My strength and Spirit to fill you. As you have harmed others, knowingly and unknowingly, they have done the same to you, and have you not forgiven their souls?"

"Of course." Dani choked out the words through hiccups, her voice thick and garbled from the emotion clogging her throat. "Of course, I do. Even when they hurt me, I love them."

Pearly white teeth showed as the Goddess grinned. "Exactly, Daniella. You are forgiven. Your debt has been paid, and you are welcome in this home." She swept a midnight-black arm toward the Pearly Gates as a resounding "BOOM" echoed through the heavens. "It is time for you to return to the Garden and resume your rightful place at My side."

Without thinking, Dani stepped forward, her soul-body moving of its own accord, as if the magic of the Garden called to it without her conscious knowing.

But a terrible thought made her pause.

"What will happen to my Virtue?" she asked. "Will..." Swallowing roughly, she cleared the dismay clogging her throat. "Will Chastity separate from me?"

Goddess smiled again, Her pearly teeth shining more brightly in the stark contrast against Her midnight skin. "Davina, perhaps you should answer Daniella after keeping your secrets for so many years."

"You act like it is my fault that *Your* Spirit stops me from telling mortals things," Hayden grumbled as she and Amara moved closer to Goddess.

Dani swallowed her fear. How could Hayden speak to Goddess that way without being pulverized by heavenly power?

"Some of my children have always been sassier than others," Goddess answered with a wink, as though She read Dani's mind... because She was *the* Goddess... of course She knew Dani's every thought.

Hayden threw her hands up in surrender. "Hey, You're the one who made me like this. I don't want to hear complaints about my sassiness—I completely blame it on my mother."

Amara snorted. "I'll be sure to tell Leyla the next time I see her."

Hayden shot her a devious grin. "As if she doesn't already know? Do you have any idea how proud Mom is that Haven inherited our sassiness?"

"Ahem," Goddess cleared her throat, but it sounded like tinkling bells.

"Oh, right. Sorry." Hayden shot the Goddess an apologetic smile. "Anyhoo. You'll regain the memories of your past reincarnations when you enter the Garden..."

"From my mortal life on Earth, when Chastity and I descended to fight the Sins."

"From *all* your lifetimes," Hayden emphasized, her tone suggesting she was hinting at, but Dani didn't have a clue.

"My child, Hayden is hinting that you will regain your memories from your immortal life, too."

Crossing her arms over her chest, Hayden grumbled, "Sure, you outright tell her, but I've had to dance around the truth for the last eight decades."

Dani froze. "My immortal life? You mean... Do you mean from when I was an angel?" Her head snapped between the three divine beings.

"And the time in between lives," Death said.

Her jaw fell open, and if flies were a thing in Heaven, she definitely would have swallowed one.

"Why tell me this now?" Dani asked, her tone pained. "Why not let me naturally regain my memories when I re-entered the Garden? Why prepare me? Was life as an angel so difficult for a mortal soul to comprehend?"

"In between mortal lives, your soul rested within the Garden for seven hundred years, living out its eternal life. Our bodies may be mortal, but our souls are everlasting, even for those of us who are divine in nature." Amara's jade green eyes landed on Hayden for a heartbeat of a second, and pity flashed in her irises. "Time does not run linearly within the Garden like it does on Earth. Everything happens all at once yet never ends and never begins."

Rubbing her temples, Hayden complained, "Don't try to understand it, Dani. It makes my brain hurt every time I think about it."

"Your soul is mortal, and as such, when you return to the Garden, what feels like thousands of years of memories will crash into you in an instant, and your soul will be overwhelmed."

"Sounds pleasant," Hayden grumbled, disgruntled on Dani's behalf.

"But I've done this before," Dani protested. "I've descended to Earth, fought the Apokalypsis War, died, and returned to the Garden every seven hundred years for thousands of years. There has to be a way to protect my soul." Dani looked to

Hayden desperately, to the woman who always seemed to hold the answers. "What makes this time any different?"

Hayden glanced sideways at the Goddess. "I'm out." She stepped backward, her hands raised. "You gotta explain this one."

It sank in then—Hayden always had the answers on Earth, because the Goddess standing beside her provided the answers through Her Spirit. Not because of Hayden or what Hayden was capable of. All her power, all her knowledge, flowed from Goddess to Salem Witch through the power of Spirit.

With a smile, Goddess stepped forward and placed a black hand of either of Dani's tanned cheeks. "I will not allow your soul to become overwhelmed by your memories, Daniella. Long ago, I assigned an angel to you. One who would guard you and care for you and hold your memories until you returned. But this time is different, Daniella. While you sought love during your mortal life on Earth—yes, you found a loving husband and had many children—but you never found the unconditional love you so craved before the war, because your soulmate was never on Earth. He was here, in Heaven, and he waits impatiently for you every seven hundred years. He is the one who holds your memories while your soul fights valiantly for Heaven. The reason your entrance to the Garden is different *now* is because your soul has fought tirelessly for My cause for too long, bearing a heavy burden."

"What does that mean?"

"It means I am offering you a choice. You may enter the Garden, as you have so many times before, as a human soul to reincarnate in seven hundred years. Or you can part ways from your virtuous brethren and reclaim your divine birthright as an angel."

Dani gasped.

"Bloody angels and their bloody secrets. I channel the all-knowing Spirit of the Creator, and I don't know everything,"

Hayden grumbled. A century old, and she still had that youthful, rebellious spark inside her soul.

Hayden exchanged an annoyed look with Amara, who looked as stunned as Dani felt. Clearly the women had no idea what the Goddess was planning to offer Dani. And Hayden knew everything.

"Part ways with Chastity?" Dani's heart sank as her expression fell. "I don't know if I can do that." She placed a hand over where her heart would normally beat in her chest. "It's a part of me. Separating from Chastity would be like…"

"Like parting from your angelic nature?" Hayden supplied, raising an eyebrow.

"Worse."

"Oooo," Hayden let out a low whistle.

"Fear not, my child," Goddess said, lifting Dani's head with a gentle hand under her chin. I would never dream to separate you and your Virtue. You were tied to Chastity long before you became mortal. Chastity is not an entity separate from you. It feels separate because Chastity is divine in nature while your soul remains mortal. If you should choose to ascend to an angel, you will never again hold a virtuous power like your nullification abilities in this past life, but you will fuse with Chastity and become one being."

Hope fluttered in Dani's heart, but…

"But what about the other six Virtues? In seven hundred years, they'd have to face the Sins without me."

Goddess smiled knowingly. "Not when there is another willing to shed his divinity to assume the burden of fighting Evil on My behalf."

"Another Virtue volunteered to become mortal?" Hayden asked with curiosity.

"Purity."

"Oh." Hayden's eyes widened in understanding. "Oh."

Amara hummed. "Ah, Zaqiel has long awaited his chance to wage war against the Sins after what they did to his mate."

"Why now?" Dani asked. "Why would this angel—Zaqiel—want to trade places with me after millennia of Apokalypsis Wars?"

"Because his mate, Sariel, has finally recovered from the first war, when the Sins destroyed her body and soul." Goddess sighed heavily. "It has taken her thousands of years to heal from the trauma."

"Why didn't You heal her?" Dani asked. "Why would You allow her to suffer?"

"Angelic wounds don't work like mortal ones, Dani. We can't heal them with water magic." Hayden whispered, wrapping her arms around herself. "Sariel was the first angel to stand against the Sins. When they attacked mortals on Earth, as the Archangel of Punishment and Death, she alone fought them off."

A tear tore from Amara's jade green eye to roll down her tanned cheek. "Enraged that they were defeated by Sariel and the humans, the Sins waited until Sariel returned to Heaven. Ambushing her, they—they—"

"They tore off her wings," Hayden finished for Death, her voice hollow as tears welled in her piercing blue eyes. "The ultimate revenge against an angel."

Dani sucked in a deep breath. "The princes didn't have wings because the feathers decayed when the original angels fell."

Hayden nodded, every muscle in her soul-body wired with tension. "Touching another angel's wings unless they are your mate is forbidden, but ripping them from her..."

"Sariel was damaged beyond her physical form. Her spirit shattered when they stole her wings and scattered the feathers across the skies of all the realms." The Goddess's silver eyes dimmed as she recounted the trauma inflicted on Her child. "While I could have healed her, for I can do all things, Sariel refused, insisting she and her mate would retrieve her missing feathers and return her soul to its unified state."

"But why?" Dani wiped at the tears rolling down her cheeks. "Why would she do that?"

"To prove the glory of the Creator," Hayden answered. "God and Goddess could heal her in an instant, but it would prove nothing to Evil. It does not fear the Creator's ultimate power. But for an angel to rebuild itself from such a tragedy…"

"It's unheard of," Amara answered. "It speaks to the power of an angel's spirit, even when broken. Sariel rebuilt her wings in demonstration of what the fallen could never do, for they do not have the favor of Heaven."

"So, Sariel… her wings… did she…?"

"Her wings have been repaired, and her soul is restored," Amara confirmed in her sing-song voice, bringing some joy to the harrowing conversation.

"Now that his mate is whole, Zaqiel insists he has many years to recompense for his distractedness in the days since the Fall. I will allow him to atone for his absence, but only if you wish to step away from your mortal existence." Goddess spoke with such assuredness and kindness, like it wasn't a conversation about angels turning against angels and breaking one another's souls.

"But won't Zaqiel and Sariel be separated?"

"It is a price they are willing to pay," Goddess answered unwaveringly. "You have fought the Sins since the beginning, so whilst the Sins focused on you, they did not haunt Sariel while she healed. Zaqiel wishes to return the favor to you, Daniella."

Hayden snorted. "Pretty sure if Sariel was a Virtue instead of an Archangel, she would shed her divinity for the chance for some payback."

"Revenge is not our way, Davina," the Goddess chastised, then pursed her lips. "Although, you are correct, which is more reason to not allow Sariel to become mortal." Hair swayed like a silver waterfall as the Goddess shook her head. "I allow Zaqiel to shed his divinity because he wishes to serve Me. Not seek revenge."

"Zaqiel will become mortal, but I'll be an angel again?"

Goddess nodded.

"Will I... will I be able to see my mortal family again?"

"Whenever your heart desires."

"But what of the other Virtues? They'll be stuck in the endless cycle of reincarnation. Who am I to abandon them?"

"Spoken like a true leader," Hayden proclaimed, her blue eyes dancing with pride. "But the Virtues voted.... They want you to make the best choice for *you*. Not the best choice for them." A pale hand landed on each of Dani's shoulders as the Salem Witch gripped her soul-body with resolve. "Listen to me, Dani. The Virtues followed you for thousands of years. Though they can be brats on Earth, they love and respect you. They're angels, too, but they don't have soulmates like you do. They haven't sacrificed as much as you and him. Part of being one of the Virtues is exhibiting selflessness, and none have done that as much as you. It would be supremely selfish of the Virtues to begrudge you returning to your soulmate."

"But what about the rest of the world? What about the next Apokalypsis War?" she whispered. She wanted it. She wanted her divinity and her soulmate so bad, she could almost taste it. But...

"But nothing," Hayden argued fiercely. "No matter our decisions, the Creator weaves them into Its perfect, eternal plan."

"Perhaps a change in leadership would be good for the Virtues," the Goddess mused, winking a single silver eye.

"The Virtues certainly fought more in this lifetime than in the rest combined," Amara agreed. "After countless lifetimes together, the seven of you squabble relentlessly."

"Daniella," Goddess sang her name. "I would not offer for you to return to the Garden as an angel if I did not *know* with My infinite knowledge that all will be well in the cosmos." She smiled a brilliant smile that was warm and motherly, and the sight of it soothed Dani's soul. "It is wise to give your soul a rest. God and I rested on the seventh day as We created the Universe. My children are not above Me, therefore, they, too, require rest. So, rest, Daniella, rest in the love you have been deprived of for so long."

"All you wanted during your mortal life was love, Dani," Hayden spoke softly, her entire body relaxing as she glowed with silver light. "This is your chance to be with your soulmate. Take your divinity and return to your soulmate in the Garden. It is not selfish to desire love, especially when he must sacrifice his mate to every war against the Sins."

"You know who my soulmate is, don't you?" In the near century Dani had known Hayden, she learned more than a few tricks to read the Salem Witch, even without Ronnie's powers.

A mischievous grin split her face, and a resounding crack echoed through Heaven as she snapped her fingers.

Brilliant light flashed, but faded as quickly as it appeared, revealing a seven-foot-tall angel with muscles bulging off his broad, wide-set shoulders standing beside Hayden.

Six wings protruded from his back. Two covered his face, two flapped behind his back, and the bottom two extended down to cover his feet.

But as the Seraph stepped toward her, his wings unfolded, the feathers rustling as the angel revealed his face and feet. A golden halo wrapped around the angel's forehead and disappeared into his thick brown hair. Enormous wings stretched to their full span behind his back, and a soft light glowed off the angel's tanned skin. Heavenly fire burned along the tops of his six white wings, adding to his light.

He would have been a terrifying sight to behold, the most imposing angel Dani could have imagined, if it weren't for those eyes. Golden irises wrapped around a white pupil. Eyes she had stared into for every moment of her existence as an immortal angel.

The sight of the Seraph angel would have petrified Dani if it weren't for the current of electricity that zapped through her as she locked eyes with her soulmate.

"Abdiel," she breathed the name. She did not know how she knew, but she knew with absolutely certainty, in every particle of light that composed her soul, that he was Abdiel, the Seraph Angel of Loyalty and Steadfastness, the first to devote himself to the Creator and defy Lucifer's Rebellion.

And he was her soulmate.

"Hello, Daniella," he rumbled in his deep timbre, sending a current through Dani's soul-body. Stepping forward, he cupped a hand to her cheek. Energy passed between them, and Dani sank into his touch, releasing a content sigh. This feeling... how could she have abandoned this feeling? The sensation of being in the presence of one's soulmate, let alone the feeling of his skin against hers?

And that energy.... Dani knew what that energy was.... It was complete, absolute, true love.

"I will respect whatever decision you make, Daniella," Abdiel rumbled, sending a thrill through her body. Did she affect him the way he affected her?

Reading her mind, Abdiel laughed lowly. "Yes, you have the same effect on me, Daniella, perhaps more profound, if I am to be truthful. There is nothing in the Universe like the yearning of two souls to be united into one as the Creator intended."

"How could I have given this up?" she whispered in a breathy tone, her voice reverent.

"Because you love Me more than you love yourself or your soulmate," Goddess answered, but Dani couldn't look at Her. It had been so long—too long—since she had been united with her one and only. "It is the greatest act of selflessness and love to place Me, the source of all love, at the peak of your affections. It is well earned for you to release your mortal responsibilities after countless reincarnations. And for the love and obedience you have shown to Me, I will bless your soul with more to come, my beloved child, whether you accept my offer or not."

"I accept your offer, Goddess," Dani spoke with the authority of the angel she once was but didn't dare tear her gaze away from Abdiel's for fear he might disappear if she did. "I will don my divine nature once more and join my mate in the Garden."

Abdiel gripped her face harder, as though afraid she might slip from between his fingers. "You will?"

She nodded, pressing her lips together to keep her sobs of joy from escaping.

"Then it is time I go," Hayden announced, sliding closer to Dani. "Nephilim aren't allowed to watch the alchemy of divinity unless we reside in the Garden." Elbowing the Seraph out of the way, Hayden wiggled between the soulmates before locking eyes with Dani.

Here stood the woman who mentored her, guided her, loved her like a sister. And all this time, Dani was an angel, bonded to a Seraph. Before Hayden knew the truth, a special bond existed between the women. She knew because Hayden had always called her Dani until the day Spirit revealed the truth to her. Only then did Hayden call her Daniella, like Goddess did. It was that thought that flooded her eyes with hot tears that spilled over the edge.

"Merry meet, merry part, and merry meet again." Hayden brushed her thumbs over Dani's cheeks to dispel the tears, then pulled her in for what would have been a bone-crushing hug in their physical bodies. "I am honored to have known you during your mortal life, but I look forward to getting to know you as an angel." Releasing Dani's soul-body, Hayden stepped away, her silver hair shimmering under the lights of heaven. "But until then... Blessed be, Daniella Sanchez."

"Davina," Abdiel rumbled. "Michael asked me to remind you to keep out of trouble."

With a mischievous grin that said she would do anything but the sort, Hayden bowed to Goddess, and in a flash of silver light, the Salem Witch disappeared.

A warm hand, twice the size of hers, intertwined its fingers with hers, bringing comfort she did not know was possible from another being other than the Creator.

"Your soul will transform into its true physical form—that of an angel, and we shall be equals in body, mind, and soul, once more, Daniella." Abdiel rubbed a thumb over the back of her hand, soothing her nerves for what came next.

With one last glance at her soulmate through the eyes of her mortal soul, Dani nodded. "I'm ready."

Teeth dazzled as the Goddess smiled, sweeping her arms wide. With a resounding clang, the latch on the Pearly Gates unhooked, and the Gates swung backward at the Goddess's command. "Welcome home, Daniella Sanchez, Chastity of the Virtues."

Without thought, without hesitation, Daniella trusted the pull of her soul and stepped into the loving arms of her Creator. Brilliant silver light swallowed her, and the deepest peace she had ever known washed over her.

And all was well with her soul.

GLOSSARY OF TERMS & POWERS

<u>Asylum</u> – Magical town hidden in a pocket of magic within Briar Woods of the human town, Salem, Wisconsin

<u>Wards</u> – Enchantments cast to protect a person or space

<u>St. Salem's Spellery</u> – Magical school constructed by Alice Parker after founding the town of Asylum

<u>The Salem Witch</u> – A witch chosen by Heaven's angels as the champion in the upcoming Salem War; the Salem Witch must master the five elements—air, fire, water, earth, and Spirit—and pass the Salem Witch Trials before their seventeenth birthday, or forfeit their life

<u>Nephilim</u> – Half mortal child of a celestial

<u>Celestial</u> – A supernatural divine entity associated with the heavens like an angel or god/goddess; possesses supernatural abilities beyond that of a mortal, but serves the Creator

<u>The Creator</u> – the omnipotent being that created the entire Universe; composed of a masculine and feminine aspect; God represents the Divine Masculine while Goddess represents the Divine Feminine

<u>god/goddess</u> – Lowercase "g" indicates a paranormal being with powers similar to an angels; gods and goddesses are manifestations of the Creator's ultimate power

Prince of Hell – Title assigned to a demon of particularly high rank; only seven demons ever serve as Princes to the Devil (Lucifer)

Sin – A demonic entity or power that dwells in the world and Hell dimensions with the intention to corrupt mortals; Sins often bond with the Princes of Hell to multiply their power

Fallen Angel – An angel who joined Lucifer's rebellion against Heaven; not necessarily a Sin or Prince of Hell

<u>Athenian Council</u> – the governing body of a witching community; comprised of seven individually elected members: Air Representative, Fire Representative, Water Representative, Earth Representative, Witch Military General, High Priestess, and Ethereal Bloodline Representative

<u>Supreme Council</u> – the governing body of the entire witching world; every Athenian Council reports to the Supreme Council in Jerusalem

<u>Ethereal Bloodline Representative</u> – a witch descended from a celestial who serves on the Council as a heavenly connection

Virtues

<u>Patience</u> – Axel Redd; Hypnosis; Red

<u>Temperance</u> – Emmett English; Shield; Orange

<u>Charity</u> – Raphaela Jacobs; Amplification; Yellow

<u>Kindness</u> – Walker Burroughs; Astral Projection; Green

<u>Diligence</u> – Milena (Mila) Wardwell; Sonic Blast; Teal

<u>Chastity</u> – Daniella (Dani) Sanchez; Nullification; Blue

<u>Humility</u> – Verona (Ronnie) Hathorne; Second Sight; Purple

Archangels
Michael – The Warrior Archangel; Archangel of Fire
Azriel – The Archangel of Death
Raphael – The Archangel of Air
Jophiel – The Archangel of Heavenly Beauty and Light
Chamuel – The Archangel of Heavenly Relationships
Uriel – The Archangel of Earth
Gabriel – The Messenger Archangel; Archangel of Water

Angel Choirs
1st Triad:
Seraphim – "Burning Ones"; Attendants of the Throne of the Creator
Cherubim – "Fullness of Wisdom"; Assigned to protect special places
Thrones – "Steadfast Love of the Creator"; Dispense justice

2nd Triad:
Dominions – Distribute the Creator's commands to other angel choirs
Virtues – Rule the operations of movement of the Universe
Powers – Warrior angels that govern the natural order & fight demonic choirs

3rd Triad:
Principalities – Care and guard kingdoms; associated with transitions in power
Archangels – Leaders to communicate and carry out the Creator's plan
Angels – Closest to humanity; Serve as personal guardian angels

Sins & Princes of Hell
Wrath – **Abaddon** "The Destroyer"; Super Strength; Red
   Renounced from Heaven by Michael & Patience
Gluttony – **Beelzebub** "The Lord of Flies"; Siphon; Orange
   Renounced from Heaven by Azriel & Temperance
Greed – **Mammon** "The Lord of Fools"; Alchemy; Yellow
   Renounced from Heaven by Raphael & Charity
Envy – **Leviathan** "The King of Monsters"; Hellmouth; Green
   Renounced from Heaven by Jophiel & Kindness
Sloth – **Belphegor** "The Corruptor"; Temporary Time Magic; Teal
   Renounced from Heaven by Chamuel & Diligence
Lust – **Elliot Fox**, Air Witch; Charm Speak; Navy Blue
   Formerly Asmodeus, Renounced from Heaven by Uriel & Chastity,
   Killed by Alice Urielson Parker
Pride – **Belial** "The Worthless"; Illusion Magic; Purple
   Renounced from Heaven by Gabriel & Humility

Read Hayden's Epic Story in Book One: The Lost Witch

Read it on Amazon today!

Book One: The Lost Witch

Five deadly Trials. An ancient, sinister evil.

**One lost witch
with the power to save the world.**

Welcome to Asylum.

Twelve-year-old Hayden Black has never been normal, that much she knew, but when her father is abducted by demons, she learns just how remarkable she truly is. Not only is she a witch, but Heaven's angels have chosen her as the next Salem Witch, destined to protect the world from evil... if she can survive the deadly Salem Witch Trials first.

Now Hayden must traverse the magical world of Asylum and learn to use her powers. If she does not master all five elements — air, fire, water, earth, and Spirit — before her seventeenth birthday, she forfeits her life.

Hayden might have started her journey orphaned and alone, but it does not take her long to forge new friendships and attract new enemies. Hayden thought her only nemesis was the residential bully, but her greatest enemy, a terrible evil lurking in the shadows, has yet to reveal itself.

Will Hayden master her air magic in time to save her friends and find her father? Or will she perish alongside them?

The Lost Witch is the first book in an urban fantasy series intended for readers ages ten and above who love Percy Jackson and Avatar: The Last Airbender.

HELP ME OUT

Thank you for reading Dani Sanchez and the Seven Deadly Sins! If you enjoyed this story, please consider leaving a review on Amazon or Goodreads.

Scan this QR code to leave a review:

Or scan the QR code to read on Amazon today!

About The Author
B. C. Taylor

Click here to view a full list of B. C. Taylor's published and upcoming novels.

Visit her on the web at:

Website: https://www.brooklynctaylor.com
Instagram: https://www.instagram.com/brooklyn_tay
Goodreads:
https://www.goodreads.com/user/show/155122248-
brooklyn-taylor
Pinterest: https://www.pinterest.com/brooklyn_tay7/
Facebook Page:
https://www.facebook.com/profile.php?id=1000845245
15084

When not casting spells, brewing potions, or flying her broom, B. C. Taylor writes middle grade and young adult fantasy with a hint of wickedness. While she currently lives in Wisconsin, Brooklyn enjoys traveling throughout the country and recently traveled to Thailand where she engaged in daring adventures like feeding elephants and petting tigers. During her travels, she pushed the boundaries of her comfort zone by learning new skills from wake boarding and surfing to country swing dancing to expanding her martial arts background. Despite the adventurousness of her reality, Brooklyn's magic power is daydreaming of witches and wizards, angels and demons, and other supernatural creatures that live within the shadowy realms of books.

She invites readers to get first looks, exclusive content, and more by subscribing to her newsletter:

ACKNOWLEDGEMENTS

Last minute like everything else I did in college. At least during Undergrad.... I swear, I was more diligent in Grad school.

On a serious note, this book was a hard one for me to write. Thankfully, despite thinking I did a horrible job initially, editing was quick and smooth, and I was surprised by how much I ended up liking the story. Hayden Black will always be my girl, but I loved the opportunity to write in Dani Sanchez's voice.

The past year—the last three, if we're being honest—has been incredibly hard on me. Life sucks, especially when everything is crumbling around you. And my love life sucks the worst. These years have been filled with more heartbreak than a heart should have to bear, so that is why I wrote Dani's character the way I did. No matter what, she always chose love. Even when she craved love and didn't receive it, she knew there was greater waiting for her. For me, it has felt like some souls just aren't fated to get a happy ending, but for Dani, she never let the brutality of life break her, and in the end, she found the love she always wanted.

So, this book goes out to all the girls whose hearts have been broken, to all the girls whose hearts will be broken, and to all the girls who have mended their hearts back together despite it all. May you find all the love in the Universe, because it already exists inside you.

To my parents, thank you for loving me throughout this journey and supporting me in more than one way. Especially by buying me chocolate muffins. I think that is my love language.

To my friends... Micah and Sam, thank you for being such a bright spot in my life, for always listening to my insane stories and drama, and for always telling me that I deserve better. Thank you for being my life long friends. I love you guys.

To Lacie... thank you for being my sister in writing. I love that we have a bond to build one another up. I'm so thankful to have a lovely soul like you to walk this road with me. Thank you for supporting me emotionally when no other friends did.

To Tessa, thank you for mending the hurt in our friendship and listening to the crap I go through, whether it's work or relationships or the other million things I could complain about.

www.ingramcontent.com/pod-product-compliance
Lightning Source LLC
Chambersburg PA
CBHW030753310726
48969CB00005B/1397